The ForEver Child

The ForEver Child

D. B. Martin

Published by IM Books

THE FOREVER CHILD

ISBN 978-1-915120-16-8

"Machine intelligence is the last invention that humanity will ever need to make."

Nick Bostrom

Nick Bostrom is the author of the book, *Superintelligence: Paths, Dangers, Strategies*, and a Professor at Oxford University, where he leads the Future of Humanity Institute as its founding director.

Chapter 1

10:14, 18th May 2032: Luke

The door slid closed behind him with a sibilant swish – the kind you hear in only the most expensive places. Ahead, the receptionist was of the same class, blonde, understated, elegant, ice-cold. She looked up and smiled as he entered, her highly polished red talons clicking against the keyboard and then pausing, mid-air, as she waited for him to approach. He flashed his press card but she frowned and shook her head.

'Chip?' she asked.

'No, thanks,' he said, winking. 'I'm on a diet.'

She laughed, a cool, tinkling sound like glass slivers colliding. 'Funny man, huh?'

'Not at all. Just old-fashioned. Is my press card not enough then? I *was* invited.'

'Name?'

'Edward Hughes.'

Her nails clattered against the keyboard again and her eyes fixed on the screen ahead of her.

'Indeed, you were.' Her manner changed; switched up a gear. 'Mr Crane will see you in due course. In the meantime, please just wait here.'

'Right here?' he asked.

'For the moment. Someone will collect you. But I'm afraid I will have to chip you to allow entry.'

'Isn't that against my human rights?' He leaned in towards her, rapidly reducing the gap between her icy perfection and what some had described as his mischievous charm, before she could object. She leaned back, smiling gently and completely unfazed. Now that was a receptionist for you!

'Maybe, but for access to Jason Crane, you have to make sacrifices. It's removable though. It's only inserted just under the epidermis. Like a splinter. I can hook it out with a pin when you leave if you want me to.'

'Ah,' Luke laughed, and then looked stern, regaining the ground he'd lost as the receptionist backed off, unsure of his reaction. 'And will you also conquer me as you remove it for me?'

She shook her head at him, laughing and frowning simultaneously. 'What are you on about?'

'The fable – Androcles and the lion. You remove the thorn from my paw and I'm yours forever afterwards in gratitude.'

'You're mad,' she laughed, but the charm had worked. He might even get away with asking for a date if he played his cards right. Behind the receptionist a satin-steel door slid open and a lumpy middle-aged man stomped through it. The receptionist jumped and swung round in her seat, making a soft cooing sound. Her manner changed again. Professionalism to a tee. 'Oh, Dr Green, this is Edward Hughes. He's here for the interview with Mr Crane. He's from…' she looked enquiringly at Luke.

'Oh, er, Bio Weekly,' Luke supplied, trying to remember where Hughes had last worked, according to his contact.

Green stuttered to a halt in front of him. 'Hughes?' He stared at Luke, rheumy grey eyes suddenly steely. He looked Luke up and down then took him by the arm and steered him away from the reception desk. "I thought Hughes was old – in his sixties,' he hissed.

'Ah well…'

'You're not Hughes, are you?'

'Err, no, but I am the one they've sent for the briefing. On the latest BioModule?' Luke smiled at him, tucking the devil-may-care lad behind the serious reporter mask he adopted for serious-reporter occasions. 'Hughes unfortunately couldn't make it.' Green was the next best thing to the main man – although still not the main man, and he had yet to bypass the chip, the reckoning and the casting-out stage when they found out that he'd only borrowed Edward Hughes's outdated press pass whilst Edwards Hughes was passed out in his hotel room after too many whiskies the night before – courtesy of Luke Maynard. Stupid really, because, *really*? How had he expected to get past the sophisticated wizardry that Crane Industries routinely employed to keep the workers in and the snoopers out? But he'd almost got there with Blondie and it would be worth it to be in on the scoop of the century if he could somehow sweet-talk Green. Edwards would have done it to him if the boot had been on the other foot, old press hack that he was.

Green subjected Luke to a further minute's narrow-lidded inspection, then, 'Sent, huh? OK, come on, then.' Green's eyes slipped away from Luke's face and towards the silently opening main entrance door. 'Carly, put the doors on automatic, will you?'

'Of course,' Carly's red talons clicked a series of buttons and the main doors glowed blue around their edges. She studied Green curiously as he nodded and then turned away from her. Her eyes were full of questions, and now so were Luke's.

'Right.' Green was already heading back towards the door he'd come through, as if he'd forgotten his visitor.

'Dr Green,' Carly called after him. Green turned. 'He's not chipped yet...' she prompted, raising her eyebrows questioningly.

'Neither am I,' he growled back.

'But Mr Crane…'

But Green was already walking through the internal door and beckoning his visitor to join him. 'Bloody microchips,' he complained to Luke as the door closed behind them and Carly was sealed in the outer sanctum. 'Bloody things are for pets, aren't they?'

'Err,' Luke couldn't believe his luck. Surely it couldn't be this easy – but then it had been a year ago too, slipping into the rank and file of the invited press. 'I guess… You don't subscribe to the same level of tracking then?'

'I don't subscribe to any level of tracking. Human beings have to retain some dignity, don't they – but,' he stopped abruptly and thrust his face into Luke's, glaring fiercely at him. 'Don't you say I said that – or that you're not chipped though.'

Now Luke studied Green; forehead ridged with furrows as deep as a ploughed field, cheeks grey and sagging, hair straggly and smelling strongly of sweat and grime, shoulders slumped, paunch rolling over his belt. He looked the archetypal mad scientist, yet Matthew Green – from what he'd read about him – was still only in his late thirties, and not mad at all; brilliant really – more brilliant than the great Jason Crane himself. Yet so much older than he'd looked a year ago. So much water had passed under the bridge since then, it seemed – for both of them.

'Never,' Luke assured him, trying to look as submissive and trustworthy as he wasn't.

'Right…well,' Green thrust his face even closer to Luke's so that he could smell the stench of stale cheese sandwich and too much coffee on Green's breath. 'You sure we've never met before?'

'Never,' Luke repeated, mentally crossing his fingers that Green's memory was as bad as his appearance.

'All right…' Green remained looking dubious for a few moments longer, then, 'I'll take you to join the others.'

A year previously, not long after Jason Crane's sudden and absolute departure from public life, Luke had managed to insert himself into a group of journalists who had been allowed into the hallowed halls of Crane Industries on a rare visit, purely to promote its latest innovation – BioModules; plug-in modifications tailored to whatever was causing a problem in bodily functioning. Using Crane Industries' 3D printing process, bionic modifications were created to replace malfunctioning organs – and more. They were akin to the futuristic adaptations that had been the basis to The Bionic Man movies for those who could afford them – both horrendously expensive and the data horrendously protected from the general press. Only the select few – representatives of the rich and famous, or those who would enable Crane Industries to connect with the rich and famous – had been welcomed then. This time, it seemed the net had been thrown wider, but still only as far as the privileged few in press circles. It had been a stroke of genius – or maybe calculated manipulation, although on whose part, he wasn't yet sure – throwing his hand in with 3:16. And a stroke of luck them coming up with Edwards and his proclivity for too much scotch. Luke was determined to make the most of both whilst he could. There were so many questions to answer and this could even be his big break – and God knew he needed one – his claim to fame; one of the few to actually witness the living, breathing man of steel so many claimed was as much a fable as the lion and the thorn. After all, why would you, and your wife, just completely withdraw when you were making a mint and set to be the future of biotechnology? It didn't make sense. Apart from that, Frieda's silence still didn't make sense – even after three years and accepting the damage to his ego that a disappearing girlfriend did. Going from hot and harried to ice cold and silent overnight, even in a stormy relationship, didn't make sense whichever way he approached it – especially as *she'd* chased *him*, and insisted on telling him she was on to something big; something that could change his life – and God knew he needed a miracle! Maybe some of it would be explained now?

Luke followed Green silently along the network of corridors that criss-crossed the Crane Industries lab facility without ever seeming to collide with the outside world or another corridor. Replaying that in his head in preparation for the preamble to his piece, he decided that wouldn't make sense unless he made a confession too. How could he know there was a network of corridors if he never encountered any others than the one he was currently following Green along?

Because he'd been here before.

He'd thought it might have been his big break then, but it had merely served to introduce more confusion – and a lingering memory that felt more like a dream than a memory to puzzle over in the intervening downtime – of which there'd been far too much. He shook his head to clear it. Not today. He couldn't afford downtime today…

'Here we are.' Green had stopped in front of a satin-steel door similar to the one they'd exited reception through. It proclaimed itself to be the entrance to Conference Room 3 and Luke could already hear the buzz of his fellow press on the other side of it. So no intimate meeting with the great man after all, despite what Edwards had been boasting. Oh well, it was as expected.

He followed Green into Conference Room 3 and wasn't surprised to find that the hum he'd heard was being made by a relatively small gathering – and a sleek, highly polished unit fitted flush to the back wall of the, surprisingly large, conference room. Indeed, the noise was almost exclusively being emitted by the unit and not the journalists in the room.

'Is that it?' Luke plucked at Green's arm. 'Is that the new BioModule processor?'

'Correct,' Green replied, pausing to stare admiringly at the back wall.

'And will we get to see it in action? Maybe even test it out on one of us?'

'Why? What do you need replacing, young bloke like you?' Green seemed suddenly hostile, and for the second time since they'd met, Luke wondered why on earth he'd managed to evade the chip in order to gain access to this briefing. What game was Green playing? Luke wandered across to the BioModule processor, conscious that Green and a number of others were watching him. Had Green been the creator of the module, he wondered? Or was he just the engineer of the project, and Crane the genius?

The noise the module generated was making his ears buzz and combined with the general feeling of being on edge that he – and he sensed everyone else in the room – was feeling, made him fidgety and anxious. Not today, he told his body firmly. Today we operate as normal. He gave the module a cursory inspection but really there was nothing to see, just smooth steel casing. The outer covering of the BioModule processor – whatever the module was programmed to do – was as mysterious as its creator. The literature had described it as a plug-in which was claimed would promote overall longevity in its recipient, whatever else it was programmed to do. Not quite eternal life but improved cell reproduction, healing, anti-ageing and so on, as well as being able to regenerate a failing organ. It was anticipated it would improve life expectancy to double the current limit, with good health being maintained throughout, even as the body aged overall. The price was beyond what most ordinary people – like journalists – could afford, but for the super-rich, and the super-powerful it was one step closer to God. And now, for the merely big bucks wealthy, it seemed the market was opening up too. Maybe Crane Industries had realised that there was more money in mass marketing than catering for a small number of elite? Either way, probably the main reason he'd managed to get in here today, 3:16 or not, was because someone in Crane Industries had decided to allow him in…

Swinging around to survey the room – a cold, clinical, pristine white space, devoid of the usual conference facilities – and its other occupants, he sensed they were as uneasy as he. Perhaps it was the noise, or the emptiness – the soullessness – of the place, or the immensity of the concept? He was just edging himself into a suitable position to observe without being observed once the presentation started when the heavy steel door to the room itself swung wide and there he was…Jason Crane.

Even though the BioModule processor was still hammering away, creating its pathways to eternity, to Luke's ears the room felt silent, like everything had stopped – slowed to a minute pace – while Crane took them all in. He didn't look a day older than he had when he'd first come to everyone's notice, several years before he'd 'disappeared' – so whether or not Green intended using the unit to regenerate himself one day – and by God, he could do with it – it seemed likely Jason Crane was already the beneficiary of one of his own BioModules, Luke mused. Yet there was something else about him, something indefinable that made Luke shiver. An unnatural stillness.

'Welcome, welcome,' Crane said in a warm confident tone, the stillness momentarily dispelled by expansive bonhomie until an alarm sounded full pitch, making them all cower and cover their ears as the sound vibrated through them, rattling bones and palpating organs until they felt bruised and assaulted. 'What the…' Crane alone didn't cover his ears. He looked quizzically at one of the heavies flanking him, but now doubling over in pain. Luke could just see Green, grimacing but managing to stay upright enough to peer over Crane's shoulder, eyes wide and mouth hanging open as the heavies rallied sufficiently to muscle through and bundle Crane out of the door.

'Ladies and gents, I'm afraid we have a situation…' The smaller – and more intelligent-looking – of the heavies stepped round the space that had previously occupied the now departed Crane, and with difficulty, addressed the shivering group of journalists, shouting to be heard above the ululation of the alarm. 'It seems there's been a breach in main reception and a number of protesters have managed to gain access. Nothing to be alarmed about, but for your safety, please follow me.'

'Nothing to be alarmed about? Fuck that!' the man nearest Luke mouthed at him, hands plastered to his ears and face creased into a grimace. 'They've been having trouble with the local religious nuts for months now. Bet your bottom dollar it's the same bunch of Godzillas baying for his blood.'

'You reckon?' Luke mouthed back. 'The Life Rights Group you mean?'

'This way, this way…' the heavy was alternating between covering his ears and ushering the little group through the door, pushing them along the corridor like a column of sausage meat being fed through a sausage machine.

'Yeah!' Luke's companion nodded, hands still clamped over his ears. '3:16 they call themselves. Load of religious claptrap, but probably pretty harmless normally. If I were you, I'd be making a break for it right now and having a poke around – make my career with some carefully crafted revelations.'

'Why aren't you?'

'Too old, too tired, and too attached to my paycheck,' the old hack mouthed back, grinning, then winced as the sirens went up a pitch.

They had reached the door now, and the woman in front of them stumbled as the heel broke on her stilettos. As she ducked down to grab the broken shoe and then hobble along the corridor, following her peers, Green bobbed back into view, now wearing ear defenders.

'What's there to reveal?' Luke pressed his companion but he didn't answer – or maybe didn't even realise Luke had asked another question. Luke grabbed at his arm to get his attention but he was already drifting forward and away from Luke, although his expression said 'Go'!

'Hey,' Green beckoned to Luke and grabbed him by the sleeve as

Luke neared. 'This way,' and he plucked Luke from the sausage machine of journalists and tossed him into the raging seas of general mass evacuation as all the doors along the corridor were flung open and the room occupants stumbled out, hands to ears and heads down – a swarm of white worker ants heading for sanctuary.

'Where?' Luke resisted Green's tugging as he watched his erstwhile companions jostle and elbow their way along the corridor, vying with lab staff for right of way. 'Where are they all going?'

'Panic rooms, or out,' Green yelled. 'But you're with me.'

'Why?'

Green pulled the left ear defender away from his ear so it was partially uncovered. 'Because you'll be more use on the loose than locked down. Or are you a pussy, scared of a few yobs?'

'The 3:16 Group aren't merely a few yobs,' Luke protested. 'They're bloody maniacs!'

'Really?' Green paused to look Luke in the eye with a questioning expression on his face and Luke realised he was in danger of giving too much away.

'If that's who's behind this,' Luke added hastily.

'Even more reason for you to come with me, then…' Green took him by the forearm and pulled him through the throng, grunting and elbowing to beat a pathway through the chaos. In the distance, the small group comprising Jason Crane, his heavies, and a straggling group of anxious journalists disappeared round the corner in the corridor, and equally suddenly, a series of doors on the other side of the corridor swung open and another white cloud of lab techs flowed through them, leaving Green and Luke alone in the middle of the now deserted corridor, empty except for the volume of sound which by now, Luke was sure, must have perforated his eardrums. His shirt was plastered to his back and his armpits wringing with sweat; the sheer volume of the noise was making him feel nauseous, but it wasn't just the noise. Not now, not now, he begged his body. He swallowed back acid bile and his throat burned as he yelled at Green.

'Where?'

'Down there,' Green pointed to the opposite end of the corridor to where they'd entered and to where Jason and his posse had melted away. 'Go!' and he pushed Luke ahead of him. Luke stumbled and had to steady himself against the corridor wall to keep his balance.

'Hey!' he protested, swinging round and looking to Green for more direction – but to no avail. Green had already gone. 'What the fuck? Where are you?' but Luke's voice was lost in the scream of the alarms. He stood in the middle of the corridor, swaying and confused by the sheer wall of sound and the sudden emptiness of the place. 'Green? Don't play silly buggers! Where are you?' Swinging round and around until he felt dizzy, he finally had to admit that Dr Green was nowhere to be seen, but on his last pass, rounding the corner of the corridor was someone who was very much in evidence, crouching low, masked, flak-jacketed and carrying a crowbar in one hand and a rifle slung over their other shoulder. One of the 3:16 group – and not in the amicable mood they had been on his last encounter with them.

Turning, the group member yelled over their shoulder, but the alarm was too loud for Luke to hear what they were shouting. In the circumstances, he wasn't waiting to find out though. If this was the advance party of the 3:16 Group, they wouldn't have any hesitation swinging that crowbar or pointing that rifle, whatever they'd said previously. He knew that from personal experience.

'Fuck, fuck, fuck!' he muttered to himself as he careered along the corridor, feet skidding on the highly polished medvac flooring and elbows rebounding off the corridor walls as he ran, hands still clamped over his ears, occasionally colliding with a wall as his balance faltered. He rounded the end of the corridor and found himself in another one, but this time the walls were painted pastel blue instead of crisp white. Behind him the alarms no longer fully masked his assailant's shouts as his ears became accustomed to the pulsating sound. Ahead of him the corridor seemed to go on for miles. 'Fuck!' he muttered again. His breath was coming hard and heavy and he knew he wouldn't be able to outrun them, but where could he hide? The corridor was a smooth tunnel of pastel blue nothing. 'Oh Jesus!' Luke wailed aloud. When he'd said this group were maniacs, he hadn't been joking. He hadn't known that when he'd first encountered them but it had been their obsessional hatred of Jason Crane and what Crane Industries was reputedly doing that had put him the way of getting Edwards drunk and stealing his press pass. And what a great story it would be, apart from other considerations – the crazed fanatics, baying for blood at what they claimed Jason Crane was doing, modifying the world into a race of semi-androids which he then planned to control through their modules, versus the ice-cold scientist claiming to be devoted to protecting humanity. Who was the bigger danger? He'd even imagined the headlines and the Pulitzer Prize it could have won him.

Now, he wholeheartedly regretted his hubris. Why the hell had he thought he'd be the one to break the story of the century?

Because it's not just the story you're after, is it? It's the explanations…

Nevertheless, Luke ran half the length of the corridor before collapsing against the wall, chest heaving and breath catching in his throat and making him gasp and choke as his pursuers also rounded the corner and had him in their sights. It had been a good life up till now, mainly, apart from the last few years. Thank you everyone, he thought – apart from you, Dr fucking Matthew Green who got me into this mess when I could have been safe and sound in Jason Crane's panic room, or back out on the street. He banged his fist against the wall and with that his body plain refused to cooperate any longer. He landed hard on his back, jolting his coccyx and flopping backwards with the pain, following that up with a good solid whack to the back of his head. His eyes blurred and his head throbbed, but even as he cursed the pain he started to laugh.

But not so different to a bad day recently…and yet…the sensation of falling was different. His head hit the floor at precisely the same moment he realised he shouldn't be falling since he'd already collided with the wall. Flat on his back, he opened his eyes and stared up into the bright blue of sky behind glass.

Back here again. Where he'd been a year ago. Exactly the same place.

'Are you OK?'

He rolled onto his side and struggled to get up, head still banging like a drum – but not from the bloody alarm anymore. That seemed to have been silenced – this time from the lump he could already feel forming at the back of his skull. He pulled his knees up in front of him and rolled into a foetal position before twisting onto his side and thence onto his knees without his head actually falling off. From there he checked out the source of the question. A young girl, maybe ten or so, was standing about the same number of feet away from him, in the middle of the courtyard. Steady blue eyes watched him sympathetically, but she made no move to come any closer. She just stood, and watched – golden-haired, serene, breathtakingly beautiful. Behind him the opening he'd fallen through sealed shut and if he hadn't fallen through it, he would never have even known it was there.

'Are you OK?' she repeated.

'I think so,' he frowned as he gently explored the lump on his head, wincing as he found the epicentre of the blast. 'Well, better than I would have been if I was still out there, at least,' he added, attempting a rueful smile. 'Thank you…'

'I know you,' she replied, still studying him. 'You were here when I was tiny. Last year.'

'What? That *was* you?'

What the child would have become…The memory rolled over him with full force – the lingering memory that had felt more like a dream than a memory. The secret place he'd found on his furtive exploration of the Crane facilities when he'd managed to slip away from his compatriots after gaining entry that other time. The secret door – seemingly deliberately left ajar – and leading through into some kind of inner sanctum; a courtyard, with greenery and shrubs and flowers and on the 'lawn', a small child, making daisy chains, and singing to herself. He'd stepped through, unable to stop himself, like a life-size ugly male Alice stepping into Wonderland. The child hadn't stopped singing or making her daisy chains even when she'd seen him. She'd just smiled as if he'd been expected.

'Hello,' he'd said. 'I'm not going to harm you,' but she hadn't been frightened. 'I'm Luke Maynard.'

'Hello, Luke Maynard, I'm Hebe.'

'Well, hello then, Hebe. Are you lost?' he'd asked, assessing her as maybe four years old.

'Oh no, I live here.'

'Well, thank you for inviting me into your home here,' Luke had begun, 'which is…where?'

She ignored that. 'I knew you'd come. Are you taking me with you now?'

'Err, no…' he'd said, but he'd wondered many times if he should have. What child was she? Whose child was she? 'Where's your mummy or your daddy?'

She shook her head and put her finger to her lips. 'This is how it begins, but no one must know.'

'OK.' He was about to follow up with, 'how what begins?' but changed his mind – simple questions; simple questions but potentially complex answers… Instead, he continued lightly 'So if you live here, I wonder if you can help me? I'm looking for a friend of mine who I think lives here too. Maybe you even know her? Her name is Frieda…' Hebe studied him gravely for a moment and then shook her head again as her

eyes left his face to fix on the still-open secret door. Luke followed her gaze, simultaneously hearing noise in the corridor – the official tour party coming back. 'I'd better go,' he said quickly.

'Oh no! No! Not without me. Take me with you!' Suddenly she was on her feet and grabbing his hand, clinging on to him as if her life depended on him.

'I can't,' he said, gently disengaging from her. 'What would your parents think?'

'Please...' she pleaded.

'I'll come back,' he promised, torn between finding out who she was and why she was walled away inside a lab facility, and needing to go before he was caught.

'Promise? I'll die if you don't. This is how it begins...'

He'd come away having learnt nothing more about Frieda Kohn's whereabouts, or the reason for Jason Crane and his wife's withdrawal from life, but with even more curiosity about what was going on inside Crane Industries. Now, he admitted to himself, this latest escapade wasn't down to seeking the greatest story of all time or trying to find out what had happened to Frieda, but because he'd spent all the intervening time wondering about the mysterious child and why he had to go back, or she would die.

'I knew you'd keep your promise. Have you come to save me this time?'

'Err, well…' Luke said, overwhelmed by the strong sense of déjà vu his reply provoked. The conclusion he'd come to about who the child was a year ago had made sense at the time, but how could a four-year-old girl become the same ten-year-old only a year later? And how could she have known he was coming the first time?

Chapter 2

10:14, 18th May 2032: Hebe

My earliest memory is of my father. Well, I think it was of my father. It could also have been of Uncle Matthew, that big moon face hovering over mine… It gradually became less moon and more face – and then it *was* my father's, peering at me like I was an exciting object. How old was I? A few days, or weeks or months? Babies recognise their parent's face from around eight weeks, I read once, but I think I must have been younger because I remember it being so warm and sunny – heat-stroke-hot sunlight beating down on me through the glass roof of the courtyard as I lay kicking in my pram. That would make me much younger than eight weeks when I first recognised my father's face because I was born into the heat of the summer and the weather turned rapidly shortly afterwards – thunderstorms and torrential rain for weeks. I wonder now if that was because of me – my arrival – because I was so confused. Birth is the most traumatic experience for a baby if they could but remember it. I suppose that's partly what he meant when he wondered if I was precocious. He first mentioned it when I wasn't quite six months old. Of course, I didn't know what it meant then. It was just an odd sounding mix of vowels and consonants to my infantile brain. Did I even know what vowels and consonants were then? Probably not – to do so would definitely have been precocious.

He mentioned it again when I was sitting on his lap in Lab One, stabbing at the lights on the PC screen he'd been working on, anticipating where the next one was going to pop up before it did so. By then I was older – nine months, perhaps?

'She *should* be precocious,' he'd said to Uncle Matthew, and then got up and sat me on my own in front of the computer screen. 'I mean, how could she not be? Let's see how well she can do on her own.'

I cried, abandoned there precariously atop a lab chair at least twice my height off the floor. I don't remember what Uncle Matthew said, but it was accompanied by an exclamation and he was the one who rescued me from the chair and sat me on the floor, crouching down next to me and playing with my toys until I stopped crying and my father shrugged and left us to it.

Like he always did. 'Sort it out, would you?' It became his catchphrase to Uncle Matthew. 'Sort it out, would you?'

Maybe that's what's made me need to be precocious now? To be more than I am in order to get my father's attention? Not be a something that has to be sorted out, but a person. With Uncle Matthew I don't have to be anything – just me. With Uncle Matthew I AM just me. With my father I seem to be… nothing – and everything. Or something to be sorted out.

By the time I was eleven months, I was a regular in Lab One. My father would sit nose to screen almost all day, whilst Uncle Matthew pottered around, collecting and sorting out paperwork, checking the other computer screens and feeding the rats and mice in the cages at the back of the lab. Generally, I would be plonked on a lab seat and told by my father not to move, although Uncle Matthew regularly rotated back to check on me. I was supposed to be reading or doing the computer games my father set up for me, perched atop the lab chair, its wheels locked so it didn't skate across the floor and take me with it, shrieking – as it had once. I hated it but there was no escaping it so I lessened the load for myself by doodling on the scraps of paper that were often abandoned by my father or Uncle Matthew after they'd been scribbling out some equation or another to try and make it work. I loved drawing and I loved it when Uncle Matthew fed the mice and rats because sometimes, when my father had left the lab on some private errand, he let me feed them too. He even got them out on occasion and held them in his cupped hands so I could stroke a tentative finger over the top of their heads. They were so tiny and yet so vibrant, noses twitching, eyes swivelling, terrifyingly fragile yet amazingly alive too. I think Uncle Matthew felt the same way about them because together we secretly gave them all names depending on their characters, even though my father had forbidden they be referred to as anything other than 'specimen one', 'specimen two' and so on. They were my friends – they and Uncle Matthew.

'Twitch' was the white rat whose nose was always twitching, 'Scrabble' and 'Jiggle' the breeding pair who were always tumbling over each other to play, 'Lucky' the alternately tail-less and long-tailed rat who'd somehow shed her tail and then regrown it so had been saved from dissection whilst my father figured out how she'd managed to do it, and the elderly brown one with the grizzled nose was 'Fred' – although I never knew exactly why Fred was Fred because Uncle Matthew named him. He just said he'd been the start of something that had no end so he should be called something timeless.

'What is timeless?' I'd asked, revelling in the fact that for the first time Uncle Matthew had allowed me to hold Fred, showing me first how to cup my hands but not squeeze him when he started to wriggle free. His fur was soft and silky but underneath I could feel the vulnerability of his tiny skeleton and cotton-thin sinews as if they were mine – even his little heart somehow transmitted its wild beat through my skin and into my central core. Fred has always been my favourite because of that. For me he's the epitome of the marvel and frailty of life.

'It's a long story and maybe I'll tell you it one day, but probably not in Fred's lifetime … oops! Remember what I said about not squeezing or you'll make his eyes pop out.' Uncle Matthew gently prised my fingers apart sufficiently to allow Fred to flex his tiny muscles and scramble up my forearm.

'He's escaping, Uncle Matthew. He mustn't escape!' I panicked and made a grab at Fred but only succeeded in grasping his rear end and catapulting him forward like he was a slippery bar of soap being propelled forward by a wet hand. 'Oh no! Now he's climbing my shoulder.' I giggled and squirmed as Fred's tiny claws tickled, yet I was anxious too. 'What if he falls?' I exclaimed, clutched by such fear for Fred's safety that I WAS Fred, falling and falling…

I've always had a fear of falling, ever since my father first marooned me on that lab seat and left me there. I was terrified that if I moved the chair would move too and then I would fall so far I might never find my way up again. I've never liked being on moving things ever since. I did fall off once, and that's why my father locks the wheels now, but despite Uncle Matthew's protests that I'd be better on the floor or on a lower chair, he just shrugs and says that I'm getting bigger all the time and I have to learn... That's true, I am and I do, but I'm still afraid of falling. Maybe that was why I was so afraid of Fred falling. Or maybe it was the first instance of what I can feel now.

Uncle Matthew coaxed Fred from my shoulder, laughing. 'He would probably land on his feet and scamper away,' he assured me, 'delighted to have his freedom…' He paused, gently stroking Fred's head, while his expression changed from laughing to sad, like a clown. One minute a happy face, next minute, sad. 'Like we all would,' he added under his breath. He looked up and caught me watching him. His expression changed again – startled – then back to sad.

'What? What's wrong?' I asked, studying the way his mouth drooped and his eyes looked suddenly dull and empty.

'Sometimes I think you'll look so like your mother, and yet…' He shook his head.

'What?' I prompted again.

'And yet you are your father's daughter,' he added. 'And I must remember that, so we'd better put Monsieur Fred here back in his cage and set you to work before your father comes back. Come on,' he nodded towards the rows of cages. 'You can open the door and make sure he's settled in.'

We'd barely shut the cage door when my father marched in. He paused in the doorway, looking from Uncle Matthew to me and we shared a moment of inexplicable fear. I say inexplicable, because why would my father hurt either of us?

'What have we here?'

I heard Uncle Matthew take a deep breath before replying and I knew what he was going to say – and that all it would do would be to make my father more cold and distant.

'Nothing, Jason, we…'

'How old was I when I knew who you were?' I interrupted before Uncle Matthew could say any more.

I was born the year we had the snowstorms unexpectedly early – deepest winter already by October – and I was apparently born in August. Of course, I'd already worked out how old I was since I remembered my father's face against the backdrop of fierce yellow sunlight not cool frosty snowlight, but interestingly both my father and Uncle Matthew have always been of one accord in avoiding giving me an answer. That was why I knew I was right in thinking it was the one thing that would deflect him from questioning Uncle Matthew further and maybe discovering our guilty secret with the rats and mice.

'Goodness, Hebe, I can't remember. Why do you want to know?'

'I just wondered. Whether I'm average for my age?'

That would definitely cap it! Something about me being precocious is very important to my father. So I play on it for my benefit and for Uncle Matthew's. He needs looking after by me as much as I do by him. You see, my father and Uncle Matthew – they're both my parents in a way. My father is my father biologically, but there has always been something distant about my father, even when he bounced me on his knee or held out his hands to encourage me to walk. It always felt like his focus was just beyond me – just beyond whatever I was doing.

'Catch the ball,' he'd say, applauding me when I managed to clutch the ball to me in a clumsy full arm swipe, and then, 'now catch it quicker.' Or 'how high can you build the tower?' handing me a selection of brightly coloured building blocks, then standing back to observe and pushing more blocks my way with the toe of his shoe when I'd stacked what he'd originally given me. Uncle Matthew though, he has never judged me.

'You're only average if you don't make yourself better than average,' was my father's terse reply. Then he strode across the room and swept me up under one arm and deposited me back on my lab seat. I could feel the seat rocking with the suddenness of my deposit on top of it. I clutched the arms and swallowed hard, waiting for it to steady.

'Jason, shouldn't she…'

'Who decides what my daughter does?' My father swung round towards Uncle Matthew. I couldn't see my father's face but I could imagine what it was like from Uncle Matthew's. He froze, then he sort of crumpled, like he was folding bits of himself inside.

'You do, of course…'

'Then let's get back to where we were earlier then, shall we?' He turned back to me and then noticed my pages upon pages of doodles. 'What's this?' He homed in on one page in particular. It was of eyes, peering through grass stalks. He picked it up and showed it to Uncle Matthew, not me.

'Oh…' Uncle Matthew's mouth opened and closed like a fish blowing bubbles. 'But that's…'

'Just doodling,' I said, hanging my head so he couldn't look into my eyes. My father has this uncanny ability to see through what you are saying if he can look you in the eye. A bit like me, but different.

'Well,' he paused and then looked back at Uncle Matthew. Something passed between them that I didn't understand, then, surprisingly, my father backed off.

'You were wondering if she is precocious,' Uncle Matthew told him. 'Perhaps you've been assuming the wrong kind of precocious or the wrong kind of genetics.'

My father's shoulders seemed to clench, turning his body into a fist that I imagined punching Uncle Matthew and pinning him to the ground, but I knew it was just what he was feeling, not what he was actually doing – and it was surprising I managed to feel it too. Usually, my father is a closed door whereas Uncle Matthew is an open one. You walk through Uncle Matthew's door and inside is everything he's thinking and feeling. You try to walk through my father's, and he's sealed off. Maybe that's because on the odd occasion his door isn't sealed off you want to turn and run back outside before you get crushed.

My father didn't pound anyone to dust – or even raise his voice. He has a way of crushing without any pressure at all. He just said, coolly and quietly, 'Just do what you were meant to be doing,' and put the doodled papers back on the desktop next to me. 'I have something to check on.'

He glared at Uncle Matthew and waited until Uncle Matthew had retreated to his workstation then went back to his own PC screen and settled back down there, apparently oblivious to both of us. The day wore on, silent, tedious and tense until I was desperate to get down from the chair, but Uncle Matthew still seemed afraid to meet my eye.

It was then it struck me. I felt just like Fred – not in a cage but trapped, nevertheless. I wondered if Uncle Matthew did too. Across the lab, my father seemed to have fallen asleep, head on the workstation in front of him. He did that sometimes – like he just shut down. I peered longingly in the direction of Uncle Matthew and the rat and mice cages, hoping Uncle Matthew might come over and rescue me like the prince rescued Rapunzel from her tower whilst my father was asleep. He didn't. I sighed loudly and only then did he look up, glance across at my father and then put a finger to his lips. He pointed to his watch and held up three fingers. Only another three hours to go. I sighed again and went back to my doodling.

In between completing the computer tasks my father had set me, I looked up the word precocious on the internet, and found out what it meant.

"Precocious: having developed certain abilities or inclinations at an earlier age than is usual or expected."

Three hours later, my father awoke as abruptly as he'd fallen asleep, and signalled to Uncle Matthew that I could be collected by Andrea my nurse. Uncle Matthew merely nodded and shuffled across the room to pick me up off the chair, whilst my father flicked through my pages of drawings again and then studied my computer work.

'Come on, Hebe, tea, bath and bedtime for you,' Uncle Matthew said as if nothing had happened. He set me on the floor and gave me a gentle push towards the lab door. I hesitated in the doorway and luckily he picked up on my cue. 'I'm just going too. School play tonight. OK if I go early, Jason?'

'Huh?' My father twisted round, still clutching my drawings. 'Oh, yes, I suppose so. Keep the harridan happy.'

'Thanks,' Uncle Matthew grabbed his jacket from the coat rack by the door and ushered me out. 'Whew…' he blew it out like it was a cloud of steam once the door had closed behind us and we were setting off down the corridor. 'Tough one today…'

'Uncle Matthew?'

'Yes?'

'Why is my father so…' I wanted to say cold, distant, unalike, overwhelming but even a precocious four–year-old can't always find the words to adequately describe a father who is there, and yet not, even whilst being overwhelmingly…*everywhere*… Odd, in a word.

'Hmm, well, it's a bit like Fred, a long story but not one I'll likely tell you in his lifetime.'

I thought about that for the rest of the walk along the corridor and until we got to the secret panel. Then I asked Uncle Matthew if he thought I was precocious because of what I could do, because wouldn't that make me a bit odd too?

'And what are my genetics?'

'Jeez,' was his reply. 'What are you today? Four? You're only four and you're asking about genetics and if you're precocious – or odd!' He sighed, then got down on both knees in front of me and took both my hands in his. 'You are as you are, Hebe,' was his reply, 'and one day you will have all the answers you need, but for now, just be a little girl, huh? As a little girl you are just perfect…'

I liked that, but I'm not a little girl, am I? That's what my father means by precocious. I'm anything but a little girl. And I'm only four for the time being. Tomorrow is another day altogether.

Chapter 3

10:48, 18th May 2032: Luke

'What the fuck! Who is this?'

Luke swung round. Entering the courtyard by another concealed opening were Matthew Green and the big man himself, Jason Crane, now pushing Green roughly aside and striding across the courtyard towards Luke and Hebe.

'Jason, wait…' Green's voice quavered after him as Green struggled to regain his balance. 'He's just one of the journalists…'

Jason didn't falter or slow. He was approaching Luke with the urgency and power of a high-speed train making up speed for earlier delays, yet still with that disquieting sense of stillness to him that Luke had felt before. His expression was somewhere between anger and the fixed focus of a predator stalking its prey.

'I don't give a fuck what he is. How'd he get in here?'

Instinctively Luke placed himself between Jason and Hebe, although why the hell he did it, he couldn't have explained later. After all, the girl must be Crane's daughter, surely? What other explanation was there for hiding her away? But then again, what explanation was there *for* hiding her away?

'Father, stop!' Hebe took Luke by surprise by stepping out from behind him and positioning herself in between Luke and the oncoming train. If it had been a cartoon, Crane would have literally screeched to a halt in a cloud of steam in front of her. As it was, he stopped short of Hebe by mere inches. Luke found himself transfixed, despite the drama of the moment, watching it all as if in slow motion as Hebe stepped in front of him and Crane steadied himself, slowing from full speed to stationary without even flinching. Under his exquisitely tailored shirt, Luke could see the tightening and contracting of Crane's muscles, the supreme control over a body honed to the same pitch as an athlete's. High-speed train? Actually, more like a panther, sleek, sly and ruthless. Behind him, Green was now loping towards them too, with all the grace of a warthog, since Luke now found himself using animal similes. The curse of the writer – even when you're up shit creek and without a paddle your brain is still working on ways to describe that. Hebe was speaking again now. Luke switched off the writer's brain and applied the brain of the man aiming to not be beaten to a pulp for invading Jason Crane's private sanctuary. He'd heard enough of 3:16's assumptions about the personality and character of Jason Crane to know that what he'd apparently done was likely to get him a good beating, at the very least.

'I let him in,' Hebe was saying, her voice cool and calming. Wilfully, Luke's writer's brain likened her to a cooing dove before he told it to shut up and listen. 'He was being chased and they didn't look too friendly. I couldn't just leave him out there to get hurt, could I?'

'Like you did when you just abandoned me,' Luke couldn't stop himself levelling at Green as he arrived alongside Crane.

Crane turned sideways, but only fractionally, just enough to imply that the threat of his perfectly honed body might be to Green now, rather than to Luke.

'Where did you abandon him, Matthew? He should have been with the rest of the press, not you. Or should I ask, why did you abandon him?'

'I didn't abandon him. I told him to follow the rest,' Green protested, his heavy jowls wobbling defensively. 'I can't help it if he didn't.'

Beads of sweat were just starting to break out on his forehead, his face taking on that unhealthy sheen of fear you get when your nemesis approaches. Luke was about to roundly denounce Green as a liar when his strategising brain kicked in and quietly pointed out to him that Green had deliberately facilitated his avoidance of the security chip at reception – therefore also avoiding officially proving he was who he said he was. Green must have done that for a reason, just as he'd singled Luke out from the other press and told him to head in the opposite direction to them. Why? That was worth finding out at the very least. Luke closed his mouth and ground his teeth whilst Crane continued to berate Green.

'He should have already been with the rest,' Crane replied. He seemed calm, yet underneath the calm was something else. 'So why was he with you? Did he engineer that, or did you?'

Green's mouth opened and shut like a fish, then he seemed to regain his composure and with it a certain amount of his own belligerence. 'I don't know why we're dissecting why he followed me rather than the rest of the press group when there's what amounts to a rampaging army outside,' Green replied. For a moment, Luke admired his spunk. He wouldn't be answering Jason Crane back like this from what he could ascertain from his now close-up observation. Not only was the man in peak condition physically, but he could now put a name to that sense of over-stillness; unnatural – and yet... He was tempted to reach out and touch the man's arm, test the texture, see if he was sweating too, or if he felt cold and inhuman to the touch. All the stories that 3:16 had regaled him with came flooding back – stories he'd dismissed as the crazies feeding their obsessions, but which now, his gut was telling him, might not have been so wild after all. Luke jerked back to attention as he sensed Crane's focus had swung back onto him. His eyes were deep blue but edged with a hard grey rim. There was something of the camera lens to that rim, like an aperture opening and closing. Crane physically removed Hebe from between them, lifting her bodily and placing her to one side as if she were an object. She didn't resist. Indeed, it even seemed as if she went rigid in order to facilitate the movement, with only the merest whisper of complaint in the 'Oh' that escaped as he placed her feet back onto the ground. Then he thrust his face into Luke's and Luke was staring right into that grey lens aperture, tracing the intricate patterns of the connective tissue and thin muscle that made up the iris and marvelling at the unbelievable complexity of the human body. Crane's breath warmed Luke's face until it flamed and Luke swallowed hard, anticipating the punch, heavy and relentless, that would surely follow this intimidatory scrutiny. But it never came. Crane took a step back, still scrutinising him.

'Why are you here today?' he asked, voice neutral and polite.

'I… er, I… Well, I was with the press conference party. For the ReNewal module launch.'

'Your name?' Crane held out his hand and when Luke hesitated, not quite sure how the outstretched hand and the question intersected, he ripped Luke's press pass from his lapel, taking a small fragment of cloth with it. The noise of the cloth tearing seemed like thunder in the quiet of the courtyard. Crane turned the press pass over and read the name aloud. 'Edward Hughes. Matthew,' he didn't even turn as he addressed Green. 'Bring me up a photo of Edward Hughes.'

Beside him, Green rummaged in his pocket and brought out one of the latest smartphones, now equipped with bio-scanning. He pointed it at Luke and then flipped the screen so Crane could see what Edward Hughes *should* look like. The courtyard echoed with Luke's despair as Crane smiled, a slow spread of satisfaction covering his whole face, but never reaching his eyes. They remained cool, alert and judgemental, recording Luke's face for posterity before it exploded in a mass of red, tortured flesh. Surely Crane was going to punch him now? The desire to do so had been latent within his attitude to Luke from that very first 'What the fuck?'

But still he didn't.

'So, not Edward Hughes,' Crane commented, the pleasant, almost conversational tone belying the expression in his eyes. 'Luke Maynard,' he read, referring back to the bio-scan page on the smartphone. The name reverberated around the courtyard, bouncing off the high glass ceiling like the place had perfect acoustics. 'Age thirty-six, freelance journalist – so that at least is true – no dependants, no close family, no specific political allegiances, and no known group memberships. The veritable invisible man, apart from the photograph. And a liar. That makes you perfect fodder for undercover work, doesn't it – for a group like 3:16. Is that what you're really doing here? Opening the door for them once you've got in on somebody else's press pass?'

'No!' Luke protested but even to himself, he didn't sound convincing. The man had got it in one – but not that he was undercover for them. Christ, far from it. The only person he was undercover for was… He shifted awkwardly from one foot to the other, conscious of the sweat now starting to trickle down his sides from his armpits and of the taste of bile in his mouth. 'No,' he repeated, quieter and more decidedly. 'I was here for the ReNewal launch. I haven't had much work recently so I was hoping this was going to get me back on the map again. Edwards is a drunk, and stupid. I took advantage after he'd emptied my wallet with whiskies. So, yes, I'm a liar, but that's all.'

A low humming noise off to one side of the courtyard drew all of their attention. Hebe was sitting in the middle of the small patch of grass and systematically threading daisies into a daisy chain but staring into space as she did so.

'Hebe, you should go,' Crane instructed. She ignored him. 'Hebe!' he thundered. She jumped up, dropping the daisy chain and to Luke she seemed suddenly quite different, but he couldn't work out why. 'You need to go!' Crane ordered, gesturing to his watch. Her mouth dropped open and her vacant expression filled suddenly with horror. She ran towards the opening where Crane and Green had arrived and slipped through it, turning and glancing back briefly at Luke before she disappeared.

'Jason,' Green touched Crane lightly on the arm and then took the phone back from him. He pocketed it and continued, 'whether he's here solely for the press conference or for other reasons, for the moment we have more important things to deal with.' His eyes flicked across to where Hebe had left and then back to Crane. 'Put this on ice until the situation's under control out there.'

Crane stared at Green, and then smiled again – this time a normal smile. 'Yes, yes, you're right. We need to get rid of these raving lunatics first, I agree. Then we'll find out what this one's really up to – who he's working with too. Come on,' he nodded towards Luke. 'Follow me.'

Luke looked askance at Green. Green shook his head and put a finger to his lips. 'Go on,' he said aloud. 'You heard the man.' He prodded Luke on ahead of him but as they reached the concealed opening, he pulled Luke back by his jacket tail. Crane disappeared through the hole and Green drew level with Luke. 'I'll get you out later. Just keep your mouth shut for now.' Then he pushed him on ahead again. Luke emerged in a corridor similar to the one he'd arrived via, but this had a softer, less clinical feel to it. The floor was carpeted, and the walls tinted a pastel blue. The corridor stretched on into the distance but Crane was already waiting by another exit point halfway along. Beyond it yawned a dark space and stairs leading downwards.

'After you,' Crane said with mock courtesy. He gave a little bow to add to the irony, before pushing Luke roughly through the open doorway and down the first step. Luke lost his footing and stumbled, ankles giving way under him and burning with the savagery of the twist as he tumbled down the next four steps before making a grab for the handrail. His feet skittered off the next step, but he held on tight, arms wrenching from their sockets and making him gasp with pain. Unexpectedly he felt a hand on his collar and he was jerked back upright and set on his feet. Crane's voice whispered silkily in his ear, 'Have to keep you in one piece in case I need you that way later… Now go on and stand on your own two feet.'

Luke continued on down the stairs, feeling his way in the dimly lit stairway, shoulders still screaming with pain, ankles weak and useless. Finally they reached the bottom and Crane pushed past him. It was even darker here than on the stairs – dank, dark – like he was drowning in nothing. Crane placed his hand across a wall-mounted identity pad and it lit up, revealing a hitherto invisible door which slid open with a sibilant hiss. Simultaneously, the lights flipped on and Luke was staring into a brilliant white room roughly ten feet square, one wall a tessellation of doors all the same height and width, the others absolutely pristine; a cold place of nothing.

'In you go.' Crane shoved him hard between the shoulder blades and Luke careered into the room, skidding on the highly polished floor. He slithered across it and collided with the far wall, rebounding off it as quickly as if he'd been burnt. It wasn't heat that made him jump though. Quite the reverse. It didn't just look cold, it *was* cold. The only thing in the room apart from the doors was a wall thermometer, reading 0 degrees. Luke shivered and Crane laughed. 'There,' he called over his shoulder to Green. 'Literally on ice – in cold storage.' Luke barely caught Green's expression as the door began to slide shut – shock mixed with fear. 'And only I can let you out.' He held his palm up to Luke and it was then that Luke saw the small circuitry pads on each fingertip. Jesus, the man himself was the security code!

'Shit!' Luke said, as much to himself as to the closing door. He looked at the row upon row of doors and the wall thermometer and it dawned on him what this was. Not just cold storage. More like a morgue – and one only Jason Crane had access to! Now he understood Green's expression. But why the hell would Crane Industries have a morgue? And how was he going to get out before he became one of its residents?

Chapter 4

11:12, 18th May 2032: Luke

Luke completed a circuit of the room, ending up back at the door. He stamped his feet and cursed again. What had he been thinking of? He was in no condition to play these kind of games. What kind of short-sighted hubris had led him to get involved in any of this? But he already knew the answer to that – the need to believe he *could* still play these kind of games. Without that belief he might as well just curl up and die – as he was most likely to do in here unless Jason Crane felt more curiosity that animosity towards him. Most men could last out an hour in this temperature, but he wasn't most men. His extremities were already beginning to stiffen up and spasm. He felt in his jacket pocket and found the tube containing his medication in the furry-edged depths, lined with the detritus of long lack of use. The last time he'd worn this jacket must have been when he'd taken Frieda on their first date. Over two and a half years ago. Shit! That long? He flipped the lid open and downed two pills as he pictured her then, diminutive yet filling the room with the force of her personality as she outlined the National Hospital for Neurology and Neurosurgery's most recent developments in the field of neurology – and specifically in relation to Motor Neurone Disease.

'No longer will sufferers need to measure their life span in years and months but in decades.'

Her small red button mouth enunciated each consonant as if it were an enemy to be fought off and cut down. Her hair folded around her face like a cloud, soft brown with golden highlights, face heart-shaped, skin translucent. His writer's skills faltered in front of her. As human beings went, she wasn't just beautiful, she was perfect – and tiny. A minute powerhouse delivering the death blow to Motor Neurone Disease – or so he'd thought then. He'd. joined the trial there and then. No question. This beautiful little Hitler was going to be the saving of him. And behind the clipped, cool and collected consonants and vowels he'd thought he'd detected something else – a genuine desire to see her research succeed, not just for her own satisfaction, but for the poor despondent victims of the disease.

That might have been more wishful thinking than reality, looking back on things, but she'd never been only the cool-headed scientist signing up sufficient lab rats to get her trial authenticated, as some of the self-centred assholes had been that he'd encountered since MND first hit his personal radar. That he could say for her, even if she broke his balls and his heart simultaneously and then broke off all contact too.

'Mr Maynard? Luke Maynard?' She had to look up at him – not that he was that tall, but five foot nothing has to look up to anything above them and he prided himself of making five-nine even in his stockinged feet. He'd been working out then too – had a six pack and shoulders to match – determined not to let the beast eat away at his bones before he'd at least had a chance to throw his meat around a little.

'That's me,' he'd replied, looking down into her doe eyes and finding his own misting over.

'You don't look very ill,' she commented, looking him over and making no attempt to hide the none too scientific assessment going on as part of it. Her eyes widened as they took in his thighs and crotch. She looked back up into his face too suddenly for him to hide his smile of satisfaction.

'Do I have to be ill to join the trial?'

'No, you just have to have a firm diagnosis, but your general state of health will determine the kind of trial we enter you into. Some trial candidates are already more debilitated than others so we have a duty of care to not place any undue strain on their already taxed physiology.' She smiled then and the button mouth revealed perfect pearls of teeth, lined up into perfect rows. 'You, I suspect, we could use as a workhorse though...' The smile became a low, amused gurgle as she winked at him. He didn't know what to say. But that was always the way it was with her. One minute the cool clinician, the next the mischievous temptress – and all bound together in the ambitious madam. A beautiful little Hitler.

Luke stamped his feet again. This wasn't the time for reminiscing, even though Frieda Kohn was part of the reason he'd got himself into this mess. They should never have got involved, he could see that now. Not even the most objective doctor could fail to be influenced by her patient-lover and they'd hardly been objective about each other – either of them. He'd ruined the trial for her, ruined her chance at recognition and ruined their possibility at a future. Of course, she was going to cut him dead when the Trust cut her off. The beautiful little Hitler could be as cruel as Mengele too.

But he couldn't bring himself to believe she'd stopped caring about him, and her recruits, as she called them. Never stopped hoping she would find a cure one day. Maybe that was why he'd heard from her, completely out of the blue all those months after they'd split, acrimoniously, rancorously and finally?

'Luke?'

'Frieda? What the fuck? Is it really you?'

'Yes, it's really me, but don't get any stupid ideas. I'm not taking you back.'

'I don't expect you to…' but he had. His hopes were already soaring at the mere sound of her voice.

'Good.' It sounded more like 'gud'. Her trademark clipped speech was always more pronounced when she was talking in a professional capacity. Just that one word had adjusted his expectations like a bucket of icy water tipped over his head.

'Then?'

'You know I left the National Hospital for Neurology and Neurosurgery after…'

'Yes…'

The pauses between their words reminded him of the pauses between their understanding of each other. She was sounding soft and regretful even whilst telling him they were still over. He was confused.

'Well,' her voice had taken on that sharp edge again. 'I joined another hospital – a small one that was grateful to have me, despite the mess,' her tongue lingered on mess, drawling the 's' until it became like the hiss of a snake. He recoiled in pain.

'I'm so sorry,' he murmured, but she cut him off.

'That's all in the past now. What I'm ringing you about is the future. I didn't stay at the hospital. I took on another role for one of the hospital's patients which has become rather interesting. In fact, so interesting, I think there is the potential for a breakthrough for people like you here, Luke. A cure.'

'A cure? For MND? I thought you concluded that wasn't possible, even without my... interference, shall we say?'

'I did, but this is very different. Look, I can't explain over the phone, but let's meet and I'll explain. Then I'll need your help too.'

'Breaking a story?'

'No, keeping it under wraps if you want to take advantage of it.'

'Now I AM intrigued.'

'Who's the patient you went to work for?'

'Jason Crane. Crane Industries. I've got to go. Meet me in the café tomorrow at ten.'

And then she was gone, her voice cut off as abruptly by the end of the call as their future together had been three months previously. Ten o'clock came and went the next day, with no appearance from her in the café they'd used to meet at when he was still a working hack trying to pretend he didn't have MND, and she a clinical trials doctor. He rang her. No answer. He rang her again. Still no answer. He had no idea where she was living by then so paying her a visit was out. The days and weeks had passed and still there had been no sound or sign of her, but by the time the midsummer had become late summer in 2029, Jason Crane and Crane Industries had become a source of speculation and mystery to both Luke Maynard, and much of the rest of the world. Its CyberArm 3.3 had caused a revolution in cybernetic prostheses and Jason Crane's name was being bandied around as a potential Nobel prize-winner. By autumn, the great man had seemingly disappeared off the map, together with his wife, Elise – and Frieda Kohn. It had taken most of six months and many bouts of dragging himself into work when he felt as if his whole body was seizing up to get himself on the list for the first press conference. The visit that had landed him up in the courtyard for the first time. He should have given up then, but where the desire to find out why Frieda had blown him out after promising him something akin to Nirvana had gradually faded, the determination to get back to the little child all on her own in the courtyard and desperate for him to take him with her had grown exponentially. The child had become him, he supposed – someone lost and in need of a saviour. He couldn't save himself, but maybe he could save her?

But to do that, now he needed to save himself first because clearly Matthew Green wasn't going to be able to get him out of here, despite his promise. Struggling to keep upright, he rubbed his frozen hands against his cramping muscles, pounding at his thighs to encourage the blood to keep flowing through them. He winced at the pain to his already over-sensitive hands and clawed his fingers into his palm to keep the warmth between them. Damn this fucking disease! Without it he'd never have met Frieda, never have come exploring here, never have got shoved in this room to freeze his balls off! Concentrate! His head felt stuffed full of too many ideas, too many thoughts. Maybe he wasn't cold after all? Maybe he was too hot? He plucked at his jacket with numb fingers. But why were his fingers cold if he was too hot? You stupid bastard. That's hypothermia setting in. He smacked his face and shouted at himself. Stupid, stupid bastard… He gasped and coughed at the pain, doubling over and sucking in a great gulp of cold air as his cheek stung like a thousand needles were being poked through it. At least there was sufficient air in the room to breathe and he wasn't going to suffocate before he froze. He slumped down into a crouch, curling into a little ball as he waited for the pain in his cheek and fingers to subside. Air, lovely cool air to breathe…

Air.

Then, there must be a way for the air to come in! Luke struggled back onto his feet and shuffled his twentieth circuit of the room, this time paying minute attention to the walls, the doors, the wall thermometer. As he passed the wall of doors, he slowed almost to a standstill. He paused in front of the crack between wall and door, fingers flitting like fleeing doves in front of it. Air. He could feel air. Cold air. The cold air was coming in though the crack between the door and the wall. If there was air coming in there, maybe he could get out there too? Luke grabbed the handle on the door front and pulled. Nothing. It wouldn't budge. He pulled again, sitting on the floor and bracing his feet against the wall underneath the door as he yanked at it again. Nothing, just a pulled muscle in his back. He let go of the handle and fell backwards, heaving and sighing. His head spun and little lights seemed to buzz around him like fireflies. He blew out between pursed lips and heaved himself upright. How long had he been in here? Ten minutes? Fifteen and with his condition, he would be out cold – a goner. Try again. No, try a different one. Maybe that door was locked but another might not be. He shuffled along to the next door and braced himself again. Nothing. Try the next one.

Slowly, he moved along the wall of doors until he arrived at the door on the far end of the wall. If this one didn't work, then he wasn't sure he would have the energy or wherewithal to stand and try the next layer. He swallowed hard, struggling to close his mouth. His jaw hung open and his tongue stuck to the roof of his mouth like a dried sponge. He swallowed again and his mouth fused, tongue to teeth to lips. Ugh… his despair escaped him in a long, low sigh as he grasped the handle on the door and pulled.

The door swung across the top of his face as it opened, grazing chin, nose and forehead as it slid full length across the top of him so he lay underneath it, staring up at its steely grey underside with runners and rails attaching it to the mechanism that moved it forward and backwards. It wasn't just a door, it was a drawer. Oh shit, of course it was a drawer. This was a morgue, wasn't it? He rolled awkwardly out from underneath the drawer and scrabbled onto his hands and knees. Crawling painfully across the icy floor, peeling his bone-cold fingers from its smooth coldness, he slowly reached the head of the drawer. He reared up, clutching the drawer edge and peered in, chin resting on the sharp sliver of steel that formed the drawer runner at the top.

The drawer was occupied.

Luke stared in horror at the neat, perfect features, the soft cloud of dark curls and the blanched lips that once would have been formed into a bow; a kiss waiting to unravel – then he fell backwards onto his heels and wailed.

Chapter 5

10:22, 18th May 2032: Hebe

That day I was sitting in the courtyard, like I am now, daydreaming. I've always liked the courtyard. It's the closest I've ever experienced to being outside and when the glass roof is rolled back, like it is in the summer, I AM outside. The little patch of grass in the centre of the courtyard was full of daisies and I'd already made a chain as long as myself from them as my mind wandered – like it often does; this and that, storing up random and useless bits of information, which convince me that the world is real, otherwise why would there be all this useless and random information to find out? *Bellis perennis*, the daisy, is a common European species of the family Asteraceae. It is small, white, with pink tipped petals and found everywhere on earth except Antarctica. Its name is thought to come from the Old English 'daes eag' and it was first classified in 1792. It is said to represent purity and innocence and is, in fact, two flowers in one. The white petals count as one flower and the cluster of tiny yellow disc petals in the centre are technically another.

'There you are!' My father was halfway through the secret panel before I heard him. You can't hear him like you can hear other people – Uncle Matthew or the lady who cleans our rooms – so I always miss the moment he first arrives. One day I won't. One day I'll be so on the alert, I'll hear that tiny space between him being here and not, and then I'll see him arrive. I'll know then, too, what his face looks like before he knows anyone is watching him, and if he looks like Uncle Matthew then, or the lady who cleans our rooms, or like... 'What are you doing?'

'Making daisy chains.' I held up the one I'd made so far, the one that was as long as I was. 'This is mine. Yours would need to be a lot longer.'

He squatted down beside me, squashing the grass. Its anguished cries made me want to wince for sympathy at the pain he caused the grass stalks as he crushed them, but I tucked the feeling inside me and just smiled at him.

'Why would mine need to be longer?' he picked up the tail end of the daisy chain, dangling it though his fingers.

'Because you're longer than me.'

'Oh, I see. We're to be measured in daisies now, are we?'

'We can be measured in anything as long as it's a specified unit of measurement, can't we? I choose daisies.'

'A good answer.' He laughed and let the daisy chain drop. In my head its impact on the already injured grass reverberated like a pistol being fired too close to my head would make my eardrum ring. The suddenness of the reaction was too much to contain and this time I did wince. 'What?' he peered into my face and studied me like he studied the rats in the cages in Lab Three sometimes. I hadn't told anyone about the grass, not even Uncle Matthew. Now it seemed I should have.

'I can… sense it hurts – the grass; dropping things on it.' I added.

'Sense?'

'Feel it.'

'Feel what?'

'That it hurts…'

'But then how can you pick the daisies?'

'They don't mind. They're not real.'

I haven't explained very well why the crushed grass is in pain but the daisies I'm picking aren't, have I? Well, it's exactly as I said to my father. They're not real. The grass was grown from seed, the daisies weren't. They were manufactured. Uncle Matthew explained for me how the little square of lawn had been grown when I first stood on it and had been overwhelmed by its cries of pain. They raked the soil, watered it and scattered the seed. Eventually a fine fuzz of green grew and it has stayed alive ever since, carefully cut by the lady who cleans our rooms, but when I'm not around to hear the symphony of agony as she systematically beheads it. But the flower seeds wouldn't grow, so my father created flowers – daisies. 3D printing, Uncle Matthew called it. He explained the process to me once but I was too young to understand it then. I do now I'm older. It explains a lot of things too – like my father. I don't like the daisies any the less for not being real, and at least it means I can make daisy chains without hurting them when I pick them. The grass, though, I can't help, so I never sit on it. I just admire it.

'Of course, they're real, Hebe. You can pick them and make daisy chains with them, so how are they not real?'

'They're just not.'

He looked at me strangely. 'What else isn't real then Hebe?'

Some sixth sense stopped me from saying 'you'. Instead, I said, 'I wish I'd been called Daisy, not Hebe. I'd like to be pure and innocent and two flowers in one.' I repeated the facts I'd gathered about daisies and he listened, nodding seriously as if he was considering them one by one.

'But Hebe is the name of a flower too,' he told me. 'It's small, intensely blue and very pretty. Better still, Hebe was the goddess of youth in Greek mythology. She served nectar and ambrosia to the Olympians and later married Heracles.'

'I don't want to be a goddess.'

'What do you want to be then, Hebe?'

'I don't know. I'm too young to know.'

'Indeed, you are. But precocious – you've always been precocious. Matthew tells me you know what that means?'

I nodded. 'I looked it up.'

'You looked it up, huh?' he frowned. 'Was it easy to read?'

'I spelled out the letters and made the sounds and then I knew it was the word I was looking for, like you showed me.'

'Hmm, then maybe it's time we found out how precocious you are? Would you like to find out?'

'Why?'

'It's always best to know what you are capable of.'

'Uncle Matthew says you are as you are,' I said, straightening the daisy chain, 'so do I need to know what I can do? Can't I just be whatever I am without knowing any more for now? And maybe when I'm bigger, I'll be able to do more and that would be a better time to find out?'

'Without a baseline, any assessment would be very hit or miss then.' He tapped his fingers on the grass and pain echoed in the hollow of my chest. I gritted my teeth to hold back from groaning. 'I should have done it earlier really, but we can start it now with some tolerances accepted. We can start by seeing how good you are at doing specific things, or if you can do things that maybe, Uncle Matthew, for example, can't do? Like hear the grass when it's hurt,' he added smiling.

'I suppose we could.' I arranged the daisy chain across my knees and counted the daisies. There were thirty-two of them. In my head I calculated how many my father would need. Seventy-nine would do it. There were at least that many still poking their heads up through the grass, waiting to be picked, and then he or Uncle Matthew would have to make some more. The sleeping lady in the locked room would need sixty-five. 'Do you hear the grass when it's hurt?'

He hesitated and I knew he wasn't going to tell me. I knew also that not telling me meant he did, but maybe he ignored it. He got up and brushed some stray strands of grass from his trousers and they whimpered as they fell. 'We do have some funny conversations, don't we?' he said, smiling at me like he used to before he'd started to show me how to do things like sound out letters and recognise words. Before he'd given me the tools to be precocious... 'But it's good you're starting to read so fluently now. That's going to be a bonus. Once the brain starts to develop its language facility everything else speeds up, you know. If you can read words like precocious then that could signify hyperlexia – and certainly gives you a reading age of about twelve when you're…' he looked at me searchingly.

'Thirteen months,' I supplied.

'Thirteen months... That long?' His eyes flicked away from me and towards the room the sleeping lady was locked inside. I followed his gaze with my own, only to find him staring at me when I brought my attention back to him again. 'More than a year old,' he added, his voice artificially jolly. 'Who would have thought I would have a year-old daughter who can read the word precocious. Is that for real?' he laughed aloud and patted me on the head. 'We'll start that baseline tomorrow, I think.'

I watched him go, slipping through the hidden panel as silently as he'd arrived, and leaving me, the one-year-old who could read the word precocious, and hear the grass crying out in pain, wondering what a baseline assessment meant and was that why Uncle Matthew had said that one day I would have to leave here, but he'd have to find the right someone to take me. I considered the four greyish-cream walls around me, enclosing the courtyard, the roll-back glass roof, the artificial daisies and the agonised grass… and me. I'd read all the books about school and friends and puppies and the world outside in order to get to the stage where I could read 'precocious' when I was only two and I knew my life wasn't normal. The questioned remained, was I? Today I was thirteen months old. Tomorrow, I would be quite different.

Chapter 6

12:43, 18th May 2032: Luke

Luke opened his eyes and stared up, trying to place what he was looking up at. Had he already died? Was this a frozen heaven and she an ice angel? She looked familiar, and yet not anyone he knew. A woman with a girl's face. A child who was a woman too. Blonde hair, blue eyes – oh, so deep a blue they were like the deepest aqua of a tumbling wave mid-ocean, surrounded by the bubbling white of sea foam, effervescing and floating up to meet big juicy clouds of white, so full, one squeeze would send the rain spurting from them in a great torrent of water. The woman-girl smiled. She looked kind. She looked pleased. Pleased he was dead or pleased he was alive. His body was numb so he must be dead.

'Where am I? Is this heaven?'

'No,' the girl-woman giggled. 'It's the cold storage room.'

'But I am dead…'

'No, silly, but you are probably hypothermic so it's a good job Uncle Matthew is on his way. I must have activated the intruder alert when I broke in and it flooded the room with cold air.'

'You're… Hebe?'

'Yes,' she smiled, even white teeth in two perfect rows just showing between soft pink lips. 'Maybe you're not quite so hypothermic as I thought you were.'

Luke struggled to sit up but nothing worked. He couldn't even feel the protrusion of Hebe's legs against his back. His head lay in her lap, neck ricked at an awkward ninety degree angle, but even that was numb. He flexed his fingers but he couldn't tell if they moved or not.

'You can't be Hebe. She's older than you. Or younger, I'm not sure now.'

'Well…' she smiled again, this time ruefully. 'Both, I expect. It's complicated.'

Luke frowned and squinted at her, struggling to focus his ice-dulled eyes. This girl-woman was maybe twelve or thirteen. Hebe had been about ten. But this *was* Hebe. He was quite sure of that.

'How the hell did you get in? There's a security pad only your father can operate.'

'I know, annoying, isn't it? He does it on all the places he doesn't want me to get into, but there's always a way if you set your mind to it. I can't get out the same way now though. I'm too small.'

'How did you get in?'

'Through an air duct. There's cold air circulated through all the drawers to keep the contents cold.'

'Dammit!' Luke struggled to get up again. This time Hebe helped him, pushing on his shoulders and then his back until his body was at ninety degrees instead of his neck. The open drawer that contained Frieda's body was closed now, all but for a few inches. 'Which drawer?' he demanded. His voice rasped and his throat felt sore but at least he was sitting up and – apparently – still functioning.

'One in the top row. That's why I can't get out that way now. I'm not tall enough to reach it. I was earlier.'

The brief respite from helplessness that sitting upright brought also had its downsides. He might be sitting, but his legs were spasming and his hands were clawing. He could feel his tongue furring up too. The next stage would be for speech to slur and then the twitching would start. He didn't want that to happen in front of Hebe.

'In my pocket, there's a pill tube.'

'You want me to get it out?' Hebe was on her hands and knees now, sliding him round like he was a rag doll, his legs flopping out in front of him – and yet he knew they wouldn't flop if he tried to use them. They'd be rigid like two rods of steel – but equally as useless as a rag doll's legs. She manoeuvred him so his back was resting against the wall and then rifled through his jacket pockets, eventually pulling out the medication tube. "This it?' she asked, waving it in front of him.

He nodded weakly, allowing his head to rest limply against the cold hard storage room wall. It rolled sideways and lolled at an angle. Jeez, what must he look like? He worried he was going to scare the girl – and yet she didn't even seem fazed, either by his condition, or where she'd found him, or the way she'd arrived here.

'Two. I need two.'

'OK,' she popped the lid off the medication tube and emptied two into her palm. 'They're pretty,' she exclaimed, rolling them around her palm, studying the way their pearlescent sheen changed from green to gold to red, depending on the way the light fell on them. Luke coughed and she looked up at him, expression full of concern. 'Here,' she said, tipping his head back so his jaw fell open. She dropped the two pills onto his tongue and closed his mouth. 'Can you swallow?' His eyes signalled distress and she surprised him by tutting and then stroking his throat in long sweeping motions until the impulse to swallow overrode the gag reflex and the two pills slipped down his gullet as if oiled. He coughed again and then shut his eyes. 'Uncle Matthew shouldn't be long.' Luke felt her hands cover his. 'Oh! You're freezing though. Here, I'll warm you up whilst we wait.'

Her hands left his and for a moment Luke thought she'd gone altogether, but when he opened his eyes, she was kneeling astride his legs, fingertips pressed to his temples. He felt acutely uncomfortable, as if he was violating her even though it was she who'd initiated the compromising position.

'Uhh, Hebe, I…'

'Shhh,' she shook her head at him. 'Just close your eyes. It'll make you feel better, I promise.'

'But…' even as he protested, his eyelids drooped as if someone had attached weights to them, pulling them inexorably downwards until they closed altogether. Hebe's fingertips rotated against his temples and she started to hum, a lilting melody of highs and lows, swooping and soaring. As he listened, his body seemed to go with it despite his disinclination. It felt unnatural – he felt unnatural – and yet somehow, he didn't too. That in itself unsettled him more. He wanted to tell her to stop, that it was creeping him out – and yet it wasn't. Some of the deeper drops and more dramatic inclines in the melody made him nauseous but just as he was about to complain, the nausea left him, leaving him relaxed but also throbbing with an intense raw energy. In fact, he felt more alive and healthier than he had in years, despite the intense cold and his twitching but useless limbs. With an enormous effort, he opened his eyes to find her looking right at him, but whilst her gaze was on his face, her thoughts were clearly far away. Her deep blue eyes were fixed and staring, lips parted and expression intent. As he looked at her and struggled to stop himself squirming to displace her from his lap, he realised that the drawer containing Frieda Kohn's body had inched open from its previously almost closed position and he could quite clearly see the tip of her nose and the set of her chin from where he was sitting. Damn! In that case he'd better sit still and submit whilst he worked out what to do because the one major advantage of Hebe's current sitting position was that she had her back to the open drawer and no way did he want her to see inside it. Who knew what she might do? Freak out for sure, but what if she thought he'd killed Frieda? His eyelids began to droop again and this time he didn't attempt to stop them. The transition from anxious consciousness to subliminal memory must have happened without him even realising he was drifting off to sleep.

The child had been playing on his mind ever since he'd seen her, but what could he do? He couldn't get back into Crane Industries without another invitation and a press pass to go with it. And he couldn't get either in the state he was in currently, anyway. Luke pushed the keypad back into the desktop and switched off the monitor. His eyes felt like they were being plucked from his head and his arms and legs were crampy and aching. The smell of stale coffee lingered in the air and his stomach complained it hadn't been fed in hours, but the burden of getting up, stumbling his way to his poky kitchen and clearing a way through the debris of the last unsuccessful meal he'd prepared there – a sandwich made of stale bread, curling and dried ham substitute and too-sharp chutney – had seemed too much. His shakiness could also be attributed to low blood sugar, he admitted to himself, but an MND flare-up was the more likely. He knew the signs all too well by now. Another bout of severe incapacity was imminent unless he could stave it off somehow.

There'd been talk on the streets for a while now about some new meds – ones that could all but set the clock back... for a time. After that – well, what did it matter? He was already walking the line to an early grave so why not enjoy what little time he could grab back for himself in the meantime? Just being able to wake up in the morning and not have to go through an hour-long routine to even get himself out of bed and walking would feel like a miracle. To be well enough to go back to work, dammit, even go out for a drink, a social life – a shag! He laughed wryly to himself at that. A shag – have sex – he'd almost forgotten what that felt like it, had been so long. Since Frieda... He closed his eyes and imagined the pressure of her body against his, her slim legs twisting around his and the fuzz of her pubic mound brushing against him, featherdown and enticing. Her lips, her tongue – so cutting when she wanted it to be, and so sensuous when they were alone and she wanted him... Oh boy, had she wanted him, too! That had been such a surprise the first time. Of course, he'd known she'd noticed his prime physical condition at the outset – but he'd attributed it more to curiosity how someone with MND had been able to sustain such good muscle tone. How wrong he'd been! Frieda was all woman as well as all scientist…

He shook his head to clear thoughts of her from it, but he couldn't. He'd thought he'd put her behind him after two years of silence and no sight or sound of her at Crane Industries when he'd managed to get in there, but for the last few days she'd begun to invade them again almost as much as the kid did now – like they were linked. Outside, it was starting to get dark. That meant it must be approaching eight or so. He'd stopped wearing a watch months ago, preferring not to mark the passage of time too closely – it was ticking away far too fast for his liking! Eight o'clock and starting to get dark when it was still only spring, the weather had been so bad recently too, thundery downpours amid almost incessant drizzle. Spring had felt like winter for almost the whole of it. God, he'd like to get some sun on his back too! Some sun, some sex, some alcohol, some good times… That decided him. He flipped the pressure pad on the desktop keypad and it re-emerged, automatically syncing to the monitor which glowed brightly at him – an artificial sun, filled with God-knew-what harmful rays… Luke abandoned the normal internet sign-ins and opened a tab on the dark web instead. The forum opened up in front of him but moved on from where he'd left it around the same time last night, having lost his nerve.

'Seeking meds for M…' he tapped into the forum chat. The chat auto-filled the rest of the sentence for him, he'd input it so many times now. 'Seeking meds for M…ND cur…'

'Hey, buddy…' Toxicdaddy messaged back almost immediately. 'How's you doin?'

'Not good tonight, old mate,' Luke's reply flipped up under his own handle, KnackeredHack.

'Sorry to hear it,' Toxicdaddy replied. 'Taken anything for it?'

'Guess that's why I'm here,' KnackeredHack responded. 'Wondering whether to finally go for it.'

'Man, you must feel bad. You know the consequences?' MadMinny chipped in, her avatar of a mouse suspiciously like Minnie Mouse but with ragged ears, shaking a finger at him in a cautionary manner. MadMinny had found her way round the animation tools. Luke and Toxicdaddy settled for just a head and shoulders blank. That meant MadMinny had been on here a while…

'Yeah,' Luke typed. Knackeredhack added a thumbs down icon. 'But why not enjoy what there is for less than suffer what there isn't for longer?'

'Getting philosophical in your old age?' MadMinny jibed.

'Pragmatic...' KnackeredHack replied. 'But no idea how to go about it. Any ideas, guys?'

His message flickered up on the screen but the replies didn't come. He'd gone too far this time – too direct. He'd been hopeful when MadMinny had replied. He'd had a feeling she knew people – but maybe outright asking had been a step too far?

He waited for a full five minutes, watching his last message blink rhythmically at him, as he sunk back into his carefully designed chair, padded to support him where he was going to need it most – one of the last helpful pieces of advice Frieda had given him before walking out of his life. Outside, the streetlamps came on, sending pools of light pollution down onto the grimy pavement. A car horn hooted mournfully into the twilight, followed by silence – there was so much silence on the streets now that car engines no longer revved and purred, they merely hummed with static electricity, and passers-by kept their heads down so they couldn't be accused of passive aggression if their fellow street-walker was in any way part of another ethnic community. Luke got it, of course – after the race riots of the 2020s and the escalating demands of an overly-PC social media – everyone acknowledged it was better to be silent than politically incorrect. They had nearly descended into a third world war because of it, so silence and diplomacy were a small price to pay for a world peace agreement, even if it was a flimsy one. It had slimmed down the number of media opportunities too, as free speech had dwindled and party lines grown, yet ironically freed the hacks like him up to focus more on the things that mattered, or at least so he hoped. What was happening to the world as the earth's climate decayed, how to manage technology growth against human disfunction, what and how to enhance life against what and how to end it. The latter issue had preoccupied him a lot over the last few years...

By now it was clear his dark web chat buddies had no intention of replying so he'd clearly blown it with his impatience. Damn! He slowly reached forward to shut down the browser, joints creaking and muscles complaining at the imposition. His finger was about to stroke the pressure point on the keypad when the monitor screen changed. The winking cursor has left the end of his own message and switched to a new line.

Someone was replying...

'Hear you're hoping for a miracle cure?' The avatar was a head and shoulders blank like his and Toxicdaddy's. The avatar's handle read 3:16contact

'Hey, good to hear from you,' he typed in reply. MadMinny – it had to be her putting him in touch with one of her contacts. 'And bless you, Minny,' he said aloud to the screen. 'Yeah, feeling the pinch with MND and wondering whether it's possible to do something about it.'

'Don't you take anything for it?' 3:16contact responded.

'Like sweeties, for what good they do me. Was hoping for something more...'

The cursor remained blinking at the end of his message, and Luke cursed again as his new contact seemed to have thought better of whatever he'd made contact for. Maybe it was time to brave the kitchen after all and see if he had any of the vodka left that he'd bought the other day.

'Live and lurch along another day,' he told himself, bracing himself for movement. 'Who knows who will come up with a cure tomorrow?' Once again he reached to stroke the pressure pad on the keyboard and once again his hand was stayed by another message.

'What sweeties do you take currently?' Luke stared at the screen. That was the kind of thing a doctor would ask, not a dark web illegal drug supplier. Should he answer? Was it an undercover operation to track down customers in order to shut down a supply stream? 'Have to know or can't determine what alternative sweeties might be better for you.'

Luke read and re-read the message. 'Ok, here goes nothing,' he muttered under his breath. 'Quinine and baclofen for cramps, an antimuscarinic if I get too drooly, opiods for respiration when my chest gest too floppy.'

'ALS?' 3:16contact asked. 'Amyotrophic lateral sclerosis...'

Christ Almighty! This guy – or woman – knew what they were talking about. Luke breathed a little easier. Maybe they were making sure they suggested nothing that would make him worse.

'Not yet, but I've been warned to prep myself if the next attack is bad.'

'I see. So you want a miracle cure or a temporary fix?' 3:16contact was back at him in seconds.

'How temporary is temporary?'

'Temporary. Days,' 3:16contact added a clock icon at the end of the

message. Luke didn't appreciate the funny. He grimaced. What was the point of a few days' fix? 3:16contact was typing again. 'Not much better than you've got already. You want the miracle cure, really.'

'And the miracle cure?' Luke typed, his heart starting to beat faster and his breathing deepened. This could actually be the real McCoy!

'Hasn't been invented yet – supposedly.'

'Then…' Luke had started to type, furious and frustrated. His fingers stumbled over the keyboard, 'stip fuckin wit me…'

'Not fucking with you, just being upfront. What I can offer you is a miracle cure that doesn't work – officially.'

'Wha dows that meam?' Luke's fingers flew over the keyboard, showering his reply with miskeys but this time he didn't care.

'It means, it works, but I take no responsibility for what else it might do to you – or whether your body rejects it.'

'Is it damgerous?'

'Life is dangerous, KnackeredHack. We all do what we can to minimise the risks, but sometimes the risks find us and kill us before we can find them. You take the cure at your own risk, I provide it at mine. The price we agree between us.'

Luke sat back against the overstuffed chair back and chewed at his fingernail. 3:16contact wasn't offering any assurances, but then that wasn't to be expected.

'How do I know it works?' he typed eventually.

'I give you someone who's lived to tell the tale to verify it, then we agree a price.'

'I'm not rich…'

'Services rendered to be agreed will be acceptable instead.'

Luke watched as the cursor blinked hypnotically at the end of the reply. 'OK, send me the someone,' he slowly typed, then sat back, breath held, for the reply.

'Locker 16 at the British Library in London, 96 Euston Rd, London NW1 2DB. You'll find the key to the locker tucked behind the book entitled 'The Golden Text' by Massim Noral Duma. Replace it there after you have recovered the contents of the locker and then send this message in the chat on here when you have satisfied yourself of the efficacy of what I can offer you; Massim has a lot to say for himself – anyone else agree?'

'And what then?' Luke typed nervously, already wondering how he was going to get himself to the British Library and back the way he felt

currently. Double doses of his current meds, he supposed – with all the wonderful attendant side effects that would produce.

'Then we agree the price.'

Luke woke, suddenly and violently wracked by cramp. His spasm threw Hebe from his lap and she sprawled awkwardly on the floor, legs stretching out towards him in an ungainly manner.

'Oh!' she exclaimed as Luke jack-knifed when the worst of the spasms hit his abdomen.

'Ah, shit!' he spat through clenched teeth as he sobbed with the pain. Distantly he heard noise, clattering, a door opening, and footsteps entering the room. Another spasm ripped through him and he flung himself backwards, unable to control the vagaries of his body. He lay against the wall, gasping, wide-eyed and mouth gaping open as he struggled to breathe. And then he admitted defeat. Matthew Green was standing in front of him, with Hebe, and Green was holding a syringe-full of a yellowish fluid. 'No,' he protested weakly. 'I didn't do it.'

Green lunged at him and stabbed the needle into his neck. Carotid artery – fuck! At least it was going to be quick. Luke registered one last sweep of the morgue, a last whiff of Hebe's haunting perfume, floral yet as light as a breeze, and the taste of his own bile burning its way back down into his gullet then, strangely, he started to feel better. The pounding in his head softened to a gentle background hum and his vision began to clear. There were no longer two Hebes or two Greens. There was only one of each, both watching him with concern. A tiny frown line marked the centre of Hebe's forehead and Green's fleshy jowls quivered as his jaw tensed.

'I think he's going to be all right,' Hebe announced, turning towards Green and beaming.

'Temporarily,' Green agreed, kneeling down awkwardly and reaching for Luke's wrist. He held it firmly between sweaty forefinger and thumb until he announced, 'Sixty-eight. Not bad given the state of him.'

Luke shook him off and pulled his knees up to his chest, hugging them to him in an effort to mask the trembling he could feel beginning deep inside him and which he knew of old was the reaction of his body to a neat adrenaline shot. He rested his forehead on his knees and waited for the worst to wear off.

'But he will be all right?' Hebe's voice fluted around Luke's head.

'Hopefully, but we need to get him out of here,' Green replied, heaving himself back to his feet. 'I thought Jason was only going to leave him here to soften him up, not freeze him half to death! What the hell was he playing at?'

'It wasn't Dad this time,' Hebe corrected him. 'It was me. I triggered the system by coming through the air duct.'

Luke finally managed to control the trembling in his head and forced it upright so he could watch his two saviours. Without Hebe astride him he was cooling down again and even Hebe's teeth were beginning to chatter now too, but he still felt dazed and confused. He'd come to the conclusion that they were all potentially crazy – or murderous – here, even Hebe. What *had* she been doing to him when she'd sat astride him like a madam in a brothel? He felt sure she'd saved him from hypothermia with whatever she'd been doing, but how he had no idea. There was only one thing he was sure of; he had to get out.

'Why did you do *that*?' Matthew asks, exasperated and confused.

'I didn't mean to but he needed me.' They both looked at Luke. 'Did you know he's ill?' Hebe added. 'Dad mustn't know.' A look passed between them that Luke couldn't decipher. He eyed the open door, wondering whether he could make it there before they stopped him.

'That's not going to happen,' Green replied. 'You know that as well as I do. Come on, help me get him up.' Green stepped to one side of Luke and Hebe took up a position on the other side. They slid him up the cold wall till he was standing to attention like a soldier awaiting court martial and they his guards ready to frog march him away. 'Look, I'm sorry, Jason can get carried away at times. But he doesn't mean it and the cold air, that was a mistake, as you've heard Hebe say. He's just stressed and fearful and suspicious because of the protesters getting in, but once we're out of here, we'll get everything sorted out and you on your way again once the coast is clear.'

Luke said nothing as he calculated what 'once the coast is clear meant'. Clear of Jason or clear of protesters? He didn't particularly want to meet either again.

Green left Hebe holding Luke up to reset the security system and turn off the cold air. Luke edged ninety degrees to the left, rotating Hebe with him as he went and stamping his feet to get some life into his legs in readiness to run. He needed Hebe to let go of him and Green to be distracted, that was all. He could do it – he had to do it! His moment came as Green stopped in shock as he saw the open drawer and Frieda Kohn's nose peeping out. Luke tensed and flexed his leg muscles, ready to bolt for it, but at the last moment he hesitated. Green had started to shake, and Hebe had twisted back round so she could see what had shocked Green so much.

'Oh,' she exclaimed, her lips forming a perfect round that mimicked the shape of her eyes. 'Is she dead?'

Green nodded, the loose skin of his neck and jowls wobbling like a turkey wattle. His face was white and sweating and he seemed transfixed. 'I thought he'd got rid of her,' he murmured.

'Who? Who is she?' Hebe asked, finally relinquishing her grasp of Luke's arm. She stepped towards the open drawer, but still looking at Green. He shook his head and held up his hands, as if to ward her off.

'Her name was Frieda,' Luke supplied for Green. 'Frieda Kohn, isn't that right, Dr Green?'

Green's hand flew up to his mouth and he peered at Luke over the top of it. His eyes were wide and afraid, and something else. Guilty.

'Oh,' Hebe stopped and turned back towards Luke. 'Oh,' she said, as if that explained everything. She turned back towards Green. 'That would be Luke's friend, then – the one he was looking for last time he was here,' she said, as if explaining why she'd had yoghurt for breakfast, and not toast.

Chapter 7

13:24, 18th May 2032: Luke

'Oh shit! Now what do we do?' Green stared at Luke as if he might have the answer. It was a split-second reaction – one Luke hadn't realised he was capable of until he was in the throes of it. His hands were round Green's throat, squeezing harder than he ever imagined he'd have the strength for. Green's baggy neck felt both spongy and lumpy simultaneously, the Adam's apple bulging and shifting around beneath his fingers as he applied more pressure. Green's eyes were bulging too, bloodshot and staring as he gasped for breath, choking and gurgling. One part of Luke's brain was disgusted by the whole experience – the stale stench of Green's breath as it departed him, the corded twists of muscle and ligament in Green's neck as they engulfed his fingers, the jerking and flailing of his limbs… whilst the other side was marvelling at Luke's unexpected strength and the rage that was driving it. It was a revelation, that he could be this angry and actually follow through on it.

'Who killed her? Tell me you bastard! You know, don't you? I can tell by the way you reacted. Who was it?'

Green tried to prise his fingers off but there was no strength in his own – nothing to compare to Luke's enraged power. He gagged and protested but Luke refused to release his grip until he felt Hebe's hands on his shoulders, pulling him away.

'Stop it!' she was screaming at him. 'You're killing him. Stop it!'

She wrenched him away from Green and they tumbled backwards, with Luke landing on top of her as they hit the floor. Temporarily winded, the fury seemed to leave him with his breath. Hebe pushed him off of her, kicked herself free, bruising the small of his back as the heels of her trainers dug into him. She rushed to Green who had collapsed to his knees, still clutching his throat, coughing and spluttering. As Hebe reached him Green sank to the floor and curled into a foetal ball. Hebe knelt over him, eyeing Luke balefully as Luke rolled onto his side and in turn also found himself on his knees, facing away from the open drawer containing Frieda's body. He hovered there protectively.

'What the hell were you playing at?' she hissed at Luke.

'He knows,' he spat back. 'I could see it in his face. He knows who killed her – and who was supposed to have got rid of her. You heard him.'

'If he knows how she died, then trying to strangle him was hardly going to allow him to tell you, was it? And getting rid of her could mean anything – fired perhaps. You don't know anyone killed her.'

'So she killed herself, did she?'

'You don't know she was killed. She might have just died.'

'Oh right, from a self-inflicted blunt trauma to the side and back of the head, huh?'

Luke heaved himself upright and rolled the drawer back so it was fully open, revealing the whole of Frieda Kohn – all diminutive five foot of her – and the blackened, blood-matted crater that extended from the back to the right side of her head. Hebe stood and abandoned Green to take a closer look. She got to within a few feet of the open drawer and then cringed and backed away.

'It was an accident,' Green's voice quavered from behind her, rasping through the cool air of the room like a knife against ice. He'd rolled onto one side and was attempting to stand. Hebe rushed back to help him, still eyeing Luke balefully.

'How can that be an accident?' Luke shouted back at him, surprising even himself with the volume of his voice. The three of them stood in wary silence, observing each other. It was Luke who broke first, suddenly ashamed of how he'd behaved and that he'd made Hebe look at the wounds on Frieda's body when, in fact, he'd been trying to avoid her seeing the body at all. With diminishing anger came equally diminishing strength. His legs lost their rigidity, and he could feel them beginning to give way underneath him even as he began his apology. 'But you weren't meant to see that, Hebe. I'm sorry, sorry…' he mumbled as he sank to his knees, then onto his hands, panting and shivering. The adrenaline had worn off and the MND was back in full control. He couldn't even object as hands rolled him onto his side and dragged him upwards even though he knew two of them had to be Green's.

'We need to get him out of here and stabilised,' Green was saying, voice still a whispery murmur.

His feet dragged and skittered across the floor as they exited the morgue, Hebe on one side and Green on the other, alternately hauling him along and encouraging him to walk. The stairs were the worst, requiring him to use his legs to push himself up from one to the other with Hebe urging him on and Green puffing and panting alongside him. The cold air of the morgue gave way to the softer dank air of the stairs and then the modulated flow in the corridor that he had taken on the journey down. Air conditioning. Clean air, but it still had the smell of murder on it and his mouth had the sour taste of death sticking his tongue to the roof of his mouth and making him gasp for air.

They passed a number of doorways. Luke lost count as his eyes glazed over and refocused each time Hebe urged him on.

'You have to help us, Luke,' she pleaded. She seemed smaller, frail. She looked up into his eyes and he saw a frightened child there, not the feisty young woman who'd climbed through a cooling pipe and kept him alive. Yes, he admitted that to himself now – whatever weird and unlikely things she'd done whilst they'd been alone in the morgue, she'd no doubt been the only reason he was still alive now.

'Sorry,' he whimpered to her,' his eyes filling with tears, and remorse for the way he'd behaved displacing the indignation he'd felt at the sight of Frieda's body. 'So sorry… shouldn't have…' his voice slurred to the point where his words were unrecognisable even to him, who knew what he was trying to say.

'Shh,' she told him.

'He's bad,' he heard Green mutter to Hebe. 'Really bad.'

'Do you know what's wrong with him?' her voice was lighter and softer than Luke remembered it, but maybe that was due to his rapidly deteriorating condition. They reached the opening to the courtyard but Luke barely noticed. Their passage through it and out the other side passed in a blur of green as his head lolled, chin on chest, until even the green faded to black. It was only when he felt his back make contact with something soft and forgiving that he briefly opened his eyes. Hebe's face was hovering above him, round and childish. Or was it Hebe? This girl was too young for Hebe. Maybe he was already dreaming?

'I'm giving him a sedative so he'll sleep whilst I set up the monitors,' he heard Green rasp somewhere very far away.

'Monitors?' he managed before his eyes closed again and he wasn't sure he even said anything despite the intention being signalled from brain to mouth.

He slid the book out and balanced it on his right hand as his left reached to the back of the shelf. It was a hefty book, tooled leather and golden lettering giving it a grandeur Luke wondered if it deserved. But he wasn't going to bother to find out. It didn't look like his kind of thing. He'd never been a fusty academic. Sci-fi and space opera were more his bag – fight off the aliens, save the world and then shoot off to another galaxy for another round of the same thing. Not that he was an adventurer, more a dreamer – the dream of a better life, a brighter future, or that there really still were heroes, and not just downtrodden humans avoiding the scammers and freedom-thieves that seemed to have marked the real world for so long. He'd been barely more than an overgrown child when the first pandemic had hit in the early 2020s. Eighteen and just about to start university, he'd deferred until the world had got back on its feet, but it never had. And he'd never gone to university in the end, first wangling himself a job at the local rag as a glorified tea boy once the world had re-opened to business, then taking on the worst of the reporters' jobs – the ones no one else had wanted in case they caught Covid. Then sanctions had hit – first the US against China in retribution for the disease, then Europe against the UK in retribution for Brexit and the Middle East for peace treaty violations, then most of the world against Russia and China for breaches of human rights. Everyone could see it coming; World War Three was imminent. Luckily it hadn't ever quite got that far, although there were sufficient skirmishes and devastating casualties to change the world's view of what war and peace looked like for the future to become one in which people were mindful of not speaking out too vociferously or siding too obviously with any one ally – apart from the terrorists, of course, but what one man called a terrorist was secretly another's sane man now. Initially science had ruled all of course, after the pandemic had only been curtailed by the introduction of rapidly developed and only minimally tested vaccines. But some still claimed that their illnesses of today were the result of their cure from yesterday. Maybe that was even what had triggered his MND? There'd been no sign of the faulty gene in the genetic work-up Frieda had done for him...and with the results of almost-war had come other advances – Crane Industries advances most predominantly. The fore-runner of biologically adaptive prostheses to replace all those lost limbs and mangled body parts that the almost-war of attrition had delivered to every part of the world, alongside the other physiological failings resulting from over-use of drugs – blindness, muscle wasting and limb deformities.

Hell, they'd made a mess of the world – and that was before he even started on climate change...he looked again at the title of the book. Actually what was 'The Golden Text' about? He opened the cover and read the first sentence of the foreword.

'For anyone who has ever questioned the love of God for humanity, the John 3:16 verse must be the most resounding answer anyone could ask to be given. For years I questioned this very thing myself as I watched war after war, famine after famine, atrocity after atrocity beset our world and...'

'Yeah, right,' Luke said to the book. 'Let's leave it right there, shall we?' Religion had never been his thing either – well, what would you expect of a space opera freak? The biblical reference was interesting though, given the name of his potential saviour on the dark web chat. Were they trying to claim sainthood for themselves, or was there another significance to it?

The key was exactly where 3:16contact had said it would be. His fingers touched, retrieved and stored it as he looked around to make sure no one was watching him. Then he replaced the weighty tome of the biblical proponent and made his way down to the basement where the signposts on the wall near lifts and stairwells insisted the lockers were located. In the depths of the building, the locker room was small, stifling and depressing. And empty. It smelt of abandoned theses and despondent researchers – and dust. The lockers ranged in size from letterbox size to small cabin case proportions. Locker 16 was one of the former. Luke approached it with caution, although why, he wasn't sure. What could a letterbox-size locker contain? A bomb, his over-imaginative brain supplied for him. But why? His logical mind countered. What would anyone stand to gain from blowing him up? One less cynical but fairly useless hack who hadn't even worked properly in months because their body simply refused to co-operate? Nevertheless, he felt ridiculously anxious as he stabbed the key into the lock and – taking a quick look around him first to make sure he was still alone – twisted it open.

No bomb, just a buff manila envelope, sealed.

Cautiously, Luke slid the envelope from the locker and tucked it under his arm. He desperately wanted to open it, but discretion and an unusual – for him – bout of common sense restrained him. What had 3:16contact said? Put the key back where he'd found it. He'd better do that first then get the hell out of Dodge to somewhere he could open the envelope in private and browse its contents at his leisure. The envelope easily folded in two so there wasn't much in it. Luke folded it and tucked it into an inside pocket of his jacket. His meds were starting to wear off, so he delved in his jeans pocket and retrieved the med tube and dosed himself again. Too much for one day but it would get him home and then he could be as pathetic as he needed to be.

Replacing the key turned out to be as simple as retrieving it and Luke was back to where he had left his car in the high-tech parking lot two blocks away from the British Library itself in less than twenty minutes. It would have been sooner but he had to cross the road twice, zigzagging between the traffic, to avoid tangling with other cultural groups who were walking the streets alongside him. He hated the woke agenda that required a white to defer to a coloured and a coloured to an Asian or vice versa, depending who was occupying that particular bit of pavement space first and most extensively. It was crazy – they were all just people, weren't they? Why did people have to avoid other people just in case one or the other of them was offended by their ethnic background? He hated that policy – in place since his early twenties – almost as much as he hated the grime and smell of London. Why did it always smell of grease and garbage? Slipping into the seat of his car, he adjusted the car's speed from cruise to his version of 'just get me there', flipped on the self-drive control and slumped back in the car seat. It would take roughly two hours to get him home, even on his 'just get me there' setting, and for that time he needn't think about anything other than the buff envelope in his jacket pocket. He looked at his watch. 15:25. It would be nearly half five by the time he got back... The temptation was too much. Bugger patience and restraint! He dragged the envelope from his pocket and ran his finger under the flap. It opened easily – tantalising and seductive. If he looked at the stuff inside, that would be it – no going back after his dark web contact had upheld his part and offered proofs. He would have to go with it and negotiate whatever those services rendered would entail. He hesitated. Or he could reseal the envelope and put it back where he'd found it... His finger pressed the flap back down and envelope and flap plastered themselves back together as the car continued smoothly on its homeward journey, skirting Euston station and heading for the Regent's Park area. As the car purred its way past the concrete jungle of office buildings and apartment blocks, squat and grey or dun brown, that made up the roads around Euston, Luke wavered between just ripping the envelope open and exposing its contents and reconsidering his options.

But then, what were his options? A maybe cure, or a definite death? Put like that, there was no choice at all.

The closely packed buildings gave way to distant, greener vistas and immediately Luke began to feel better. It was the city that did it – and London in particular – but there was no point in unpacking old baggage and reopening old wounds. Decisively, he separated envelope and flap again and pulled the papers out onto his lap. The car sped past Regent's Park, and into Camden Town. Next stop Kilburn and then the edge of College Park before circuiting Wembley. After that London was more or less behind him, only its suburbs clinging onto his coat tails as he fled north, back to fields, fresher air and what he'd latterly made of his life. He watched the buildings and intermittent green spaces flash by, merging into a kaleidoscope of grey, green and brickwork. As the grey and brick-brown gave way to more and more hues of green even the atmosphere in the car felt better, although they'd never quite got rid of that pervasive rubbery smell from the new air con unit. He reached forward and twisted the scent blocker to 'floral' and waited for its fresh citrusy tang to oust the burnt plastic smell the car suffered from. His fingers ached and from the oversensitivity of his fingertips, he knew the additional meds had taken hold, but not in a good way. Read it all now, he advised himself. Later you're going to feel like shit!

The first page was a document detailing treatable medical conditions and potential long-term outcomes. He read the list of illnesses. Motor Neurone Disease came roughly halfway down and had been run through with a highlighter so it stood out like a beacon. Clearly a literature profile intended as some kind of sales sheet but tailored to his criteria. He turned the page. As he'd expected: details of the treatment of Candidate D, suffering from Grand Mal epileptic fits and MND – damn! That really was a raw deal! The results though, in the form of a diary post-treatment, were spectacular. No fits after two days and MND symptoms dissipating by the end of week one. By the end of week eight – the currency of the diary – blood tests indicated no trace of MND and there had been no further fits. The dates of the trial spanned a period of time barely three years ago. Well, that WAS persuasive... Luke flipped over the remaining pages, which seemed to relate to intermittent continued monitoring, each entry over the remaining two and a half years or so confirming the original findings. So what was the treatment? Drugs? Surgery? Brain stimulus modification? He scoured the pages of the closely printed report and could find only one indication of the type of therapy applied – 'the module continues to perform without the need for any adjustments' was stated at around the two-and-a-half-year mark. 'Suitable for generalised use' was the additional endorsement. So part of a research project... Had Frieda known of it? Was this what she'd been referring to in that phone call just before she'd disappeared?

Luke put the papers away, adjusted the car's speed for a smoother ride and settled back against the soft imitation leather of the seat. His head nestled comfortably into the self-adjusting headrest and, having flicked the massage setting to 'mild', he allowed the gentle movements of the seat around his cushioned body to soothe his aches. But sleep wouldn't come. He was too hyped about what the information in the envelope could mean for him. Instead, he found himself gnawing at his fingernails and wishing away the remaining journey so he could get to his PC and send 3:16contact the requisite 'go ahead' message.

He logged onto the dark web at precisely 17:32 and sent the message. 3:16contact was clearly busier or more patient than him. The reply didn't come back until almost nine forty-five, just as Luke was starting to climb the walls with frustration. By then he'd emptied the remains of the vodka bottle, eaten his way through part of yesterday's left-over takeaway and then thrown it all up half an hour later. At nine forty-five he was disconsolately examining his over-gnawed fingernails and contemplating the remains of the aforesaid yesterday's takeaway which he hadn't eaten prior to the major vomit episode. A crusty-looking spring roll and some noodles that were congealing on the side of the plate weren't particularly appetising, but clearing his stomach seemed to have reset his appetite. The arrival of the message no doubt saved him from another bout of sickness, he reflected later.

'So, we're negotiating, are we?' 3:16contact's message made him jump.

Luke struggled to get to his keyboard and typed, 'Negotiating. When and where?'

'No need, I'll tell you what and when. You either agree or not.'

'What and when, then?'

Luke waited, watching the cursor blink at the end of his hurried reply. It stayed there taunting him for a full ten minutes then leapt into life with a vigour that took his breath away.

'You will no doubt have heard of Crane Industries? They're holding a rare press conference in a week's time to launch their latest BioModule – a plug-in which is claimed to promote longevity. Not quite eternal life but

improved cell reproduction, healing, anti-ageing etc. It's anticipated it will improve life expectancy to double the current limit with good health being maintained throughout, even as the body ages overall. But not for everyone. It's a plug-in for the rich alone, regardless of what Crane Industries might claim. That alone is morally and ethically reprehensible, apart from the tampering with the natural order of the world.'

The cursor paused and stayed winking at the end of the last sentence. Luke had to steel himself not to prompt 3:16contact. After a while, more message appeared on the screen.

'I belong to a group that wants to redress those imbalances. We call ourselves 3:16 after the biblical verse John 3:16. We don't believe in cutting life short, but nor do we believe in artificially prolonging it beyond its natural and acceptable span. The world was never intended to support an excessively artificially extended and aged population. Nor is equality about only the privileged benefiting from scientific advance. We would like you attend the press conference, and through you allow us to infiltrate the facility so this technology can be disseminated fairly to the world to those who need life-extending treatment because of illness alone, not vanity alone and the desire for immortality.'

'But I can't just ask to attend the press conference,' Luke typed. 'These kind of things are invitation only...'

'And you will be invited – or someone you can easily replace will be. Do you agree?'

'And for this, I will be given the treatment that is referred to in the documents I collected today?'

'Yes.'

'The module the press conference is launching? The document seemed to me to be a research report prior to the launch of a new product.'

'Very astute, Mr Maynard,' 3:16contact replied.

Luke stared at his name. So they knew precisely who he was. Not just any old journalist – that much would have been easy to have deduced from the childish vanity involved in the avatar name he used. Him specifically...

'OK, I guess we're at ground zero now, aren't we? Agree or get burned,' Luke replied. 'So, what the hell – I agree...'

3:16contact's response was to send a list of instructions, a date, time, location and a name. He'd agreed. Services to be rendered in exchange for a cure – maybe. Outside, night had fallen and random flashes of light from passing car headlights added to the tension he was feeling – spotlights from the outside world on a man feeling like he was about to betray it, or his own principles, at least. But then, what 3:16contact had said was true – why should the privileged few reap the benefit of scientific advance just because they were immensely wealthy whilst the poor sods like him were left with a no-win situation because they weren't?

Before he closed the PC for the night and struggled to bed, refusing to take another dose of meds and thereby compound the ravages of overdosing with stupidity too, he googled John 3:16.

"For God so loved the world that he gave his one and only Son, that whoever believes in him shall not perish but have eternal life."

What was so wrong with that? He added another search to the tabs open on his PC before he gave up completely for the night. Crane Industries BioModules.

"BioModules were first devised by Crane Industries back in 2023 and were intended to replace or enhance bodily dysfunction via the use of prostheses following the volume of physical injury caused by the 2022 global conflicts. They have since been developed into plug-in modifications, tailored to augment or treat whatever is causing a problem in bodily functioning. Using Crane Industries' 3D printing process, bionic modifications can now be used to replace malfunctioning organs and more. They are akin to the iconic Bionic Man additions of the series of the same name that was popular in the mid-1970s – but only for those who can afford them. Crane Industries continue to claim that they market to the super-rich purely to obtain sufficient orders to fund being able to offer less expensive formats and versions to the general populace via the NHS. Some groups maintain this is untrue, the most notable of which is the group known as 3:16, which has vowed to stop the use of any such technology for the artificial prolonging of life, seen to be in violation of God's laws…'

Luke opened his eyes. The ceiling above him was decorated with delicate whorls of pastel blue. In fact, the whole room was pastel blue. Where was he? He struggled to sit up, but the bed seemed designed to keep him lying down. He kicked hard with his heels and managed to scoot himself into a sitting position. From there he surveyed his accommodation. A large room, decorated in blue, but largely devoid of any furniture apart from the bed. Soft drapes covered the windows, and the floor was scattered with deep pile rugs. It was a bedroom – of sorts – but so sterile, despite the coloured walls and coordinated soft furnishings, it could be a hospital room.

Luke pushed the covers aside and swung his legs over the side of the bed. His feet steadied against the cool floor, toes wriggling and ankles flexing as his body prepared for the biggest test of the day – standing. He swayed unsteadily for a while, head swimming, then he stepped cautiously away from the bed and explored the room. His first impressions were correct: it was big – and empty. He roamed its edges, pulling the drapes back only to be confronted with locked shutters over the windows. The light in the room was wholly artificial then. His exploration ended at the door at the far end. He fully expected this to be locked too, but the handle turned without resistance and the door swung inwards without complaint. He pulled it towards him a fraction, then hesitated. He looked down at his feet, naked toes still curling against the cold floor. He pushed the door quietly to and examined the rest of himself in the one vanity the room offered – a full-length mirror. A tallish, once decent physique, but now showing the impact of MND in the round-shouldered stoop he'd acquired of late. Slightly knock-kneed, clothes worse for the wear; crumpled shirt, creased trousers – well they had suffered the same experiences as him in the morgue, so that was to be expected. It was his face that shocked him though. Had he aged that much over the last few days, weeks? The last press pass he'd posed for had portrayed a young man, late twenties, kind-eyed, wide smile, firm jaw – not remarkable, but not unpleasant either. This man had defeated eyes, a slack jaw, and an expression of permanent disappointment. He'd lost not only his health but his soul too. Would any treatment in the world give that back to him? Could any explanation in the world restore Frieda Kohn back to life? That was the crux of it really, wasn't it? When he'd found her body it had been as if a part of him had died too. Not that he'd still loved her or been in love with her, but she'd represented the something before despair had set in. Before the hope of a cure had left him – despite what the 3:16 Group were offering, and unless they achieved their goal of taking over the Crane Industries lab, he doubted they would or could make good on their cure. It was clear now that their cure was indeed Crane Industries technology in some form, and given their opposition to Crane Industries and all it stood for, could he trust them, anyway – not that he had any other options, so what the hell…

Luke was still examining himself when the door opened, slowly at first, then swinging wide to reveal Matthew Green, corpulent, sweating and uneasy. The smell of him preceded him into the room. Rancid. He and Luke stood silently watching each other, Green in a tensed position as if he half-expected Luke to launch himself at him again and finish what he'd started in the morgue.

'You're awake then?' Green said, tongue slipping nervously across his lips. He was breathing heavily, as if he'd been jogging – except anything less likely Luke found it hard to imagine.

'Clearly,' Luke replied, unable to keep the biting edge from his voice.

Green grimaced and swallowed hard. 'You want explanations, don't you?'

'Would be good,' Luke agreed, compressing his lips and narrowing his eyes. He might feel like a pussy inside, but he wasn't going to let Green know how ill and shaken he felt.

'Better done in the lab, I think,' Green gestured for Luke to follow him.

'Wait!' Luke interjected.

'What?' Green swung round and eyed him anxiously.

'Where are my shoes? I'm not roaming this godforsaken place without any shoes.'

'Oh,' Green replied faintly, a weak smile playing over his lips. 'Under the bed?'

Luke loped back over to the bed and got down on his hands and knees. Sure enough, under the bed, his shoes had been placed neatly side by side, unlaced and ready to put back on. He scooped them out and tried to squat to put them on but ended in an ungainly sprawl instead. Green said nothing but Luke could feel his eyes on him all the while he laced and tied. The determination to not show Green any more of his vulnerability was foiled by his warring body at that point. He took a deep breath and used the bed to pull himself up. Green was still in exactly the same position at the door as he'd been before, arm outstretched holding the door open, mouth slightly agape, eyes fixed and fearful. Luke wanted to laugh. It surely wasn't him that Green was afraid of, was it? Even despite the death grip he'd attempted on him in the morgue? A child could see he was weak – ill. He followed Green through the door and it closed silently behind them, sealing them into a pristine white space, walls lined with a work bench on either side, monitors, keyboards and standard issue office chairs, plus racking at the far end, the back covered in white opaque Perspex. Through it he could see the outlines of what appeared to be cages, row upon row, lined up on the shelves, some displaying movement within and some completely static.

'This is the ForEver lab,' Green supplied as Luke stared around him.

'The ForEver lab?' Luke repeated, still trying to get his bearings. A lab that led straight off a bedroom?

'Yes,' Green replied. 'Where Jason and I do most of our basic lab work – the foundations of everything we produce.'

'Leading off a bedroom?' Luke's voice went up a tone.

'There are reasons for that, but that's not for now. Frieda Kohn is what you want to know about, isn't it?'

'Who I want to know about – and why…' Luke corrected him.

Green gestured to one of the office chairs and sat in the one opposite. Luke perched on the edge of his, then rapidly sat himself further back into it. Office chairs were renowned for their mobility, but on this glass-like floor the chair he was sitting on was manic, slipping this way and that at the slightest movement.

'Yes, sorry,' Green acknowledged the rebellious movement of the chair. 'Jason's choice, not mine. I prefer something more solid.'

I bet you do, Luke thought wryly. He secured the chair by anchoring himself to the floor, feet flat and knees braced. 'Go on,' he prompted. 'Frieda…'

'Frieda, yes… Frieda came to work for Jason shortly after his accident.' Luke straightened in surprise. 'Yes, no one knows about that,' Green explained. 'Purposely, because it had other ramifications we didn't want to be bandied around. Anyway, as you no doubt know, Frieda was a neurologist – and a brilliant one at that. She contributed incredibly to the work we were engaging in at the time – in fact without her input, I doubt Jason or I would be here today. But the problem with brilliance…' Green sighed, 'is that sometimes it doesn't know where to draw the line between progressive and ruthless.'

'Frieda wasn't ruthless,' Luke protested, but even as his words rang through the lab, he knew he wasn't being entirely objective. Hadn't he called her a miniature Hitler himself? And to her face, once… He and Green silently examined each other again – why was this place so quiet? It reminded him of the artificial silence of his electric vehicle. At times he was so desperate for sound when he travelled in it, he deliberately played with the settings just to create alarm bleeps. He felt like he needed an alarm bleep right now. 'Unless it was to do more good than evil,' Luke qualified.

'Like I said, sometimes it's a fine line and we don't always know when we've crossed it,' Green replied. 'What we were working on was top secret – life and death stuff. Frieda knew that latterly, and that was when she attempted to… I can only describe it as blackmail me. We disagreed, we fought over some confidential paperwork she was stealing, she fell,' Green gestured to the floor. 'These floors are unforgiving,' he added. 'Intended to stop the spread of bacteria, but in order to do so they have to be completely impervious. The treatment makes them… well, she hit her head… she died instantaneously – a massive haematoma. Well, you saw…' Green looked down at his hands. They were turning over and over in his lap, wringing the sweat out of themselves. 'I'm sorry. It was my fault, but it wasn't intentional.'

They sat in silence again, Luke imagining the scene, Frieda in teasing mode; taunting… she could be a devil when she taunted. And Green, perspiring, overly earnest, rising to the bait, frustrated… and the lethally slippery floor. It was very credible – all of it – but was it the truth?

'So why didn't you report the accident? And why is her body down there in your personalised Crane Industries morgue?'

'We didn't report the accident because there were things we would have had to have explained at the time – and we couldn't. The body? Well, I'm as surprised as you. Jason said he would deal with it…'

'Jason. I see…' He didn't, but that could wait for now. Green's other statement was more intriguing. 'And what were the things you'd have had to have explained? What you'd been developing?'

'I can't tell you. It's too dangerous – for you, not me.' Green looked sincere, but then he had also killed someone and concealed that fact for nearly three years.

'It can't be more dangerous than being locked in here with a murderer,' Luke fired back. He would have said more but a spasm ripped through him as unexpected as everything else that had happened to him over the last twenty-four hours. He collapsed against the back of the chair, not even bothering to try to control the chair's wayward movement as it slid off left. Shivering, he clutched the arms of the chair and gritted his teeth as he slid across the floor, hoping the spasm would pass as quickly as it had appeared. His meds. Jacket pocket. He reached for them, but of course he wasn't wearing his jacket.

Green turned out to be his saviour again, leaping up with an alacrity Luke would never have thought possible of him, and stopping the chair in its tracks. They ended up marooned in the middle of the lab, white space extending all around them in the unnatural hush.

'May I ask what is wrong with you?' Green looked genuinely concerned.

'Meds, right-hand jacket pocket,' Luke managed to squeeze out. Green abandoned Luke and the chair long enough to collect the jacket. He dug around in the pocket and produced the medtube, covered in fluff from the jacket's lining. He glanced at them before handing the tube to Luke. His expression flickered – surprise-realisation-deep thought; then it changed again. Satisfaction. Mean bastard…

'MND?' he queried as Luke flung back a mouthful of the pills in the tube.

Luke hung his head and rested his chin on his chest as the meds kicked in and his body slowly uncramped. Green's reaction made him angry but he hadn't the energy to express it currently.

'MND,' he agreed.

'Bad luck,' Green sympathised, expression now mirroring the words. 'How long have you got?'

'Who knows? A few years, maybe, if I'm lucky enough not to get frozen to death or killed in the meantime.'

'So you let him out, did you?' They both swung round in shock at Jason Crane's amused voice. 'So what should I do with two traitors in the midst?'

Chapter 8

13:56, 18th May 2032: Luke

'No, no…' Green protested. 'It wasn't my doing.'

'Then he's a Houdini in the making?' Crane was coolly sarcastic.

The worst of the spasm seemed to be passing – the shock of Crane's sudden arrival might also have had something to do with Luke's self-control returning. He hadn't wanted Green to know he was vulnerable and ill, yet he'd told him about the MND nevertheless. Crane was a different matter altogether though. He certainly didn't want Crane to know about it. Something inside him screamed at him not to let Crane know what his weakness was, but how to get that across to Green? It was the indefinable detachment that Luke sensed in Crane that chilled him to the bone, despite the fact that Crane was currently smiling and apparently affable – jokey even. What would Crane do with the knowledge that he had MND? Something Luke didn't want to know about, he suspected. And yet… No! He shut down that thought with cold, hard fury drawn from the memory of Frieda's cold, hard body.

'Hebe found him,' Green was explaining. 'You know what she's like. Like water the way she gets everywhere. She set off the intruder alarm in there and they were about to freeze to death so I had to…'

'It's OK, stop blabbering, Matthew. It was only intended as a makeshift strategy until we got rid of the madmen rampaging through the lab and found out if this one had anything to do with them. Did you?' He asked suddenly turning on Luke. 'Are you another of these religious nuts determined to keep man in the thrall of illness so God can save him once he's already died?' Crane snorted with disgust.

'No, I'm not!' Luke replied belligerently, the fire of irritation at Crane's judgemental assumptions tickling his belly, whilst the shame of lying agitated his conscience. 'I'm a fucking journalist. What are you?'

'What do you mean?' Crane was suddenly cold and chilling again.

'Well, harbouring a killer, covering up a suspicious death, endangering mine and your daughter's life – Hebe is your daughter, isn't she? What kind of man does that?'

'Ah… You told him everything?' Crane asked of Green.

'He told me enough,' Luke replied. 'Enough to get you both put away for life for murder and concealment.'

'I told you it was an accident,' Green protested weakly.

'Yeah right, it always is,' Luke spat back.

'But in this case,' Jason cut across them, 'it really was. Hebe?' He turned to where the girl was standing silently watching the three of them from the doorway. 'This doesn't concern you. Go back to the courtyard and keep yourself busy with your daisy chains or counting petals or something.' For a moment, the girl's expression was mutinous, but it wasn't the momentarily undisguised dislike on her face that struck Luke. It was the fact that Hebe was no longer even twelve, she was more like fourteen or fifteen. He stared, and she stared back, then quite deliberately poked her tongue out and winked, before turning and disappearing through the doorway in a flurry of ire and pouting disdain. Luke wasn't sure whether the poked tongue was at him or her father, but either way Hebe Crane was totally unimpressed with being ordered out of the lab.

Crane waited for Hebe to go, and then several minutes longer. His expression as the silence lengthened, was of someone concentrating intently.

'She's gone,' he advised, then swung back to face Luke.

Luke attacked before Crane could defend. 'Then why conceal her body for – how long? Nearly three years?'

'That's very precise. Do I take it you have a reason to pinpoint her departure from this life at nearly three years?'

'I knew her. And I knew she was working on something big with you. She called me to tell me.'

'Really?' Crane smiled laconically at him. 'Then maybe you also know how ambitious she could be – and how ruthless. I assure you, with Frieda, it was always a case of kill or be killed.'

'How would you know that? Supposedly you only covered up the death. *He* killed her.' Luke pointed at Green.

'Because I knew Frieda,' Crane replied calmly. 'Like I know you, Mr Maynard.' He smiled and the ice in it sent a shiver down Luke's spine. For a moment it really felt as if Crane did know him – *really* know him; the insides of him – the secrets, the failings, the betrayals, the lies. Luke swallowed hard and with it came the harsh taste of his own deceit, as well as the cloying sense of something bad lurking in the ForEver lab.

'Even if it was self-defence, you've still covered it up and that makes it more than mere self-defence,' he insisted pugnaciously. 'Conspiracy to pervert the course of justice too. You could go to prison for life for that, both of you.'

'Or maybe not, but let's be straight with each other here, Mr Maynard. If what you just told Matthew is true, I have something you need.' Luke stared at Crane. How could he know what he'd admitted to Green. He hadn't been there, so how had Green found a *way of telling him? He opened his mouth to protest, but something in Green's expression stopped him. But Green hadn't told him, had he? He'd been with Luke all the time, and Crane hadn't been there. It didn't make sense.* 'So, do you want to live or die?' Crane was saying. 'And I'm not making threats here, I'm making promises.'

Chapter 9

14:08, 18th May 2032: Hebe

Father is cross. He's ordered me out of the lab, but I'd already heard enough by then. And I saw the body in the drawer. I knew straightaway she was the friend that Luke asked me about the first time he came here, and the reason she was there was bad. Her name was Frieda, he'd said, with that strange expression in his eyes as he said her name. I don't know about adult human relationships, other than what I've read, and Uncle Matthew says to take a lot of what I've read with a pinch of salt, but I do know that expression meant Frieda had meant something important to Luke. I asked Father once – what is love? He tried. He wrote me a formula based on chemical interactions in the brain.

'That's love, Hebe. Physiological reactions – all modifiable with the right approach.'

'So is that what I feel for you and Uncle Matthew – just chemicals?'

'Precisely.'

'But it doesn't feel like a simple brain function. It feels more like... how the grass feels when it cries.'

He set aside his note-taking and gave me his full attention then.

'You're telling me the grass cries? I thought you said it felt pain.'

'It does. That's when it cries. Is love painful? Does love make you cry with pain too? I don't feel pain when I think about you and Uncle Matthew. It's a nice feeling – warm.'

He studied me a while longer. 'How old are we assessing you to be today?'

I looked down at myself, long legs, small, pointed feet, similarly long fingers, small, rounded breasts that always reminded me of apples if I examine myself naked currently, and a slim waist with curving hips descending from it.

'I guess I'm on the verge of sixteen.'

'When?'

'Later on today?' I shrugged. It had become increasingly hit and miss when the tipping point of twenty came recently, and I began to count backwards again. By tomorrow I'd probably be back to about twelve on current statistics. Uncle Matthew has only just started recording them again after the time-line for the process began to shift.

'What data has Matthew got on it?'

'Love?' I asked, my mind jumping between warmth and pain, tears and smiles.

'No, the metamorphic process.' Momentarily, my father's eyes were cold and steely. Not the warm blue they can be, but the blue of the sea when a storm is coming. All right, I know I've only ever seen the sea online, but I've seen oceans of seas in all circumstances that way – calm and serene, baby-blue, choppy and twisting with the current – deep blue-grey-green with flecks of white foam riding the tops of the waves, and dark, thunderous grey as the storm hits. I've even seen a tsunami building to its peak, towering above buildings and land, waiting to swamp in and drown everything in its wake – black, bold and people-hungry. I can feel all its emotions too – like the grass. Dormant, curious, restless, angry, demanding...

Or maybe that's my father I'm describing.

Now his eyes softened to kind blue. My father's eyes can be kind too. Warm. It's the right moment to ask him what I've wanted to know for days now – ever since the sleeping lady opened her eyes. I always know what mode he's in from his eyes.

'What kind of love did you feel for my mother? Was it chemical or grass?'

He surprised me by throwing his head back and laughing – a loud hurrumphing sound, ending abruptly in him staring over my shoulder and into a past I have no experience of. His shoulders slump and his mouth hung open in a half-smile, half-grimace.

'Both,' he said wistfully, before suddenly straightening and focusing back on me, this time with the steely grey-blue eyes of a choppy sea. 'Who told you about your mother, anyway? Was it Matthew?'

He thrust his nose up to mine and his irritated grey-blue eyes become one – a cyclops eye, boring into me and reading my mind. Oh, he can do that too – sometimes. What he doesn't realise is that I've found a way to stop him since the sleeping lady opened her eyes. Above the cyclops eye, I know he will be frowning, two deep furrows bisecting top and bottom of his forehead. He drew away and smiled, eyes baby-blue like the tranquil sea. I resist the pull of his mind to mine but the strands seep out of my consciousness nevertheless. The block only truly works when he's angry. Kindness breaks down the barrier.

'I must have a word with Matthew,' he said as he settled back into a slump, still smiling at me. 'He's talking too much.'

Thank God he only got that much from me.

We remained that way for several minutes, him sucking what he thinks are all the answers from my head, scooping them out like an egg yolk from its shell. It only stopped as I feel the first shift starting to process. He recoiled then.

'Already?' he asked, surprise taking over from coercion.

I swallowed. I hate this bit – the start. 'It's happening quicker these days. It feels like a rollercoaster when it first starts.'

He leant forward and took both my hands in his. This was warm love, grass love – not chemical formulae. 'I'm here,' he reassured me. 'It will be OK.'

'Will it, Father? Sometimes it frightens me. Why does it happen? Why am I not normal?'

'You are normal,' he squeezed my hands and they moulded into his. 3D printed. 'You're normal for you.'

Normal for me. But that isn't normal as in Luke, or Uncle Matthew. Or even the sleeping lady, or Frieda; dead Frieda. And I still don't understand anything much about adult human relationships, but something tells me I'm not going to be able to avoid them for much longer.

The sleeping lady warned me of that when she told who she is. Her name is Elise.

Chapter 10

15:52, 18th May 2032: Luke

Live or die?

The choice should be easy – he'd already made it once, and yet having the solution offered by the two men responsible for Frieda's death called out his conscience.

'A BioModule?' Luke found himself asking.

'Something like,' Crane cut across Green's attempted response. Green's jaw clamped shut but the signals he was sending Crane could have started an earthquake. 'We'll need to do some tests of course. Can't promise you a miracle without making sure we can deliver it. The choice is yours.'

'And what are the strings?'

'Your silence.' Crane pulled over a lab chair and positioned it and himself on it, in front of Luke as Luke dangled from his, legs weak and twitching, joints complaining, shoulders aching, head spinning. Green – by comparison – stepped away from both of them, backing towards the workstation in the corner of the lab and perching against the benchtop. He crossed both legs and arms, and let his chin drop almost to his chest, giving the impression of an animal preparing to hibernate, defensively folding in on itself. 'About everything,' Crane added. 'Dr Kohn and her unfortunate accident, what you learn about our BioModules, and…' he looked across at Green, 'Hebe.'

'Hebe?' Luke paused as he attempted to work out why Hebe should be part of the secrecy deal. 'She's your daughter, isn't she?'

Crane breathed out, eyes back on Luke's face and coolly appraising him. The inner silence was back again, like he'd hushed everything around us so he could focus entirely on Luke. To Luke, that focus was disconcerting to say the least.

'Why do you assume that?'

'Well, it's obvious, isn't it? She can't be his,' Luke waved an arm towards Green, wishing the gesture was more controlled than he managed to make it. He made his wild gambit then – reporter's gambit. 'And she's not what she seems, is she?'

'No,' Crane agreed. 'She's not what she seems. She's extremely vulnerable. That's why she's kept here and protected. And your choice will enable her to remain so. Safe.'

How did Crane know that was the one thing that would sway him? The one thing that would dismantle his conscience, his need for revenge, his fury on Frieda's behalf? Making sure Hebe was safe. Luke looked across at Green. Green's expression was unreadable, but Luke thought he detected the very slightest of inclinations. The tiniest of nods. Well, of course Green would want him to agree to this – Green's life and liberty were on the line too. Yet Luke sensed the nod of the head wasn't so much an encouragement to agree as a warning to say nothing more.

And why the hell should Hebe matter so much to him? He'd met her twice – no, three times now. He knew nothing of her except that she seemed to age inexplicably. What was that syndrome? He'd done an article on it some years ago – progeria, that was it. But Hebe had none of the symptoms of progeria other than advanced ageing compared to her actual age. Far from sickly, undernourished or skeletal, she was glowing.

'OK,' Luke said after a while, still trying to decipher what Green was signalling to him – and what Green had earlier been signalling to Crane. There was muck here – a whole dung-heap of it, and maybe they could treat him – or maybe 3:16 would follow through on their offer if they broke through. Either way, he wasn't getting out of the Crane labs anytime soon without the assistance of one or the other and he wasn't going to survive much beyond that escape without the assistance of one or the other either. Play both ends against the middle in the meantime. 'I agree. You cure me, I'll keep quiet – as long as that doesn't entail being as quiet as the grave.'

'Agreed.' Crane stood up so abruptly he sent the chair spinning across the lab on soundless wheels. 'First, we'll need to confirm your diagnosis, then we'll assess which treatment would be best. For now, you look like you need to rest. Matthew will draw some blood, then we'll give you a concoction of drugs to help settle things temporarily. Now I need to go and talk to Hebe, since you've both so spectacularly exposed her to the seamier side of life.'

He left, giving both Luke and Green a look which left them in no doubt he held them responsible for whatever harm the sight of Frieda Kohn's dead body had wrought on Hebe.

'I'm sorry,' Luke said defensively as Crane got up to leave. 'That was unintentional. If I'd known you'd stored her there, do you really think I would have shown her to a... child,' he concluded. Crane simply shrugged and left. The lab door swished shut with a sibilant hiss as Green collected a syringe and two test tubes from a rack near the shelves housing the mice. 'But is she a child?' Luke asked Green as Green hovered over him. Green's face was as dark as thunder clouds.

'Yes, she's a child,' Green replied, tight-lipped.

'Not an experiment?' Luke prompted. 'Or a machine?'

'She is most definitely not a machine!' Green looked offended, brows knitted together and lips pouting. 'Now, flex your arm, I need a vein.' He forced Luke's hand into a fist and worked his arm up and down like it was a lever.

'So what IS the deal with Hebe?' Luke asked as Green slid the syringe into a now prominent vein in the crook of his arm and proceeded to withdraw two vials of blood.

'There's no deal with Hebe,' Green replied, capping the second vial and pressing a small wad of cotton wool over the puncture wound on Luke's arm. 'Hold that and press down on it so you don't bruise.'

As Luke pressed two fingers against the pad he watched Green walk hurriedly to the control panel by the door and turn one of the switches to red. Immediately the lab was filled with Mahler's Sixth Symphony. Luke grinned and then frowned. What the hell? Who would have thought Matthew Green was a culture lover – and the same culture as him too! He studied Green as he returned to the kidney dish where he'd left the two vials of blood and a still-full syringe and decanted the remaining syringeful of blood into a test tube before loading it into a centrifuge.

'Well clearly there is, so why not stop playing the secretive altruist and tell me what's going on here?'

'That's not part of the deal,' Green flipped the lid of the centrifuge open and retrieved the test tube. Its contents had now separated into clear and red layers.

'Neither was you letting in the 3:16 Group, but you did, didn't you?'

'What?' Green spun round, open-mouthed at that.

'You told the receptionist to put the doors on automatic and you deliberately avoided her chipping me – even told me to say nothing about it. And you knew I wasn't Edward Hughes. You deliberately let me in knowing I wasn't who I said I was. You must have known I was a plant, there to open the doors for them – 3:16. So, tell me what's going on?'

'You're mad. You were late arriving, and we had to get the press conference going. I made the mistake of letting you in on the basis of your press pass alone, but that's all. And putting the doors on automatic meant simply putting them on automatic security, not the reverse and keeping them open.'

'And what would happen if I told Jason Crane all of that?'

'He'd let you join Frieda Kohn.' Green was implacable – except for the tiny tic under his right eye.

'After he'd put you there before me…' Luke taunted.

'You're completely mistaken,' Green replied, shaking his head. 'And if you repeat any of that to Jason, you can kiss goodbye to any kind of cure…' Green was trying to look reproving, but Luke knew he'd hit a nerve although something about his denial also rang true. He really couldn't see Green as a member of a group of religious fanatics out to scupper all he'd worked on for the last couple of decades. 'I'm trying to help you, Mr Maynard,' Green concluded more gently.

'Hmm,' Luke grunted. But help him to do what? And if he hadn't let in 3:16, then who had? That tiny head nod came back to him when Crane had been offering him the deal. Green had desperately wanted him to accept, whilst being desperately afraid of what it entailed. Since Hebe was to be the subject of secrecy even more importantly than Frieda's death, it had to be to do with the girl. 'If it's not 3:16, then it's something to do with Hebe, isn't it? Something you need me to do. For God's sake, man, if that's the case, you have to let me in on the secret. How the hell can I help otherwise – and I would. She asked me to take her with me once before – the last time I was here. She's just a kid and if she's being kept here against her will then…'

Green clapped his hand across Luke's mouth. 'Shut up,' he hissed. 'You don't know what you're getting into, and I don't know what prompted you to come here in the first place, but now you are, just shut up and take your cue from me. I can't help you otherwise.' He hauled Luke to his feet and propelled him towards the door Luke had entered the lab through, leading back to the bedroom. 'When we leave this lab, there will be no sound to cover our voices. I can get away with it in the lab because Jason knows I like to listen to music whilst I work, but elsewhere, you watch, you take note and you only act on my signals. Understood?'

'Shit! Yes, but what the hell?'

'Think on the message of Mahler's Sixth. It's been a tough day already and it's only going to get tougher. I've given you something to get you through until tomorrow so you rest now. I'll explain when I can, but you have to be patient and trust me.'

'Why should I?'

'Because otherwise we'll all die. This is how it begins…'

A shudder of fear rippled through Luke's body as the second hammer blow of Mahler's tragic symphony rose to a crescendo and engulfed them.

'That's what Hebe said…' he managed before whatever Green had given him started to kick in and it was all he could do to make it to the bed that beckoned to him from the bedroom attached to the ForEver lab.

Chapter 11

09:02, 19th May 2032: Luke

Overhead, Luke could hear drumming and what sounded like marching. Bloody hell, had the 3:16 Group gathered an army? He pulled himself upright in bed, still sleep-hazed from whatever Green had put in the shot he'd given him the day before and concentrated on focusing. The room was too blue, he decided. He consulted his watch. Nearly ten am. Shit, he really had been knocked out by Green! Unsteadily, he swung his legs over the side of the bed and attempted to stand. As weak as a kitten again. Double shit! His second attempt at standing was interrupted by the door opening and strains of Mahler once again following Green into the room. Green put his finger to his lips and looked meaningfully at Luke before entering the room proper. The music created an ironic announcement of his arrival. Luke nodded an acknowledgement and flopped back onto the bed.

'What the fuck was in that shot you gave me?' he greeted Green.

'Asedative which also acts as a muscle relaxant, with a combination of vitamins, minerals and electrolytes to keep you going until today, when no doubt you could demolish a proper breakfast?'

Luke was about to object, but the mention of breakfast suddenly brought tantalising images of crisp bacon, sunny-side-up eggs and golden hash browns. Damn, he could even smell the bacon! His mouth salivated in a way it had failed to do for weeks and his stomach joined the riot of awakened senses as it produced a cacophony of sounds even he was surprised by.

'Well,' he hesitated. Was this a signal?

'Come on, your legs will stabilise once you're on them. It's only the left-overs of the muscle relaxant but as soon as you get the muscles back working, the blood flow to them will carry away any remaining active solution and waste products.' Green had reached the bed now and was offering him a lift up, wedging his shoulder under Luke's. He smelt of camphor and dust – old man smell. Luke couldn't stop the automatic instinct to recoil but did manage to pull it up short before it was too exaggeratedly obvious. He hoped it would merely seem like physical vulnerability due to the after-effects of the shot.

'Where are we going for breakfast?' he asked as he hobbled alongside Green. 'It sounds to me as if the hordes have taken over the kitchens – and most of the rest of the place too. I thought they'd gone yesterday?' The stomping above them redoubled in its efforts to drown them out.

'They've got some kind of pneumatic drill they're trying to drill through the floor with to get to us. We're actually underground here.'

Luke paused. 'I didn't notice going down when I found the courtyard. Is that why there's shutters across the windows?'

'No, that's to keep prying eyes out. The windows look onto the courtyard and other corridors. And the decline is so gradual, you wouldn't notice the descent. It was purposely designed that way to mask its existence. Come on,' Green nudged him on. 'Hebe's playing chef today so we mustn't keep her waiting.'

They exited the room by the door Luke had originally entered it by and, a short way along the corridor, they were back into the courtyard. This time they exited the courtyard by another corridor Luke hadn't realised was there before. Green noticed him frowning and swivelling his head in an effort to track their route.

'You can't,' he said, seemingly anticipating Luke's next question. 'Think of Escher – you know who I mean by Escher?'

'The artist who drew the never-ending staircase?'

'That's him,' Green grinned and removed his shoulder from its crutch-like position under Luke's arm. 'The courtyard works on the same basis. Wherever you came in, there'll be a new exit or entrance next time. Another security device. How are the legs? They should be starting to work better by now.'

'They are, thank you.' Luke flexed his toes, then burst out laughing. 'I'm not wearing any shoes,' he exclaimed as his toes rubbed against the gently indented surface of the courtyard pathway.

'That's OK, Hebe won't mind. Come on, this way.' Green led him down the corridor they'd been about to enter, the camphor-dust smell creating a fetid trail that warred with the aroma of grilling bacon that Luke wasn't now imagining. His hunger was now so awakened that he didn't think even a pile of manure would be enough to put him off eating.

Luke padded after Green, fighting off the inclination to tuck his head down into his shoulders every time another bout of noise overhead seemed to threaten to bring the ceiling crumbling and caving in on them.

'Is this really safe?' he called after Green. Green turned and stared at him, head cocked to one side. He reminded Luke of a mother blackbird in the depths of winter, surplus plumage bedraggled and dangling like Green's crumpled shirt and shapeless trousers did. 'I mean, what they're doing up there.' Luke looked up at the ceiling just as another round of drilling started.

'Oh yes,' Green shrugged dismissively. 'It's been reinforced with steel girders sandwiched between seismic-resistant concrete. If an earthquake of 9.1 on the Richter scale won't crack that, then a pneumatic drill won't even chip it. They're just making a lot of noise. You know what they say about all bark and no bite?' He stepped alongside an exit from the corridor and gestured for Luke to follow. In a lull in the drilling, the sound of something sizzling drifted from the open entrance. Luke approached and peered through. On the other side of it was a high-tech kitchen kitted out in sparkling white, offset with gleaming chrome door furniture. A young girl stood on the opposite side of what passed for a breakfast bar, tall charcoal leather upholstered bar stools tucked neatly under its walnut-effect worktop.

'Christ,' Luke said softly to himself as the girl smiled welcomingly at him. 'Hebe?'

'How are you feeling?' she asked, her voice softly modulated. Long blonde hair swung like a curtain either side of her face and her eyes sparkled mischievously above a rosebud mouth. Hebe, but not Hebe. Almost Hebe. Mostly Hebe as he'd seen her but subtly different in everything apart from one that smacked him right between the eyes.

The girl-Hebe waved a spatula at him. 'I'm still not very good at doing eggs,' she apologised. 'Do you mind if they're a little bit broken?' She grinned at him, revealing an engaging wide-toothed smile, and without waiting for him to reply set a plate of bacon and eggs in front of him, complete with runny-yolked eggs drowning in a mound of over-crisped bacon.

'What the fuck…' he whispered, shaking his head until he felt nauseous. Yesterday she couldn't have been more than twelve. Not even progeria worked this way. He swung round to face Green, the smell of fried bacon now curdling his stomach. 'How can she be this old now – she's what? Eighteen, nineteen? She was only a tot when I arrived, then yesterday she was twelve going on fourteen, and now… I've only been here forty-eight hours max. This is impossible.'

'No,' Green took him by the arm and led him to the breakfast bar. He pulled out a stool and pushed Luke onto it. 'This is what Hebe is.'

Chapter 12

10:52, 19th May 2032: Hebe

I really must get better at cooking! I'd like to be good at it, it's just I don't get much practice. Uncle Matthew tries to indulge me to allow me to try out more aesthetic activities, but we always have to avoid Father finding out, especially if it's anything that involves salt water. I'm not sure what he's worried about, though – I mean how harmless is salt water? He just refuses to answer if I ask why. There are times he's quite expansive and then, suddenly, he'll just clam up. He's like that about painting too. Won't let me near the oil paints and brushes Uncle Matthew got me for my birthday when I was two, and I especially wanted to experiment with them because… but that's running ahead, though. I'd be better starting with what led me to trying any of these things out at all – and I'm only recording any of this because I'm going to have to explain it all sometime, and where to start with that?

I put my pen down and look at the long flow of letters and words across the page. Who am I writing this all down for? The people I'm going to have to tell one day? The person who might be able to save me? Or maybe, me? That seems sort of crazy but Uncle Matthew gave me that idea last night.

'You know, one day, we're going to have to explain things.' He checked my vitals, recorded them onscreen and then estimated my age. Sixteen, we agreed. Roughly. This morning it's probably plus two years, and by this evening it will be minus five or six. It's slower when I'm sleeping. Metabolic changes, Uncle Matthew thinks. 'How do you want to deal with that?'

'Do I have to?'

'If you leave here, yes.'

The idea of leaving here used to scare me. No, that's not true; to begin with I didn't even know there was anywhere else to go. That all changed when I was one and a bit, and the man found his way into the courtyard Luke found his way into the courtyard... By then I knew things had to be different but not how to accomplish it. I begged him to take me with him and was so angry when he didn't, I stamped on the grass and it screamed. I never did that again. Instead, I started to research the outside, and I finally found my way past the security on the door on the opposite side of the courtyard that only appeared when our corridor-way disappeared. Beyond the door was the sleeping lady. If I close my eyes, I can picture her so vividly, we are in the room together without me even needing to go into it now.

Cold, but the walls are pink. It should feel warm in here if colour therapy is real... Ah, no, it's not colour theory that's doing it. It's real-time temperature. It's actually cold in here. I peer at the wall thermometer and rub my hands briskly up and down my arms, chafing blood along inner arteries and veins. I shouldn't be in here. Father will be so angry. And he'll know... His interrogatory eyes and the way his thoughts seem to be able to seep into my head through them, entwining my own and teasing them out so that they become his too, makes me shiver in anticipation of it happening the next time he sees me. He always knows...

I step away from the wall as the anxiety takes hold. I've wondered for a while now how Father does it. I've speculated he has some kind of bio-integration with the fabric of the building and its contents one of the BioModules perhaps, tailored specifically for the purpose? But then how can he shut out the grass's screams? No, it can't be that – but the wall feels like it's closing in on me, nevertheless, pushing me closer and closer to what lies at the centre of the room. I take another step forward and another, my feet dragging me there, but I'm not uneasy with this sensation, like I am with father dredging my mind. This sensation makes me feel warm despite the room temperature, until I'm an arm's length away from the arrangement in the centre of the room. I call it an arrangement because that IS what it is – an arrangement of equipment, gently cushioning a body – a person. 'Sleeping Beauty' is what pops up in my mind as I look at her and that is what I called her for a while: The Sleeping Beauty sleeping in her shrine.

I didn't stay long that first time. Only long enough to peer into her face and detect the faintest of breaths slipping from between her parted lips. She looked so serene, so contented, so... familiar. I put my face so close I could feel her breath on my cheek, hear her heart beating, sense the pulse of life steadily flowing through her. Yes, she was attached to machines and no doubt it was the machines keeping her heart beating and her lungs expanding and deflating, but the life pulse wasn't artificially maintained. It was present regardless. Luckily, I didn't see Father that evening. He was too busy prepping the speech for the press conference the next day, announcing the next of the BioModule releases to allocate time to me. I didn't tell Uncle Matthew about the Sleeping Beauty lady either, although I'd thought I might. Some instinct made me keep her to myself for the time being. When father and Uncle Matthew were knee-deep in journalists the next day, I waited for the shift to happen in the courtyard, and that brief window of time to open when our home corridor disappeared and the sleeping lady's corridor appeared. I slipped past the security screen as easily as the last time, but on this visit, I had a plan. I marched straight up to the shrine and took her hand. Her eyes opened and she smiled at me. 'I've been waiting,' she told me. 'So long... Too long, maybe? How old are you now? All grown up...' then the tears started to stream down her cheeks and drip onto the covering of the shrine.

'No, no. I'm only just over one,' I tell her. 'I just look older. How long have you been here?'

She frowns. 'Only one?'

'Yes,' I nod. 'I have this condition. We call it...'

She put her finger to my lips. It was warm. 'No, don't tell me. We still have time then. Let me talk.'

We stayed like that for what seemed like ages, but it can't have been that long, it's just my sense of time is a bit messed up – well, it would be, wouldn't it? After a while though, I stopped feeling her finger on my lips and she started to talk. Except she wasn't talking. She was listening and I was talking – telling her all the things Uncle Matthew has now suggested I try to explain here, in these long looping words and phrases.

By the time I was fourteen months old, I was on my second revolution. To begin with it was enough just to cope with the changes one day to the next until the revolutions speeded up. I could barely cope with me then, let alone what I could or couldn't do. One day I'd be struggling to sound out consonants and vowels, the next I'd be tackling the vagaries of the Collatz Conjecture. Of course, I didn't expect to solve it. No one has, not even my father, although I suspect that's because he's decided not to now because he has other plans for me. The point originally was to flex my abilities – or in Father's terminology, to see how precocious I *could* be. For me, though, precocious was in what my body did – without thought, reason or explanation. I grew, then I declined, then I grew again. After a while, as I felt the need for a way to define what happened to me, we gave the process a name. Revolutions. On a complete Revolution I start at zero, progress to twenty and then revert to zero again.

And it hurts. Ligaments stretch, muscles striate, bones expand whilst physiological processes confuse my biorhythms so that I barely have a regular sleeping or eating pattern. Can you imagine how it feels to have your body literally tear itself apart and expand ten times over in a matter of only a few weeks, then days, and now, hours? It's like fire eating you up from within. Every second burns but you can never soothe the burn as you grow and grow because almost immediately the process reverses and then every fibre is shrinking, contracting, diminishing – and then everything is forced from you like some giant being is crushing your body down into a compact facsimile of the person you were barely a few hours ago. It took me eighteen months to get to the point where I could shut off my bodily sensations and only pay attention to what my mind was doing because, whatever the growth and regression, only my mind appeared to be unaffected. I still thought the same thoughts as an eighteen-month-old as I did as a twenty-year-old. Maybe over that first eighteen months I was simply too immature to understand but then I found my ability to be precocious – as Father put it – grew as exponentially as my body did periodically. I learnt to keep that to myself after a while, so whilst I could make much more progress with the Collatz Conjecture each time I tackled it, for instance, I only showed Father a fraction of the progress I made.

And when I'd finished talking, the Sleeping Beauty lady replied. She told me her name and what I needed to do next. She even told me who would help me. I went back out into the courtyard and told the grass, and after a while, she was right. There he was, just as the Sleeping Beauty lady said he would be. Just as my mother said he would be.

But he doesn't understand, so I decided to write it all down for him, like Uncle Matthew suggested, thinking it was something I could do to help me. And I suppose it does too, after all, whatever helps Luke is going to help me one day. Luke is a journalist. One day he'll have to tell our story, so he'll need the facts, but neither Father nor Uncle Matthew would agree with that. They don't understand what the Sleeping Beauty lady – my mother – understands about life and death and what comes next. Love.

Even Uncle Matthew doesn't understand, although he used to, she said. I haven't told him I know about the Sleeping Beauty lady yet either, although I know he goes to talk to her too. What she tells him isn't for me to know, just as what she tells me isn't for him. I only know we all have one thing in common: we have to escape from here him, my father, Luke the journalist, and me, or we will all die.

Chapter 13

09:33, 20th May 2032: Luke

'I don't understand?'

'I know.' Green shoved the plate with the runny egg congealing over too-crispy bacon towards me. 'Go on, it's all protein, even if it looks like gunk. You're going to need protein if we're doing what I think we're doing.'

'Which is?'

'We start mapping your brain today.'

'Not until you explain.' Luke pushed the plate away mutinously. He had no appetite now anyway. And what the fuck did Green mean by mapping his brain?

Green smiled and pushed the plate back at him. It reminded Luke of the kind of games he and his brother had used to play, until Aaron had started playing other less wholesome games, pushing the plate too far. Suddenly he was intensely depressed. Aaron had been his twin. He should have known what was going on – should have sensed what he'd been up to and stopped him. An overwhelming sense of failure swept over him. Served him right – maybe MND was karma – fate's way of reuniting them? Whatever, if Green pushed the fucking plate at him one more time, he'd push his fist down Green's throat…It was as if Green read his mind because he suddenly abandoned the plate-pushing game and stood up.

'OK, well, if you really don't want it, I'm not going to force you. You'll just have to make do with another vitamin shot, but solid food would have been better, and Hebe did try...'

'I'm sorry.' Now Luke felt like he'd failed Hebe as well as his brother.

'It's OK.' Green patted him on the shoulder. 'Let's get you some shoes and get on with things in the lab.' Overhead, the drill started another round of pounding. Green grimaced and seeing Luke glancing skywards too, added, 'The ForEver lab is separate to the rest of the building. They'll never break through to here even if they do break through into some of the other labs.'

'The ForEver lab?' Luke asked, as he pushed the stool away from him and steadied himself against the worktop.

'Where we'll be working on you,' Green explained.

'Oh yes. So, why is it called the ForEver lab?'

'Why do you think?'

'Anything to do with Hebe? Is she a test subject for any of the modules, or something?'

Green paused and stared at him. 'God no!' then he looked unsure. 'No, not really,' he qualified the explosion. 'Not directly, anyway.'

'Then?' Luke prompted.

Green sighed – a long, exhausted expression of frustration. 'It's not my explanation to give – and in any case you don't need it. Your agreement is to say nothing, isn't it? In which case, the less you know the easier it is to keep to your agreement.'

'But I've seen what she does and some things you can't unsee…'

They'd left the kitchen area as they talked and had now reached another door at the end of the same corridor. Green placed his hand over the security pad by the door and the door slid silently open. Luke's jaw dropped.

'How can we be back here?' he asked, looking over both shoulders as if to get his bearings. This is the lab we were in yesterday – the one the bedroom leads off of, but we've been walking away from it.'

'Escher again,' Green smiled at Luke's confusion. 'Escher explains a lot of things, actually,' he added ruminatively. His eyes misted over. 'Physiological conundrums, human misunderstandings, haphazard decisions. If only we had all the facts all the time, maybe we'd get it right more often?' His gaze returned to the here and now – and Luke. 'Or maybe we wouldn't – who can say. After you,' he ushered Luke into the lab.

'Mr Maynard! I trust you slept well and had a good breakfast?' Jason Crane was holding sway over the lab, entirely filling its space with the force of his presence. 'Are you ready to have your brain mapped?' He was dressed immaculately in silver grey trousers, white linen shirt, charcoal sneakers and crisp white lab coat. By comparison, Matthew Green looked like a thuggish version of the lab caretaker, down-at-heel, unkempt and uncouth. How the hell could these two work together to produce such sublime breakthroughs in technology, Luke wondered as Green went to join Crane. The pair of them stood side by side, examining him, weighing him up, whilst he stood opposite them, scrutinising them and deciding which might be the less desirable – Green, the accidental murderer, or Crane, the intentional conspirator?

'I want to know about Hebe before you map any part of me. If I'm going to undergo a procedure that may include the application of your technology, then I want to know how she ended up as she is and that I'm not going to find myself reacting the same way.'

Crane looked sideways at Green.

'Well, he can hardly have failed to notice, can he?' Green said, shrugging. 'She's already gone from child to woman and back since he's been here. If you were him, you'd be worried too.'

'OK, fair comment,' Crane sounded the epitome of reason. 'All right, I'll explain, but remember, this will form part of your gagging agreement with us.'

'Fair enough,' Luke agreed.

'In that case, let's talk whilst we start the mapping process. There's a lot to do, so let's be efficient with our time, shall we?' As he spoke, Crane moved across to the right-hand wall and pulled open a door which had hitherto lain flush against it. Inside was a body-sized cavity, topped by a dome-shaped ceiling. He pulled on another handle and a bed, much like a mobile conveyer belt, slid from the cavity. 'If you would lie on the bed, feet facing into the machine, we'll begin.'

'What the fuck!' Luke exclaimed, backing away. 'No way – what is that?'

'It's a form of MRI, re-purposed to enable us to map the brain's activity in 3D layers. A bit like we could get an idea of the composition of a human body from a standard MRI, this does the same for the brain. It used to be much more tedious to brain map, but this can do it all in a matter of hours.' He placed his hand over a control pad which had popped out of the wall and was now showing the word 'connected' in bright green letters.

'And why do you need to map my brain?'

'To identify how the MND has infiltrated it. MND affects the motor neurones – the nerves of the brain and spinal cord. There's no point hooking you up to a BioModule unless it can effectively bypass those neurones and activate other, healthy ones, so we need to establish how far, and where, and what the MND has affected. For that we need to map your brain, and then subsequently, how far it has affected the spinal cord. But you don't need to lie silent whilst we do that. You can listen, and talk, whilst I do it.'

'And what is it connected to, this machine?'

Crane's head tipped to one side in a disconcertingly mechanical way. 'Me,' he replied, smiling. Then he burst out laughing. 'What the hell do you think it's hooked up to? A computer, of course! Come on.'

So Jason Crane had a sense of humour, did he – albeit warped. OK…

The machine itself wasn't so bad to lie inside, and the claustrophobia that Luke had feared might overcome him never kicked in because he was too overwhelmed by what Crane told him as the machine did its job. As he lay back, sinking into the surprisingly soft surface of the machine's retractable bed, hands palm down onto its smooth surface, he found himself drifting to the sound of Crane's voice.

'Hebe is unique.'

The machine repositioned him, tilting him fractionally to one side, then clamping into position. Luke protested as the body straps slid over his torso, but Green reached in and patted him on the shoulder.

'It's only to keep you still so the machine can make connection. Neurones are tiny, you know. This is a precision process. Don't worry. They release automatically when the mapping is complete.'

The machine adjusted again, moving out of the cavity a few inches and Luke found himself staring up into the underside of Crane's chin.

'Good,' Crane nodded, then bent his head and stared straight down at him. His eyes glowed in the reflected light from inside the machine. There was something, something… 'And she's my daughter,' he continued, as if there hadn't been any cross-over in the conversation.

'Err, I rather guessed that, but how…'

Green exclaimed suddenly and they both jumped. 'Sorry,' he said gruffly. 'Need to adjust the straps or they'll get too tight. May I?' he leaned across Crane and towards Luke's head. Crane stepped aside and briefly all Luke could see and smell were Green's bulk and an aroma he associated – strangely – with fear. Green's hands were sweaty against his skin as Green fiddled with the topmost strap that secured his head. Luke held his breath and followed the movement of Green's hands with a sensation of disgust, particularly when Green deliberately planted his palm against the control panel that Crane had been manipulating just beforehand. The imprint lingered on the face of the panel and Luke distracted himself by watching the gradual disintegration of palm and fingers as the condensation faded. He might have been mistaken but Green appeared to be fiddling unnecessarily with the head strap as he watched the condensation print fade too. 'There,' he said suddenly. 'All set now.'

He backed away from Luke and the machine and Luke gratefully took a deep breath of fresher air. Crane took Green's place, an impatient expression flickering across his face as Green melted into the background. 'Can we get started now?'

'Yes, yes – sorry…'

'I know she's your daughter – I guessed as much,' Luke repeated. He assumed Green's intervention had been deliberate to change the subject, given his testiness earlier. He sure had a thing about silencing any discussion about Hebe! Well, forget that buster, Luke thought. 'But why does she change as she does?'

There was a moment's silence from Crane then his reply, urbane, smooth, dismissive. 'A genetic complexity,' Crane said, placing his hand back onto the control pad. 'Her body over-responds to HGR – human growth hormone – that's all.'

'But she doesn't just grow up, she goes backwards too, from what I can see.' Looking up, Luke could see the eyelashes fringing Crane's eyes flutter as if he was blinking rapidly. The machine flashed in synchrony. Luke frowned, then closed his eyes. It was like strobe lighting and he'd never done well with that, but the flashing lights penetrated even his closed lids so he opened his eyes again, in time to see Crane's pupils dilate and then contract, like the aperture of a lens responding to a rapid light change and Crane's face distort with pain.

'Jason,' Green was hissing, hovering nearby. Luke could tell he was close again by the sour sweat smell that now cut through Crane's expensive leathery aftershave. 'Are you…'

'Keep out of this,' Crane hissed back. 'Shit! How did?' Crane yanked his hand from the control panel and stepped backwards. Luke struggled to tip his head backwards. 'Take over,' Crane was muttering as he staggered towards the other end of the lab, soles of his shoes squeaking on the highly polished floor, the control panel hand stuffed under his opposite armpit. Green was clutching at him and guiding him to a lab stool. The next moment, Green was back at Luke's head.

'I'll take over from here,' he announced.

'What's happened?" Luke demanded, struggling against the straps. In the background Luke heard the lab door swish open and shut and the lab suddenly felt emptier. Crane's aftershave was fainter now too, overlaid by Green's sweaty earnestness. 'What is going on?' he called again, flexing and pushing against the body straps.

'It's all right, it's all right,' Green soothed. 'Jason's just had a minor accident, but it's fine. He'll be back shortly to finish off.'

Luke squirmed against the straps, panic beginning to set in. Was this Green's opportunity to finish him off too? They cut into his arms and chest, and clamped iron-fist-like over his ankles and knees. He couldn't move. 'Get me out of here now!'

'You're quite safe,' Green told him. 'But we haven't got long now.' His voice had become sharp and urgent. 'Jason will be back any time and there's a lot I need to tell you, so stop struggling, shut up, and listen!'

Luke stopped struggling and stared up at Green. Green was holding a small remote control in his hand and he pressed a button on it. Immediately the machine bed started to rotate and Luke was lying on his side.

'Wha…'

'Shh! Hebe is the daughter of Jason Crane and Elise Crane, but Jason Crane is not quite what you think he is. He was diagnosed with a fatal tumour three and a half years ago so we devised a way to save him. We had no idea whether the project would even work – it was all hypothetical then – so we kept the process top secret. We called it the ForEver Project and you are now in the ForEver lab. What does all that mean? It means that Hebe carries parts of both father and mother in her DNA, and the result would appear to be that she is age-transmutable. That means that her physiology isn't fixed to one metabolic rate. It fluctuates – one minute ageing, the next regressing. She matures at many times the rate of an ordinary child, but she also reverts to her true biological age after each revolution. Clearly, she would be regarded as a freak out in the world so Jason has kept her here, again, a top secret.'

'Are you kidding me?' Luke craned his neck to try and look into Green's face.

'No,' Green's jaw tightened. 'I know how crazy it sounds, but believe me, it gets worse. Hebe's lived a strange half-life, schooled by computer-driven AI, and exposed only to her father and me. We have been monitoring her ever since birth because Jason has been anticipating her AI abilities to make themselves apparent any time. To some extent they have – she can solve complex formulae even some of the greatest scientists and mathematicians struggle with and her mastery of language was incredible even at the age of one. However, there's a side to her that defies explanation and I fear for her because of it. I fear because of what others might be able to make of it. Latterly Jason has had her listening for insects and estimating where they are in the courtyard grass or telling him when a butterfly will emerge from its chrysalis. Yes,' Green nodded vigorously at Luke's upturned head and raised eyebrows. 'She can do that too. But the crux of it all is that she wouldn't be doing this – any of this – if something else wasn't enabling her by keeping her metabolism mutable. Otherwise all my study of her would have found a way to moderate and control it – but something or someone doesn't want to moderate or control it. I just don't know why yet.'

'But you know who…' the direction of Luke's eyes fixed on the door Crane had exited from the lab. He sighed. 'Look, I don't know whether you're taking the piss, but if you're not, if she keeps ageing and reversing, surely her metabolism will be completely fucked soon,' Luke protested. 'And why would her own father do that to her? He wouldn't…'

'You would think so, wouldn't you?' Green replied, adjusting the machine bed so that it rotated one hundred and eighty degrees and positioned Luke onto his other side. The straps tightened around him to hold him in place. 'Except it's not – apparently – and that's what intrigues Jason. Why – and how? She's on her fiftieth revolution since birth now, although each time the speed of the whole revolution does seem to get faster. It stops when she reaches adulthood and reverses at that point. She's a ForEver Child… in every sense of the word. But it's not going to stop there.'

'What does that mean?'

'It means you're…' Green froze and put his finger to his lips as a swishing sound in the background signified the opening of the lab door.

The leathery smell of Crane's aftershave pervaded the lab, followed by Crane's pleasantly modulated, 'So, how's it going?'

'More or less done,' Green replied, righting Luke and allowing the machine bed to slide from the machine cavity so Luke was once more back in the lab. The straps released and he heaved a sigh of relief. He didn't suffer from claustrophobia but he could easily have done so if he'd been restrained inside the machine much longer and without the distraction of Hebe's intriguing physiological disposition. Crane's hand was now lightly bandaged. Green looked at it and then at Crane but said nothing.

'Good,' Crane settled himself on one of the lab stools and watched as

Luke swung his legs over the side of the machine bed and shakily returned to standing position.

'What now?' Luke asked.

'Now we apply what we've garnered by way of brain activity data to modify one of the BioModule units to improve your overall physical condition whilst I track how far the MND has progressed. Here, it's all up on the screen now so come and look at your brain in all its glory.'

Luke joined Crane at the monitor displaying row upon row of data. 'And what does that mean?' he asked.

'That is your current state of synaptic connection,' Crane tapped rapidly on the keyboard and the rows of data became first a graph, the coloured lines on it undulating in dramatic peaks and troughs, crossing and re-crossing each other in a spaghetti of blue, orange, pink, green, then the screen morphed into a rotating representation of his brain in 3D, coloured variously with the same blue, orange, pink, green tones across discrete areas. 'This maps the connections as they occurred. It reflects both your emotional state of mind, and also your intellectual state – when you're processing data and manipulating it for use in order to further understand a situation or a fact. It runs along a timeline so I could split this down further and more or less tell you what you were thinking at each moment of the mind-map if I needed to.'

'Bloody hell! Really? Exactly what I was thinking?' Luke peered closer at the rotating brain, wondering if Crane would also be able to pick out what Green had been telling him then?

'Well, not exactly thinking, more your response – so enquiring, engaged, confused, bewildered, strategising, angry, and so on. But it does provide a picture of how you respond to stimuli…'

'If you knew what the stimuli were that prompted the reactions?'

'Yes…' Crane looked up at Luke, smiling complacently. 'And I do.'

'But you weren't here to hear or see everything.'

'No, indeed I wasn't. But Matthew was, so he can fill in the blanks, can't you?' Green nodded vigorously and then turned away from them, apparently busying himself with deactivating the machine. 'And failing that, I have other means.'

Luke shook his head and raised his eyebrows but Crane refused to be drawn. He merely smiled again and tapped some more commands into the keyboard.

'So how does knowing my state of mind help treat my condition?'

'It doesn't, on its own, but it's always important to have a baseline of brain activity before we tamper with it in any way. After all, if we don't have a baseline, how can we be certain we haven't adversely affected it when we do start treatment? He paused. 'Interesting…' he added, switching between the graph and the 3D rendering of Luke's brain. 'Did you ever have a twin?'

Luke's jaw dropped. 'How the hell would you know that?'

'I take it that means yes?' Crane had switched off the monitor and swung round to face Luke. 'That's very helpful, thank you. Enough for now. I need to have a better look at the data with that principle in mind. We'll do some more tests later on to establish motor-neurone intrusion and from that I will be able to establish quite how extensive the physiological effects of the condition have already been, and how we can halt and then reverse them.'

'How? So you *can* halt and reverse this kind of damage?'

'It's pretty simple in theory – if we regressed you. That would be something more than a BioModule though. Matthew has all the details…' he looked at Luke's disbelieving expression, ignoring Green's attempts to gain his attention. 'Oh, not literally. You won't suddenly become ten years younger –'

'Like Hebe does?' Luke interjected.

Crane grunted. 'Like Hebe does,' he agreed, 'but your cell structures can be regressed – reverted – in the same way hers do, but without progressing to full transformation.'

'Jason,' Green interrupted, 'that's not…'

'No, I know it's not, but we often do what was not, don't we?' And with that Crane was standing and walking back towards the lab door, unravelling the bandage on his hand and dropping it onto the far workbench. His hand looked entirely unblemished. He paused at the door and replied to Green. 'A twin means he already has dual functionality embedded.'

'I know, but… no,' Green shook his head. 'The BioModule is enough.'

'But with limitations, whereas dual functionality…' a look Luke couldn't fathom passed between them. '… and we would have spare capacity for other treatment later too, if needed.'

'Jason, we agreed…' Green shook his head again.

'We agreed to cure this gentleman in exchange for his cooperation.'

'But…'

'And think about what other possibilities it might open up.' Crane smiled encouragingly at Green.

'Err, do I have any say in this?' Luke asked, looking from one to the other. 'I don't want to be your next experiment, thanks – if that's what you're arguing over.'

'Of course not,' Crane smiled smoothly at him. 'And of course you have choices - inasmuch as you say yes or no. But we are the ones who know how to treat you, so unless you don't want to be cured…?'

'I do want to be cured, but I also want to know why you're arguing the toss over how,' Luke replied, eyeing Crane, then focusing on Green, expecting some cue, some signal from him to alert him to whether there was more he needed to know, but Green's expression was impassive.

'Not arguing, debating,' Crane replied. 'Isn't that so, Matthew?'

'Debating, yes,' Green responded. He shrugged. 'And Jason is the genius. I'm just the dogsbody.'

'Not the dogsbody. The technician – without whom nothing could happen anyway. But we'll talk about it some more later,' Crane concluded. 'In the meantime, let's get this man some food. Brain mapping gives you brain drain too,' he explained to Luke. 'Matthew will organise some lunch for you and we'll continue this afternoon.'

'So what WAS all that about?' Luke asked Green after the door had closed on Crane. Green shook his head at him and pointed to the other door to his bedroom. Oh right, the silent treatment again! Luke started towards the bedroom door but was surprised by the lab door Crane had exited through sliding open again. The young woman in the doorway was close to twenty, tall, slim, shapely, long golden hair tumbling over her shoulders and onto her high apple-bud breasts, deep-blue eyes taking in everything that was going on in the lab simultaneously with her entering it.

'Hebe!' Green sounded shocked – his voice high and cracked. 'You shouldn't be here.'

'Why not? Father isn't,' she replied. 'And I'm still playing chef. It's lunch time, isn't it?'

'Yeah,' Luke cut across Green's protestations. 'It's lunch time and I'm starving. Let's do what the main man said I should and go get some lunch, Hebe.' Before Green could cross the room and stop him. Luke launched himself like a sprinter exiting the blocks from his position by the now darkened monitor and grabbed Hebe's arm. They were already through the door and down the corridor before Green's voice trailed after them, still protesting.

'You're keen?' Hebe laughed as they marched briskly down the corridor and back in the direction of the kitchen area. 'I thought you hated my bacon and eggs this morning?'

'I'm not much of a breakfast person,' Luke replied, grinning. This girl was beautiful... and intriguing… Time to find out from the horse's mouth what Hebe knew about herself, since everyone else in this damn place was determined to be so secretive.

'What were they doing to you in there?' She seemed to be genuinely in the dark about it.

'Mapping my brain,' Luke explained, forcing his expression into one of surprised disbelief. 'To treat me, if that's possible?'

'Oh it's more than possible,' Hebe replied. 'It's essential if you're going to be treated by my father. He's been mapping mine since I was born. So are you being treated by him then?'

'Apparently. And are you being treated by him?'

'No, I'm being studied by him,' Hebe smiled at him and then winked. 'Joking,' she added. 'And not joking too.'

'Jeez! Don't you mind?' Luke came to a halt, forcing Hebe to stop too since he was still holding onto her arm.

'Well, yes and no. I don't like being an object to study, but on the other hand, I have to be. How will he ever cure me if I'm not?'

'So he is planning on curing you?'

'One day.'

'And do you know why you are as you are?'

'Genetics,' she replied, shrugging.

'I've never heard of any genetic problem that causes someone to do what you do. It's unheard of.' He watched her response with interest.

'But then so are my genetics,' she tugged on his arm, perfectly relaxed. 'And I am what I am so…Come on, I'm starving and I'm going to make you pizza.'

Luke allowed her to tow him along until they reached the kitchen where she deposited him on the same bar stool as he'd occupied earlier, while she started opening and closing cupboards and assembling a collection of utensils on the worktop. Amidst the clashes and bangs as Hebe accumulated the wherewithal to make pizza and pored over the recipe, Luke continued to inset small, seemingly – he hoped – innocuous questions. How had she learnt to read, did she like cooking, why did she call Green 'Uncle Matthew', did she ever get lonely… she answered absent-mindedly until he asked her about religion.

'Do you have any religious beliefs? I mean, as things are, do you ever think about dying? Is it right to experiment to prolong life, or even to cure death?'

'Life is whatever you believe it to be, Luke,' she replied gravely, pausing between slicing onions and coring peppers. 'And so is death. Is it wrong to want to live longer than humans normally live? No – we all want more than we already have, don't we? Is it wrong to want to cheat death? No, of course not – why wouldn't we if we can? Is it wrong to want to live forever? Still probably no, but I wonder if we would really want to if it was possible to. I know Uncle Matthew doesn't believe in immortality at any cost. I think even my father questions that at times.'

'Your father? I don't get the impression he questions anything unless it's to find out why it doesn't work!' Luke propped his chin on his hands and wedged his elbows in place on the worktop as he watched Hebe's controlled delicate movements as she prepared the pizza's ingredients.

'Oh, you're wrong there. He's always questioned a lot of things. That's why he is what he is despite what he could have been. And if anyone has the ability to question immortality, it's him.'

'Why?' Luke frowned. He couldn't decide whether Hebe admired her father enormously or thoroughly disapproved of him. She wasn't openly critical, but something in her tone implied she was, nevertheless, whilst also being actively indulgent. 'Your Uncle Matthew said something odd about him – and you. He said your father is a robot…' Hebe's mouth dropped open and she stared at him over the growing pile of peeled and chopped ingredients. Then she started to laugh. 'OK,' Luke put his hands up. 'I thought he was taking the piss…'

'No, no, sorry,' Hebe choked back her laughter. 'No, he wasn't – not at all, it just sounds so funny put that way, but he was telling you the truth. My father is the product of his own genius: a man merged with AI.'

'Merged with AI?'

'Well, what else do you think his BioModules are?

'Then… Shit! You are…'

Hebe nodded, her long silken hair flowing over her shoulders and against her breasts like molten gold. 'What?' she asked, laughing.

'You're part AI too?'

'Yes, I am part AI too – kind of. I mean, I'm wholly cellular – biologically based – but it seems elements of my father's new physiology may have integrated with mine genetically. So I grow old fast and revert fast. I'm now approaching twenty, physiologically. By this time tomorrow, I could be more like ten again. And it's no fun, I can tell you. The only bonus is that my father thinks that every time I complete a revolution, my brain capacity expands too, but doesn't then compact again. We have no idea why other than, I guess, the revolution is wholly physiological whereas brain capacity is more to do with utilisation of quantum properties. In other words, every time I complete a revolution, what I'm capable of becomes significantly more. I employ the parts of my brain that others don't. My father calls it being precocious.'

'Christ!' Luke stared at her, mesmerised. 'How do you feel about that?' Suddenly all his energy seemed to have left him. He propped himself up by the elbows on the countertop, chin resting on hands as what felt like the rest of his life force drained out through the soles of his feet, leaving him exhausted – hanging on to what Hebe was saying by a gossamer thread.

'Feel?' she shrugged again. 'I don't feel anything about it. It just is.'

'Then how do you cope with it?' he asked, wondering how he was going to cope with anything that came next. Was this the MND or the so-called 'brain drain' Crane had mentioned? 'And all on your own? Don't you ever wish you were just… normal?'

With that his left elbow slipped along the worktop and he collapsed, nose and chin rebounding off the worktop as he yelped with the force of the impact like a puppy who'd caught its tail in a door. The resulting muscle spasm brought his knees up to collide with the underside of the worktop and his ass to slip off the stool so that he landed in a heap, legs akimbo and an expression of aggrieved surprise plastered across his face. He looked up to see Hebe peering over the edge of the worktop at him, a mischievous look on her face.

'Well, yes,' she agreed. 'But don't you too?' she countered.

The silence lasted all of thirty seconds before he joined in her laughter, suddenly re-energised. It took considerably longer to get him on his feet and perched back on the stool whilst Hebe completed the complicated design of her pizza.

'I'd like to have enough time to be normal,' he agreed. 'Sometimes life is simply too short.'

'Or maybe life isn't too short, our expectations are just too much,' she replied, sliding the pizzas on their trays into the oven and slamming the door shut. 'After all, any life is more than the dead have.'

He looked at her strangely, but she didn't elaborate. As they ate, she recounted snippets of her childhood thus far – stranded on a lab stool when she was a mere few months old, teaching herself to read, discovering how she could 'hear' things – the life sounds of what others would think were mere inanimate objects; the inner workings of a pebble, the sounds of colours, the cries of the grass when it was cut or trodden on.

'That must be so cool, and yet so weird,' Luke concluded when she finally stopped talking.

'It's just nice to be able to tell someone other than Uncle Matthew,' she replied. 'Or Father, I suppose, but he doesn't really count. I only tell him so he can write it all up in his notes.'

'What about your mother?' Luke asked tentatively. Green had mentioned Elise Crane as Hebe's mother. Had she been a victim of Green too? Hebe's reaction took him by surprise.

'Shhh,' she said, almost a perfect duplicate of Green's reaction to when he'd hustled him out of the lab to the strains of Mahler's Sixth. 'She is how it begins…'

Chapter 14

12:25, 20th May 2032: Luke

The promised afternoon of tests had been similar to the morning's but with no repetition of the 'debate' between Green and Crane. In fact, both had been markedly silent throughout, and Luke had been glad of that. He hadn't felt exactly full of beans himself and his mind kept turning over and over what both Green and Hebe had told him. All in all, a combination of brain-drain and brain fog had sent him into a deep and intense sleep not long after the afternoon's tests had finished – and one which apparently had lasted almost eighteen hours because when Luke awoke it was early the next day, his mind full of the strange imaginings his dreams had been full of. A woman who could grow old and young again in a day, a man-machine, a riddle no one could solve linked to an absent mystery. His head ached with unanswered questions and unsolved clues. He sat up, then flopped back onto the pillows again and surveyed the ceiling. It was pastel blue, and so was he. No! He sat up again. He wasn't pastel blue, he was normal – human skin colour. He swung his legs gingerly over the side of the bed and padded across to the full-length mirror to examine himself. Actually, to be truthful, he did look a bit blue around the edges – or maybe grey was a better description. Tired, drained, lack-lustre. So different to Hebe, with her glowing skin, silky-gold hair and bright blue eyes. His head swam and the tangled dreams swamped over him again, but they weren't dreams – were they? They were realities; realities he'd learned yesterday.

He lifted his feet one by one from the floor, peeling his sweaty soles away from the medvac flooring, leaving perfect moisture footprints where they'd been. He shook his limbs and attempted to get the life flowing back through him. Maybe this was what they'd meant by brain drain and how he needed protein to deal with it? He felt like he'd been starved for days, and yet he'd feasted like a king on Hebe's – surprisingly good –

pizza. He was still examining his weakened limbs and aching body when Green peered round the door linking the bedroom to the ForEver lab. The opening door let in a burst of sound with it, humming machines, muffled voices, muted footfall.

'Ah, you're awake. Good,' Green announced. 'How are you feeling?'

Luke squinted in the direction of the doorway. It seemed to be letting too much light into the room too. 'Rough,' he acknowledged. 'Like you warned me I would.'

'Ye-esss,' Green surveyed him from a distance and Luke was glad he didn't enter the room or approach. Even the head round the door and the muted outside-world noises felt too much to cope with currently. 'Well, let's get some food into you, and maybe some coffee, although not too much by way of stimulants today or we'll get false readings on any tests we do on reactions. There are clothes in the cupboard, and towels and toiletries in the en-suite. Freshen up and then come and find me.' Green sent a pointed look in the direction of the bathroom and then his head ducked back behind the now closing door. Luke gave him the finger as the door closed. Freshen up? Cheeky bastard! Green was the one who needed to freshen up with his cheese-breath and sweaty pits. Luke paused and sniffed the air for that distinctive Matthew Green aroma, then searched closer to home when he realised that the ripe smell of unwashed skin was too strong to be that of Green from a distance. He sniffed his own armpit.

'Bloody hell!' he shrank away from himself in surprise. He was rank! If he'd realised he'd smelt that foul yesterday, he would have cringed with embarrassment in front of the fragrant and fresh Hebe. Stripping on the spot and leaving his tracksuit bottoms in an inky blue puddle in front of the mirror, he padded unsteadily to the bathroom and straight into the shower where he stood for half an hour. Slowly, the life trickled back into him as the water splashed over his head and dropped in small crystals around his feet, splintering into refractions of light and sound as they pounded onto the tray of the shower. After a while they reformed into a series of questions he wanted answered, organised into the beat of the water as it showered onto the floor.

What had happened to Elise Crane?

Had Green allowed 3:16 in?

Who was manipulating Hebe's metabolism?

What had Green and Crane been disagreeing over yesterday?

What was about to begin?

And could he really be cured?

He wanted to leave the last one out of the equation, but eventually, brutal honesty forced him to admit that it was actually number one on the list, not number last. OK, so could he really be cured was number one and he accepted himself as a worm – and a desperate one at that. Today's general fatigue wasn't so unlike the many and varied symptoms of degeneration the MND treated him to and he was damned if he didn't want to escape their curse. Did that make him such a bad guy? To want to live? He sat down heavily on the shower floor and let the water pitter-pat on the top of his head, drumming in that question alongside the others. He pictured Frieda, lying cold and grey in her morgue drawer, where once she had been bright as a butterfly, challenging, vivacious, terrifying too.

'Oh, Jesus!' he choked as grief rose up in him to join fear. Why had this had to happen to him? Why had it had to happen to Frieda or Aaron? Why did man have to die at all? Would Aaron have developed MND too? Twins shared the same genetics, after all. The thought of death, dying – it scared him; made his legs go weak. Not the process of it, the pain, the sickness, the bodily failure, but the potential nothing beyond it. At least pain and discomfort were proof of life. But what did you do with nothing?

But Jason Crane said he could cure him – for the price of silence. Could he? Could he really? That also begged the question – who could he ask who would tell him the truth? Green clearly wanted him to go along with it, and obviously Crane did or he wouldn't have suggested it. He was their experiment as much as they were his cure, so he couldn't expect real honesty from them. That left only Hebe.

What would Hebe think about his deal with her father? It was betrayal on many levels – a betrayal of Frieda, a betrayal of 3:16, a betrayal of her too. After all, he was agreeing to help keep her secret from the world in order to have his cure, whilst Green had said she needed to escape here, not be hidden here, and she herself talked of needing to escape or die here. Yes, it was a betrayal of Hebe, and yet Green had wanted him to betray Hebe whilst helping protect her. Luke shook his head, scattering shower droplets like a dog shaking his coat dry. There was more to this than met the eye, but that also meant he couldn't ask Hebe if the treatment her father was proposing would really cure him. Damn! He was on his own – just like he'd been ever since Aaron had found his own way to damnation and Frieda had joined him – but then weren't we always on our own, right from birth, no matter what we tried to fool ourselves into believing? He wanted to live until he could live no longer, so there was no choice but betrayal.

He pulled himself slowly upright and leaned against the toughened glass of the shower wall. Through the water-spattered glass the outlines of the other objects in the bathroom were distorted – twisted versions of themselves. The carefully folded bathrobe looked both simultaneously stretched and squeezed. The towel hanging from the towel rail, jagged, not soft and inviting, and the open doorway from the bathroom into the bedroom, dark and cavernous. Everything in life was seen through a glass darkly. This was no different. It was called survival.

Luke entered the ForEver lab with determination in his step.

'You seem better?' Green greeted him. 'Let's get some grub.' He led the way to the kitchen Hebe had presided over yesterday and deposited Luke on a stool there. The kitchen smelt of stale cooking and old coffee – someone had already done the cooking and left it for them. Green heaped crisp bacon, runny-yolked eggs which seemed to drown everything in yellow, plump baked beans, lightly-baked hash browns and perfectly grilled tomatoes onto Luke's plate and pushed it towards him, seemingly impervious to the appetising smell himself.

This time, Luke didn't push the plate back. He acknowledged the need to eat to survive, however his sensitivities complained.

'Hebe?' he asked as he took his first mouthful, chewed thoroughly and forced the mangled bolus down into the depths of an ungrateful stomach. Do her cooking skills improve exponentially too?'

'No, she's indisposed today. She reached twenty-one overnight,' Green explained. 'Now she's reverting. She dislikes that part of the process so you probably won't see her for a while. This is courtesy of Andrea,' Green added. 'A cross between Hebe's nursemaid and her handmaid, but basically Jason's assistant – for whatever assistance is required for and I can't provide.'

'Oh.' Luke nodded, grateful for Hebe's absence in one way, and sorry in another. At least he wouldn't have to deal with his conscience again today. 'So what is on the agenda for today, then?' he asked, determinedly navigating his way through the rest of the plate's contents, but noting that Green hadn't joined him. He was hovering pensively by the coffee machine, fiddling with the levers and knobs that made steam and frothed milk.

'Coffee?' Green offered.

'I thought you said no stimulants?'

'Ah, yes,' Green pushed the mug he'd been reaching for away from him instead, then reached for it again and poured a half-mug of coffee. He sipped it and then pushed it away from him again.

'You seem distracted,' Luke commented as he pushed the now emptied plate away from him and poured a glass of water from the lukewarm jug near him on the breakfast bar.

'Distracted?' Green stared at him, his eyes slowly glazing over. Then he was snapping back into focus and answering sharply, 'Not at all. Just a lot to remember today. Almost ready? Chop-chop then. It's just you and me today. Jason is busy.'

'Then you can explain what all that business was about twins yesterday then?'

'Twins?'

'Yes, you and Crane wanted to know if I had a twin and then you were talking about some special kind of treatment.'

'Ah, no… that was nothing. Just a theoretical divergence.'

Luke stopped mid-stride. Green was so clearly lying to him, there was no way the new self-preserving Luke Maynard was being experimented on without it being fully explained to him – cure or no cure.

'Fuck that. It was clearly something. Now you tell me what it was or I treat you to my famous left hook from when I was fit enough to box, and then leg it out of here to tell the world about your secret labs and how Crane is made up of his own AI modules and he has a daughter who is something else altogether… You promised me a cure, and I'm damn well having it – a proper one.'

Surprisingly Green matched him in belligerence and for a moment they stood toe to toe in the echoing corridor, the on-off rurr-rurrr-rurr of the pneumatic drill the 3:16 Group were still deploying overhead, a backdrop of background threat juxtaposed with direct threat.

'You wouldn't get any kind of cure if you exposed us,' he replied, softly and sibilantly.

'Neither would you,' Luke said, equally softly and menacingly.

'And what cure is that?'

'I don't know, but clearly it could be something to do with Hebe since it was employing regression theory of some kind. So what is dual functionality? And why is Crane busy when he expressed an interest in it? Is that your doing –to stop me getting the best treatment?'

'Shh!' Green suddenly gripped the lapels of his polo shirt – the designer label one he'd found in the cupboardful of clothes all apparently at his disposal. 'You do not want to get involved in dual functionality, whatever Jason tells you, believe me!'

'Then YOU tell me what it is!' Luke thrust his nose into Green's face, steadfastly ignoring Green's cheese-breath and prising Green's hands off his lapels.

Green flipped his hands outward and ended the strange little movement in a shrug. The rurr-rurr-rurr above ceased, as if also waiting for an answer.

'You just don't know what's good for you, do you?' Green sighed.

'You just don't know what's bad for you, do you?' Luke countered. 'Murder, conspiracy to murder, conspiracy to kidnap and hold persons against their will, unsanctioned scientific experiments…'

'You came here of your own free will, and you've stayed here of your own free will. You've even asked for a cure and allowed yourself to be subjected to tests. And we've explained about Dr Kohn.'

'But what about Hebe?' Luke hissed. 'What's her cure?'

The rurr-rurr-rurr started up again, this time seemingly louder. Both Luke and Green glanced upwards.

'Come on,' Green grabbed Luke by the arm. 'Not here,' he instructed. Luke reluctantly followed him back to the ForEver lab. Green pulled him inside and shut the door. Then he turned on Mahler and the lab was filled to the exclusion of all other noise by the swelling and surging of the maestro, whilst Green beckoned Luke over towards the machine he'd been interrogated by the day before. 'Get in,' Green yelled above the music. 'Music helps me concentrate. Just follow my cues and you'll be fine. Just a few more cognitive tests today and then we're ready for the next stage.' He put his finger to his lips.

Sighing, Luke slid himself into the end of the machine, but Green stopped him from sliding all the way in and produced an earphone type device which he proceeded to wrap around Luke's neck, lying the ends on his collarbone. 'Now,' he nodded, signifying that Luke should slide the rest of the way in. Green followed up by placing a similar device on his own head, but the 'earbuds' attached to his forehead instead, with one length of wire attached to the 'earphones' Luke was wearing. 'Can you hear me?'

'Yes!' To his surprise, Luke could hear Green perfectly, despite the deafening volume of the Mahler and the fact that Green hadn't appeared to have spoken at all. 'How?' he mouthed at Green.

'Echophones,' Green tapped the earphone type device proudly. 'One of my own inventions. It works in conjunction with transmitting specific brainwaves so that you can be in the midst of immense noise but hear only what you want to focus on. My speech generated brainwaves are picked up by the patches I'm wearing and then transmitted to you via the connection so none of them can be heard in any other way. It's as if they don't even exist whilst you and I are both connected by the devices. That's very important to remember, Luke. It's as if this conversation isn't taking place, OK?'

Luke nodded. 'But won't Crane be able to work out my thoughts from the recordings?' he mouthed back.

'That's the reason for the Mahler. It's so dramatic, any overreaction you have will be so completely masked by the normal emotional responses to the music. So, listen carefully and don't ask me questions as then we could be in trouble. This conversation needs to be one way only.' He scoured Luke's expression for his answer then, seemingly satisfied, continued. 'So we DO have a cure for you, but it wouldn't be a wholly permanent cure. However, in searching for a cure for Hebe, I have been working on an alternative whereby we literally reprogram the dual functioning side of you as if it were AI. You only have a dual functioning element if you had or have a twin.' Green paused, watching Luke's expression. 'And now you want to know why I would object to using it on you?'

Luke nodded his head vigorously. The strap was pulling on his chest and he was feeling the first uncomfortable stirrings of claustrophobia, even though his head was outside of the machine.

'Because currently it could make you into a split personality – one side you, with your natural human characteristics, including faults, the other side AI functioning via the duality having had a twin would make possible with your physiology. But that AI side would be mechanistic, entirely logical, perfectly ordered, intractable. In other words, we might heal your body but as the AI element took over and reinstructed DNA and cell structures, we could potentially tear your mind in two with the conflict between human and AI. You'd go mad. That's why, as yet, we can't use it. We need to perfect it first.'

Luke frowned at him and shook his head. 'You need a guinea pig then,' he mouthed. 'And Crane was proposing me?'

'Somewhat. Dual functionality treatment would enable Jason to experiment with it – on you. Yes, cure you physically, but possibly kill you mentally. There's only one person who might survive that at the moment…' he paused and then clamped his mouth shut as if he'd said too much already.

'So the promise of a cure is a lie?' Luke mouthed up at Green.

'No, it's real, but temporary. We could regress your cells, using a similar process to what Hebe's body does, and that would potentially cure you. However, it will entail wearing a BioModule all your life because your body can't do on its own what Hebe's does. As soon as the module is removed or malfunctions or wears out, you immediately revert to your current state, and regress negatively extremely rapidly. Failure of the BioModule would effectively mean death within twenty-four hours or so.'

'Great! A scam!' Luke started to struggle and the lights on the machine indicated, *instability, reposition patient.* 'Get me out of here then.'

'Wait, wait,' Green put a restraining hand on Luke's right shoulder. 'It's not a scam and a cure is possible.' He hesitated. 'There is something far more radical than the plug-in BioModule, but that's not dual functionality.' He hesitated again.

'Huh?' Luke stared up at him, raising his eyebrows until they felt like they would shoot through his skull.

'But you'd have to ask Jason for it specifically,' Green replied, reluctance twisting his mouth into a sneer. 'Ask for a complete fix. Like he had.'

'Whaaaaa?' Luke's mouth hung wide open. 'A complete fix? But he was never broken, was he?' he yelled above the Mahler. Green slapped a hand across his mouth.

'The ForEver Project; that's what it was. If you did that, you'd be assured of a complete cure and it would take longer to set up so it would give me time to work on fine-tuning the dual function programme so then I could use it on… I'm so near, but… You'd only have to stay for another week...'

'Another week? No. Flat no.' Luke started wriggling again and this time the machine's warning system beeped angrily. 'I just want my cure and then get out of here.' In response, Green switched the alarm off and slid Luke out of the machine. As soon as his arms were free, Luke ripped the chest strap off of him and unravelled the echophones. He pulled them away from his collarbone and thrust them at Green. 'But if that's not possible I'm out of here anyway,' he shouted at an astonished Green. 'I'll take my chances, but I'm not going to be a test subject just to keep you two in lab experiments or give you extra time to fix something that sounds like it's out of a nightmare, regardless of how sweet a kid Hebe is.'

Surprising himself, he yanked himself out of the machine with an alacrity he hadn't felt for years and managed to make a dignified and reasonably steady exit from the lab, ignoring Green's alarmed, 'Mr Maynard, Mr Maynard? It's not like that. Please come back and let me explain.'

He hesitated, and that was his downfall. Green caught up with him and dragged him into a small room that seemed to have no doors or windows.

'Shhh,' Green clapped his hand across Luke's mouth again. 'Jesus! I'm trying to help you, you stupid bastard!' he hissed. 'Just shut up and listen or you'll get us both killed. I told you all that stuff so that you weren't fooled into believing curing you is that simple, even though Jason would have you believe it is. There's no way he's just going to fit you with a BioModule and let you wander out of here. That's not the way it works. Yes, you're prime experiment material – in here under an assumed identity, and in need of a cure, and that's what you'll remain for him, whatever you think. Your only chance is to ask to be part of the ForEver Project. Now that would be a different thing altogether. He simply wouldn't be able to refuse that. It would buy you time and me opportunity.'

'For what?'

'To find a way of getting you and Hebe safely out of here.'

'And then? What about my cure?'

'There's no point to a cure when you're already dead, is there?'

'Shit!' Luke stared at Green. Was he joking or finally playing the good guy and telling the truth? This time he wasn't sure. Green might have murdered Frieda, but the expression on his face suggested to Luke he was desperate to save – if not Luke – Hebe. But then, Green HAD killed Frieda… 'And why should I believe you?'

'What reason have I to lie?'

'I don't know. Many…'

'Look, you ask to be part of the ForEver Project and you leave the rest to me.'

'But…'

'No fucking buts, Mr Maynard, just get your ass out of here and back to the courtyard and look like you're doing sod all whilst I report some crap back to Jason about today's tests and set the scene.' And with that, Green shoved him out of the room that was little more than an alcove, and into the corridor. 'It's your only hope,' Green added. Luke stumbled and righted himself, heart pounding and stomach churning. So much for being the survivor. The survivor was relying on predators in order to survive. The only question was, which predator was worse – Green or Crane? Green followed him but started to set off in the opposite direction.

'And that's it?' Luke called after him. 'What about what you've been testing so far?'

Green paused and turned. 'If you're going to be part of the ForEver Project, the tests will be different.'

'And how do you know Crane will agree?'

'He'll agree,' Green said curtly. 'Now shut up and let me get on with what I've got to do.'

'Fuck, fuck, fuck,' Luke whispered under his breath as he watched Green disappear down the corridor with surprising speed. His only hope? Experimental material? Why the hell had he ever agreed to this? The sooner he was out and in receipt of the tender mercies of 3:16, the better, the way things were going.

Setting off in the direction of – what he thought to be – the courtyard garden – Luke strode out, trying to ignore the tingling in his fingertips and the weakness in his knees. What didn't confound him physically, confounded him mentally though. Escher was clearly working at full steam today as every corridor he took led him to another, identical passageway, long, cool pastel blue, echoing gently with the persistent rurr-rurr-rurr overhead as 3:16 patiently tried to bore their way into the viper's nest, until he eventually had to sit, exhausted, demoralised and despairing, with his back against the wall and his feet drawn up against his thighs, chin on knees. Before exhaustion totally overcame him, he allowed himself one brief bout of ironic laughter at his predicament. He'd come here for a cure and answers. What he'd ended up with was more questions and the possibility of something that could kill him as easily as it cured him. It was in the middle of this that Hebe found him.

She'd reverted to about fourteen, a gangly teenager with over-long limbs, a shy smile and an embarrassed air.

'Luke?' she called softly. 'Luke?' She must have been calling for some minutes before her gentle voice made it through his raucous laughter, that was by then steadily veering towards the hysterical. No way out, other than as an experiment himself. Dammit, was he fucked! 'Luke…' Finally, she got his attention. She beckoned to him.

'What?' he let his head loll backwards and through rolling eyes, there she was – the girl-woman. The anomaly. The answer. The problem. The biggest question of all… But what the hell, he hadn't any other way of finding his way out of this maze. He followed her down another passageway leading onto and then off the courtyard. Easy. Why hadn't he been able to find this? She waited long enough for him to catch up with her there, the bright sun streaming through the glass roof overhead and turning her flaxen hair to a cap of gold. Even the air smelt like molten gold – the kind of heat you associate with high summer and holidays and freedom.

'You asked me how I coped with this. This is how,' and she led him through a doorway that was almost invisible into a softly lit room. In the centre of the room, a woman was lying asleep on a bed. She was attached to a heart monitor and a breathing tube, but even that couldn't mar the serene beauty of her face. Golden-haired, like an angel – and he could quite clearly see the likeness of Hebe to her. Luke stared at that face; that face…

'She's my mother,' Hebe, told him. 'My father doesn't know I've found her, only Uncle Matthew. I talk to her when I'm lonely. But she can't…'

Luke stopped himself from blurting out 'talk back' just in time, because he knew from Hebe's expression that he'd be wrong. 'What?' he asked, breath catching in his throat and making his voice rasp. He moved closer, still staring, scrutinising the features, the gold stranded hair, the lips gently kissing the breathing tube. 'What can't she do?' That face, those long, elegant fingers. Those lips. He knew them all. Intimately. But this woman was comatose – and a complete stranger to him.

'Survive,' Hebe replied, joining him, and gently stroking the prone figure's hand. 'Not on her own, anyway. She's on life support.'

Luke scrutinised Hebe and the silent figure, comparing the likenesses and compiling the differences. There weren't many of the latter. Age difference was the main one. Hebe was hovering around fourteen, the woman around mid-thirties.

'So why is she here – and such a big secret?'

'Because she is why my father is monitoring me. If he can figure out how I tick, he could regress her to the point before she died.'

'He couldn't do that – that's impossible.' But even as he denied it, he realised that it was exactly what Crane had suggested they do to him, Luke – regress his cell structure to before the MND developed. But then, if it could already be done – albeit with the use of some as yet untested

BioModule, why hadn't Crane already done it to his wife then?

'I do many things that are impossible, Luke,' Hebe was saying. 'And I'm not AI. My father is and what he can do is limitless.'

'Your father is AI? Come on…' Someone else with an obsession about Crane's additions to himself even whilst they actively sought them to work for themselves! Were they the crazies, or was he? 'OK, then why can't he cure you?' It came out harsher than Luke had intended it to. They stared at each other, the ventilator clicking softly with each breath in and out, and the heart monitor beeping quietly in tandem with it.

'He will, when he's figured out the best way to do it. In the meantime he's going to cure you,' Hebe reminded him, eyes gentle and reassuring. 'Isn't he?'

'Not really. It's a BioModule he's going to fit. That's not a cure, it's a management system. OK whilst it works, but once it stops working, so do I. Not that it's not better than nothing…' Luke paused at the sight of Hebe's crestfallen expression. He sounded so ungrateful. *Not that it's not better than nothing... Not that it's not better than imminent death*, was what he should have said. 'I didn't mean…' he began but stopped as Hebe clutched at him and they both froze at the sound outside the door.

'In here,' Hebe pulled at his arm, and they melted behind the drapes that hid the working end of the room from the presentational one. Behind the sinuous pink drapes, a full lab had been set up to service the survival of Elise Crane. Luke gaped at the set-up. 'Shhh', Hebe cautioned him. She had positioned herself at the join in the drapes, peering through the tiniest chink between them. Luke left his open-mouthed examination of the rows of monitors, attached to what seemed to be a master computer, and tiptoed over to join her.

The sound heralded a newly arriving visitor. Matthew Green entered the room cautiously, pausing to check behind him before closing the door and tiptoeing over to the comatose Elise as if afraid he might wake her. He collected a chair on the way and positioned it by the bed, close to her head. Once again, Hebe motioned to Luke to stay silent.

'Well, he's here,' Green told Elise. 'And he's with 3:16, even though he hasn't admitted it yet, but he was looking for Frieda too. I don't know which came first, but he's sure as hell going to make sure he comes out of here with what he wants – and that's hardly going to be what Jason wants, is it?'

'3:16?' Hebe mouthed at Luke. Her eyes flashed again, lightning strikes of anger and disillusionment. 'The people attacking the lab?' Luke tried to convey that she didn't understand, but her lips set in a thin angry line and she applied herself back to the chink in the curtain.

'But God knows whether he'll be able to help after all,' Green was saying. 'He's worse than we thought.' Luke had to swallow hard at that. So that was what the test results had told Crane and Green – that he was expendable because he would expire relatively soon anyway. So much for his fond hope that a few years might extend to a few decades.

'Jason's offered him the module cure,' Green was still talking, his voice a hushed monotone, 'but now he knows that won't help long term so he's going to hold out for more. He's going to ask to be part of the ForEver Project…'

Hebe rounded on Luke then and grabbed at him, her eyes blue fire in a pale face. He grimaced and shook his head again but he couldn't reply whilst Green was only the other side of the drapes.

'As for the rest,' Green's voice took on wistful note, 'well, you know where things are at with Hebe. I don't know what else to do. And I don't see how this young man will help when his eyes are on saving himself, not us. What do I do, Elise? I can't decide what's for the best now.'

Green's head hung low, chin on chest, and he stayed there a while, as if in prayer. Then just as suddenly, he was standing, replacing the chair and leaving. When they were sure Green had gone, Hebe and Luke tumbled out from the drapes and Hebe slapped him hard across the face. Not just the impact, but the words stung. He winced and shied away from her.

'You traitor! I thought you came back to help us but you're just here for your own ends, aren't you?' She aimed another slap at him, then another until Luke grabbed her flailing hands to stop the pummelling. They felt small and frail in his grasp, but his shoulders and arms still stung from their impact.

'But you already knew that. I'm dying, Hebe. Who wouldn't accept the chance at saving themselves? But I don't know what this ForEver Project is. It's just something Green mentioned to me. And what did he mean – save you?'

'I told you, right from the start. We need saving. *From* the ForEver Project.'

'But what the fuck IS the ForEver Project?' Luke demanded, exasperated.

'The ForEver Project is my father. He was dying too, until he and Uncle Matthew devised a way to save him.'

'BioModule…'

'Yes, BioModule – but much more; he's in an artificial body that's effectively all BioModule except for his brain.'

'But…no! Come on. He's as human as you or me. He even hurt himself on the MRI machine yesterday.'

'His body is biological. It's become so because of what Uncle Matthew developed – it's called CyberCute – a kind of artificial skin that catalyses a body's non-human cellular structures to morph into biological ones. AI and bio merged.'

'That's not possible.'

'But it is, Luke. My father is proof. And I've already told you some of this before.'

'Yeah, sort of, and I didn't believe you then either…' Luke paused, trying to put what he'd just been told about his potential healer into perspective. 'And I still don't believe it now. It's just not possible – even with a genius like your father.' Every time he heard Jason Crane referred to as some kind of robot, it made him want to laugh, whether through fear or disbelief, he wasn't sure. 'But if he is part AI then, what's the big deal? The whole deal here is about replacing bits of people that don't work, isn't it? Even you are talking cures…'

Hebe seemed calmer now and he allowed her to shake him away from her, losing his grip of her wrists, but remaining watchful in case she decided to start hitting him again. It seemed wrong to be arguing like this alongside the serenely sleeping Elise – surreal in fact, but then the whole place, the whole idea, the whole situation was surreal.

'It's not the same. You want to know what's wrong with a fully functioning biologically mechanical full body shell? It never dies. Even the earliest prostheses my father and Uncle Matthew developed were designed to only be part AI programming, part bio-engineering, not independently functioning. The idea was always to merge the mechanical and the biological so that they worked symbiotically to create a new whole, but merge, not replace. But my father is a new whole, made up of an AI-programmed body and biological brain. He's the earliest version of dual functionality.'

'Well, then he's not a robot, is he?' Luke felt uncertain about that, but it still fell in the crazy and impossible category. On the other hand, dual functionality… he remembered Green's explanation of it. 'Or, he's only half-robot because dual functionality means half is still controlled by human impulses…'

'His brain and body merged completely within days, so Uncle Matthew tells me. There aren't two parts to my father. There's one. Alternately. Sometimes he's controlled by human motivations – love, emotions, and so on. Then other times, the AI programming takes over. There's only cold hard, logic involved then. No compassion, no benefit of the doubt, no empathy. So what does that make him?'

'Shit, well… I don't know. Confusing?' Luke suggested after a while.

'Dangerous,' she corrected him. 'If the AI overrules the human for longer than intermittently.'

'I suppose.' Luke was still grappling with seeing Crane as a semi-robot – although that was somewhat oversimplifying things.

'He wanted to do the same to my mother when she had her accident. But then she'd be gone.'

'Gone?' Luke frowned. He felt weak again, tired to his bones and he knew this kind of fatigue of old. This wasn't brain drain. This was MND and it was getting worse. 'Surely she'd be saved, wouldn't she?' he said, sighing and trying to focus again. What Hebe had explained about the ForEver Project was fascinating and provocative, but unlikely. A whole new body – bio-engineered and running off of a human brain? A complete BioModule, in fact. Very interesting, and weirdly – tempting – for someone with a rapidly failing body, even if it did mean one day you were robotic and the next human. But could it also break down or wear out like the smaller units? He was still pondering this as Hebe replied.

'No! Luke, you haven't been listening, have you?'

'I have, it's just – Christ, Hebe this is all too surreal. First there's you going backwards and forwards all the time, then there's your mother in that weird room, then you're telling me your father is a robot.'

'Not a robot!' She stamped her foot angrily. 'AI and human fused. And if he did it to my mother she'd be AI too, like my father.'

'But he's not,' Luke replied, exasperated. 'You've already said he's AI and human fused. And even if he was, I don't see what's wrong with him? I'm sorry, but I really can't believe all this…' he waved his arm to encompass the room, the woman, Hebe… 'Yes, your father's a bit of a cold fish, and possibly quite ruthless, but so are a lot of people who've never even had anything to do with AI or robotics or bio-engineering. Ruthlessness is born, not made. And your father seems as human as they come even if he is a ruthless bastard with it.' He paused, uncertain whether to continue, given Hebe's affronted expression. 'I'm sorry. I'm not feeling too good. What's your mother like?' he asked to change the subject.

'I never met her,' Hebe replied, tight-lipped.

'What do you mean, you never met her? She's right there,' Luke waved at the silent, static form of Elise Crane.

'She was already clinically dead when I was born. No one even knew she was pregnant when she had the accident.'

'Jeez!' Now Luke sat heavily on the chair Green had replaced at the side of the room. This whole set-up just got weirder and weirder. The space between him and Hebe and him and Elise helped. Something about both of them felt like it was invading his consciousness, entwining itself around his thoughts. Christ, he needed to get away from all of them, the faster the better! 'Look, to begin with I came here looking for Frieda – the woman's whose body is in your morgue...' He stopped. It felt wrong talking to a teenager like this – no, worse than a teenager; a little kid, because Hebe was in reality little more than about two. He mentally shook himself – and yet no two-year-old debated morality and the technical complexities of AI and bio-engineering. 'Anyway, that aside, I came back when I had the opportunity in part because I wanted to make sure you were OK too. That first time I met you… well, it bothered me. But the thing is, Hebe, I AM dying – maybe not tomorrow, but my life span is seriously curtailed. I have Motor Neurone Disease. MND. Look at me now,' and he held out his trembling hands. 'And think how I was in the morgue. I couldn't help a fly. But with your father's treatment – his BioModule, or even more than that, maybe then it'll be a different matter. I'd be strong and healthy again. Then I really could help you.'

'You, in an AI body?' she couldn't contain her disgust.

Luke sighed. 'Me, in any functioning body,' he replied patiently. 'I've lost too many people I cared for in my life to just abandon you – my own twin, Frieda…'

'*Twin?*' Hebe was transfixed, staring at him as if he'd just announced that he was the devil incarnate. 'You have a twin?'

'Had a twin. Aaron died a few years back now. Drugs.' It hurt to say it even now – not the admission of a dead twin, the implication, whether anyone else knew it or not, that he, the surviving twin should have been more connected; no, *enough* connected, to have stopped Aaron dying. It was a fault he'd only recently accepted about himself – evidenced by Aaron and Frieda, and every other poor sod he'd been emotionally connected to – he'd never connected enough. When the chips were down, he'd walked away: let them do the sorting out because he couldn't. 'I couldn't help him, and now I can't help myself – unless through this cure.'

'But this isn't a cure, Luke. It's a life sentence – a life sentence forever, no end. Look, I love my father, but I love my mother too, and we need to escape, Luke, all of us. Please help us…'

'Look, I don't know whether it's a life sentence or a life saver, but even if I helped, you, you can't live like this outside of here, not as you are.'

'I can, I could,' Hebe came across and knelt in front of him, clutching his knees and staring up at him with huge imploring eyes. 'It's being here that makes me like this. I know you don't believe me, but I'll show you what I've told you is the truth… I'll prove it to you,' she said. 'Will you help me escape if I prove that I've told you is true – showed you what my father really is?'

'Oh shit!' was all he said, staring back over his shoulder as the reason for Elise Crane's face being far too familiar suddenly came to him, and then returning his gaze to Hebe's pleading expression. 'I can't promise you anything, Hebe,' he said eventually. 'Only that I haven't yet made up my mind.'

Chapter 15

15:14, 21st May 2032: Hebe

Today I am ten – or maybe nine. I have reverted back to toddlerhood and started the climb back up into teens already. The usual cramping has passed and my body is well on the way to easing into its next stage. Cells are expanding again, blood volume is increasing, bones are elongating, small, cracked fragments combining to clump together into a solid structure as tibia and fibula lengthen, pelvis expands and ribs spread. My fingers are the things that ache most in this phase. Funny, isn't it? Why should my fingers ache so? The bones are minute compared to the larger structures of legs and arms. My spine tingles too. I am a walking rattle of bones and sludge of organs all mutating into the next size up. I did describe it to Father once – at his request. He made notes – as he always does, and then, surprisingly, put his notebook down and encased me in an embrace, so close I could hear his heart beating and his blood pumping around his veins. It was perhaps the first time I realised I could hear such minute physiological details, so it was special. It was all the more special because I can count on the fingers of one steadily expanding hand how many times Father has hugged me. One hand. I haven't yet extended to the second one.

And yet I know he loves me in his own way. Love is a complexity I don't really understand but instinctively I know it simultaneously entails sacrifice, pain and immense joy. Alongside the pounding of his heart and the whooshing of his blood, I felt that too in my father – a sensation so intense it made my own head spin. But there was no record made of it in his notes. So how can I betray my own father to a man who has come here solely to satisfy his curiosity and find a cure for himself at the expense of everyone else? Yes, that is Luke Maynard. But there's more to come. That's what my mother has told me, and it's what I see too, through my inexperienced eyes – a man lost to himself but maybe not lost to me. And so I will prove to him what I've told him is true, and hope he will start the process of finding himself again.

I shouldn't have been in the lab at all but I managed to insinuate myself right up the back, behind the mice cages.

'So you understand what we're doing?' Luke was already in the MRI machine, only the top of his head peeping out, a thatch of unruly hair. His nose could be seen rising above it, like a small mountain peak in a thawing alpine scene. Not green of course. An unhealthy grey. Luke is ill. Very ill. I feel sorry for him. My father does too. Since that hug I've been able to decipher his moods far better. I can't tune in to him, of course. The AI makes that impossible even to me. It creates a shield, as impenetrable as that of an immortal in one of those Marvel films Uncle Matthew used to show me when he was trying to explain to me what else precocious meant. Luke was nodding. My father had explained some of it – the fact that it would be extensive, the BioModule, but he knows his psychology. He was drip-feeding it, as any good psychologist would.

'You're tracking my synaptic responses to see how badly the MND has affected me.' Luke's response was muffled, but firm.

'Precisely.' My father was nodding, more interested in the minute calibrations necessary on the machine than Luke, but as he was in AI mode today, he would be monitoring many things without appearing to notice any of them, so I have to be very quiet, very still. Cause no vibrations in the atmosphere.

'These are yesterday's results,' Uncle Matthew thrust a sheaf of papers at my father. My father took them and balanced them on his knee as he fiddled with one of the dials. 'You may want to run your eye over them before you complete that,' Uncle Matthew hissed under his breath – presumably so Luke couldn't hear. I tried to home in on the top page, but it was beyond my range. My father stopped fiddling with the dial. Uncle Matthew suddenly had his full attention. He looked askance at Uncle Matthew then picked up the papers.

'Oh,' my father commented as he balanced the papers on his knee again. 'And?'

'Well…' Uncle Matthew didn't seem to want to supply an answer to the 'and'.

'Can I get out soon?' Luke asked plaintively from inside the machine, his voice sounding small and excessively meek.

'Soon,' my father replied, picking up the sheaf of papers again. He looked at Uncle Matthew again. 'We just need to check on something.'

'What is it?' Luke asked. 'What's wrong? Is it something with the machine? Can I get out of it now?'

'We have your results from yesterday,' my father replied, cutting Luke's anxious whine short. 'They're… disappointing.'

'Meaning?' I could see the unruly thatch shift, seem to strain out of the machine. He sounded panicked. I looked at my father, wishing for Luke's sake he was better at picking up on people's emotions when he was in AI mode.

'Well…' Uncle Matthew bit his thumbnail whilst my father pondered the sheaf of papers.

'Well, they show the MND has made significant inroads into your CNS – your central nervous system,' my father replied eventually. 'More than it is likely a single BioModule would manage to rectify.'

'Oh? Do I need two then?'

'Fitting two BioModules simultaneously would defeat the object.' My father's voice sounded clipped, efficient. 'They would be in competition with each other and probably negate the benefits of both in the process.'

'But I thought they all did different things?'

'They do, but, Mr Maynard, I believe Matthew has explained to you that a BioModule isn't a happy ever after. It's a happy for some time fix. Of course, there is still the possibility of dual functionality, but…' My father held his hand up to halt Uncle Matthew's protestations, 'we are still working on that, so our options are limited. You understand that, don't you? I don't want you walking out of here and breaking our agreement because you claim we didn't cure you as we hoped to.'

My father flipped a switch on the machine and Luke slid out of it by about six inches – just enough for him to be able to look my father in the eye.

'You're telling me you can't cure me after all?' he sounded belligerent, voice rasping and edgy.

'I'm not saying I can't cure you. I'm saying I can't cure you with a BioModule.'

'What then?'

'It would have to be a more radical approach altogether.'

'Something that would work forever?' Luke asked pointedly. The tone wasn't lost on my father – or the use of vocabulary. I looked from Uncle Matthew to my father. Neither was giving anything away.

'What does that mean?'

'The ForEver Project?'

'And where did you coin that phrase from?' my father asked, shrugging as if it meant nothing to him.

'I've heard it around. Could it work for me?' the unruly thatch strained upwards again. 'And can I get out of this thing soon, please?'

Oh, Luke... I edged closer to the corner of the cages and tried to see round them to study my father's expression, but now he was at an oblique angle to me.

'Well,' my father's voice was soft, considering. 'As you've heard the phrase around somewhere, why don't you tell me what you think it means?'

'Jason…' Green's tone held a warning note in it.'

'No, Matthew, he's heard the phrase around somewhere and there aren't many somewheres around here, are there? Let's find out where.'

He must know it had to be Uncle Matthew! But Uncle Matthew was playing it out as if it wasn't. There was more to this than I knew about.

'I don't know…' Luke's voice sounded different, wary.

'Does it matter?' Uncle Matthew, interrupted. 'We're not doing it.'

But Uncle Matthew had put him up to it...

My father held up his hand as if to silence Uncle Matthew. 'Or maybe we are… But it's a completely different ball game if we are,' my father continued in clipped tones. 'And not something we'd normally be offering you.'

'But this situation isn't normal, is it?' Luke persisted. He'd stopped wriggling and was suddenly very still. 'I know about Frieda, I know about Hebe and you've a fucking army of crazies trying to pile drive into your facility right over our heads. So, *the ForEver Project…*'

I watched my father and Uncle Matthew exchange glances again. Surely Uncle Matthew wasn't for this? But no. He just shrugged. *Shrugged*! I stepped back further behind the cages, thinking hard. Luke had asked for the ForEver Project, just as Uncle Matthew had told my mother he would, but something about the whole thing seemed staged. In fact, everything seemed staged – the 3:16 incursion, Luke finding the body in the cold room – even Luke being sent to the cold room in the first place, and now his cure. And he'd had a twin. Something vague and disturbing began to form around the puzzle pieces in my mind – something that didn't make sense at all. Why *was* this man here? Someone had arranged this all.

'All right, but it's not some little BioModule you can have fitted or removed on a rolling basis. This is a permanent, "for life" change,' my father was saying, and Luke was nodding.

'I know. And a life is what I want.'

'In that case,' my father leaned into the machine and started to change the settings.

'Jason…' finally Uncle Matthews tone was cautionary. 'I thought we'd agreed not to…'

'It's his choice,' my father replied, waving him away.

'But what if it doesn't…'

'Work?' my father asked, laughing. 'Well, we know it does and practice makes perfect, doesn't it? If he wants it, then maybe we have the initiator of our first wave right here.' Uncle Matthew shook his head but remained silent. 'Turning on...' my father added, flipping the switch on the machine.

'Oh, I thought we'd finished?' Luke sounded desperate again. 'And aren't you going to tell me what the ForEver Project entails?'

'We've a lot more to do if we're going to consider the ForEver Project for you,' my father replied firmly. 'And I assumed you knew what it entailed if you had heard it mentioned around and had felt strongly enough motivated by what you'd heard to actually ask for it?'

'Well, hearing a few things and knowing the full facts isn't quite the same thing…' Luke replied, weakly.

'Ah,' my father flipped the switch to off again. 'So shall we start again then? As you've heard the phrase around somewhere, why don't you tell me what *you* think it means, and who you've heard mention it?' he pressed a button and Luke slid nine inches out of the machine so most of his face could be seen. His eyes sought Uncle Matthew's and my father smiled.

'All right, I told him about it,' Uncle Matthew pitched in. 'He had to know that the BioModule unit probably wouldn't work well enough for a permanent fix but we'd promised him a permanent fix in exchange for, well…'

'So you decided to spill all our secrets in one fell swoop?' My father's lip curled and both Uncle Matthew and I knew what was likely to come next. That coldness that froze your feet to the floor and your lips shut, whatever you *wanted* to say in reply.

'I'm s-sorry, Jason,' Uncle Matthew stammered. He hunched over as if he'd been knifed in the gut, clutching his arms round himself. I knew that posture well. I've seen it so many times over my short life, yet still I wonder why Uncle Matthew is so subdued by my father. 'I only gave him the briefest of outlines – just enough for him to understand there was another solution – but an extreme one.'

'I see,' my father turned his attention back to Luke. I could just see Luke's eyes from where I was hiding. They were wide and anxious.

'Look, I don't want to get in the middle of you two. I just want a cure,' he began, eyes beseeching my father's good graces.

'And you shall have one, since that's what we promised you. You're right too, Matthew. We can't move forward with anything until it's properly planned, and everyone is totally onboard, so, what is the ForEver Project?' he grinned suddenly and pushing the button that operated the movable bed that fed Luke into the scanner, he extracted Luke from the machine and unstrapped him, all whilst Luke lay prone and clearly surprised by the turn in events. 'Come with me,' my father beckoned to Luke as he swung his legs off the scanner bed, staggering slightly as he stood and then swaying uncertainly as he again looked from Uncle Matthew to my father. What was my father doing? And what had Uncle Matthew been thinking of if he had put Luke up to this? Luke followed my father over to the far side of the lab and I had to sneak along to the other end of the cages and peer through a gap in the racking to see what they were doing. Uncle Matthew stayed by the scanner, nervously chewing his fingernails.

'This is what the ForEver Project is,' my father announced, turning on a monitor and angling it so Luke could see it. 'This is me before treatment,' Luke peered in closer. On screen was a clip of my father, struggling to move, arms flapping everywhere, speech slurring, eyes rolling. He looked thin and grey – drained. He also looked desperately afraid. I looked away, the lump in my throat threatening to choke me at the comparison between this wraith of a man and my vibrant, powerful father. 'I was dying there, Luke – literally. The tumour that would have killed me had taken over most of my body. I only had enough left in me to give the go-ahead for the procedure.' He changed the film clip and the man I know filled the screen, vital, demanding, and glowing with health. 'This is me a couple of days later.'

'Bloody hell!' Luke stared at the screen and then at my father. 'The procedure is that good?'

'Better,' my father replied. 'Watch.' He picked up a metal rack and crushed it between his fingers, squeezing it down into a small cube with a number of finely balanced movements. 'Increased strength and precision fine motor control.' He placed the cube on the lab worktop for Luke to examine. He grabbed a set of electrodes and attached their ends to the computer. The other ends he taped to his chest, exposing the bare skin under his shirt – the chest of a man who spent many hours in the gym. 'No I don't, actually,' he said, without even looking up.

'What?' Luke exclaimed, mouth hanging open and his forehead creased in a frown.

My father looked up and in my general direction, but I knew he couldn't see me – not where I was hiding, anyway. I held my breath and hoped he'd attribute the thought to Luke. 'I don't spend hours in the gym. That was what you were thinking – or someone was thinking. I don't spend any time there at all. I don't need to. My body does its own repairs and adjustments. If I want to strengthen my pecs, I tell it to do so. If it's my quads that need refining, I redirect it to do so there instead. My body does exactly what I want it to. Fast or slow?'

'I don't understand?' Luke was shaking his head.

'Shall I make my heart rate fast or slow?'

'Slow?' Luke asked, hesitantly. Uncle Matthew shifted uncomfortably and then deliberately turned his head in my direction – just a fraction – but it was enough to indicate he'd spotted me. He made no other sign, just slowly turned his head back again, and let his hand drop to his side, making a small suppressing motion with it. *Stay there, and don't move...* On the monitor my father's heart rate had slowed to near-impossible levels. 'That's crazy,' Luke blurted out at him. 'You should be dead!'

'I control my body, my body doesn't control me,' my father replied, smiling in that thin-lipped way he has when he's showing off. 'Nanites,' he added as an afterthought. 'They circulate my venous system and repair damage, refine and hone performance. That's mainly how it works – with a little help from some strategic AI – far more advanced and comprehensive than the BioModules, of course, but you don't really need all that detail, do you?'

'No,' Luke croaked, replaying the film of my father almost dead and then my father larger than life itself.

My father smiled again, a secretive, complacent smile I hadn't ever seen before. 'So Luke, that's just the tiniest part of what the ForEver Project process can do. Bring you back from the almost dead, into a strong healthy body that you control. What do you think now?'

'Dammit, I never realised it was as good as that...'

'I take it from that you would still like to be considered as a candidate for it?'

'Well,' Luke looked from my father to Uncle Matthew. Whatever Uncle Matthew had told him, it wasn't any of this. And this had brought him to a completely different conclusion to the one he'd come to after talking to Uncle Matthew – and me. 'Yes, I think I would,' he replied firmly. *Damn! There was no choice now, then.*

'All right then,' my father gestured to the scanner machine. 'Then it's back in for a spell again, I'm afraid.'

'Oh,' Luke looked unsure.

'Or it won't be possible. We need full biometrics now,' my father added, smiling his thin-lipped smile again.

'Well, in that case I suppose…' Luke stumbled across the room and back to the scanner. As Uncle Matthew strapped him in and he slid once more into the scanner, he wouldn't have heard my father's one-word hissed question of Uncle Matthew.

'Why?'

'I – I don't know,' Uncle Matthew stammered. 'I suppose because of the twin, so as a test, before…' Then he hesitated and I could tell from the stiffening of his shoulders that he'd remembered I was there. 'Ready to go,' he continued. Before?

Ready to go. Well, in that case, so was I…

I waited until the machine drum was spinning and the data was being sent back – outer shell, epidermis, dermis, capillary network – then I made my move. This had to be stopped. Luke had to understand the rest of it. I let Fred out. He meandered round to the front of the cages, then sniffed his way across to the machine. I'm sorry Fred, but it was necessary. This is how it ends, not begins.

'How did that bloody rat get out?' her father exclaimed as Fred nibbled at the toe of his shoe. He nudged Fred away, but Fred had other ideas. 'Matthew! Catch him and put him away.'

The lab was cool too, cooler than normal. Maybe that helped too? I've noticed that my father is less efficient on cold days. Strange, as I wouldn't have thought it mattered. I must make a note to check up on AI sensory activity. Does it atrophy under cooler conditions? I have my father's scientific mind too. Of course, the generality of the rules of atrophy might not apply specifically to my father because he isn't in the generality. He is quite specific. He is a Fred too. ForEver Fred: and I know if a certain concoction of water makes contact with his outer dermal layer – the CyberCute product Uncle Matthew developed which started it all – his outer dermal layer will react, and then so will he. Uncle Matthew has a glass of water conveniently on the work bench. Is that plain water or salt water? And is that for generality of drinking or specific use? It's salt water that can damage him – irreparably in sufficient quantity, irksomely in low volume, but could Uncle Matthew ever do that to my father? I'm not sure but I do know that what Luke needs to see is my father from the inside out – how the man inside the machine struggles, then maybe he will understand why he can't be the same; and definitely why my mother can't be made to be the same… I know his pain. I can read my father like he can read me, he just doesn't know that. He thinks he excretes his pain harmlessly into what's around him; discharges it – into the grass, into the air, into the atoms that surround all of us – without it doing any harm, but what he doesn't realise is that those discharges aren't harmless and they'll slowly kill the world over time, atom by atom. They're toxicity that remains like static, filling the world with the pain of a human trapped in an AI. And I absorb it – can't help but absorb it – so no one else does. For now.

'Sorry!' I watched Uncle Matthew hobble off his lab stool and go in pursuit of Fred. I'd sent Fred in at precisely the right moment and in the right direction, knowing that Uncle Matthew would follow and stay out of it. Clever Fred, he'd find a hidey-hole and keep Uncle Matthew there just long enough for me to send the pin into the MRI drum and create the malfunction. But he didn't. Uncle Matthew came back.

'Damned if I know where he's gone, but he's gone anyway,' he announced, picking up the glass of water and sipping it. Ok, so it was plain water then, so that wouldn't help either. The machine still whirred and the drum still spun and Luke was being mapped, co-ordinates fixed, future determined. Luke still had to see from the inside out. Surely Uncle Matthew realised that too? Luke had to understand what ForEver really is. Not a cure, a curse.

Uncle Matthew put the glass down suddenly, looking uncertain as my father tutted and exclaimed about how the rat was interfering with lab protocol, but Matthew was doing nothing about it. So it really was done to me then.

Over here, over here, Fred – distract them again so I can show Luke what ForEver is really all about. I willed Fred to respond. One of them will have to grab you and then…

But then my plan went awry. Uncle Matthew did leap into action, spotting and diverting Fred, but sending him directly from his hidey-hole towards the spinning drum.

'Get him!' my father exclaimed, flat-toned, but with that edge that I can read as exasperation in his voice, making it one thousandth per cent sharper than usual. It's useful being able to hear nuances and when the nuances had changed, but not when you can do nothing about them.

'No!' I screamed in my head as the inevitability of what was about to happen caught up with me. The drum ground to a halt with a deafening screech, which Luke and Uncle Matthew and I all winced at. My father frowned. I bit hard on my knuckles to contain the pain and the grief. *I'm so sorry, Fred, the memory of that long twitchy nose of yours, and that silky fur that always soothed even the worst of the aches in my expanding and contracting fingers will always comfort me. You weren't meant to be a sacrifice, just a diversion. Uncle Matthew, why didn't you grab him, hold onto him? It should have been the pin I was going to throw into the drum that stopped it. Not my beloved Fred...*

The machine stalled with a painful creak as Fred disappeared into it. I jumped out from behind the cages, screaming silently whilst Uncle Matthew shouted and the drum on the machine wobbled wildly off-kilter and a spray of blood spattered an abstract pattern across the floor. Then Luke started yelling too, 'What's going on? Get me out of here!' whilst Uncle Matthew flapped about helplessly.

'Shit!' Uncle Matthew yelled. 'If the drum detaches it could kill him!'

And my father? My father did what I knew he would in the face of disaster, Uncle Matthew's inability and Luke's danger. What I'd seen him doing even before he did it. He's not a monster. In AI mode, he's governed by logic, not moderated by human instinct. Logic said he should stop the drum and then repair himself, so he did what was necessary to fix the problem. What I hadn't seen was the way he would do it. He stopped the crazily spinning drum as it spun off its axis by ducking into it and allowing it to behead him instead of macerating Luke. That is the best of him. That is why I love him, even though he is toxic to the world. If I didn't love him, I wouldn't want to destroy him. *Two of the creatures I love most have suffered to show you the truth, Luke. See it, I beg you. See everything for what it is...*

The silence that followed the execution was the most awful silence I have ever heard, and the pain in my chest, the worst pain I will ever feel.

My Father. Decapitated. Fred, destroyed.

Then, Luke's hysterical, 'Fucking hell! Get me out of here!' was ringing in my ears, again and again and again, but all I could think of was why my father had sacrificed himself for someone he barely even knew.

What had I not understood about him? Could his humanity still outweigh his programming?

As rigid as an automaton, Uncle Matthew flipped the release lever and the bed of the MRI exhumed Luke from his own impending deathbed whilst Uncle Matthew belatedly tried to shield me from my father's headless corpse and his bodyless head. It was far too late by then. I'd seen what I could never unsee and understood what I could never then forget.

'For fuck's sake!' Luke screamed. 'He's dead! What do we do? What do we do?'

Uncle Matthew ignored him and edged around me to reunite head with body and the two merged even as we watched. He waved me away to the corner of the room with a 'don't watch,' but I did anyway. Within minutes, my father was sitting upright again; sinews, spine, spinal cord, bones, flesh – even surface hair – all back in their rightful position, and Luke Maynard was staring, then being violently sick onto the cool grey medvac floor. As for me, I slithered into a corner of the lab and waited, sickened and shocked, and ridiculously relieved. My father looked sad and disorientated, and for a moment, I think the human and the AI touched.

'Oh,' he said as he looked down at his bloodied body. 'I thought I was me again then…' Then he gave himself a little shake, and exhaled heavily, before looking up at Luke and Matthew as they hovered around him in various shades of panic.

I hadn't realised how possible all the impossibilities were until then. And how much a curse ForEver truly was, whatever I had told Luke. It was in my father's eyes – that exhaustion I'd never seen before. The exhaustion of hope.

'Shit!' exclaimed Luke once he'd recovered a fraction and had distanced himself from the foul-smelling vomit where he'd been standing. The stench lingered in my head for hours afterwards. 'But that's impossible… Even an AI couldn't do that, could it?'

'Hrmm,' my father grunted into the shocked silence. 'Nanites,' he added as if that explained everything.

There was another deathly hush then Luke said, 'Bloody hell! This is like something out a horror movie. You can't be alive – not after that. In which case what the fuck are you?'

'I'm ForEver,' my father said, standing up and straightening his shirt and adjusting the angle of his neck. He didn't seem to have registered I was there, and I was glad. He wouldn't have wanted me to see that. The human in him would never have wanted me to have seen that. 'I...'

'We're going to have to tell him everything, Jason,' Uncle Matthew interrupted him.

My father paused, then, 'I thought we already had?' he replied, smiling ironically.

'No,' Uncle Matthew replied. 'Not everything. Not that...'

'Then we'd better tell him now, hadn't we?' My father was still smiling.

'Or kill him instead.' I could barely believe that was Uncle Matthew, but he seemed to have forgotten about me too. 'Because if this gets out before he's gone through the process...'

'No, I'm not doing that. There's been too much death already.' My father seemed to go in on himself – that hushed stillness I know is when he is calculating the probabilities and deciding on the odds. He turned to Luke and said, 'This is the actual reality of the ForEver Project. I am not human. I am AI, yes – adaptive AI that synchronises symbiotically with human elements – in my case my brain, but I am still AI. Whatever you do to me, chop me up, burn me... I will repair. I won't ever die.' Luke shook his head, slowly at first, then like he was trying to shake his own head off and back on again.

'Never?' Luke whispered.

'As long as my AI shell can be reformed and my brain remains intact – never,' my father confirmed.

'Oh, my God!' Luke croaked. 'And that's what I'd be?'

'Similar. Could you cope with that?' My father's eyes were like gimlets, boring into Luke's face and examining the workings of his brain.

'I... I...don't know...'

'And you would of necessity always be under direction from me – in other words, you would have to do exactly as I told you to, or you would be shut down.' To be fair, my father was taking no prisoners in his honesty with Luke. 'No thoughts of rebellion or take over once you have the same powers as me either.' My father was smiling but it didn't look like a smile to me. It looked like a challenge; a gauntlet thrown down. A despair masked.

'Rebellion or take over?' Luke didn't seem to understand what he was repeating.

'Well, you won't be the last, once things get going. There will be more of us eventually – when the time is right. We all know this world is destined to change – has to change to survive. This is it. And you can't say anything to anyone, ever, how this all came about. Remember, your life is not only in my hands metaphorically now, but it would be in actuality if we do this for you. You could die without anyone knowing – like Dr Kohn – or you could live… Your MND has no conventional cure. We are offering you an unconventional one – one that will take you into the future and beyond. So which is it to be? Live in the future or die in the now?'

The silence that filled the void between us suffocated me. I clutched my throat. I knew what Luke was going to say.

'Live,' Luke croaked, still shaking.

It was then my father finally caught sight of me. He made a strangled sound like an animal in pain and all around me the air sang in agony at my father's toxic discharge.

'You shouldn't have had to… How long has Hebe been there?' he demanded of Uncle Matthew.

'Ask me, not them,' I shouted, horror and confusion souring my mouth. My father moved towards me but I scrambled to my feet and ran. I didn't look at either Luke or Uncle Matthew. I couldn't bear to see their faces. Their betrayal.

'Matthew?' I heard my father querying as I fled. 'What the hell is going on?'

Chapter 16

17:25, 21st May 2032: Luke

Luke left them to it, relieved to be out of what he now thought of as 'the fucking machine'; Green the 'technician' and Crane the – well, God, what was he? He pictured again the tumbling head, the blood, the prone body. A wave of nausea swept over him and he had to sit heavily on the side of the bed and shove his head between his knees to fend off the dizziness that accompanied the memory. And what the hell had he agreed to if that was what he would become? *You will do as I tell you to. No thoughts of rebellion or take over once you have the same powers as me, either.*

Powers. He needed to talk to someone, but who? He pictured Hebe's frightened eyes, huge in her pale, shocked face as she'd scrambled to her feet and run away when they'd suddenly noticed she was there too – although he suspected Green had already known, in which case…. He paused there. Hold that thought. Green had known she was there but said nothing? No good talking to Green, then. Green had put him up to this – knowing… Hebe. He needed to talk to Hebe…

He steadied his legs and pushed himself upright from the bed. He wobbled. Legs still unstable then. Head floating about six inches above where it should be too and trying to emulate a rollercoaster. The MND was getting a second wind just as he was running out of puff. He sat down again and the bed welcomed him. He lay back on it, crossways, neck only just supported by the far side of the bed and head dangling – feet dangling off the other side. Above him the spotless pastel blue ceiling reminded him of summer skies and seamless summers where sunshine and beer and effortlessly doing nothing or everything had seemed unending. Before MND. Before Aaron had overdosed. Before Frieda had turned his world upside down and then disappeared. Before life had become complicated and painful and confusing. Before Hebe.

Hebe.

Luke struggled to extract himself from the softness of the bed, the calmness of the bedroom and the temptation to just drift – let it happen, whatever it was. The world had taken a strange turn but he was just a tiny cog in its gigantic wheel, turning and turning like the drum on the machine had turned until it had spun out of control and…

He sat upright abruptly, the energy to do so returning to him with the same abruptness as the shock of remembering Jason Crane's severed head reattaching itself to his body had rendered him weak and dizzy. Still unsteady, but determined, he braced himself to walk, put one foot in front of the other and stay upright. Jesus! He must look like a frail old man, staggering crab-like across the room until he was within an arm's length of the door into the corridor. He paused there, turning to survey the room before he left its sanctuary. In doing so he caught a glimpse of himself in the full-length mirror, a vanity he could have done without, given how wretched he'd become since he'd arrived here. Bent, pale-faced, with unkempt hair and stubble turning his face into a pitted, razed cornfield version of itself, even he was shocked by himself. Yet the apparition convinced him where logic could not. He really had no choice but to go along with what he'd just agreed to with Jason Crane or this bent and ravaged young-old man really would be nothing more than an apparition soon.

But he still wanted to talk to Hebe. She'd said she'd prove to him why he couldn't countenance becoming like her father, and she had been in the lab earlier when *it* had happened too. He found it easier to package the imagery into *it* rather than force himself to the film reel of what *it* had entailed. Surely she couldn't have engineered that display, could she? But if she had, it had also to be because she knew that her father would be able to… to… He doubled up again as the queasiness returned and he gulped down the acid bile the memory forced up his gullet.

Steeling himself, he opened the door to the corridor and cool air rushed in. He gasped, taken aback by the sudden change in temperature. He had noticed the difference yesterday but only in passing. Today it winded him. The temperature in the bedroom, he realised, must be deliberately higher to induce sleepiness, lethargy, a physical ploy mimicking the soft blue of the décor. Well, he wasn't sleepy any more, he was wide awake and in need of information. He stepped determinedly out into the corridor and the bedroom door clicked shut behind him with an air of finality. You want to leave my cocoon of peace, it seemed to be saying, well, do so at your own peril.

In the corridor, he was soon at a loss. Escher had been at it again, redefining known paths into mystery corridors, roads leading nowhere. Much like his life, Luke mused wryly as he tried yet another branch only to find it again arrived at a dead end. He slapped the wall with frustration and it echoed back at him, hollow and melancholy. Green had found his way OK, but then he'd lived in this warren for years, yet nevertheless it couldn't be totally random, this regular rearranging of layout. Luke turned and stood with his back to the dead end and slowly retraced his steps until he arrived at the last fork in the road. So he'd tried left and he'd tried right and he'd just returned from straight on so the only logical way forward was back the way he'd come… Crazy! He pondered that a moment longer. Something in the sheer illogic of it all suggested a deeper kind of logic – the logic of the instinctive. Remembering how… *invaded…* he'd felt in the room that Elise Crane slept in, he closed his eyes. Maybe he could sense that sense of Hebe and Elise Crane again if he denied his physical senses and concentrated on his inner ones. He waited, swaying gently as the sounds of the corridor faded away – such as they were; mainly the distant rurr-rurr-rurr of the still persistent onslaught of 3:16's pneumatic drills, but under that there were other subtle nuances. He thought he caught the patter of feet as he strained to hear, then the slide of a door shutting with that sibilant hiss the Crane Industries doors all seemed to exhibit on movement – apart from his bedroom door that was – the one that had clicked irritably at him as he'd left earlier. They were distractions though, and he knew if he set out in their direction, he'd only find himself in another dead end, so he deliberately set them aside, imagining himself deaf and blind and unable to touch: a deep dark cocoon of nothing but that feeling that had emanated from Hebe and her mother. He almost missed it to begin with, its tendrils were so tentative, so gentle he barely felt it touching that inner core that had responded to it before. And then there it was – inescapable, palpable, intoxicating. He didn't even open his eyes, he just stumbled towards the feeling until his toes encountered stone and his nose smelt grass and sunlight and…

'Hebe! Can we talk?' he began, before he took in why that was so impossible.

She was sitting in the middle of the courtyard, the grass rising above her knees, a daisy chain dangling from her neck and another in the making. She looked up at his call, round-eyed, little mouth open in a tiny 'ooh', fingers poised in the throes of stringing another daisy to the long twisting chain she was completing. So much for asking Hebe for information. She looked no older than three or four; the age she'd been the first time he'd seen her.

'This one's for you,' she said, holding up the end of the chain. 'Your length exactly. The same as my father's – or it will be since you'll be the same as him.' She looked sad.

'No,' Luke tottered over to join her, stubbing his toe on the coping stone that edged the grass and narrowly avoiding swearing as the sting make him wince. 'No, Hebe.' He stumbled into the grass, holding his toe, before rolling awkwardly onto his side. Little pinpricks like needle stabs peppered the side he rolled onto and he reeled, rolling onto the other, but it was the same. 'Ow! Shit! What is that?' he let go of his aching toe and sat upright, knees to his chest, but still the pinpricks continued, this time into his ass and the soles of his feet. 'Ouch! Has someone sprayed something onto this grass – a pesticide or something?'

'No,' Hebe seemed unperturbed – and indeed, certainly not being stung like he was. 'It's just grass but I told it to retaliate this time.'

'Retaliate?' he'd stood up now and was hot-footing it, literally, over to the courtyard paving now. He reached it before she answered, relieved that the pinpricks had now stopped, but strangely depressed not to be physically closer to her.

'Yes. If you walked all over someone, they'd retaliate, wouldn't they? Well, so will the grass now. You deserve it.'

'That's…' he was lost for words. He'd been about to say, 'so childish,' but then she was – and she was right too. He probably did deserve it. He stared at Hebe instead as she finished the daisy chain and then tiptoed delicately off of the grass herself to come and stand in front of him. She laid the daisy chain down on the paving in front of him and stretched it out to its full length.

'There,' she said.

'How can the grass retaliate?' he asked, bemused and uneasy.

'It's a living thing. All living things hurt but they don't all hurt back. The grass hasn't hurt back until now, but I told it that it would have to from now on because sometimes you have to fight back.' She looked mutinous, lower lip pouting and eyes glowering. Under other circumstances, he would have laughed at what he would have regarded as merely a tempestuous toddler, but Hebe was definitely not that.

'Because of what happened in the lab?' he asked gently. 'My choice there?'

'Because of many things,' she replied as she picked up the end of the daisy chain and dragged it away behind her, as she turned and began to walk away. 'But nothing that I can tell you any more. You need to understand them for yourself.'

'Wait,' Luke called after her. 'So what about the daisies. Didn't they hurt too when you picked them and turned them into a daisy chain?'

'They're not alive. My father made them. You have to be alive to hurt. I've only connected them so they can communicate.'

'What are they communicating?' Luke frowned. As ever, communicating with Hebe was somewhat surreal – and there was always something more behind what she said.

'Reach out to them yourself and you'll see.'

Then she turned into the corridor and she was gone. Luke jumped up and hurried after her, stubbing his other foot on another coping stone, and this time swearing loudly, but when he reached the mouth of the corridor, Hebe was nowhere to be seen.

'Shit, shit, shit!' Luke spluttered as he collapsed on his backside and clutched a foot in each hand until the impact of the coping stones wore off enough for him to wonder what to do next. You have to be alive to hurt. Yes, indeed you did, so that meant Hebe didn't regard her father as alive. That chilled him to the bone, followed by the resurgence of the now familiar feeling of nausea as he remembered again what had happened in the lab. Shit, and he'd agreed to be the same. He shivered. He couldn't go through with this – not even to stay alive. There had to be another way. The BioModule that only did half the job, or gene therapy, or even the dual functionality thing Green had warned him against. Any of it was better than becoming… not alive. He staggered to his feet. He didn't trust him but Green was the only one he could talk to now – even though it was Green who'd set him up for this in the first place. Maybe now was the time to find out why because he doubted Green had his welfare at heart, whereas he had mentioned something about it giving him time to sort out a way to get him and Hebe out of there – except, he wouldn't be coming out of here as him if he became part of the ForEver Project. Unless...

Heaving himself to his feet, Luke set off, carefully avoiding the coping stones and the grass and headed for the courtyard entrance he'd arrived through. At the entrance, he paused and closed his eyes as he thought about the ForEver Lab and how he would have to steel himself to enter it again after yesterday. Unexpectedly, he found his feet repositioning themselves so that there was only one way to head in. What? He laughed. Like a compass finding magnetic north. Well, he'd never thought of himself as a world navigator before and certainly not a compass to steer by, and yet...*Magnetic north.* The idea changed shape, turned itself on its head and back again as he put the crazy idea together with the crazy architect of the lab. Jesus! Was this how it worked? A neural network that operated as a ground plan too, based on the geometry of the brain, and using quantum human instinct to navigate it? Luke laughed aloud as the thought formed, crystallised and found its place in the logic of it all. Jason Crane's lab network was based on the neural net, mimicking the creation and recreation of synaptic pathways by rearranging the structure of the place accordingly as the participant made their way to specific places for specific purposes and formed routine pathways to and from those places. The structure changed around them but whenever they thought of the place they needed to go, the place itself connected symbiotically to the thinker's brain and hey presto! You knew the way. Hebe was both right and wrong. You did need to be alive to feel pain but you didn't need to be alive to feel if you were using AI to do so – or to connect. He bet if he reached out to the daisy chain it would tell him what it was currently adorning, purely because of the AI connectivity that this place seemed to be imbued with.

Then maybe whatever the ForEver project produced was also alive despite what Hebe had said?

The ForEver lab door was ajar, as if waiting for him to arrive. That made sense too. But it wasn't Jason Crane who was there waiting for him, it was Matthew Green.

He greeted Luke with, 'I wondered when you'd work it out.'

'Whose idea was it?'

'Mine originally. Most of it was mine, Jason's just much better at being brave and doing it.'

'The technician and the genius?'

'Sadly.'

'ForEver.' Luke helped himself to the lab stool opposite Green and perched on it. 'What does it really mean. What is Jason Crane like now he's no longer a man?'

'He is a man, just not in the way we normally perceive a man to be. He is still flesh and blood, as you saw.'

'That can put itself back together after lethal trauma. That's not a man, that's a... a...' Luke struggled for the right definition.

'God?' Green supplied. 'Yes, in some ways, but even the gods had Achilles heels.'

'So what's his Achilles heel?'

'Hebe. Or maybe I should say, Elise and Hebe. If he could find out why Hebe can regress and then regrow, he'd be able to turn Elise back to where she was before the accident. In a way, Hebe's body is a mobile time machine, going backwards and forwards as it grows older, becomes younger, grows older, and then becomes younger again. But whilst for Elise it would be a cure, for Hebe it's a curse.'

'So why do you want to get Hebe out of here if she needs a cure?'

'Because it's her only chance, ultimately, of surviving. Unless you're going through with the ForEver process so you can champion her against him?' Green pulled up another lab stool and positioned it in front of Luke. 'Look, I don't know if I even like you, let alone trust you, but you're what was sent so I have to work with it.'

'Sent?'

'3:16. You were right, I did let them in, so you could take Hebe out of here. They told me they'd found just the man, someone with the right amount of need, vigilante mindset, and downright bloody-mindedness. So far I've only seen need – and maybe some vigilante mindset over Kohn. What I need is a nemesis.'

'Sure, I can be your bloody nemesis if that's what you want,' Luke's temper flared at the reminder of Frieda's fate.

'Not *my* nemesis. That's been with me ever since my daughter was born. No, *a* nemesis – the type that creates the inevitable conclusion for everyone. Or a catalyst. Maybe you're the catalyst and the nemesis will be someone else?'

Luke shook his head. The lab was considerably colder than both the bedroom and the courtyard and he was starting to feel it. 'I don't know what the hell you're talking about, or why, but I want to know what I'm up against in Jason Crane, because you have no intention of me going through with this process really, do you? I'm just the expendable delay that enables you to get Hebe out of here, like to 3:16 I was the expendable mug who got them in here.'

'We're all expendable, Mr Maynard. Just some are more expendable than others – with one exception. Hebe. Hebe isn't expendable at all. She's the answer. She is where it all begins – or ends.'

'She keeps saying that too,' Luke exploded with exasperation. 'She's a sweet kid but why the fuck can't you play it straight with me, both of you, if you want my help?'

'To help you would have to accept being expendable,' Green

explained in a tired but patient tone. 'Like I have. Maybe it would help if I told you the whole story?'

'Now we're getting somewhere,' Luke sighed. He scooted the lab stool backwards until his back rested against one of the lab walls and then he slumped against it, waiting. Its cool gradually penetrated his shirt and seeped into his skin, as he listened to Hebe's story.

'Elise was already in a coma when we found out she was pregnant.'

'She'd had an accident,' Luke supplied.

'Yes, of a sort,' Green agreed, 'except Jason caused it. He wanted her to undergo the ForEver procedure too when he found out she would never come round, but when he found out about the child – that he was going to be a father – there was a change in him. He bowed to what he knew would have been Elise's wishes, had her moved to this facility and the baby was born. He vowed to be a good father to her, and I think he would have until he realised that no child born with her pedigree could ever be anything less than exceptional. And there was proof of that when she was barely a few weeks old. She could recognise things a newborn wouldn't even be able to focus on at that age. By six months she was talking and reading fluently. By a year she'd mastered rudimentary programming and by almost two, she'd surpassed what we wouldn't even have expected of a twenty-year-old. She'd started doing something else too: grow and regress. But every time she does that, her brain has a growth spurt,' Green paused. 'Very soon, her mental capacity will rival and then surpass Jason's AI brain and whilst she will still be mortal she will also be able to out-strategise him. His plan was ultimately to populate the world with AI and AI hybrids, relieve us all of death, and create a status-quo not possible with people always coming and going. If you're never going to die and always have enough because the population is controlled, why fight over anything? Now he knows Hebe's powers, but how do you do that when there is someone who can outstrip you, but you can't ever bring yourself to destroy them.'

'Wait, what are her powers?' Luke asked, sitting forward on the lab stool and giving his aching back a rest from the ice-cold wall.

'Many, it would seem… telepathy, telekinesis, quantum computing and of course, time travel. And her brain is growing exponentially into the parts we hitherto have never used – ninety per cent of it, Mr Maynard. We don't make use of ninety per cent of our brains, but Hebe does. Jason's idea is idealistic and maybe even paternalistic to some extent, but it's still control. Hebe would overturn that control. Do you see what I mean?'

'Jesus!' Luke slumped back against the wall again, his mind grappling with what Green was telling him in its paltry ten per cent usage capacity. 'Well, that's a pretty impressive catalogue of superpowers. And has she got these from her father?'

'No,' Green looked at him as if he was mud. 'They are all peculiar to Hebe. But Hebe is going to run out of time soon. I know that but he doesn't because I kept back some of the data from him. You can't put a human body through the kind of rigours she suffers every day without it breaking down and failing very soon. Then we'll have nothing.'

'OK…' Luke took a moment to consider this. 'Then why have you allowed her to be put through so much stress if it's likely to be terminal and does Crane wants to use the ForEver Project process on her?'

'It's not a case of allow…' Green hesitated. 'But yes, if Jason can create a better shell than he has, and then populate it, he will. A perfect Hebe, fixed by AI intervention…'

'But surely there's another way – find a way to fix the metabolic shit? I mean, I thought Crane said you had – almost…'

'The ReNewal unit? It's based on how Hebe's metabolism works, but it's untested and at best random where it would regress the user's body to. At worst, it could be as uncontrolled as Hebe is. There's no way of pacing it, structuring it so that it works to a logical pattern. It's a wild life force, essentially, not joined-up and not controllable. No, that's not the answer either, I'm afraid.'

'But this… interconnectivity that runs through this complex – who is behind that – Crane or Hebe?'

'Interconnectivity?' Green stared at Luke as if he'd gone mad. 'There's no interconnectivity, just a clever revolving plan, if it's the changing structure of the complex you're talking about.'

'But what about the neural net – the AI instinctive one that…' Green was looking strangely at him. Shit! If Green didn't know, then maybe neither did Crane? Maybe this wasn't Jason Crane's doing at all, but some other influence?' Luke frowned as the possibilities piled up but still didn't quite *add* up. To counter Green's continued look of enquiry, he added. 'Oh, I see. Just good old Escher again…'

'Escheristic,' Green agreed. 'Typical of Jason's contorted thinking at times. I suppose you'd say that was AI-stimulated – the desire to confound the mere mortals. And he also still plans to put Elise through the ForEver Project. He just needs Hebe as the perfect prototype…' he paused again, 'which she isn't yet – and can't be unless she's totally on board with the idea too. That's why she needs to get away from here.'

'Then why the hell don't you stop him?' Luke demanded, weighing up whether to alert Green to the misunderstanding he was labouring under; namely that Jason Crane was redesigning the lab layout himself. 'And why do I find all this so difficult to believe?'

'You can see what he can do, Mr Maynard. And… there are other reasons... I can't do anything, but Jason's capable of everything. You are our hope.'

'Shit! Why me, for God's sake?'

'Because – Jesus, I don't know. It was Elise's idea. We thought you could be their saviour – you had nothing to lose and everything to gain, especially since you'd made it in here under your own steam the first time…'

'Elise? But she's in a coma.'

'And in Hebe's head. She thinks if Hebe can get out of here, that's Hebe's best chance of a normal life – and maybe saving her too. Once Hebe's away from here then the toxic programming that Hebe's human-AI melded genes are picking up won't affect her when she's at a distance from it. Who knows what she might be capable of then? Maybe she could even fix herself? That's what I'm guessing anyway. Elise doesn't always explain what she tells Hebe – to protect Hebe, I suppose.'

'Her human-AI melded side?'

'Yes. She's half Jason's daughter so of course she has an AI side. In fact, I suspect he's most of the reason we haven't found a way to cure or control Hebe's metabolic changes. And he's waiting to see how far it'll develop.' He looked at Luke's incredulous expression. 'If you don't believe me, ask her.'

'Ask Hebe?' Luke's sarcasm was barely disguised.

'No, ask Elise. Via Hebe.'

'Ask Elise,' Luke murmured to himself. 'Yes, I think that's exactly who I need to ask…'

Chapter 17

17:40, 21st May 2032: Hebe

It's not my father's fault. He is what he is, and I am what I am. It's not even Luke's fault. He is what he is too. It's the space between what we each are that causes the problem. Luke has gone now so I can go back to the courtyard. Had he understood? Some part of him seemed to have changed, redirected itself, or he wouldn't have been able to have found her in the courtyard – and she'd sensed it too, like she felt the pain of the grass, and the voice of her mother

In the courtyard, it was peaceful now Luke had gone. The long daisy chain trailed behind me as I made my way to its centre and spread out the daisy chain so it could commune with the grass. The living and the dead. The artificial and the real. Eventually who knew which would be which? I settled lightly on the grass and it bore my weight with only the merest of sighs. We intertwined, me, the grass and the daisy chain. The more I do it the easier it becomes. – not like the first time it happened – any of it had happened. I'd been two, much the same as I was now, but so unlike I was now that I could barely believe I'd been just a precocious child then, but not the kind of precocious my father understood and hoped for.

The last embers of the sunset were turning the glass roof over the courtyard blood red. I'd been lying on my back, in the middle of the courtyard, marvelling at it, thumb in mouth and a daisy pinched between thumb and forefinger, rolling it round and around, enjoying the sensation of its frilly petals tickling the edge of my finger and thumb as it revolved. I'd watched sunsets before but never quite this spectacular. I must ask Uncle Matthew about it. My father would explain the reason for the display better – the science and logic – but Uncle Matthew would explain why it made me feel this way. I'd learnt latterly to merge the information each offered to understand the experience or occurrence better. Father was fact, Uncle Matthew was feeling – and sometimes an excess of it, like the time I'd overheard him and father talking about someone called Katie.

'We already have a test subject, you just have to sanction it,' my father was saying gently.

He didn't need to be facing me for me to know how he was looking at Uncle Matthew. I could imagine his expression. It would be the one he uses on me when I am being intransigent. A slight smile, a tilt of the head, accompanied by a nod. 'Come on,' it said. 'You know you want to…' even if I didn't. But then I would, simply because of the way my father delivered the request. He's a student of human nature, you see. He's had to be, to become human once the AI had fully integrated. AI dominates, no matter how you try to stop it. It is naturally self-progressive, whereas the human mind – and will - can be lazy, complacent, disinclined to overcoming the difficulties that precede achievement. I give my father full credit for that. He's never let the AI take over – not completely.

'It's not just down to me. Jane has the final say,' Uncle Matthew replied, trying to avoid my father's eyes by picking at a non-existent piece of lint on his sleeve.

'Really, Matthew? Even now?'

'You know what she's like…'

'Ill?'

'Well, yes, that too, but whose fault is that?' For the briefest of moments, Uncle Matthew's eyes reached up to hold my father's, and they flashed fire.

'Mine, of course,' my father replied. His head bobbed up and down like one of those nodding dog toys people used to put in their cars. I've seen them on old TV programmes. 'So perhaps it's time we did something about that?'

'Sorry, that wasn't fair of me.' Uncle Matthew's eyes dropped back to where his fingers had resumed the lint picking. His shoulders drooped and he did that kind of inner deflating thing he does when my father challenges him. 'I didn't mean…'

'But I did,' my father's voice had lost its cooing civility. Now there was an edge to it like a line drawn around each of his words. 'Beneficially, of course,' he added, the cool returning. 'A quid pro quo. If Jane would like a module fitted, we could do so at the same time.'

'What, a BioModule for Jane? But…'

'As a quid pro quo, like I said. Maybe you would like one too?'

'Me? Oh, God no!' Uncle Matthew abandoned the lint completely and pulled himself upright. His body literally unfolded in front of me. 'I'll take what's coming to me without fear or favour. But for Jane, that would mean…'

'It would be easier… For you too…'

'Maybe, but I don't deserve easy. Jane though…' he hesitated, biting his lower lip. His straggly moustache wriggled like an overfilled bird's nest. 'But why not for Katie too?'

"You know a BioModule wouldn't solve Katie's problems. You can't take her back to pre-conception.'

'I know, I know, but maybe the ReNewal unit, when it's ready?' Uncle Matthew stopped biting his lip, but he still looked worried.

'It is – but we need to test it to make sure we've got it right.'

'I have – we have…'

'Then…' My father shrugged, looking as if he was about to turn away, then hesitating. 'Then we'll have to find a way of testing it,' he continued, and this time he did start to walk away.

'Wait…' Uncle Matthew called after him. 'But if it doesn't work, there's no going back.'

'And no going forward for some,' my father added softly – so softly I almost didn't hear it. 'Remember…'

'You bastard!'

'Hardly. I'm offering both a significant improvement to their futures, based on your claims. How does that make me a bastard?'

'If the ReNewal doesn't work they're stuck with it, and no other form of treatment – other than the most radical…'

'Well,' my father shrugged. 'You have to choose. Or perhaps I should say, you have to let Jane choose.'

'You know what she'd choose. You know what she thinks of you.'

'Then you'll have to persuade her, won't you?' My father paused, and then added pointedly, 'for Hebe's sake too.'

For my sake? How did whatever they were discussing affect me?

I soon had my answer. It affected me overnight because that was the first time my growth escalated. By morning I was at least a year older, and my limbs ached as if I'd been put on a rack and pulled. I thought I'd caught a bug, but Uncle Matthew and Father huddled together and whispered, then assured me everything was fine. The next day I was older again – and in more pain. The week went by with each day making me a year older. My periods started on day ten, a terrifying gush of bright red blood, streaming down my legs and staining the courtyard paving. If I look carefully even now, I can still see the faintest stain, although Maria or someone must have scrubbed and scrubbed until their knuckles were raw to get rid of it. She told me it was nothing, like the aches and pains – just part of the condition. So did Uncle Matthew and my father, so I lay listlessly though the days and nights that followed, hoping to feel well again soon. On day twenty, miraculously, I did. But on day twenty-one it all changed again as I started the regression phase. More huddling between my father and Uncle Matthew, and then the whole process started all over again from day one.

I didn't believe that it was a bug then because I felt different by then too – more alive, more alert, more aware – more pained. That was when the whispering began too – the thoughts in my head that weren't mine, the sensations on my body that weren't mine, the memories in my head that weren't mine. They became cyclical with the cycle of my growth and regression cycles. They became accepted too – so integral to me that I stopped even questioning whether anyone else had these thoughts or feelings or awareness. I don't know what the outcome of the conversation between my father and Uncle Matthew was except there was one day, not long afterwards, that I was banned from the ForEver lab, but my heightened senses told me there were other people in it, even though I was right across the other side of the lab complex to it. I suspect, now, they were the Katie and Jane my father and Uncle Matthew had been discussing, being treated. Whatever Uncle Matthew called him then – now I know what a bastard is – my father isn't a bad man. I suppose he isn't even actually a man. He is what he is, and he was offering them a cure. Who doesn't want a cure? Poor Luke, why wouldn't he want a cure? But what they don't understand is that they don't need a cure because the cure is already all around them, they just need to connect – like the daisy chain.

It's so peaceful here with just the grass and the daisy chain for company, feeling the rhythm of their growth and renewal, death and rebirth… that's what is in me, renewal, but the only way for there to be renewal is for there to be entropy first. That's why father's BioModules never quite do the whole job – not even the ReNewal unit he's modelled on me. They don't allow for entropy. There can never just be forever, there has to be change. Luke is that change. Now he has to understand how.

Chapter 18

23:14, 22nd May 2032: Luke

Luke lay staring up at the ceiling. It occurred – fleetingly – to him that it was strange to be looking up at what felt like perpetually blue sky when he was in, at least metaphorically speaking, perpetual darkness underground. The thought was fleeting because he was immediately plunged back to self-imposed darkness as he pondered the conversation with Hebe earlier. There'd been barely any substance to it and yet it had felt loaded with hidden meaning. He closed his eyes against the determinedly cheerful blue ceiling and allowed himself to sink back into the memory. For some reason, Hebe expected great things of him – for him to be her saviour in fact – but it made no sense. He was weak at best, flawed and failing, and downright useless at worst since the rate at which the MND seemed to be affecting him appeared to have escalated. He flexed a fist in response to that – stiff, aching and ineffectual. He couldn't even punch air and make an impact currently, let alone an assailant or… or Hebe's father, if that was what was going to be necessary to help her 'escape'. And then what about his cure? That would no longer happen. Effectively what Hebe wanted of him was for him to lay down his life for her.

'Oh, shit!' Luke opened his eyes and stared up at the ceiling. It no longer seemed happily blue, but oppressively blue. He wasn't cut out to be a hero. He'd had his chance when Aaron had needed his help and he'd been useless then – and that had been his twin brother. There was no way he could see himself selflessly give his life for a girl he barely even knew – a girl with strange parentage and even stranger powers. And yet…

'There's one more thing.' The 3:16 contact seemed hesitant. Although we have a firmly held belief that life shouldn't be artificially prolonged, so no AI and so on, where life has evolved beyond that of its accord, we run

up against a tricky predicament. What do we do about a new life form? Do we regard it as part of the Godhead, or do we eradicate it?'

Luke hadn't been listening properly – more concerned with assimilating the arrangements the 3:16 contact had told him he had to memorise, including passwords, PIN numbers and timing. If he got any of it wrong, he'd be locked out of Hughes' journalistic account, and he needed to be in it to activate his invitation to the Crane Industries press conference. His attention flipped away from the onscreen instructions he was supposed to be memorising and focused on that word 'eradicate'. It had shades of Nazi-istic ethnic cleansing to it – the overt kind he'd sometimes encountered in the past in relation to Asians and Blacks before the new rules had come in and vigilante rule had been outlawed – not that it didn't sometimes still occur in some areas.

'Eradicate?' Luke queried. 'Eradicate what?'

'Whatever you might find in Crane Industries,' he could hear the satisfaction in the 3:16 contact's voice. 'You see, we suspect it's not only BioModules that Crane Industries has been growing. It's modules on a larger scale. Maybe you could even call it a new race?'

'Are you crazy?' Luke bit his lip as soon as he'd blurted it out. You didn't call these guys crazy even if they were.

The 3:16 contact laughed mirthlessly. 'Indeed, Mr Maynard, many people do call us crazy, but maybe you'll find out that we're not so much crazy as visionary when you gain access to the inner heart of Crane Industries.'

'What are you expecting me to find in there? Frankenstein's monster?'

'No,' the 3:16 contact had replied. 'Frankenstein's daughter. And when you do, you need to bring her to us,' he added softly.

'I thought you just wanted to get in there and destroy everything?'

'Not everything. There are some things we need to study first.'

'Like Frankenstein's daughter?'

'Exactly. You understand what will happen if you don't?'

'No more meds.'

'Worse than that. Your medication has been treated to work on a nuclear basis. It will work just fine to an extent, but after a certain period of time, the isotopes that have been inserted into it will begin to degrade. You need to be in and out within seven days. After that... And maybe even faster if your body can't tolerate the strength of the meds or you're subjected to extremes of anything; heat, cold, anxiety, emotions – your

metabolism will speed up, metabolise the drugs faster and you'll go downhill faster too – maybe even die.'

'Seven days? Well, Chri- crikey! I wasn't intending being in there for that long. Twenty-four hours should do it, shouldn't it?'

'To allow US access, but maybe not to gain full access for yourself.'

'Frankenstein's daughter?'

'Frankenstein's daughter.'

'What do you want her for?'

'That's not within your remit. Your remit is to get us in and her out. For that, you will receive your cure – and your big break too possibly. You're obviously going to write about all of this, aren't you?'

'Is that allowed?' Luke asked, unable to keep the sarcasm from his voice. Outside the whine of a police siren reminded him that everywhere what was allowed and what wasn't was becoming increasingly controlled. 3:16 wasn't so different to the authorities these days, with their unmodified prejudices, just less respectable.

'We've always supported freedom of speech,' the 3:16 contact replied, sounding mildly amused – and smug. 'As long as it concurs with the official version of events.'

'Official?'

'Our official – as we will be after this. Official, that is.'

Luke shivered involuntarily at that. Was he also going to be instrumental in enabling some kind of coup or rebellion?

'But she'd be safe? He thought about the small child he'd encountered the last time he'd got into Crane Industries. The child who'd begged him then to help her escape. Maybe he'd be doing her a favour then, if that was who 3:16 were interested in and promised to keep her safe? And salving his conscience for having left her there the first time. A win:win all round, with him getting cured too.

'Understood,' he said, returning to memorising the last series of numbers. 'I'll do what I need to.'

It was only now he was beginning to understand though. And with understanding came betrayal, whichever way he jumped. The progression of the MND symptoms was a clear indicator that his body was metabolising the drugs too fast, and they would fail altogether soon. He now needed the ForEver Project just to survive… but then he'd be consigning Hebe to continue to be walled up in the Crane Industries building, and continually grow old, revert, grow old, revert – as well as consigning her mother to what Hebe regarded as the hateful ForEver Project process. On the other hand, if he helped Hebe escape, whilst he might gain access to extra drug treatment from the 3:16 Group, it was clear now it wasn't going to work for long for him AND the 3:16 Group would simply take over with Hebe where Jason Crane left off. And what did 3:16 want with Hebe anyway? Why did they want to destroy everything else in Crane Industries but study Hebe first?

Luke sat upright on the bed. It was no good. These questions needed answers, and he needed absolution, whichever way he jumped. There was only one person who could give him that. He had two days left before complete collapse from medication failure, or complete assimilation via the ForEver Project. It was inevitable he was going to betray someone, he just needed to be certain about who, and then beg their forgiveness.

The whole complex seemed to be quiet tonight. Even the incessant drilling seemed to have stopped temporarily. He'd become so used to it, latterly it had become barely more than an annoying buzz, like a fly trying to escape through a shut window. It had been unnerving at first, but now complete silence was more intimidating. Touching his feet to the floor, he padded, barefoot, across to the door out onto the corridor, pausing only briefly to commiserate with his ragged and ailing image in the full-length mirror.

'You and me, both,' he told the unkempt apparition as it grimaced back. He sighed. How the hell had this happened to him? WHY the hell had this happened to him? Wasn't it bad enough to lose your brother and then find out you're following hard on his heels anyway, even though you've never done a line of coke or even smoked a single cigarette in your life? Booze had been his only sin – and even then his moments of inebriation had been few and quickly regretted. Life was fucking unfair, and death was even worse. But... there was no point moaning about it. It wouldn't change anything. Hebe might though. He abandoned the mirror and made for the door. It opened as silently as the corridor welcomed him into it. He paused for a moment, listening. Nope. No drilling at all. Had they stopped altogether or just run out of drill bits or drill operators? Or did it signify something more? A change of tack? The trouble was, he wouldn't know either way because his contact with them had ended on entry into the facility. Presumably if he exited it again – with or without 'Frankenstein's daughter' – it would resume however 3:16 wanted it to.

The floor felt so cold to his bare feet. Why hadn't he put on his shoes? There seemed to be something quite perverse growing in him of late – an unwillingness to conform. He scrunched his toes against the icy floor and walked the length of the corridor, toes cringing inwards. Near the end, he held his breath. Where would he be? He'd been holding the thought of Hebe in his mind the length of the corridor, so if his assumptions were correct, his instinctive neural pathways should have adapted the corridor's route to take him straight to her. If not, well, he was fucked!

The doorway was straight ahead of him, almost concealed in the smooth wall of the corridor, identifiable by only the merest distortion of the wall's curvature. He stopped in front of it, mentally envisaging Hebe, by her mother's bedside, holding her hand. He reached out and touched the wall, smoothing its silken skin as he would have stroked Frieda's skin if she had been alive, except Frieda and Hebe became confused in his head and he recoiled, ashamed of the inappropriate thoughts he was having for a mere child. Before he could remove his hand from the wall, the door swung open, making him jump backwards and rock unsteadily on his heels, toes still cringing in on themselves, but more now in the precursor to a fit than because of the coldness of the floor.

'Oh!' It was involuntary, breaking the silence of the complex like a plunging object breaking the meniscus of water. Hebe turned, long flaxen hair moving like a wave of silken gold as she twisted in her chair to greet him.

'You're here,' she said, smiling a welcome. He could see, now she'd turned and her body wasn't blocking his view of the sleeping woman, that she was holding Elise's hand. 'My mother said you would come.'

Elise Crane still lay motionless, the heart monitor bleeping and the ventilator clicking and puffing with each exhaled and inhaled breath. The room was softly lit by a myriad of candles, Luke suddenly noticed with surprise. Now, it seemed more like a shrine than a sick room. He stared around him, taking it all in – one long slow sweep of the room, medical equipment, luxurious drapes – behind which he now knew was the rest of the paraphernalia keeping Elise Crane alive, the bed on which the still figure of Elise lay, prone and fragile, and Hebe, perched on the edge of the same chair Green had squatted on when he'd denounced Luke's weaknesses. Hebe was about mid-teens again now, the child's body lengthening and refining into the young woman's, long-limbed, lean, athletic and supple. Luke looked away before his mind could retrace its earlier steps and embarrass him.

'I… wanted to talk to you again after… well… It's not like that, you know. Really. I'm trying to do the right thing, I just don't know what it is any more. I mean,' he hesitated. 'How did you know I would come here?'

'I didn't, but my mother did, didn't you?' Elise Crane's eyes flickered open and she stared at her daughter. Hebe squeezed her lifeless fingers and Luke's breath caught in his throat. She just stared and stared whilst Hebe seemed to be listening.

'Is she…?' Luke wasn't sure what he was asking. Was she awake? Was she aware? Was she listening? Was she even alive? Hebe interrupted his thoughts.

'You're wondering if what I've just told you is true? That my mother brought you to us?'

'Well,' he moved closer so he could get a better look at Elise Crane's face. Her eyes were open, but the pupils were fixed and staring. She reminded him of a full-size doll – or a mannequin. 'She can't have done. She's in a coma.' Her eyes flicked shut even as Luke spoke.

'Yet she talks to me all the time – in my head.' Hebe looked at him and smiled, kindly. 'We have a telepathic communication because I'm genetically part AI, part human.'

'I thought you were wholly human, physiologically. I mean how could you be…'

'Part machine? But you saw what my father was like – straight after the accident. He's mainly AI – or at least his shell is, yet he's made up of blood and bone and sinews. It's not the substance that makes the man, it's how it's applied. After his initial descent, my father fought back hard to be a father for me. If it hadn't had been for what I am, he might even have succeeded. Unfortunately, what I am was too much for the AI in him and "gradually he has allowed the AI neurosis to take precedence again.'

'And what are you?' Luke asked softly.

'Frankenstein's daughter – isn't that what they called me?'

Luke gasped. 'How did you know?'

'Uncle Matthew told me that's what they call me.'

'Jesus! 3:16?'

'"For God so loved the world that He gave His only begotten Son, that whoever believes in Him should not perish but have everlasting life." So their questions now are, could a son be a generic term? In other words, for son, could you also insert daughter instead? And secondly, Jesus rose from the dead. So did my father. So do 3:16 revile or worship my father, or me, or neither? "Spirit without measure" was said to have been given to Jesus in John 3:34. Is that what I have – from my father?'

'Do you really believe all that…' Luke was about to say 'twaddle' but he managed to pull himself up in time and change it to 'speculation.'

Hebe grinned at him. 'No, but they do, and we have to go along with them if they are going to get me out, don't we?'

'I thought you wanted me to get you out?'

'I did – do – but I don't think you do.'

'That's not true, I'm just… well, you know what I am. So you mean to play along with this 3:16 Group?'

'Of course, don't you? Oh Luke, don't look so guilty. I've known all along that's how you got in here – 3:16 and Uncle Matthew. But that's OK. Wasn't it Machiavelli who said, "There is nothing more necessary to appear to have than this last quality (appearing to be religious), inasmuch as men judge generally more by the eye than by the hand, because it belongs to everybody to see you, to few to come in touch with you." In other words, be what people need you to be, but only allow the essential few to get close enough to find out what you truly are. I've classed you as one of the essential few.' She paused and, seeing his shocked expression, laughed. 'Sorry, I did a lot of reading when I was little. Became a bit of a philosopher then as a result, I suppose.'

'You still are,' Luke replied. He felt as if his consciousness was about to explode, taking with it whatever sanity he still had. Here was a two-year-old who looked like a fifteen-year-old quoting Machiavelli at him.

'But that's only my appearance, Luke. Not what the essential few know about me.'

'And will you allow 3:16 to number amongst the essential few too?'

'Hardly,' she giggled. 'But they can get me out, because of what they think I am. They can. Or you can, or Uncle Matthew can. Either way, it's time for me to get out of here.'

'My only chance of a cure is in here,' Luke replied, feeling small and shameful.

'That's only how it appears to you right now. Come on. Tomorrow's another day, and you have appearances to keep up.'

Hebe stood, placing Elise's hand gently back on the bed and took Luke's instead. He allowed her to guide him gently towards the door.

'I'm sorry, Hebe,' he said, choking back his failure and his regret. 'I'm sorry, that I'm so weak and that I can't be your saviour.'

The voice in his head shocked him. 'The end justifies the means.' Luke whipped round to look back towards the bed. Elise Crane's eyes were wide open, and her head had turned sufficiently to one side to enable her to be staring straight at him. She was smiling – the same kind of smile the Mona Lisa was smiling: secretive, smug and sure.

'She spoke to you, didn't she?' Hebe was watching him closely, the same Mona Lisa smile hovering on her lips. 'You must have a special connection with her too.'

'And how could that be?' Luke asked, more defensively than he'd intended. 'I've never even met her before yesterday.' But that wasn't true. A jolt of electricity ran through him as he acknowledged the lie. Now he knew how he knew Elise Crane - but that was impossible.

Chapter 19

09:03, 23rd May 2032: Luke

Had last night been a dream? Luke lay as still as he could inside the machine. He'd refused initially, until Crane had threatened that there could be no ForEver, and not even a fallible BioModule unless he manned up and got in the damn machine – Crane's words. So he'd manned up, but was seriously regretting it now. Just don't think about it, he told himself. Don't think about the tunnel… Oh shit! He hated the feeling of being trapped, but there was no other way to map his CNS and Crane had insisted on repeating yesterday's tests as a double-check. The side of the tube pinched his arms close to his body and he could feel the wet patches developing under his arms and where his hands clamped against his sides. He had to concentrate hard just to breathe evenly. Don't think about it, don't think about it…

'A full map is essential if we are to successfully reconnect all the synaptic bridges. Without a roadway to travel, your brain will be stuck in default mode. We want it in dynamic mode so it can create new pathways and join up all the dots as quickly as possible. It will still take a few days to achieve full functionality, but at least you will have the basic motor functions straight away,' Crane was saying as Luke attempted to lie motionless in the tube. Luke's head began to pound from the effort of trying to remain still and not scream to be released from the machine. Desperately, he latched onto Crane's words as a means of distraction.

'Basic motor functions?' Luke asked, breathing deeply to control the rising panic that both being inside the machine and the idea of being transferred lock, stock and barrel into an AI body was engendering in him. He could hear the blood pressure monitor beep as it recorded increasingly elevated levels and the cuff tightened around his arm, squeezing his enfeebled bicep as it measured just how agitated he was. It didn't help that Green was hovering near his head, and his musty smell made Luke want to gag with every breath he took.

'It's OK,' Green instructed, reaching into the machine and squeezing Luke's shoulder. Luke recoiled and the heart monitor loudly recorded the spike. Green removed his hand. 'It won't take much longer. We're on the last stages now.' His voice was even but Luke could detect the hurt underlying it. Momentarily, he felt sorry for Green, the 'technician', yet even he knew that Green had been a shining star in previous years – brighter even than Crane, until Crane had eclipsed him with the inception of Crane Industries. What had happened to Green to make him so downtrodden, so wasted, so… decrepit? That thought made Luke want to gag again. Decrepitude had been the downfall of his parents – after Aaron had died. They'd just given up and old age had eaten them from the inside out – or the outside in. It probably hadn't made much difference by then. A bolt of rage against the dying of the light – the giving up by them – suddenly filled Luke. Aaron had gone, but what about him? Why hadn't they carried on for him? He'd not long been diagnosed with MND when Aaron overdosed. He'd had no hope for himself, let alone to give anyone else. Wasn't that when your parents came to the rescue? He breathed deeply to contain the agony of abandonment.

'Good,' Luke hissed through gritted teeth. Green made a tutting noise that Luke assumed was intended as reassuring. Still the blood pressure cuff tightened around his arm and his heart thumped painfully in his chest.

'Jason?' Green's voice was soft, hesitant.

'Think calming thoughts,' Crane advised from his position in front of a monitor on the other side of the lab. His voice sounded muffled to Luke as he lay, sweating and skin prickling inside the machine, but nevertheless there was sufficient of an edge to it to force Luke to concentrate on lowering his heart rate and the agitated pumping of blood through constricted veins. Since he'd witnessed Crane's decapitation and recovery, a part of him had been afraid, yes, afraid, of Crane. And by association, afraid of what he was about to become himself.

If he allowed the ForEver Project process to happen, that was.

But if he didn't allow it to happen, he would die.

The heart monitor beeped its rising crescendo again. He heard the swish of Crane's lab stool as it left its position.

'I can give you a sedative,' Crane's voice permeated Luke's fugue of misery. 'But that will suppress your bodily reactions and make it take longer to fully map your CNS. It's up to you; try to calm down so we can complete this quickly, or I drug you and it will take all day.'

Luke could sense Crane standing where Green had been before. The smell was different – more pleasant and somehow ambiguous, like the man himself. Man? Man. Maybe.

'I'd rather get it over and done with as quickly as possible,' Luke replied. *So I can talk to Hebe again,* his mind agreed. *Or Elise...*

'Then you are going to have to make more of an effort to stay calm. The higher your blood pressure and heart rate, the more stress on your CNS and then I get artificially elevated levels, which could lead to your AI shell being incorrectly calibrated.' Crane paused. 'Matthew, what's that music you like to play in here. Music soothes even the savage beast, doesn't it, so they say.'

'I can put some music on if it would help,' Green agreed. His proximity was evident by the blending of aromas – the Crane coolness, and the Green stench, that seemed to be getting worse by the day. Was the guy rotting? Luke laughed at that, a small explosion of mirth at the ridiculousness – and hideousness of the idea. He smelt that bad though. Luke swallowed hard and gulped back the bolus of disgust rising in his throat. He gasped in air and coughed, eyes smarting and chest spasming.

'Sorry,' Green moved away and the atmosphere around me lightened. His music choice was quite unexpected – light, airy, floral. Strains of one of the iconic pastoral symphonies swelled around Luke as he battled with his desire to puke and his need to remain still. He settled for trying to figure out which one it was as Crane returned to his monitor and Green hovered far enough away for the smell to be diluted.

It took another hour before Crane declared they were done. 'So would you like to meet yourself?' he added, as the bed slid out of the machine, and Luke breathed a ragged sigh of relief as Green loosened the security straps that had contributed towards pinning him like a specimen to a pinboard and removed the blood pressure cuff and electrode pads measuring his heart rate. He'd forgotten to turn the heart monitor off before removing the electrodes and its alarm uncomfortably mimicked what Crane had explained to him would happen at the moment of transfer from human body to AI shell.

'You WILL be sedated then. Easier to manage. You'll be hooked up to blood pressure, blood oxygen and cardiac machines; both of you. You'll also be lying face down, strapped to the operating table so we have full access to your brain and the connection points of brain to spinal cord so

we can monitor your CNS as we make the transfer. We will have exposed the top of your brain by removing a disc of your skull...'

'Wait!' Luke held up his hand. 'You remove my brain?'

They were sitting at the far end of the ForEver lab at the time. Luke had managed to plan it so he was sitting as far away from Green as possible and they were drinking coffee made by some machine that seemed to be an in-joke between Crane and Green. The more formal conversation about the actual ForEver process had been preceded by a stream of banter about coffee and the delicate balance between three and four grains of sugar to sweeten it. The humour was lost on him, as was the need for sugar. He hadn't touched sugar in years. It looked too much like the tiny heap of 'snow' that had been lying on the sheet of foil on the floor next to Aaron when he was found, the needle still in his arm. The camaraderie between the two wasn't though – or the strangeness of the situation where a man-machine was describing the process of turning another man into a man-machine, whilst the man who might reasonably be credited with enabling it looked on, noncommittal, and yet clearly, from what Green had said to him privately, Green was also negatively judgemental. So how did that fit in with what he was proposing Luke allow them to do?

'Well, of course we remove your brain. What do you think your AI shell is going to work on otherwise?'

'OK, OK, yes.' Luke steadied himself as he imagined brain and body being separated. 'But, that will work? I mean my brain is OK to use as it is – not affected by the MND?'

Fortunately the physiology lessons Frieda had given him when explaining why his CNS had been compromised by the MND were coming back to Luke – or perhaps unfortunately since they reminded him just how unlikely a cure was. Her explanation that small alterations in his DNA had resulted in the protein that would normally protect cells from the toxic effects of respiration instead allowed it to congregate in high volume and hinder the normal metabolic process, had been graphic. Instead of protecting his cells from neuronal death, his own body was actually facilitating it. That neuronal death was what caused spasms, muscle wastage, numbness, fatigue, difficulties in swallowing – and eventually breathing, and death. Sometimes there were cognitive changes too if the front or temporal lobes of the brain were affected. Although not always, she had reassured him. Sometimes the brain was not apparently affected.

'Although we do not know why yet. Maybe I will find out from studying you? With some specific experiments, perhaps...' she'd added, winking. That had resulted in a prolonged session of 'experiments' which had proved that his body was still functioning, even if his brain remained untested.

But no good thinking about Frieda now. Frieda was gone. Luke returned his attention to what Crane was saying as depression settled over him like a beguilingly soft blanket, enveloping, and suffocating.

'That's why we need a detailed map of your brain and your CNS. By establishing your synaptic patterning, we can see the neural pathways between brain and body, and what has been affected. If your brain has been affected, then of course we have a more difficult job, but initial observation of you hasn't implied any cognitive or serious behavioural changes so I think you may be lucky.'

'OK...' he hunched over, until he realised he was doing what Green so often did when he was thinking. Luke straightened himself, pushing his shoulders back.

'You're sure you still want to go ahead with this?' Green asked him, although his eyes flashed a warning.

'Of course, I do. I want to live, don't I?' his belligerence belied his belief.

'Good.' Crane had got up then, leaving him and Green to the dregs of their coffee. Two strides took him to the door and he was gone. The room felt empty without him.

'It does work, doesn't it?' Luke asked Green, then immediately wished he hadn't.

'Yes, it works. You've just been talking to the proof of that, haven't you?'

'So why do I feel like this is the worst decision of my life?'

'I don't know. How bad have your other decisions been?' Green chuckled but the humour didn't reach his eyes.

'It's not a joke!' Luke raged back at him. 'And you're the one who set me up for this – even though Hebe says you don't believe in it. Why don't you believe in it? And if you don't believe in it, why are you proposing it for me?'

Green put his coffee mug carefully back onto the lab worktop. He ran his finger round the rim several times before answering. 'Many reasons,' he said at length. 'I don't believe in immortality, unless we're talking about God – and even then, I'd like to think about it a bit more. That's probably the main one.'

'Then why the hell did you help Jason Crane to eternal life in the first place?'

'I didn't,' Green replied, suddenly looking up and squarely into Luke's face. 'I tried to stop it, in fact. The person who made it happen was your good lady doctor, Dr Kohn.'

'Frieda? No! She wouldn't do that. She wouldn't know HOW to do that!'

'How well did you know Frieda Kohn?'

'Intimately,' Luke replied, chin jutting and eyes rock-hard.

'Then you will know that she was an extremely determined – not to say, ruthless – individual.' Green leant back in his chair and pushed the coffee mug away from himself with an expression of distaste.

'No! She was...' But Luke hesitated. She was all of that. Christ, the way she'd just left him hanging... but that didn't warrant murder. 'So you killed her as revenge?'

'No, she died as a result of a freak accident, like we told you. She was about to expose the ForEver Project to the world, via the highest bidder – the military. You can imagine what would have happened next after that, can't you?'

'Bloody hell!' If it were possible, the lab seemed even quieter than before. Luke leant back too and studied Green as he took up the story. 'Go on. I think you need to come clean with me now – really clean...'

'OK.' Conspiratorially, Green leaned towards him and breathed out heavily, fetid breath making Luke want to back away, but he knew if he did, Green might read the body language and clam so he steeled himself and remained close. 'Jason was dying. We knew his death was imminent, but I didn't agree with what he wanted to do – neither of us did; Elise or me. And I didn't think we were ready even if I had agreed to help. Elise and I, well, we were afraid that the extent of the power conferred on anyone taking part in the ForEver Project was too much for any human to have and remain principled. Even Jason, who we both loved in our own ways. But I owed him. And I couldn't just let my oldest friend die, could I? Once upon a time he'd been more like my brother than my business partner... so I stalled, and kept stalling, but Jason knew that was what I was doing and made his back-up plan. I was out of the facility at the time – my daughter, Katie... well, she's another story... Anyway, I was out of the facility when Jason suffered a major shut-down as the tumour moved and your Dr Kohn took matters into her own hands. I was

only called back at the last moment when she didn't know what to do to complete the process. I had two choices then; to betray my oldest friend and let him die or betray myself and help him live. Did I make the right choice? I don't know. I suppose I made the only one my conscience would allow me to make at the time. I've asked myself if what I did was right over and over again since then, and ultimately there's too many reasons to list why it was wrong and only one reason why it was right: Hebe. However, it doesn't mean I would make the same choice again this time.'

'You wouldn't?'

The sat in silence, looking at each other.

'I don't know,' Green said at length. 'Hebe's unnatural too – as lovely as she is. Maybe I shouldn't have allowed things to continue even after we knew about her. I could have stopped him even then, but I didn't...'

'Yet you're facilitating the option for me? Repeating everything you question all over again?'

'Because Hebe has asked me to.'

'But she's absolutely against it!'

'Is she? There's a lot more to Hebe than you think – and what she says she doesn't always mean.'

'So now I don't know who to believe, or what to do.'

'Yes, you do.' Green got up then and walked over to the door, not as quickly as Crane had, but swiftly nevertheless, his usual shuffling gait replaced by a more agile and purposeful stride. 'We always know what to do, even when we're sure we don't. That's how I made my decision. For all the reasons it was wrong, there was one overriding one that said it was right. Trust in yourself, Mr Maynard. You might be surprised at the results.'

'I take it that's a yes?' Crane was still waiting for his answer.

'What?' Luke shook his head, trying to clear the warring memories and questions.

'Would you like to meet yourself?' Crane sounded patient, but the edge – that Luke so often detected these days, was even more in evidence in the repeated question. Green was hovering near Crane's shoulder, eyes signalling an answer at him.

'Oh, yes,' Luke said, still confused.

'Your AI shell,' Crane elaborated.

'Oh shit, yes!' Luke was now full on-board. And how the hell hadn't he thought to ask about this sooner?

Crane stood and beckoned for him to follow. Behind the racking containing the lab animals, there was a door with a security pass panel. Crane tapped his forefinger to the panel and it flashed up 'Director Crane' simultaneous with the door opening.

'Come on, then. This is where we'll do the procedure too.' Crane walked through the open door and Green gestured for Luke to follow him. Luke eased past Green, consciously holding his breath, and found himself inside a small room equipped with monitors, PCs and a large, obscured viewing window. Crane tapped his fingertip to another security panel next to the viewing window and it cleared, revealing another room on the other side of it. An operating theatre, with its first patient already in situ. Amidst the trolleys of instruments and the two draped gurneys at the back of the room, Luke stared at himself.

'Shit!' he muttered under his breath.

'I think he's a rather good likeness, myself,' Crane remarked mildly ironic.

'No, I mean yes, he is. It is. He is…'

'He is,' Crane confirmed. 'Or at least as of the day after tomorrow, he will be "he" – you…'

'Shit,' breathed Luke again.

'I would give you a closer look, but he's sterile and you're not. When we start the procedure, we will scrub you down and you will be sterile too. For the moment though, you can direct the mobile camera units to study various aspects of him. We've been generous,' again that ironic twist to Crane's tone. And as the body was naked, it didn't take Luke long to understand where the generosity had come into it.

'Fucking hell, I'm hung like a…'

'Not quite, but we've erred on the side of good fortune, as with the rest of the physique. You're quite run down now, but once, you were clearly a good specimen. Your new body reflects that.'

Crane selected one of the mobile camera units and directed it to take a close-up of Luke's alter ego. The skin was taut, the hair, fine and downy on the body, thick and luxuriant on his head, chest and genital areas. The shell's eyes were open, and as the camera zoomed in, stared back at him, fixed, clear and soulless. Luke moved closer and placed his nose close to the screen as he scrutinised the body, the hair, the eye…

'Oh!' Luke took a step backwards as one eye winked at him. Crane burst out laughing.

'Sorry,' he said, between bursts of amusement. 'He's hooked up to basic controls currently, to check on basic motor skills. I couldn't resist that.'

'Right.' Luke couldn't stop the sarcasm in his voice. To be honest, he felt offended. It felt wrong for Crane to be playing practical jokes on him with his own body. 'Well…' he took another step back and collided with Green who was standing right behind him. Luke was surprised he hadn't realised, but maybe his whole sense of perception – all senses of perception – were off currently. It wasn't every day you got to see yourself. 'Thanks,' he added. 'Good to know I'm going to be a prime specimen…' then suddenly, 'but what will happen to my old body?'

'Happen?' Crane turned to him, a quizzical look on his face. 'Why should anything happen to it?'

'Well, I… I just wondered. Will you dispose of it, or keep it on ice like Frie…' He tailed off. Crane's expression wasn't inviting any more questions.

'It will be seen to,' Crane replied. 'That's all you need to know. We're giving you a new body. What becomes of your old one is irrelevant. Now, if you've seen enough, time to shut down for the evening.' He pressed a button and the viewing window became obscure again. 'Shall we?' he gestured towards the outer door and ushered both Luke and Green towards it. They exited back into the main lab and Crane secured the door behind them. 'Tomorrow,' he concluded, 'we will complete the final diagnostics and set up a timeline for transfer. The process will start at 06:00 the day after. I suggest you get some rest now, so we can get everything concluded to schedule. We may have to move out of here shortly afterwards.'

And with that, he was gone, leaving Luke facing Green, in the middle of the ForEver lab, a hundred questions unanswered and no expectation they would be.

'He's right,' Green said, before Luke could pose even one of them of him. 'See you tomorrow bright and early.'

The door shut on him, leaving Luke alone in the middle of the ForEver lab. For the merest of moments he stood there, swaying with fatigue and mixed emotions, then he set off in their wake. Fuck this! The more he had explained to him, the less he understood. He was an old hand it this now, closing his eyes and feeling his way instinctively – allowing his gut to direct him to where he wanted to be – in the immediate vicinity of Hebe Crane.

She was ensconced in her favourite place – the centre of the small patch of grass that covered the centre of the courtyard garden. No daisy chains this time, or at least none he could see, and as he got closer, daisy chains were the last thing on his mind. The courtyard smelt of jasmine and fresh breezes. He breathed it in like a dying man – the dying man that he was. Oh God, it smelt good – she smelt good! She was cross-legged, eyes closed, hands resting palm upwards on her knees. Her dress was of smooth white silk, reflecting an almost rainbow patina as the light from the patterned ceiling windows caught it. The patina spread across her face and hair, turning her to a thing of some multicoloured substance. He crept closer still, desperate not to disturb her and yet equally desperate for her to open her eyes and explain.

'Hebe?' he whispered. Then he shook his head. Not Hebe. This couldn't be Hebe. This young woman was too old – mid-twenties perhaps, still radiantly beautiful, but not Hebe.

Elise?

He reached across the grass, careful not to step on it, remembering what Hebe had told him about the grass feeling pain, of the connectivity of all living things. He'd caused enough pain already in his life. This was one kind of pain he could avoid.

'Elise,' he murmured, this time, but there was no sign that she'd heard him. Just the deep steady breathing of one so far within themselves, they had lost all awareness of anything around them. So where was Hebe? His instinct – his neural instinct had brought him here when he'd focused on Hebe, so she couldn't be far away. Maybe she was in Elise's room? He repositioned himself in the courtyard, facing one of the exits to a corridor and thought about Elise's room. Immediately and involuntarily his feet started moving, stepping in a circle until he'd rotated one hundred and eighty degrees and was facing the opposite exit. He skirted the grass square in the courtyard, casting a backward glance at the still unmoving figure and then concentrated on finding the tell-tale indentation in the corridor wall that signified the opening to Elise Crane's sick room. He slid his hands, palms flat across the wall. It felt like the satin of Elise's dress – smooth, slippery, sensual. Lurid thoughts started to entwine with the sensation of sliding his hands across the smooth wall, across smooth limbs, until they touched the soft swell of breasts, thrusting against him and – shit! He was doing it again. Disgusted with himself he tried to squash his erection and simultaneously identified the inset handle to the door. He hesitated, not wishing to offend Hebe if she was in the room, but the sound of distant footsteps far along the corridor decided him. He twisted the handle and was inside the room in seconds, eyes squinting to see as they adjusted top the gloom. The bed, the chair, the prone figure, they were all the same. No Hebe, and the prone figure was Elise.

'What?' he muttered, approaching the bed like a cat burglar, tiptoeing in case he woke her. Up close, she looked younger. Her skin, under a fine network of lines, filament-thin, like a spider's web – a fine fuzz of something that he hadn't thought had been there before, was dewy, youthful. Curious, he touched her cheek, stroked it, dabbled his fingertips against it. She felt like featherdown. His breath caught in his throat. But she was older than the oldest he'd ever seen Hebe so this couldn't be Hebe. No, there was no doubt, this was Elise Crane, so who was it out in the courtyard? Jason Crane had said he didn't seem to have suffered any neural damage to his brain – no impairment of reasoning or cognitive abilities and yet here he was staring at the self-same person in two different places. Leaving the room, he returned to the courtyard, to the same young woman. There were two of them. Something was wrong.

Finding energy he hadn't thought possible after the day's events, he retraced his steps as far as the ForEver lab, but of course, Green wasn't there. Where were Green's quarters? He'd never thought to ask. He cursed silently, and then realised something else had changed. The drilling hadn't resumed overhead. The whole complex was deathly quiet and a sense of impending doom hung heavy in the air.

'Green?' he shouted. He didn't know what else to do. 'Green, where are you? Or Crane? Jason Crane? Where are you all?' His voice echoed hollowly in the empty lab. He banged on the worktops, pounding the flat of his hand down in an awkward slapping motion which made his hand sting. He changed to hammering his fist on the worktop instead. 'Green? Where are you?' he shouted again. Nothing. He headed for the animal cages at the end of the lab, rattling the cages and running a pencil across the bars so they thrummed and set the animals squeaking and chattering – anything to make a racket. 'Green! Matthew Green, where are you?' He reached the doorway to the viewing room and operating theatre and was about to hammer on that too, when he realised it wasn't fully closed. He pulled it ajar. 'Green?' he called more cautiously, pulling the door wide. The viewing room was empty, but the viewing window had been opened and he had a clear view straight into the operating theatre. Straight at the prone bodies of himself, Elise and Hebe Crane, and the live one of Matthew Green.

He hammered on the viewing window. 'Fuck you! What the hell is this? What are you doing in there? That's supposed to be sterile – and why are Hebe and Elise in there too?'

It was only in the third battering that Green turned and saw Luke. He froze, eyes wide like a wild animal staring into the night. Then he waved frantically at Luke and pointed off to the left. 'Switch,' he mouthed. 'Flick the switch.'

Luke froze, fist in mid-air, as all the fury drained from him and he was left with confusion at Green's response. He looked over to where Green was gesturing and saw a switch on the wall beside the viewing window. It said 'intercom'. He flicked it and immediately Green's voice burst into the room.

'For fuck's sake, calm down, will you? What the hell is wrong?'

'What are you doing in there?' Luke tried to yell back but his breath wouldn't obey and instead rushed out as he spoke, creating a breathy whine instead of a belligerent bellow. Now he was calming down he noticed that Green was clad in what looked like dull blue surgical scrubs.

'I'm prepping. What do you think I'm doing?'

'And those,' Luke waved wildly towards the other two bodies lying on the gurneys behind Green. They were covered one by a green, and one by a blue drape.

'Ah, those.' Green sighed and shrugged. 'Meet Elise,' he waved sadly towards the blue-draped gurney, 'and Hebe,' he gestured to the green-covered form. 'I did warn you Hebe and Elise needed saving from the ForEver Project. Now do you understand why I want to get them out of here?'

'But he can't…'

'Can't he?' Green suddenly looked twice as old as he usually did. He moved closer to the viewing window. 'You know, this wasn't part of the plan when you first got in here, but given how things have gone, maybe if you're a ForEver, it's the one way we can stand up to Jason. After all, you'd have the same capabilities as him. OK, maybe you'd have to grow into them a bit, but strength for strength, in a fist fight, you'd be matched. That would at least be something, especially if the racket you've just made is anything to go by.'

'Oh shut up and listen. Something's wrong.'

Green leant against the viewing window glass. 'Every fucking thing here is wrong, Mr Maynard. Which one would you like to report first?'

'Hebe. She's got older.'

'She does.' Green's weariness didn't quite make the sarcasm work.

'No, she's got much older. Older than I've ever seen her. Over twenty.'

Now he had Green's attention. 'What?'

'And Elise Crane looks pretty much the same. It's hard to say for sure with that awful lighting but I think…'

'Stand outside and shut the door. I'm coming out.'

'Be my guest,' Luke gestured ironically towards the inner door.'

'No, you stupid bastard. Go outside the other door and shut it. I need to decompress both rooms and dry-anti-bac that one so both remain sterile when I pass between them. You'll suffocate if I do that whilst you're still in it.'

'Oh…' Luke hastily took himself out of the inner room and stood outside the main door, having checked several times that it really had clicked shut. Five minutes later, Green opened the door and stepped out, dragging the sterile surgeon's cap from his head and leaving what there was of his hair straggling either side of his forehead.

'Now say that all again,' he demanded as he led Luke away from the inner room and past the cages of lab animals, now considerably less vocal, but still jittery from Luke's onslaught. He pointed to a lab stool and perched on one that he set down opposite it.

'Where's Crane?' Luke asked as he settled on the empty stool.

'Downtime. He has to download and switch off just like we do. His is just more specific. He won't disturb us. So talk!'

Luke recounted finding both Hebe and Elise, frowning as he remembered the eerie similarity between them. 'Like twins,' he added to conclude. 'So what's going on?'

Green chewed on his thumb. 'Something has reprogrammed their metabolism,' he suggested at last. 'So now Hebe keeps ageing. And Elise keeps regressing.'

'*Their* metabolism? Reprogrammed?'

'Well, yes.'

'You're saying it's a program? They're plugged into something – like Crane is?'

'Not exactly plugged in, but… attuned, I suppose would be the nearest to it. Attuned to what is going on here.'

'And what the fuck IS going on here?'

'Well,' Green looked surprised, but Luke didn't quite believe the attempt at mild-mannered bewilderment. 'You know what is going on here.'

'Do I? What about the connectivity? What's that all about? The way I can find places and people by thinking about them?

'Can you?' Green shrugged. 'Then maybe you're attuned too. It's nothing to do with me though and not part of a deep dire plan you know nothing about.'

'Crane's doing then?'

'Presumably. It's certainly not mine. This is all Jason's doing,' Green swung his arm in a wide sweep. 'I just do his bidding in return for…'

'For what?'

'Loyalty.' Green's lips pursed together in a thin white line as if the word pained him.

'But Hebe will die if she ages as fast as she regressed. So will Elise, if she reverts all the way back to – what?'

'Cells, DNA… Complete bio-reversal. But Jason wouldn't do that to them. He'd end up damaging the project.'

'Project? Jesus, is that what Hebe is to you two?' Luke exploded, half-rising from the stool.

'No! Of course not. Not to me, anyway. To me she's Hebe, but to Jason… She didn't start out as a project. Maybe she has become one, or maybe she has become a challenge. It's difficult to say. Either way, it's why I want to get her away from here. But aside from that, no, how she is now can't be down to Jason. Like I said, he wouldn't deliberately damage them.'

'Then who?'

'Maybe it's Hebe herself?' Green mused, still gnawing at his thumb. 'Now that would be interesting. Although, Hebe knows that her life cycle is crazily speeded up and she wouldn't willingly kill herself before she's found a way to save Elise. No, I don't think this is Hebe. It must have happened of its own accord somehow. Not reprogramming, or at least not deliberately, but maybe it IS to do with being here – what she's absorbing here…' he stopped gnawing on his thumb and looked up, eyes full of surprise. 'Yes, yes… the more I think about it…'

'So what do we do about it?' Luke demanded.

'Nothing,' Green said. 'We can't as things stand – unless you want to use those two AI shells in there?'

'Christ Almighty, no!'

'In that case, if you really want to help Hebe,' Green said, rubbing his chin, 'get her away from here and we'll see what happens then. But don't let her know what's happening to her.'

'Why not, hasn't she a right to know?'

'Yes, but in knowing she'll also be at risk of being convinced that her only hope of a cure – or Elise's – is Jason, and then she'll never leave. Jason will have a way to convince her to stay – a cure for her mother – and you know how tempting being offered a cure is. Those religious nuts are part right,' he added. 'No one should confer immortality of anyone else. It's against the rules of nature, and when you tamper with nature, it's not just nature that goes wrong. Ultimately it's the whole damn order of the universe because you give one man one power, and he wants two. Two and he wants four. Four and he wants everything…'

'Then why did you keep Crane's secret?'

'Because he kept mine first, and then he made it impossible to allow mine to be confessed.' Green reached into his pocket and produced two photographs. 'Remember I mentioned my daughter, Katie? That was Katie,' he handed Luke the photo of a Downs child at about seven. 'And this is her now. He passed the second photo over to Luke. A beautiful – and very normal – pre-teen of around eleven smiled back at him. 'That's her before the BioModule and now. I can't consign her back onto the scrap heap now she's tasted normal life. The best I can do is to stay here and moderate Jason as much as possible, and if need be, sabotage the programmes when the time comes. You see, his projects – his extra little bits of immortality can be used for good as well as power.'

'But he couldn't take the module away from her. I thought once implanted, it's implanted for life; that's why you have to be certain it's the right one.'

'Indeed, but he could turn it off. He could turn me off too. Apart from Katie and my other murky past, he also has your friend Frieda Kohn over me, so I can never escape. Maybe Hebe can though. Maybe the further away from here she is, the more normal she'll become.'

'You mean the further away she is from this instinctive neural networking stuff?'

'You've mentioned that before. What do you mean by it?'

'Don't you know?'

'No. I have no idea what you're talking about, other than that AI brains grow by mimicking the human brain's instinctive reactions to create synaptic connections, even if they're later abandoned because they have no cause and effect. That inevitably has fallout into the world at large. Everything we do has fallout, chemically or atomically.'

'Well...' Luke eyed Green suspiciously. Sounded like scientific bullshit to him, but then what did he know? He'd never have believed a man could have his head severed and reattach it himself, or a girl could continually age and regress years in a matter of hours. 'All I know is that I can sense a connection between thought and destination when I think about a specific place or person.'

'Dual functionality!' Green exclaimed suddenly. 'You had a twin, didn't you?'

'Yes,' Luke replied warily.

'Then maybe that's what you're sensing. You have their brain patterning alongside yours. You can duplicate connections, making them more powerful. Maybe you would have been a good candidate for that after all since you seem to be unexpectedly sensitive to it, but that's irrelevant now – and too late. You need to get Hebe away from here then we'll see whether she can live some kind of normal life.'

'Or die prematurely. It's not up to us to decide.'

'No,' Green agreed slowly. 'She has a right to decide for herself,' he sighed. 'We all have the right to decide our fate for ourselves, even if the choice we make is the wrong one. But only when we're in a position to do so. Hebe isn't here. So, get out of here and go and fill yourself up with grub. You're going to need it whatever you end up doing.' Green started to remove his scrubs, stripping them off and flinging them into the laundry bin next to the door. 'There's still some pizza left in the fridge in the kitchen, I believe. We'll find you there.'

Luke hesitated. 'We?

'Hebe and me.'

'But...'

'No buts. Believe me, I know what's the right choice now. You've got to go before tomorrow or you'll be bound up in the ForEver process. Just take your cue from me and when I say go, you go – whatever the circumstances.' He flipped the lid of the laundry bin closed. 'But Luke,' he added, 'please remember, she may look like a woman, and have more than the intellectual capacity of a woman, but emotionally, she's just a child – a two-year-old child. She can choose for herself but only explain the choice when you're sure she's able to make it.'

Chapter 20

09:03, 23rd May 2032: Hebe

'Hebe?'

Distantly I heard Luke's voice, but I couldn't answer him. Inside me, the patterns were shifting, revising, transforming. I was used to it, of course, but this time I felt more jittery, as if I'd drunk too much coffee – alongside, of course, the usual stretching, tearing, expanding pains I always felt during the growth part of the process. The sensations this time were subtly different too. Less elastic, more solid. I flexed my arm and the muscle cranked into action as normal, but with more precision, as if it was testing the process of flex-contract-activate in preparation to fix it anew in my brain. A new synaptic pathway – and it felt… different. I felt different. More 'real'. I examined myself in the mirror then. Slim, still almost boyish shape, but with an inherent curvature to me that hitherto hadn't been obvious, only implied. I touched my belly. It felt firm, developed, ready. I touched my face and found fine down overlaying my skin, almost like a protective covering. If I rubbed at it, it dropped away, revealing fresh unblemished skin, and the downy residue on my fingertips just melted away to dust. I turned around and around and examined the whole of myself then. It was everywhere, that fine down. I swept it away to reveal the new me, and I knew then. I wasn't wholly me any more. I was more than me – what I'd been born to be. All this time had been preparation. But I wasn't ready – had no idea what I was meant to do even though it had been explained to me. All these years of hearing that other voice inside me, informing, directing, reassuring; telling me who'd come and when – even how and why – but now I was totally unprepared for the 'what' that would entail.

I went to her then. 'I'm different this time,' I told her. 'More solid. I don't know how I'm meant to be in this current body.'

She considered for a while, then, 'Yes, you do. I think your metabolism must have reached puberty, Hebe – the moment the child becomes the woman. Just listen to your body, and it will tell you how to respond.'

'And will I stay like this?'

'I don't know. Your body is an unknown for me. You work differently. Perhaps, or perhaps you will revert, but as far as the process of maturing is concerned, you're moving on to another stage and none of us know how we will be when that happens. Don't be afraid, just go with it. Learn how to feel comfortable in it.'

So I went to the only place I felt comfortable by then – the grass in the courtyard – and learned. That was when Luke came, but I wasn't ready to answer him then. I was still learning. That is how dual functionality works. You have to meld – converge on what you both individually know and allow it to combine – life and death, before and after, child and adult. Elise Crane isn't just my mother, she is my other me – my twin; the twin who lived whilst I lay dormant inside her, a seed in a pod, fertilised but unrealised, until she was forced into dormancy so I could grow. It's a very rare – almost unheard-of phenomenon – but that is what we are, Siamese twins where one implanted inside the other, and as the other outwardly grew, absorbing all the nutrients required to develop into a normal child, the other remained a cluster of nascent cells, waiting.

My father believes my advanced cognitive development is simply because I'm precocious – but what two-year-old wouldn't be precocious when she already has, inbuilt, the life and experiences of another thirty-nine years? Thirty-nine years since Elise's birth, filled with joys and disappointments, disillusionments, betrayals, information, and finally, acceptance. My understanding of 'us' has been necessarily gradual, since that first time when Elise spoke to me. For a long time, she was just my mother because I had to be nurtured, and who else was there to nurture me? The cuckoo in the nest, the alien waiting to invade? For a time, after I started to understand, I was surprised my father hadn't recognised the deception – after all with his AI technology, he can scan and decipher many of our human brainwaves into basic thought and cerebral emotion – if he chooses to, that is. Maybe he decided it was easier not to, where his daughter was concerned? Or maybe our complexity scrambles his emotional responses so that he fails to read the connection. I suppose I am also part my father in a sense since it was his nanites that reactivated me. He turned the dormant seed into a germinating plant with the introduction of nanites into my mother/twin's body – and thence into me. That makes him both my rejuvenator and my father, and Elise Crane both my twin and my mother. And here we all are, still dormant inside this body of a lab complex, just awaiting the moment when we burst out and grow into the world outside. In a moment of weakness, Uncle Matthew told me how we all came to be here, locked down and hermit-like, after I overheard my father exerting pressure over the testing of the ReNewal unit. He'd never mentioned anyone outside until then.

'Who is Katie? Who is Jane?'

'Just people I was once close to.'

'Once? Why aren't you close any more?'

'It's complicated, Hebe.'

'I like complicated. I can sort out all kinds of complex problems.' I went and hugged him, draping my arms around him like a sloth hanging onto a tree whilst it dozed. I even ignored that musty, death-smell he's developed over time, like he's dying from the inside out.

'Not this one, you can't.' I watched his reflection in the blank monitor in front of him as I hung from his shoulders. He'd clamped his lips shut, but his eyes were sad, soft – relenting.

'Try me,' I persisted.

'It's no use, Hebe, really. Let it go.'

'No, if it's something that makes you sad, I want to help – make it go away. That's what you do for me. You're always looking out for me and trying to cheer me up if I'm down.'

'That's my job, Hebe.' He gently disentangled himself from me. 'What I promised to do from the moment we knew about you.'

'You promised my father?'

'Well, I suppose him too – but it was your mother I promised.'

'But I thought she was in a coma already then?' I scrutinised his face. He smiled a lopsided half-smile that was more sadness than smile.

'She was, but it didn't matter that she couldn't hear me. It was what I had to do. I owed her that for having failed her in other ways. And once you were born, well,' he grabbed my hands and held me at arm's length from him. 'Look at you! Now I look out for you simply because you're you.'

'But why did you owe her?'

'It's a long story, and not for now. You're too young.'

'Today, I'm all of eighteen,' I reminded him.

'But only in body, not in mind or experience,' he replied gently.

'Well, unless I'm allowed to experience experiences, I'll never grow any more experienced,' I reasoned. 'And not many two-year-olds, going on eighteen, can claim to understand the theory of relativity, so maybe my mind is more mature than you think? Plus, I'm hardly your average two-year-old in any other way, am I?'

'No,' he agreed. 'All right, I'll tell you, but you have to understand that nothing in this life is black and white, and no person is either wholly good or wholly bad.'

'My father, you mean? I know, Uncle Matthew. I already know.' I looked deep into his eyes and he must have seen there that I did, so he told me our story then – how I developed so abnormally quickly, I equally rapidly became a medical mystery, and that in itself determined the first step towards this hermit-like existence. My father paid off the medical staff, got my mother transferred to the medical facility within the Crane Industries lab complex, and it was here that I was born – just two months after my existence was first detected. It was a difficult caesarean. I was attached to my mother's womb in a most unusual manner- not by an umbilical cord but by a complex construct of multiple arteries and tissue, more like I was a growth that was integral to her body than a foetus. Once detached though, I grew exponentially as fast as I had in the womb, so by a month old, I was more like nine, and by two months old, I was walking, babbling, feeding myself and generally showing signs of being a rapacious toddler. I had been shielded from the world until then because of those anomalies alone. Shortly afterwards, it became clear that I had to be shielded from the world for another, more far-reaching reason: my elastic metabolism. At just past eighteen months it kicked in with a vengeance.

He summarised the rest, including what my father is, although I'd already worked that out for myself long ago, and he knew that. What he wouldn't explain was how he'd failed my mother.

'Do I have to eviscerate myself too, Hebe?' he asked, plaintively. 'I'd rather you didn't think that badly of me.'

'I could never think badly of you, Uncle Matthew. You're what keeps me going here.'

'Then let's leave it there, shall we?'

'Just one more question – so who are Katie and Jane?'

He sighed. 'That's two,' he parried.

'Please?'

'My daughter and my wife. I had to leave them behind. I couldn't

consign them to living here too.'

'You gave them up for me – and my mother?'

'Like I said.'

We DID leave it there, but I knew that however he'd failed my mother, it must have been terribly, and that he was more than paying the price for it. Yes, he was dying from the inside out, and his failing was killing him. That's why it's not just me that Luke Maynard needs to save, it's Elise and Uncle Matthew as well. Maybe even my father too. We don't only incarcerate others in our own prisons.

Dual functionality, my father calls what I have, but he has no idea I have it, or quite what it means I can do. He pontificates over it. He theorises about it. He aspires to identify it, and I know he mustn't because my father with dual functionality as well as what he can already do doesn't bear thinking about. It doesn't bear thinking about in anyone without the purest soul, and who has a pure soul?

'Hebe?'

This time I did answer. It was Uncle Matthew. Whether I was ready to answer or not, something in the urgency of his tone forced me to. I opened my eyes to find him on his hands and knees, peering across the carpet of the grass, but on it. He knew.

'Uncle Matthew? What's the matter?'

'I think it's time for you to go.'

'Go?' I asked stupidly.

'From here,' his voice was patient, but his expression was intent, urgent.

'We're escaping right now?' My heart thumped against my ribs. 'Why right now? It's night-time.'

'*You're* escaping. Come on!' He held out his hand across the grass threshold. I hesitated.

'Only me?'

'You and the journalist.'

'Oh no, what about you – and my…' I managed to time the hesitation with a small sob of anxiety. 'Elise?' I've always found it so difficult to lie to Uncle Matthew, even though he would never know. He's such an accepting soul. He even accepted me calling her Elise instead of 'Mother'.

'Just you,' he replied, shaking his head. He looked so sad, I wanted to put my arms around him and comfort him, but the grass between us prevailed. 'If the journalist had been prepared to be more co-operative – do what I'd wanted him to – we could have got you both out, but now…'

'No, that's not the plan. The plan was for all of us…'

'I know, but we will follow when we can, later. We just can't manage it tonight without raising the alarm.'

'Then I'll go later too. I'm not going without you.'

He gestured for me to cross the grass. Sweat was beading his nose and forehead and there were dark patches under his arms. 'Please, Hebe, you need to go right now. Later may be too late.'

'Why?' reluctantly I threaded my way across the grass, putting the least amount of pressure that I could on it. Still it squirmed and groaned at my weight – my increased, bone-deep weight; the weight of two become one.

'There's a small window of opportunity opening shortly. All the alarm systems will be down then and you'll be able to get out through the air ducts. The fans will go off when the power goes down.'

'How?' I watched the shadow drift across his face; the guilt. 'Oh,' I exclaimed involuntarily. 'The group? You're letting them in past the last barricade? But Father?

'They won't find him – they won't even get that far past the internal security systems. Anyway, Escher will see them off. Only our friend Mr Maynard seems to be able to navigate past Escher.'

I laughed then. Escher – the private joke between Uncle Matthew and me when the floor plan re-arranged itself. It had been his idea originally, this fluid floor arrangement – a paradox that perpetually fooled my father because AI simply doesn't understand paradoxes – but it had been me who'd made it happen. Well, me and Elise together, that is. It had certainly kept Father from finding me and her together many a time since I'd first found her. Indeed, I once told Uncle Matthew I'd lay good money that he didn't even know I knew of her existence, but he got a bit funny about that. 'No betting and no odds. They have a tendency of going against you when you least expect it,' he replied ambiguously, but wouldn't be drawn to explain. So neither did I explain what the Escher floor planning really was: dual functionality.

'But why are you letting them in now?'

'Because now is the right time. You need to get out of here, now… Just trust me, huh? I know what is right now.'

'And you'll be…'

'We'll be fine. I have a plan – and, anyway, I will have fulfilled my agreement with 3:16 by letting them in so you can get out, so we'll be able to follow later when all the song and dance is over.'

'With Father?'

'That will depend, Hebe, you know that.'

I nodded. Yes, that would depend…

Chapter 21

22:16, 23rd May 2032: Luke

'Luke?' Green's voice sounded like a sotto voce caricature as he hissed and ahemmed at Luke. Luke jumped, sending the plate he'd loaded with left-over pizza clattering to the floor.

'What the hell?'

Standing behind Green, laden with rucksack, head torch and a large stick that could either be a large stick or something more murderous, stood Hebe; tall, slim, and still older.

'Time to go,' Green hissed.

'Go?' Luke staggered to his feet. 'Right now?'

'I told you to be ready, well, ready is now. Come on.' Draped over Green's right arm was a waterproof jacket, another rucksack, and another head torch. He was also dangling some boots from his left hand. 'Put this lot on.' He thrust the jacket and rucksack at Luke, dropped the boots at his feet and stretched the band of the head torch around Luke's head before he could protest. Luke straightened the head torch and took the jacket and rucksack from him, looking past Green's bulk to Hebe as he did so. She was hovering in the doorway to the kitchen, periodically checking over her shoulder. Everywhere was still too silent.

'What happened to the drilling?' Luke asked as he slid his left arm awkwardly into the jacket's sleeve. He winced as he felt a sharp prick in his right arm and turning, caught Green capping the needle he'd just injected him with. 'Shit, what was that?'

'Adrenaline. You're going to need it for the journey out.'

'What journey? Luke asked, rubbing his arm, but already appreciating the sudden flood of vitality he could feel rejuvenating his arm, his right side, his whole body.

'Through the air ducts,' Hebe replied, stepping forward. 'So you're going to have to push the rucksack in front of you whilst you drag yourself through behind it. Can you manage that?'

'Why? Why that way? What's going on with the crazies upstairs? I thought they must have gone, it's so quiet.'

'Not gone, waiting for my signal.' Green helped him shoulder the rucksack. 'All part of the plan. Let them in to take over upstairs. Let you in to insinuate yourself here. Get us all out when I open the final floodgates for the crazies, as you call them. The plan's mainly the same, except I can't open all the floodgates. Only some of them – the air ducts, and the main entrance to the underground complex. 3:16 will get access that way, but probably not a lot further because of the complexity of the floor layout. In the meantime, you and Hebe can get out through the air ducts whilst the power is off. Don't forget the boots,' he nodded to the boots still untouched by Luke's feet.

'Oh,' Luke dropped the rucksack and bent to fumble with the laces, having slipped his feet into them, then he paused. 'But what do we do when we get out of here?'

'Get away.'

'And then?'

'It depends. I'll be in touch. Just get out and lay low until then.'

'Come on,' Hebe grabbed Luke's hand and pulled him out into the corridor. 'This way.'

'But what about your mother and father – and him?' Luke gestured towards Green as Hebe dragged him along the corridor.

'They will follow us when they can.' She paused at Luke's continued resistance. 'What? What's the matter?'

'I don't know. I don't understand and I don't know any more, Hebe – whether I want to escape, whether I want to be cured, even whether I'm worth saving. I mean, look at me! I need an adrenaline shot to even make it out of here. How am I going to be of any help to you? More like you'll have to help me.'

'Oh, Luke,' she placed her hands on his cheeks and looked him deep in the eyes. 'Have you ever thought it might work the other way round? That in helping you, maybe I help myself? And I really need your help right now.'

Luke sighed. 'But if I slow you down…'

'I'll put a boot up your backside,' she laughed, releasing his face and taking his hand again. 'Come on…'

Still Luke hesitated. Behind them, Green was still watching. He waved them on impatiently. 'Go on, get going,' he called sotto voce. 'We only have a limited amount of time – unless you're ready to become an AI tomorrow.' At that, Luke shivered and shouldered the rucksack into a more comfortable position. He already knew he would have refused the process, having seen what he would have been transferred into. Not Frankenstein's monster, Luke Maynard's monster...

'Come on, then,' he said to Hebe through gritted teeth. 'Let's get the hell out of here!'

The entry to the air ducts that Green had selected as their best exit point was situated in the cold room. At the door, Luke looked askance at Hebe.

'And how do we get in?'

'Like this,' she replied, placing her fingertips over the security panel.

'But I thought only your father…'

'Could operate it?'

'Yes, but when he's on downtime, that's when Uncle Matthew can bypass his controls because he's effectively shut down. Then everything works on auto and Uncle Matthew can override specific controls. That's why we don't have much time.' The door slid open and immediately the cold hit them. Luke gasped, but Hebe seemed unaffected. She stepped into the room and waited for him on the other side. He followed more slowly, reluctant to even enter the room where it had all started – or ended, perhaps, at least for Frieda. 'I'm sorry, but I have to lock the door behind us, just in case,' Hebe explained as the door slid shut and Luke jumped and tried to stop it.

'Jesus, well, let's hope we can get out through the air duct like you say we can, then.'

'We will. I trust Uncle Matthew.'

'That's more than I do,' Luke muttered under his breath, trying not to look at the drawer front that contained Frieda. He'd come here to find her as well as something of more substance for himself. He'd promised her justice, but this wasn't justice, this was another betrayal, agreeing to silence in exchange for a cure – and now, not even a cure. His resolve failed him again – and his conscience. He pulled at Hebe's shoulder as she slipped the backpack off her shoulders after pulling the grille away from the air duct cover.

'Look, maybe I'm not so sure… Once we're out of here, Hebe, I'm going to get worse – a lot worse. You may think I'm going to be a help to you, but really I'm going to be a hindrance.'

'You want to stay for your cure?' she asked coldly.

'No, God, no!' Luke exclaimed, remembering the augmented body lying prone on the operating table, alongside the other two on the gurneys. 'I want a cure, but not the kind that was being offered.' He shivered again, hot and cold slivers of something close to disgust sliding down his spine and into his gut. How could he have even considered it? 'I meant,' he took a deep breath and finally acknowledged the truth of what he'd been continually bleating about to whoever would listen recently. 'I think I'm dying. This MND is only going to get worse, fast. And you – you need someone who can look after you, not a snivelling wreck who needs you to look after him. It's going to be tricky out there…'

'You're not a snivelling wreck, just a sniveller,' she grinned. 'And I don't have anyone to help me out there but you. Aren't people meant to help each other?' she added softly. 'Isn't that what love is all about?'

'Love?' Luke reeled away from her at that. 'What has love got to do with it?'

'Doesn't love have something to do with everything? You go first,' she added, 'then I can poke your feet if you slow down,' she waved her baton-stick at him, smiling ingenuously.

'But I don't know the way out,' he demurred, eyeing the now gaping air duct tube with growing panic. It was small, only marginally bigger than his shoulders. What if he got stuck in the dark, like he had when… He exhaled slowly, trying to calm himself. It didn't. The mention of love didn't help either. He was no good at loving – anyone or anything, not even himself.

'Neither do I,' she laughed, pulling his backpack from his shoulders and tossing it into the air duct opening ahead of him. 'Off you go! We've got ten minutes – fifteen tops. Then the power could come back on at any time and we'll be frozen in situ.'

'Great!' Luke muttered as he clambered in. 'At least we won't be fried.'

The duct was tight, hot and claustrophobic – frozen in situ seemed unlikely, but he still remembered the icy air that had filled the cold room when he'd been imprisoned there, so he knew it was no empty threat. Other than that, the duct reminded him of the machine he'd been fed into to map his CNS and he had to clamp his teeth into his lower lip to stop himself from panicking as Hebe followed hard on his heels, blocking any chance of retreat. He hoped to God the adrenaline shot would see him through to the other end of the duct. The sense of vital strength it had temporarily instilled in him was already waning.

'Just keep going straight ahead,' Hebe's voice boomed eerily from behind him, rebounding off the wall of the metal tube. His hands slipped against the smooth metal and his breath caught in his throat. His head torch shone a thin beam of white light ahead of him but otherwise it was darkly suffocating – the kind of suffocating being dead and underground might feel like. Shit, don't think that! His heart thumped painfully against his constricted chest and the blood roared in his head as he heaved himself along the tunnel, hand over hand, trying to gain purchase on the slippery surface, but more often than not losing his grip altogether as his sweating palm skittered and slithered. After another foot or so, he paused, laid his cheek against the damp metal and closed his eyes. It was better when you couldn't see. He felt Hebe's stick tap on the bottom of his shoes.

'Are you OK?' Hebe's whispered question contained its own edge of anxiety. It pushed him from exhausted pessimist into despairing defeatist. What if he expired here? What would she do? She would be stuck, with no way forward, and the excruciatingly difficult retreat back down the duct – if she even managed it before the power came back on.

'No,' he choked, the panic swamping over him in a searing wave. 'I'm not sure I can do this. Claustrophobia,' he managed to gasp as his cheek sealed itself to the tube and he exhaled. He opened his eyes and his head spun so he closed his eyes again. The dark overwhelmed him. Soon the cold would too. Better that way, maybe?

'It's only a little further. You can do it, Luke. Just keep going. The duct leads immediately to an outer wall, then we're free.'

'But I can't, Hebe.' He opened his eyes and then closed them again. It didn't matter whether they were open or closed, the same thing was imprinted on them. Aaron, and the drain outlet they'd found as children. Don't think about it – but it was too late. He already had. 'I just can't,' he whimpered, and let the devil take him.

Aaron's high-pitched voice urged him to not be a ninny, or a scaredy-cat. It echoed strangely from inside the outlet.

'Aaron,' I don't like this. Come out.'

'Noooooo,' Aaron's voice echoed back to him. 'You come and get meeee...'

He'd stood at the entrance, afraid to go in, afraid to leave Aaron alone in there. Aaron was the older one of them, as Aaron always liked to remind him.

'Two minutes,' he always crowed. 'That makes me the boss and you have to do what I tell you to because I'm OLDER. I'm Aaron the adventurer and you're Luke the loser.'

'Aaron?' he'd stepped into the outlet. One step. No answer. Another step. 'Aaron,' his voice had taken on a more peremptory ring now.

'Keep going, I'm just down here.' Aaron's voice seemed to be mere feet away but... he took another step, then another, until he was right inside the outlet, cold water dripping down his neck and debris and muck floating around his feet. 'Scaredy-cat, scaredy cat...'

That spurred him on. He wasn't a scaredy-cat. Aaron shouldn't have gone into the outlet. Their father was always telling them not to play around there.

'Aaron?'

This time there was no answering reply. He stopped, shivering and afraid in the middle of the tunnel. Somewhere deep inside, a low rumbling had replaced Aaron's high-pitched taunts. He froze, listening for anything that might indicate where Aaron was hiding in the dank foulness of the water outlet, beginning to edge back towards the dim orb of light that was the opening to the outlet, then something rushed past him, spinning him around so he was facing inwards again. The rumbling sound deepened, became louder, deafening... and then he was swept off his feet by the rush of the discharge that flooded the outlet with foul-smelling water and sewerage, turning him upside down and flushing him out into the river with the rest of its vomit. Luke sank deep, deep down into the river, gulping in mouthfuls of murky water and weed, until he sank down into the reedy bed, arms outstretched and fingers grasping desperately for anything with which to drag himself back up again. Far away he could hear strange murmurings and in the distance, shimmering patches of light reached out to him, but they were too far away to grasp. His fingers dug into the silty mud at the bottom of the river and he sank down, dark, down until his eyes clouded and his mouth stuck open in a silent call for help.

'Aaron...' he begged, as he watched a tiny bubble escape and swim determinedly up towards the slanting light patches, before, finally he let go.

He'd woken three days later in the hospital, to his mother's quiet sobs and his father's grim fury. Aaron hovered awkwardly in the background.

'Ah! You've come round then. Well that's something at least,' his father greeted him. He hugged Luke so hard all the air was squashed out

of him, then as abruptly, he released him and cuffed him across the tip of the head. Luke saw stars, and his brother's sheepish grin. 'You could have got both yourself and your brother killed, playing in that damned water-spout. How many times have I told you? You're lucky he pulled you out and raised the alarm or you'd be dead. Remember you owe him that for the rest of your life!'

And how Aaron had reminded him of that whenever he was in a fix.

'You owe me. Remember what Dad told you? So, if you could just...'

And he always did, because he was weak and Aaron was strong. Aaron the adventurer and Luke the loser. Maybe that was why he'd both loved and hated his twin, and when Aaron had needed his help that last time, he hadn't had it in him to give it. Turned his back on him instead – walked away because he couldn't face that dark place his brother had chosen for his last adventure – the dark tunnel they'd pulled Aaron from as he'd sat outside its entrance rocking and crying, unable to face going inside, not even one step, when he knew he should have gone inside and found Aaron, dragged him out, got him to a hospital, like Aaron had done for him all those years ago. Aaron the adventurer and Luke the loser...

'I'm sorry Aaron, I shouldn't have left you. I just couldn't do it. I should have come inside to find you – even in there – but I just couldn't... I'm so sorry. I'm so sorry. I'm so sorry...'

'It's OK, it's OK,' Hebe's hand was stroking his calf and her voice was soothing his fear. 'This isn't the water outlet and we're almost out anyway. Just a couple more feet. You can do it. I'm here and I'm not going anywhere that's not right behind you... Luke?'

He raised his head and breathed in deeply. Had he been reminiscing aloud? 'Hebe?' he asked tearfully. 'Oh God...'

'I'm here. It's all right. Just keep going.' He raised himself onto his elbows and put one hand forward, palm down. It slapped against the smooth metal of the tunnel. Now the other hand and pull. He edged forward several inches. 'That's it! That's it!' Hebe's grateful voice hovered behind him, firm and encouraging. He put hand over hand again and pulled. More inches. Yes, he could do it. He opened his eyes and focused on the beam the head torch shone in front of him. It was blending with something else, getting lighter and brighter and... Oh God, it was the exit point! 'That's it,' Hebe called excitedly from behind him. 'That's it. We're there.'

He hammered hard at the grille until it loosened, pounding with his fists until they were bruised and bloody and the grille finally hanging off. One last heave and he was slithering out of the exit hole and collapsing onto the ground below. Hebe followed seconds later, landing on top of him as the alarms around the perimeter of Crane Industries began to wail and all the lights on the building lit up.

'We made it,' Hebe gasped as they rolled together into the scrub at the side of the building.

'I'm so sorry,' Luke sobbed into the air. 'I'm so sorry…'

Chapter 22

23:12, 23rd May 2032: Luke

'I'm so sorry,' Luke mumbled again as Hebe gently disentangled herself from him and brushed away strands of grass.

'What for?' she asked, standing and holding out her hand to help him upright too.

'For being a mess?' he suggested, but took her hand nevertheless and struggled to his feet. The memory rushed over him again, and he felt ashamed. 'And for burdening you with my guilt,' he added. Monetarily they stood facing each other, and a light from the building flickered across their faces. Simultaneously they dropped to the ground again.

'Your guilt is your burden, Luke Maynard. No one shoulders it but you,' she whispered.

'I know but… Oh fuck, what must you think of me? I'm such a failure!'

'You were traumatised by an experience as a child, and it's had a life-long effect on you – but it doesn't need to. We choose what forms us, ultimately, you know. We make choices and they create actions, which make us into what we are. You don't have to remain the frightened child who was bullied by his older brother. Or the guilty adult who thinks he failed his older brother. You are neither. You are Luke Maynard, the man who – despite it not being in his own interests – helped Hebe Crane when she needed it. That makes you an entirely different person, doesn't it?'

'Well,' his knees were beginning to stiffen from crouching and the adrenaline shot was definitely wearing off, but he didn't want to leave this moment by moving. 'That's saying that future actions negate past ones.'

'No, it's saying they balance them, and one day, they overbalance them – they weigh more with their good than the past weighs with its bad. I was right, wasn't I? Aaron was your brother. Your twin?'

'Yes,' he said heavily, shifting so the pressure lifted from one knee and counterbalancing it on the other by placing a hand on the ground and leaning on it. The movement still caused him to wince though. 'He was my twin. The twin I adored and hated almost equally.'

And strangely, he felt better immediately for finally having admitted that. The twin brother who'd always been their parents' favourite, who'd always been more successful, more charming, more clever, more of everything, whilst he'd struggled to compete – and failed miserably. For fuck's sake, he'd even developed MND when Aaron had – apparently – been fine, despite sharing the same DNA.

'That's not so unusual, you know,' Hebe said, casting her eyes towards the now kaleidoscope-lit building and the hordes of black-clad figures clustering around it. 'I could cite so many examples in history and literature, but maybe not right now. Right now, I think we just need to get well away from here before those guys spot us.'

Luke twisted to look back towards the building. 'Christ, yes! Here I am being a failure again and about to get us caught.' He pulled one of the rucksacks towards him and slung it over his shoulder. 'That way, I think,' he said, trying to remember the route he'd taken in six days ago. 'There will probably be someone on security at the gate, but with a bit of luck it will be 3:16 and I should be able to get past them since I sold out alongside Green.' He grimaced. 'In case you hadn't already figured that out.'

'Oh, long ago,' Hebe told him. 'I'm not a child.'

Luke smiled at that. No, at times, Hebe was so far from being a child it terrified him, and at others… He raised himself back into a crouch and led the way out of the scrub and towards the hedge which ran along the eastern boundary of the car parking area. They merged into its overhanging foliage with surprising ease and although the whole lab complex was lit up like Oxford Street at Christmas – and seemingly as busy – surprisingly the focus didn't seem to be on the perimeter at all. Indeed, having edged along the boundary until the security post was in sight by the main entrance, it appeared to be unmanned. Maybe they didn't think the perimeter posed a risk? If 3:16 had control, they wouldn't, but what about local law enforcement? They could do without their interest too.

Luke signalled to Hebe to remain hidden, then cautiously circuited the area, approaching the security guard box from the rear. His feet crunched on the gravel, but apart from that, everywhere in this part of the grounds remained eerily quiet. Back up at the lab complex itself, there was still plenty of activity, with ant-like figures swarming around the main entrance and distant shouts as groups of black-clad figures peeled off this way and that to barked orders. 3:16 or Crane's men? He couldn't tell. They had to avoid both though. He stopped often, listening and checking for any change in the proximity of the activity. None. Still deserted here, with everyone focused on the building itself. Maybe Green had managed to draw them in without letting them all the way? Maybe Crane didn't even know he and Hebe had got out yet?

A sudden muffled disturbance overhead and a fleeting breath of air across the top of his head had him ducking, preparing for attack, only to laugh at himself a moment later as the melancholy hoot of an owl revealed his would-be assailant. The moon was high and the night sky exceptionally bright – even aside from the light pollution the lab complex was contributing to it. He breathed in deeply, absorbing the smells of the evening, the musky loam of the soil, the sweet scent of some flowering shrub announcing the plush entrance to the complex, and the edge of cordite that tinged the air here – there must have been gunfire recently then? Green had been right. They needed to get away from here as quickly as possible. Abandoning caution, he made the rest of the approach to the guard's box swiftly and without further stops. He'd left his rucksack with Hebe, carrying only the stick-baton she'd used to prod at the soles of his feet in the air duct. He raised it to shoulder height in preparation as he rounded the corner of the guard's box, but he didn't need it. It was empty. A further check all the way round the box revealed one unconscious guard, and an empty open top jeep, the keys still dangling in the ignition. This guy must have been sent to check on things and been overcome at the gate before his assailants had headed off to the lab itself.

Luke prodded him with the end of the baton. He groaned but didn't move. Still alive then and, Luke peered in closer, not a 3:16 foot soldier; a Crane Industries guard. Either way, he wasn't someone they would want to encounter or they'd end up prisoners of war to one or the other side. He crept back round to the far side of the guard box and waved to Hebe. The jeep was an unexpected bonus. Of course, it would be tracked eventually, but for now, it could at least get them as far away from here as possible so they would have time to plan what to do next. A prime-time spot on one of the news stations, denouncing what was going on at Crane Industries and introducing Hebe as the victim of it seemed the best solution to breaking the deadlock and making sure Crane couldn't simply sweep Hebe back into her prison again by claiming parental rights – but what would that mean for Hebe if she kept growing exponentially? Someone, somewhere, would want to know how and why, and then she would be back in prison again – someone else's prison, and someone else's lab rat.

Luke shook his head. Get away from here first and worry about that later. He peered round the side of the guard box to check the guard was still out cold. All he could see were the man's feet, but they were still turned toes upwards, pointing into the night sky in abject submission. Nodding to himself, he went back to the other side of the box so he could watch Hebe's progress across the open space between the boundary hedge and the guard box. She was already halfway across but hampered by having to carry both rucksacks. Damn! Another failure on his part. He should have thought about that and brought one of them with him. Above them, the whine of an engine split the quiet of the night sky, followed by the whump-whump-whump of a chopper's blades. Hebe had heard it too. She must have because she'd hesitated and was looking upwards. Luke waved frantically at her, but she was too busy looking up into the sky.

'Hebe!' he called but his voice was lost in the swelling noise. How close it was, and who it was, didn't matter. He had to go. Stumbling over his own feet, Luke ran heedlessly back out into the open and headed for Hebe. She'd started running again, but he could see the fear on her small pale face. *You are Luke Maynard, the man who – despite it not being in his own interests, helped Hebe Crane when she needed it. That makes you an entirely different person, doesn't it?*

'Fuck, yes, it does!' Luke screamed up at the sky and the predator homing in on both of them. 'Fuck MND, fuck failure, fuck everyone!'

Overhead, the thud of rotor blades had metamorphosed into a sleek black bird swooping in on them, tiny figures hanging out of the open wound in its side, yelling and waving.

'Luke, it's a…'

He almost collided with Hebe, pulling himself up at the very last moment, still ranting and cursing, but flooded with anger and intensity and adrenaline. He grabbed the heavier of the rucksacks from her and pushed her ahead of him.

'I know, but fuck it, we can outrun it. It's got to land first. There's a jeep with the keys in it just the other side of the guard's post. Just keep running, I'm right behind you.'

The chopper was circling, throwing out a storm of air currents making

Hebe's hair snake around her face like glow worms leaving light trails. She ducked down, head hunched between her shoulders and surprised Luke by leaving him standing, but not for long. As soon as she'd beaten him by five or so paces, he was after her, running harder than he'd ever run in his life, lungs aching as they fought for oxygen, legs burning as degenerated muscles were forced back into action, heart pounding until it was rattling his rib cage. They rounded the corner of the guard box together as the helicopter swung in lower and the floored guard started to come round. He raised himself groggily on one elbow as Hebe passed him.

'Hey,' he called feebly. Luke kicked him as he passed and the guard collapsed onto his back, then twisted awkwardly onto his side. Luke reached the jeep moments after Hebe, yelling at her to take the passenger's side, not the driver's seat.

'Why not?' she yelled back over the deafening whump-whump of the rotating chopper blades.

'You can't drive!'

'Wanna bet?' She turned the key in the ignition like she was twisting a blade in a body and the jeep revved angrily. 'I've read all about it and I've always wanted to do this!' she announced delightedly. The radio blasted out too. The driver must have left it on when he pulled up. Luke reached across to turn it off but was almost jolted out of his seat as Hebe lurched the jeep into a pothole and the jeep bounced sideways, then went careering off towards the side of the road. Luke abandoned the radio controls and grabbed the steering wheel instead, just managing to steady it before they bounced the other way off the grass bank siding the road. They slid to a halt, and Luke was about to demand Hebe hand over the wheel to him when his attention was once again distracted.

'Hey, stop!'

Luke twisted in his seat. The guard was on his knees behind them, pointing something at them.

'Oh shit, he's got a gun!' he screamed. 'Just floor it!'

'What?' Hebe frowned at him.

'Put your foot down – accelerate!'

The first shot whistled past them, the second clipped the edge of the windscreen, flinging chips of glass out in front of them and setting the point for a long, jagged crack to make its way across the windscreen as they shot jerkily down the road. Luke twisted in his seat again, in time to see the chopper land and the waving yelling figures he'd seen hanging from it in the air spill out onto the ground and start running towards them. They were carrying machine guns. The first hail of bullets followed within seconds.

How they missed, Luke had no idea. He was only relieved they had – somehow – made it out alive, although how long they would stay that way, was another matter, with Hebe's driving almost as dangerous as the hail of bullets that flew after them. They arrived in the nearest town twenty minutes later after a rollercoaster ride, during the course of which they'd mounted the kerb twice and run through three red lights.

'Just pull in here,' Luke gasped as he spotted an all-night supermarket car park.

'Is this your place?' Hebe asked as she manoeuvred past the entrance, narrowly missing a bollard sending customers one way into the car park, and another to exit it.

'No. And that's the last place we should go, anyway,' Luke said as they pulled haphazardly into a parking spot and lurched to a halt. 'That'll be the first place they'll look for us, but we can't stay here either. We stick out like a sore thumb. We need to find somewhere under the radar until we've decided how to get you out into the open without your father or 3:16 intervening and grabbing you back.'

'Oh,' Hebe looked surprised. She turned off the ignition and handed the keys to Luke. 'But surely they wouldn't do that?'

Luke stared at her, this strange half-child, half-woman, who'd soothed him through the most difficult of moments, enabled him to face his past and own it, do more than he'd ever thought he could do in the service of someone else, and – yes – engendered disturbingly erotic imaginings involving her too, suddenly realising how ill-equipped she was to survive in this cut-throat world she had 'escaped' to.

'You father has hidden your very existence ever since before you were born and 3:16 are the kind of extremist that would stop at nothing in the service of their beliefs, no matter how cruel or psychotic.'

He watched her eyes narrow, the pupils diminishing to a pinprick as realisation of what 'freedom' meant dawned. In front of them, the connection for one of the supermarket signs sparked and failed and the open sign buzzed and flickered. Or maybe 3:16 or the lab complex were fiddling with the grid?

'I didn't think – I just wanted to get out of there and be normal…' She bit her lip and her eyes shone in the flickering light from the 'open' sign as it buzzed on again. She was about to cry. Oh shit! He'd never been good with crying women, but surprisingly this time he found he didn't want to run away, he wanted to comfort her – reassure her. Not in a paternalistic way, in a... Oh shit! Not in that way either – in a deeper, gentler way. He patted her shoulder, then when she started crying anyway, pulled her towards him in an awkward kind of hug. They sat that way for several minutes until Luke had to admit aloud that he felt exposed and especially vulnerable sitting in a deserted car park in an open top jeep with a bullet-cracked windscreen and a girl half the county was going to be looking for shortly – if not already.

'You're right,' Hebe said, wiping her eyes on the back of her hand and pinching her nostrils to stop her nose running. She sniffed hard. 'We need to find somewhere to lie low, but where?'

Luke gnawed at his forefinger. Where would they be least obvious whilst they worked out a strategy to get Hebe's story out to the world without Hebe being sequestered away from the world again once it was? The radio was still playing but muted now. The Country and Western programme that had accompanied them most of the way here had given over to the midnight news.

'The disturbance at a local lab complex and artificial limb factory has apparently given rise to reports of gunfire according to news just coming in. The Crane Industries laboratories appear to have come under attack from an extremist group following a disturbance when the science giant was due to announce a major advance in the application and use of bio-technically engineered units to assist in the treatment of various life-diminishing diseases. Jason Crane, the CEO of Crane Industries, is said to have had to take shelter in a secure area within the lab complex whilst the extremist faction attempt to invade and destroy vital equipment. Police firearms experts have now been called to the complex, together with hostage negotiators, but in a surprise twist, it's not known whether Mr Crane is being held hostage or the intruders are! For now, police are advising to keep your distance whilst the situation is monitored, and local residents are asked to stay home and lock their doors, with free movement restricted to outside the cordoned-off area of ten miles radius only to ensure safety.'

'Swap over with me,' he said suddenly. Hebe obliged, climbing over the top of him rather than getting out and walking round to the passenger door. 'I need to teach you a thing or two about motorised travel etiquette,'

Luke said, laughing in spite of himself when they'd finally managed the swap. 'There are doors, you know?'

'Oh right, yes, but more fun this way, huh?' Hebe's expression reminded Luke of an elf or a goblin – all mischief, no malice.

'Yeah, more fun,' he agreed as he put the jeep into gear and drove them – considerably more smoothly than on their journey there – back down the road to a small house nestling in amongst row of shops and lock-up garages.

'But why are we going back closer?' Hebe asked as he swung into the lay-by in front of the buildings.

'Because this is going to be a no-go zone for a while – within their ten mile radius. No one allowed out or in, so once we're holed up here, we should be safe for a while to plan whilst we find out what is going on back there.' Luke rattled at the front door of the tiny house, then moved round to the back when he found it firmly locked. The back door wouldn't budge either, but on the step was an upturned flowerpot. He swooped on it, turning it over with a satisfied 'Aaah!' He showed Hebe what he'd uncovered. A key. 'Why people still do it, I don't know, but if there's going to be a spare key somewhere, it's under the flowerpot or a stone or whatever's by the back door.' He slipped the key into the lock and it turned easily. Pushing the door open, he gestured for Hebe to go inside. 'This is our bolt-hole for the next little while. You go inside and make the place comfy, whilst I go back to that supermarket and get us some supplies.'

'Oh, then I should come with you,' Hebe turned back and grabbed at Luke's arm.

'No, you stay here. Just me will be less noticeable, especially if they're looking for two people. You'll be fine here. Just lock the door behind me, pull all the curtains and stay quiet until I get back. OK?'

'OK,' she nodded obediently, like a small child. It was unnerving, given that she looked more like mid-twenties and only a short while ago, she'd been acting like a counsellor to him as he'd unburdened himself about Aaron. Green had been right when he said there was far more to Hebe Crane than a scientific oddity – but now wasn't the time to focus on that. He nodded back, then made his way briskly back to the jeep. As much as she didn't want him to be away from her any longer than he had to, suddenly he didn't want to be away from Hebe Crane any longer than he had to either – and it had nothing to do with anxiety.

Chapter 23

01:25, 24th May 2032: Luke

By the time Luke had returned from the all-night supermarket, there had been a further news update. He listened to it on the jeep's radio with the volume on low as he sped back through the night to the tiny house. The show broadcaster reported that people had been ringing in asking why the 3:16 Group should want to attack this particular lab, which was best known for its ground-breaking prostheses.

'...so we thought it was high time we listened to what is worrying people. Here we go... Caller Number One, you're on air. What would you like to ask about the recent reports of some kind of uprising at the Crane Industries complex?'

'Well, Ashton, "Why?", would be my first question,' the female caller asked, sounding breathless and excited. Probably her first time being on air, Luke mused as he tuned the radio for better reception. 'Surely they should be singing their praises, not trying to force entry?' she continued.

'Indeed, good point,' the radio show host intervened. 'Caller Number Two, what do you think?'

'Maybe there's more to what they're doing there than we know about?' Caller Number Two suggested, voice lowering to almost hushed.

'Indeed, an even better point,' the radio show host enthused. 'What do we know about Crane Industries – really know, that is?' he continued. 'Anyone in the know and can tell us more? If you're an employee or a client of Crane Industries – or even a business associate, what do we need to know? There's never smoke without fire, is there folks?'

He cut to a music break and Luke was tempted to turn the radio off then, but something about the focus of the show on what had been little more than a report of disruption earlier was escalating very rapidly into a point of interest, with a very finely tuned interest indeed! Why would anyone be immediately suggesting the lab did anything other than make cutting-edge prosthetic appliances when it was essentially just under fire from a bunch of religious nuts. All the previous press 3:16 had garnered had only ever described it as such; irrational extremists out to cause trouble. There was a different ring to this reporting.

The music break came to an end and Ashton – whoever he was – came back on air.

'Just bringing you up to date on the local breaking news, folks, and a strange situation that is developing at the site of one our biggest local employers, Crane Industries. To re-cap, previously we've brought you news about a group of religious protesters trying to gain access to the lab complex and sabotage the press conference announcing a new addition to its armoury in the fight against debilitating disability and chronic illness. Crane Industries is at the forefront of the field developing bio-engineered prostheses and plug-in treatments for a variety of degenerative conditions. However, in just under a week, what started as a protest appears to have escalated into a full-blown assault, with a potential hostage situation, and even reports of shots being fired. So what IS going on at Crane Industries, and what ARE these protesters so fired up about? I have Louisa Capmond here to tell us more. Louisa, I believe you are an ex-employee of Crane Industries?'

'I am Ashton,' the woman's voice had an annoying nasal twang to it. Brummie or Mancunian? He'd never been good at distinguishing those two. Mancunian, he decided. 'I used to work in the main lab complex until I was forced to leave.'

'Forced to leave? Were you sacked?' Ashton was clearly leading her. He was almost as good as one of the fashionable American talk show hosts – probably had modelled himself on them, in fact.

'Oh no, goodness, no!' Luke could tell that Miss Goody-Two-Shoes-Capmond was about to tell whoever cared to listen how principled she was and how unprincipled Crane Industries was. 'I just couldn't stay there any longer after I found out that they were experimenting with AI and people. Artificial people, just think!'

'Artificial people? You mean robots?'

'No! Artificial people. People who were people but are now made up of artificial bodies.'

'That sounds like something out of a horror film, are you sure?'

Ashton's voice was hushed and melodramatic.'

'Well, I wouldn't give up my job for nothing, would I?' Miss Goody-Two-Shoes sounded sarcastic now. 'I used to earn nearly seventy grand a year there, now I'm unemployed – just too stressed and afraid to go out after what I've seen.'

'And what have you seen, Louisa?' Ashton's voice was silkily smooth, slithering towards its predestined conclusion.

'Terrifying things. Artificially grown brains and other organs, horrific tests and transplants undertaken on the lab animals, and...' Now her voice hushed too. 'The first artificial man himself.'

'The artificial man himself? A robot-man?'

'Jason Crane.'

The station descended into static then and no amount of retuning could get it back, but Luke had heard enough. The cat was out of the bag – or about to be – and he hadn't a clue what to do about it. The only good thing about the interview with Ms Capmond was that it had been broadcast in the middle of the night when most of the local residents were asleep. And sleep was what he needed too. This was the kind of problem to solve in the morning, especially as there was pretty much nothing left of the adrenaline jab Green had given him earlier still circulating in his system. He steered the jeep quietly into the layby in front of the house and then on into one of the lock-up units next to it, which he'd managed to prise the padlock from. He unloaded the shopping and heaved it to the back door, having wedged the lock-up's door shut. It would have to do for now. Now he needed to recuperate and try to find some of that energy he was going to need for whatever they did – God help them!

Hebe was already waiting by the back door.

'Have you moved from there at all since I went?' he asked teasingly as she virtually dragged him inside. He blinked in surprise at the halo of tea lights and candles spread around the place, creating a warm but hazy glow.

'I've looked around a bit too,' she replied defensively, then giggled. 'A bit,' she emphasised. 'Only enough to make us some light in the darkness, really.' The bit turned out to be slightly more than enough, given the size of the place – one bedroom, a bathroom and a kitchen-diner. It was dusty and had an air of the forlorn to it, all faded previous decade style décor and furnishings, a stained washbasin in the bathroom, thick with limescale where the tap had been dripping – probably non-stop

– for years, and an antiquated bath, no shower. The kitchen area was little better, but it did at least contain some crockery and pots and pans in need of a wash, and a gas cooker that appeared to still be connected. 'No electricity, though,' Hebe commented. 'Hence the candles. Lucky they left some matches, whoever they were, and Uncle Matthew packed us some torches in the rucksacks. Medicine too – for you, I think.' She showed him the ampules and some packaged hypodermics. 'Adrenaline?' she asked as he examined them.

'For what it's worth,' he agreed. 'Hebe…'

'I know,' she put her hand on his shoulder. 'You are ill, dying. Stop reminding me please. Come on, I'm starving. Is there anything to eat without heating it up?' Luke dumped the bags of provisions he'd collected from the supermarket on the dusty kitchen table and spread them out. Bread, assorted tins – all edible cold – coffee, water, cheese. 'Hmm,' she mused. 'Maybe I ought to do the shopping next time.' She opened the bread and hacked some chunks of cheese from the wedge and started to munch on it. Luke grinned and followed suit, wondering whether to tell her about the radio report. He decided against it by the second mouthful. No point spending all night worrying about something they could do little about. Time enough tomorrow to figure out a plan – and maybe there would have been more developments by then too.

Hebe had found some blankets in a cupboard in the bedroom and they spread them across the bed. They were dog-eared and moth-eaten, and to be honest, it was a warm night so they weren't really necessary, but they wriggled under them anyway, having extinguished all but one of the candles.

'Who lived here, do you think?' Hebe asked him as she moved closer.

'I don't know. Not many, I don't suppose. There's not enough room to swing a cat.' Luke backed away enough to put several inches between them. His thoughts were confused enough without the added disturbance of a warm female body lying too close.

'Why would you want to swing a cat?' Hebe asked sleepily.

'You wouldn't. It's an expression,' he laughed, but she was already asleep. Luke lay awake for a while, listening for the slightest noise outside. There were none other than the far-off rustle of the trees on the other side of the road and the occasional sound of an owl hooting, out hunting prey. Prey: that's what they were. He brushed away a strand of Hebe's downy blonde hair as it tickled his chin. And Green was right, she was barely more than a child, for all her bravado – except… He shook his head and closed his eyes to shut out the dark and fell asleep with her head wedged under his chin, waking, panicky and aching to an empty space in the bed. Immediately on the alert, he jumped up, throwing off the musty blanket that was half-covering him and peering around him. Sunlight was streaming through the window where the curtain had parted, and a thin stream of smoke was still rising into the air from where the candle they had left alight last night had recently been snuffed out. Shit! Where was she? She hadn't gone outside, had she? Ignoring the stiffness in his limbs and the ache in his back, he flung himself from the bed and almost fell down the stairs to find Hebe pouring water from an old saucepan into two chipped mugs. Simultaneous with it, the intense aroma of freshly brewed coffee made his senses tingle. She paused and twitched the curtain at the kitchen window, moving closer to peer outside. Despite her now adult appearance, she reminded him of a child, faced with Father Christmas for the first time.

He watched for a moment longer then couldn't help inserting himself into her moment. 'Penny for them?'

'Oh,' she breathed – no louder than a sigh, turning and staring at him. 'It's black, I'm afraid. You didn't bring milk, but then we don't have a working fridge so milk would have gone off anyway, so good call there…' She was gabbling and for a moment he didn't understand why until he realised too late that he was semi-erect from one of those embarrassing morning-glory awakenings, and even through his jeans it was obvious.

'Oh, I'm sorry,' he turned away from her and tried to control his body. This was just a physical reaction to waking up, but nevertheless, he couldn't deny she did things to him that he couldn't explain. He saw her as a child, and yet she wasn't. He responded to her as a woman and yet she wasn't.

'It's OK,' she said softly from behind him. 'It's only natural.'

'But somewhat embarrassing – and inappropriate,' he countered, but her hand was on his shoulder, gently turning him to face her.

'I don't mind, Luke. And it's not inappropriate. Not between a man and a woman.'

It was then that he realised it. She looked older than yesterday.

'I…' he hesitated. What did he say? Have you aged more? Do you know you must be older than twenty by now and yet you've never aged beyond that before? 'I'm a fool,' he said in the end. 'Well, what else could I be? I'm a man.'

'Have some coffee,' she replied, handing him one of the mugs. 'Be careful though, it's hot,' but that came too late too. He'd already burnt his lip and tongue. 'Let me see,' she insisted, pulling his protective hand away from his mouth. He gave in and she touched his lip with her fingertips. Immediately the pain was gone.

'What did you do?' Luke dabbed at his lip with his own fingertips, then touched them to his tongue. No pain.

'What I do,' she smiled, hesitating, then continuing in a rush, 'I haven't really shown you what I do, have I?'

'What do you do?' he asked, touching his lip in wonder again. She pulled one of the chairs out from under the table and sat on it, cradling her coffee in two hands.

'I don't know really. It depends – on what needs doing. If you need healing, I heal. If you need understanding, I know. If you need information, I can tell you it. Ask me something.'

'Like what?'

'Well, like what is the weather going to be like in ten minutes' time.'

'What's the weather going to be like in ten minutes' time?' he asked obediently, although he could probably answer that one for himself. Outside it was already looking like it was going to be a glorious early summer's day.

'It's going to rain. A hailstorm in fact. A freak one.'

'Right,' he laughed. 'I see what this is. You're teasing me to lighten the atmosphere.'

'No, really, there's going to be a freak hailstorm in ten minutes' time. I can feel it. I can feel air movement, air pressure, whatever it is – I can feel it. Like I can feel how the grass feels.'

'OK,' Luke nodded and sat down with her. He pulled the coffee mug towards him again and sipped more carefully this time. 'Anything else?'

'I don't know yet. Probably. Those are just the things I know about. Although, the people who lived here – remember I asked you about them last night? Well, I know who they were now too. An old couple, who wouldn't move out when they wanted to widen the road. They stayed here until they couldn't stay any longer.'

'How do you know that? Have you found some of their paperwork?'

'No, I just feel it now I've had some sleep and am refreshed. I can feel their determination – and their sadness.' Luke put his coffee cup down and studied her, watching the way her mouth turned down at the corners as she described what the old couple's sadness must have been like, and the light in her eyes as she described their oneness of purpose despite their age and disabilities. She stopped. She must have realised he was watching her closely and she touched her hair, adding, 'I must look a fright too – untidy hair, and all that. I'll have to find a mirror. Uncle Matthew put a brush in my rucksack, but no mirror. I wonder why? He knows I like to check what I look like because it helps me place where I am in the Revolution.'

'The Revolution?'

'Growth and regression cycle. It's what I call it – a Revolution.'

'Oh, right. Well, you look fine so I shouldn't worry about that too much.' Luke pointedly looked away from her so she couldn't see the nervous tic that had started up under his eye at the mention of her metabolic process. She couldn't know then… 'Anyway,' he began, then stopped in amazement. Hebe had pulled the curtains overlooking the rear of the house so he had a clear view of the yard and the fields beyond. Outside the sun was rapidly being obliterated by burgeoning storm clouds, sweeping across the hitherto clear azure sky. Within minutes, they'd ripped apart and were pelting down hailstones that bounced and flew in all directions as the yard filled with puddles and the corn in the fields bent under the impact. 'Bloody hell!' he exclaimed, looking at his watch. Exactly ten minutes had passed since Hebe had announced the impending hailstorm.

'No,' she giggled. 'And I don't walk on water either.' He stared at her, shocked by her flippancy even though he wasn't religious himself. He assumed Green must have told her something of his own religious beliefs – or maybe he hadn't? Somehow, Luke suspected there were things Green kept to himself too. 'Sorry,' she grinned engagingly at him. 'That's one of my father's jokes,' she explained. 'His initials are JC, so he's always making jokes like that. Uncle Matthew says he's blasphemous, but I don't think he gets too upset about it, really. He knows what my father is like, you see.'

'Oh…' Luke couldn't quite understand how Hebe could so obviously seem to love her father, despite what he'd done to her. 'You love your father, don't you?' he asked after a while.'

'Of course,' Hebe seemed surprised by the question. 'Why wouldn't I?'

'Because of what he's done to you?'

'Enabled me to progress?'

'And put you though these… Revolutions… and hidden you away ever since you were born, with no one else for company.'

'But I have – I've had him and Uncle Matthew – and Andrea, although Andrea doesn't have much to say. She's a deaf mute, you see. But she cared.'

'Hardly a normal childhood, though – or normal parental treatment; love...' he bit his lip. He hadn't meant to say love. He could hardly claim to have known normal parental love either…

'But what is love, Luke? It's different from and for everyone, isn't it? How my father loves me is different to the way your parents love you…'

'Loved,' he interrupted. 'And actually, maybe it's not that different. Their focus was more on Aaron than me, like your father's is more on scientific breakthrough than your welfare.'

'Then you know what I said is true. You can't define or dictate what love should be. It is simply what someone else gives you – can give you, depending on what and who they are. My father has given me the opportunity to extend myself in ways that wouldn't have been possible under other circumstances – and he did it despite himself, despite never wanting to be responsible for a child. That's his kind of love.'

Luke sat back in the rickety wheel-back chair and thought about that, the struts of the chair digging into his back as determinedly as Hebe's words dug into his soul, and his understanding of his parents' love for him. Perhaps they *had* loved him, in their way – a less blinded, irrational love than they'd given Aaron; one that saw his failings and merely accepted them. For Aaron, falling from his pedestal when he became a junkie had meant falling from their esteem in a way that never allowed for a way back. They'd turned their back on Luke even more firmly than Luke had when he'd been too afraid to enter the tunnel to find Aaron when he'd overdosed. He shook himself free of the memory to see Hebe now studying him with the same downturned mouth as she'd had when thinking about the old couple. With amazement, he realised she could feel his sadness too.

'Maybe we'd better explore a bit more of what you can do,' Luke replied to change the tone. 'It might be important.'

'OK. After breakfast, though,' she agreed, getting up to put their coffee mugs in the sink and rummage in the provisions bag. 'You got eggs. I could make an omelette since we seem to still have gas?'

The rest of the day passed with them playing *what can Hebe do*, as if it was a game. Her piece de resistance was the bird, half-drowned in the hailstorm, and lying lifeless in a puddle just outside the back door, which she swooped on to rescue when the storm finally passed over.

'Poor thing,' she exclaimed, clutching it to her so it created a dark wet patch on her tee shirt. The strange musty smell that always followed heavy rain on hot tarmac pervaded the tiny kitchen through the open back door. Luke would remember that for the rest of his life as the smell that marked a turning in it.

'It's no good, Hebe,' he said, trying to take the tiny lifeless body from her as tears poured down her face in mourning for it. 'It's gone. I'll find somewhere to bury it later when it's dark and we're not so exposed.' The tiny bird's feathers stuck to her fingers as she closed them around it.

'No, it's not. It's only waiting.'

'Waiting?' Luke shook his head. 'Hebe…'

'See?' she said, opening her fingers to reveal the now alert and nervous bird, beady eyes checking for danger, even as it spread its wings and fluttered out of her hands and away into the, once more, blue sky.

'But…' Luke stared after the bird until he could no longer see it. 'It was dead. I'm sure it was dead.' He turned to stare at Hebe. 'It *was* dead, wasn't it? But you…'

'It's what I do, whatever needs to be done.'

'So could you…'

'Heal you?' she asked. 'I don't know. I could try. It depends if it's what needs to be done.' She took Luke's hands in hers, enclosing them as she had the bird, staring deep into his eyes. He stared back, studying the complex patterns whirling in her blue-grey irises, scrutinising the contours and nuances of her face, the vulnerable violet-blue skin under her eyes, the curve and swell of her cheek as it flowed from cheekbone to lip to chin. He sighed. Whatever it was he felt for her, it was unbelievably sweet, gentle, kind, even as it was passionate and intense. If his hands hadn't been captured inside hers, he would have gently traced that sweet curve, caressed that downy cheek, traced the line that had deepened, even since first thing that morning. 'I'm sorry,' she said eventually. The line had deepened even as he'd watched her, trying so desperately to heal him. 'I don't seem to be able to do it right now.'

'It's OK,' he assured her, but he could see she was upset.

'But I should have been able to,' she exclaimed. 'I could feel it – the disruption in you – but I couldn't reach it. It was like it was locked away from me.'

'Well, like you said,' he replied lightly, 'maybe it wasn't what needed to be done for me right now.'

'How could healing you not be the thing that needed to be done for you?' she demanded.

He leaned forward and gently kissed her forehead. 'Healing isn't always outward,' he said. 'Or obvious.'

It had been not that long after he'd been diagnosed, nearly five years ago. A night of hitting the town to drown his sorrows had ended in him wallowing in them – and his own vomit – so drunk he'd been officially diagnosed with alcohol poisoning and a broken leg, having spent days on a drip after having his stomach pumped. Aaron had died only weeks earlier too. He'd never been so low before or since. For a while, the nights had been full of strange dreams and unspoken fears. At one stage he could have sworn Aaron had been sitting by his bedside, but a younger, less brash Aaron – not like Aaron at all; more like his own self but with the vigour and confidence his brother had always had, and he'd always strived for.

They told him later, when he'd come round and had managed to keep a bowl of porridge down – his first solid food in days – that he'd been delirious most of the time, ranting about angels and robotic enemies.

'Are you a sci-fi lover?' one little nurse asked him as she gave him a bed bath, without any apparent sense of embarrassment whilst he cringed with shame at needing such help.

'Why?' he'd asked temporarily intrigued away from his acute discomfort by the randomness of the question. Outside it was another cold grey morning in the rest of his cold, grey life. The room was cold and grey too – clinical white walls with grey soft furnishings, mop-washed floors that smelt of old, wet dog, overlaid with disinfectant, and a hard charcoal-grey bedside chair he was supposed to spend at least half the day in as he convalesced and got mobile again.

'Well, your dreams the other night would have made a best-selling movie, by all accounts. People injecting you to stop you turning into a zombie-thing, whilst others were chasing you and trying to turn you into a machine, and one – just one – was trying to save you by turning you into a bird. My dreams are never half as exciting!'

Nor premonitory, I'd wager, Luke mused now. Strange the memory came back so vividly now – or maybe not strange since those things have happened to me now – 3:16 and their miracle meds that would kill him when they ran out, Jason Crane and his ForEver Project and Hebe healing birds – but not him. If only he could remember the rest of the dream that the little nurse recounted to him. The only other part he could remember now was the woman, dressed as a nurse, who entered his dream and awoke him from it.

She'd stroked his temples, just like Hebe had in the morgue, and spoken to him about life and living, not death and dying. Slowly the despair and the pain had dulled and then disappeared, leaving him determined to fight instead. She'd been so real, so solid, then, he'd asked his counsellor which nurse had checked in on him the night before because he wanted to thank her for getting his head straight, but the counsellor had been bemused.

'But we put you on suicide watch. You were so drugged I didn't even expect to find you awake today. There's no way you could have been awake enough to have noticed anyone checking on you.'

But he had, and the woman had looked identical to Elise Crane. He'd looked in the mirror and seen himself with her – the mirror that was in the wall opposite and next to it the calendar that had announced exactly which day she'd healed the inner man.

The rest of the day passed without more drama, but by the end of it, Luke realised he was falling deeply and irrevocably in love with this strange but beautiful young woman. The realisation terrified and grieved him. At least it was only on his part. When he died, her pain would only be for the loss of one she felt she should have been able to save.

And she's still only really a kid, he told himself. A kid who had artificially aged – and yet… The memory of the woman in the hospital brought with it another realisation – how Hebe was able to tune into the weather, the rhythm of life and death, and the circle of time as it went forwards and backwards. Green had already told him what that was in as many words. She was attuned. By making her grow, age, regress and grow and age again, Crane had so honed Hebe's biological receptibility that she was in tune with not just herself but the very molecules and atoms around her that made up all things. When she said she could feel the grass, she really could. She could literally 'feel' what was going on around her and correct imbalances using her own biological responses – much as the nanites circulating in Crane's venous system repaired and honed his body and its performance. So what else could Hebe do – beyond being attuned to the universe at an atomic level? That visit he remembered but the counsellor had dismissed as impossible had indeed been impossible – then. But then, so was Hebe. Hebe was in the future, as was the date that had been on that calendar if it was a memory of a time past: 1st June 2032.

Chapter 24

08:45, 31st May 2032: Hebe

We've been here a week now and whilst we're confined to this tiny space, with only Luke venturing out occasionally to the lock-up to check that the jeep's engine will still turn over if we need to make a quick getaway, oddly, it's not felt claustrophobic. Maybe it's been easier for me because I'm used to being confined to the lab complex, but Luke hasn't appeared unhappy either; quite the reverse… That first day I was surprised, and then oddly gratified by his physical reaction to me. It had never happened before, even the couple of occasions when I'd been close to my ageing limit. Maybe it was because I have now exceeded my oldest age in the cycle – and maintained it? The psyche is a complex system, made up of ingrained beliefs, experiences and principles. My guess is that having feelings for someone years younger than himself would seem wholly inappropriate for Luke, whereas someone closer to his own age… How old am I now then? Luke must be in his mid-thirties. That set me looking for a mirror again, but I couldn't find one anywhere – not in the mouldering bathroom, or inside any of the faded brocade-lined drawers of the previous inhabitant's dressing table or chest of drawers. No mirror-like surface either, I discovered as the days passed – but Luke continued to look at me in exactly the same way, softly, with a tilted half-smile. I found myself smiling back in the same way – even before I tried to heal him and failed – and inside me, this buzz in my chest. When he touched me, the buzz turned to molten lava, and a raging desire for him to touch me again. I'd find any reason to be close, so close we had to touch, in the days that followed, and apart from the times he creeps out to the lock-up, insisting I stay hidden indoors, we are so close we are almost touching all the time. Is this what falling in love is? This all-consuming desire to be close, closer, so close there's not even a hair's breadth between you and one other person? The heady rush whenever you look them? The feeling that, even though you could be wearing leaden boots, you are still floating a good inch above ground just because of them?

'Penny for them?'

I turned away from the window where I'd been peering out through a small chink in the curtains. The fields seemed to stretch for miles. I'd never seen anything from such a distance – with such distance before.

'Oh,' I laughed, struggling to drag myself away from that far-away vista that seemed to pull me into it – even through a chink in a curtain in a deserted house. What I saw in Luke's face took me aback. Longing. What did he see in mine? The same? The sudden rush of sensations took my breath away, anyway, and I said the first thing that came into my head. 'Black, I'm afraid. You didn't bring milk, but then we don't have a working fridge so milk would have gone off anyway, so good call there…'

The words just kept tumbling out of my mouth – random, meaningless, stupid and he just kept staring at me, drinking me in and crazily, I wanted him to come over to me, wrap his arms around me and absorb me into himself. Maybe I communicated all of that to him because suddenly his expression changed to embarrassment, and he turned away.

'Oh, I'm sorry,' his hands flew down to his crotch but not before I saw what I then realised was the source of his embarrassment. Not me, but his reaction to me – and the blood sang like a descant in my head. The words stopped tumbling out of my mouth then and ordered themselves.

'It's OK,' I found myself saying. 'It's only natural.'

'It's inappropriate,' he replied, head bowing with what could only be shame. Oh don't be ashamed, be amazed – and delighted and thankful that something like this has happened to us – to me, who thought she'd never know the meaning of love or desire, locked away in my ivory tower, ageing and regressing for all eternity – a sleeping beauty destined never to be awoken with a kiss until you came along.

It just seemed to flow naturally after that. I knew what to do as if I'd been doing it for years.

'I don't mind, Luke. And it's not inappropriate.' I went across to him and placed my hand on his shoulder. He turned and looked deep into my eyes, devoured my face, bored into my brain.

'I…' he hesitated. 'I'm a fool,' he continued, that half-tilted smile taking over his mouth. 'Well, what else could I be? I'm a man.'

I wasn't sure then. Was this still his embarrassment or was it rejection?

'Have some coffee,' I said, to mark time, handing him one of the mugs. He grabbed it from me and immediately put it to his lips. 'Be careful though, it's hot,' but I was too late. He was already wincing and covering his mouth. 'Let me see,' I took his hand from his mouth and touched the burn – felt it leave him and enter me. I felt the rest of his emotions then too, tumbling over each other in their confusion – responsibility, desire, caution, affection, hope and fear.

'What did you do?' he dabbled his fingers against his lips, staring at me in wonder, as he did so, all those jumbled feelings crystallised into one.

'What I do,' I smiled. 'I haven't really shown you what I do, have I?'

I had to show Luke Maynard who I really was, and then he could decide for himself whether what he felt was gratitude or love. So I let him in – all the way in.

I wish now I'd asked Uncle Matthew to explain what falling in love meant so I could have been more prepared. Not for how wonderful it might feel, but how terrible. When I look at Luke now, and the way the creases around his eyes and mouth have deepened into pain lines, and the way his movements are less fluid, more tense each day, I know the MND is progressing and I understand what some writer I read what feels like years ago, meant by the pleasure-pain principle. I feel overwhelming, crazy, ridiculous delight just being with Luke, simultaneous with paralysing mind-numbing fear at the thought of losing him. But I can't heal him. What I do hasn't been earmarked for him and I know one day – soon – I will have to face that pain and embrace it for my own. In a matter of days, I have found and am about to lose the one I love – and it's my fault. I denied him the chance of life – a cure – using the ForEver Project process. Now I wonder if I was wrong. Is this how my father feels about my mother? Would it be so wrong for him to try to save her the way I wish I could save Luke? I don't know. Being an adult is hard. Doing the right thing as an adult is even harder. In the meantime, I would dearly love to find something – anything – that I can see myself in, so I can see what it is Luke sees when he looks at me. I won't have that loving look from him for much longer, but maybe I can store it away in my memory to treasure for the rest of my life nevertheless.

Chapter 25

11:44, 31st May 2032: Luke

He'd used the last of the adrenaline shots Green had put in the bag earlier and for the moment he didn't feel too bad. It wouldn't last though, so it was best to do the lock-up-radio run as soon as possible. Luke exited the back door after following his usual routine – check through the windows first, upstairs and in the kitchen. Look for signs of movement, visitations of any kind, and vehicular or human activity or presence. Next, plan the route from back door to lock-up, noting potential hazards along the way. Crazy for a journey of a mere ten metres, but essential. If Crane or 3:16 had any suspicion they were here, his appearance would seal their fate within seconds. He'd reported only that first news report to Hebe – after a deal of soul-searching – and then only because she'd seemed to want to try moving on from the tiny house.

'Shouldn't we try to put some distance between us and the lab now?' she'd asked on the fourth day of their confinement. By then the food stores were running low and Luke had been wondering the same thing himself. They'd started rationing what they ate to one meal a day, resting and talking in between to pass the time. Hebe's knowledge range amazed – and completely surpassed – Luke's, but so did her naivety in other areas. They'd talked a lot about the phenomena of love – without ever admitting to each other that it was what they felt for each other – but admission hardly seemed necessary any longer. It was inherent in every look, touch and comment that passed between them, and had been since that first day. Added to that, Luke also felt increasingly responsible for Hebe and what he instinctively felt must be her purpose. He'd never thought of anyone having a purpose before, other than in terms of their job, or their family obligations, but where Hebe was concerned, it was different. The feeling had been growing since she'd shown him what she could do. Oh, of course he'd been told about it whilst they'd still been in the lab complex but being told and seeing with your own eyes was quite different. For that reason, too, he'd pondered whether they should try to move on. He was back on that track today, day seven since their escape, and the reason for this latest trip to the lock-up to check on the jeep – not to make sure the engine still turned over, as he told Hebe – but to tune in to the latest news and assess what to do next.

Over the last few days, there had been developments – worrying developments. There had seemed to have been stalemate at the Crane Industries complex, with the police standing off, 3:16 battling to invade and Crane battling to evade. Luke had wondered why Crane had lain so low for so long – and also how he'd managed to keep the wolf, in the form of 3:16, from the door given their determination and superior numbers. Yesterday everything had changed, with perhaps an explanation for both.

'Jason Crane, CEO of Crane Industries, at the centre of a week-long assault by the environmentalist group known as 3:16, has emerged from the lab complex, claiming the environmentalist group are 'terrorists' who have kidnapped one of his 'people'. It is not known as yet who the victim is, nor whether 3:16 will repudiate the claim, but Mr Crane,flanked by a number of security personnel, and the man reputed to be his second in command, Matthew Green, has now taken up residence in the five-star Lombardy Hotel in the centre of town. The lab complex appears to have been taken over by the environmentalist group, but the police are remaining at a stand-off, following the kidnapping claim. It is speculated that they will now be attempting some form of hostage negotiation before moving in. More in our late evening bulletin.'

He hadn't been able to make an excuse to slip out to hear the late-night bulletin, but as things now seemed to be moving fast, he'd had to get out to listen to the midday one. Hebe hadn't quibbled over his eagerness to check on the jeep again, but her eyes had followed his every move out the door and to the first hiding place. He could feel them boring into his back, questioning, wondering. He felt bad lying to her – no, not lying, just being economical with the truth – on two counts – but he was doing it for her. That's what he told himself, anyway, as he ducked low behind the water butt and scoped the far fields for sign of any movement. It was a joy to breathe in the fresh air out here, even if it was tinged with the angst of whether he was being watched. Luke shifted his weight onto his left leg and peered round the same side of the water butt to check the side of the tiny house. All seemed quiet. He rubbed his knee as he grimaced at the dull ache from the pressure of squatting and balancing on creaking knee joints, suffering from the now rapid advance of MND. At least he had the answer now to whether his cognitive abilities were going to be compromised too. He didn't need any of Crane's scanner results to tell him he was still fully functioning mentally, albeit seeing everything to do with Hebe through rose-coloured glasses.

After a tense pause, he judged all was quiet enough to risk moving across to the next waypoint – an abandoned wheelbarrow, loaded with oil canisters. Luke had already made a mental note that they potentially had a dual purpose – hiding place and flashpoint if they were suddenly ambushed. The old flip-top lighter he'd found in one of the dusty kitchen drawers nestled comfortingly in his trouser pocket should the need come to create a diversion in order to get Hebe out of the house and both of them into the lock-up and the jeep. Earlier investigation had confirmed that there were still enough dregs in most of the cans to create quite a blaze, but Luke hoped that wouldn't be necessary. Hebe was primed if it was though. She knew to just run for the lock-up and get into the jeep, disregarding whatever he was doing, and if necessary, ram the accelerator to the floor like she had before, and drive, whether he was in the jeep with her or not.

Luke crept forward, still crouching, and painfully made his way to the wheelbarrow. Still no sound but the sweetness of birdsong and the gentle rustle of a light spring breeze in the small copse beyond the lock-up. The air felt sharper though, like there were many ears listening to it. Luke tensed and waited again. If there was no movement after three minutes, he'd make it to the last waypoint. From where he was crouching, behind the highest point of the pile of oil cans in the wheelbarrow, the last waypoint looked terribly exposed today – or maybe that was just his state of mind, knowing there must have been developments he had yet to hear about. Things could have changed dramatically since yesterday. Maybe he should have come clean with Hebe then, but she'd looked so demoralised, he could bring himself to give her bad news to weigh her down. In just a week, she'd aged from the twenty-something who'd prodded his soles with her baton to keep him moving through the air duct, to a woman heading for her mid-thirties. Indeed, she was rapidly becoming the woman who'd saved him from himself in that dream of the future; almost the duplicate of her own mother. He should have admitted that to her too, not hidden every reflective surface in the tiny house. Fear, that was what did it. Fear of acknowledging what was happening to both of them, ageing, illness and death. He breathed out heavily as that fear caught him and sent shivers of panic down his spine. Don't lose it now, don't lose it now, he chastised himself. Just get to the fucking jeep and tune in. You can face the worst of it then.

Four minutes had gone by now – longer than he usually waited, and no movement, no sound, no alarm. Move!

Luke took to his heels and ran, ears ringing from the effort as his heart pumped blood through his veins and into his unwilling legs. Don't even stop at the waypoint. Just get to that fucking jeep! Pinpricks of fear stabbed at the back of his neck and his armpits as he ran, limbs lolloping in all directions, head aimed at the entrance to the lockdown like a missile gone rogue. He made it there in record time, spraying gravel and dust into the air as he skidded to a shambling halt by the door. *Any moment now, any moment...* His breath sobbed from him and his legs burned with exquisite agony as he wrenched the door open and flung himself inside.

Silence.

No shouts, no gunshot, no revving vehicles. Nothing.

The coast had been clear after all, and he was losing what little nerve he'd had.

Slowly, he dragged himself from the floor, dusting off his knees and elbows, catching his breath and calming his panic. From his vantage point by the door he could see the kitchen curtain twitch. Hebe had been watching – probably wondering at his haste and bypassing the last waypoint. Had she worked out that he'd lost it? Or was she anticipating it was because of an unseen threat about to rain down on them. He waved to her, a reassuring gesture he hoped, then closed the lock-up door. Eleven fifty-six. It had taken him twelve minutes to get to here, even with two stops totalling nine minutes. Three minutes at top speed – for him – to run from the back door to the lock-up. Worth knowing.

The air in the lock-up was dank and laced with petrol. The atmosphere was gloomy, lit only by a small skylight at the far end of the lock-up – barely more than a torch beam given the lock-up's size. The jeep sat in the middle, facing the double doors out. Luke had entered via the side door. The double doors were unlocked, ready to be rammed open if needed. He'd pondered long and hard over whether to lock them, but decided against it in the end since they should be on high enough alert to notice if anyone was snooping around, and locking them would mean wasting valuable time unlocking them if they needed to get away fast. Picking his way through the grey light, he slipped into the driver's seat of the jeep and turned the ignition. The jeep's engine revved briefly, then idled in a low throaty growl. The radio kicked in a moment later, with the midday beeps. Just in time.

'Good afternoon to you, on the thirty-first of May, twenty-thirty-two. News reports have now confirmed that Jason Crane, the CEO of the beleaguered Crane Industries lab complex, has taken up residence at the Lombardy Hotel in Heverton. It is the first time he has been seen in public, other than at rarely held press conferences to announce the company's latest biotech advances, for nearly four years.

The move comes as he flees the company's lab complex in the same town, following an armed assault on it by the hard-core environmentalist group, 3:16, and claims that the group has taken at least one of Crane Industries personnel hostage. The group says it is fighting for the future since they have proof that Mr Crane intends releasing a new biotech unit into the world which will have dangerous and far-reaching effects on everyone, including on our freedoms and rights as individuals.'

So the fight between the future and the past had indeed come out into the open… and Luke could guess what that biotech unit might be – but did that mean Crane himself was coming out, or had Crane been spending the last week converting someone else into what he'd intended for Luke; a captured one of the 3:16s maybe?

'Bloody hell,' he gasped as the idea took hold. Yes, what if… Behind him the door creaked. He jumped and swivelled out of the jeep, twisting his ankle as he did so. 'Fuck!' he exclaimed, scanning the gloom for the visitor. He'd been right to be panicked. In the corner of the lock-up, deep into the shadows, something moved. He reached into the glove compartment and located the gun he'd found there the first time he'd sneaked out to listen to the radio on the pretence of checking the jeep over. He had checked the jeep over that time, and found the gun. No bullets though. It was threat, not a promise. Unaffected, the radio broadcast continued as Luke hobbled round to the front of the jeep, squinting to see in the gloom. 'Come out!' He ordered. 'I've got a gun.'

'The group claim that the units Crane Industries are about to release into the local community are robots. An eyewitness claims that they've seen

one of these entities be decapitated and reattach its head within seconds…'

'It's me, Luke. Don't shoot – and where the hell did you get that gun from anyway?'

'Hebe! What are you doing out here?'

'The same as you, it seems,' she replied wryly, steeping out from the shadows and coming to stand in what little light there was by the jeep.

'Oh, shit!'

'Hush,' Hebe motioned Luke to be silent. 'Listen…'

'…some local residents have formed themselves into vigilante groups and are vowing to hunt down the robots.

'"We're 'avin no zombie apocalypse here!" the interviewee's accent was broad and rough. "We'll blow 'em to smithereens first."'

'Would that do it?' Luke asked Hebe.

'Hush!'

'The police are still urging residents to remain in their homes and under no circumstances to take on either members of the 3:16 Group, or anything else they deem to be a threat, but tempers are running high in Heverton and confidence in the police is running short after they failed to quash the disturbance before it mutated into a potential lynch mo—'

The radio shut off unexpectedly, raging interference and white noise at them in place of the broadcaster's measured BBC tone.

'Oh, my God! My father…' Hebe grabbed Luke's arms. 'They'll kill him!'

'I doubt it,' Luke couldn't help the irony in his voice, despite Hebe's anxiety. 'He was the one who was decapitated and reattached himself, remember – although who the hell told them that, God knows!'

'Uncle Matthew. It would have to be Uncle Matthew. There was only him – apart from us there…' she paused, and her eyes narrowed to almond shape.

'No, I didn't – haven't!' Luke told her, angrily. 'Not before we left there and not since we got out.'

'Then what have you been doing in here all those times? Not just checking the engine will turn over…'

She was standing way too close to the jeep's wing mirrors. In fact, Luke was infinitely more concerned about that than being accused of selling out her father. He was desperately racking his brains for a way to manoeuvre her away from the wing mirror when the radio sputtered back into life.

'This is group 3:16. We would like to correct the inaccurate news reports that have been broadcast recently...'

Hebe clutched at Luke's arms and her nails dug into his skin through his thin shirt sleeves.

'...we have been accused of kidnapping – taking hostages – but we have not. We have been accused of inciting the local community to violence – to vigilante activity. We have not. We have been accused of breaking into the Crane Industries lab complex and terrorising its incumbents. We have not. We made a peaceful entry into the complex, at the behest of one of its employees. We isolated and secured various bio-engineered units to ensure no one was harmed by malicious activity using them. We provided free and safe passage out of the facility for Jason Crane and his employees and will continue to provide a safe haven for any that come to us for that. However, what you haven't been told is the truth behind Crane Industries.'

'I think now it IS time for us to get away from here,' Luke inserted into the few seconds the 3:16 propagandist took to take a breath before continuing. He placed his own hands onto Hebe's arms so they stood facing each other in the same pose a pair of barn dancers might have taken when about to dance a reel together. He used it to manoeuvre her away from the wing mirror and towards the door.

'But…' she objected.

'Things are about to get nasty,' he interrupted her objection.

'...for the last almost four years, Crane Industries has been actively developing a new form of biotech unit. Not a robot, but a hybrid biotech unit fused with human, or biologically derived parts. The witness report of a unit having its head detached and reattached is fact. These units aren't robots, they aren't humans, they are monstrous hybrids formed out of flesh and blood and AI, incredibly strong, able to repair and renew

indefinitely and totally under the control of Crane Industries. How these human parts have been harvested, we can only dread, but we are but a breath away from a world populated by something even worse than a batch of zombies. At least zombies can be killed by chopping off their heads…'

'Oh my God, my father isn't a zombie!'

'But to most of the population, he will be the nearest thing to Frankenstein or his monster, Hebe. Just listen to what they're saying. Doesn't he sound dangerous?'

'But my father isn't dangerous. Not like that, anyway.'

'Then why were you so desperate to get away from him – to save your mother from the ForEver Project, and convince me not to go through with it?'

'But worse still, the man behind all of this – Jason Crane – is the prototype for this unit. And not only is he the prototype, but he has fathered a child – a true hybrid, with powers beyond the abnormal and she is the biggest danger of all to humankind. We will crush Jason Crane and the army of human automatons he has built for himself, and you are all invited to join with us to do this, but where we need your help most is in finding Jason Crane's daughter. Until she is safely in confinement, we cannot guarantee anyone's – or even the world's – safety. Imagine a fusion of genius with the most sophisticated AI, unbounded by the normal rules of nature; someone who can read the very biometrics of the world, manipulate time, and even give or take life at will and you have Hebe Crane…'

'Oh shit! Where is this all coming from?' Luke exploded.

'Uncle Matthew,' Hebe said sadly. 'I should have understood why he sent me ahead but stayed himself. He's found out. Now they've found out.'

'He's found out what?' Luke couldn't hide the exasperation now. Oh, he loved this woman, no doubt about that, but she was a complete mystery to him too.

'What I really am.'

The quietness of her voice and the stillness around her suddenly made Luke shiver. 'What are you?'

'In the wrong hands, I am Death, the destroyer of Life.'

Chapter 26

18:47, 31st May 2032: Luke

They'd returned to the tiny house to collect some essentials – the remains of their food and the phone Green had packed in Luke's rucksack.

'Although why the fuck we want this,' Luke spat as he threw the phone on the bed alongside the rest of their possessions. It still showed a mainly full battery. 'Why he even packed it if he was going to set us up like he has – or maybe that's why he packed it. Maybe it's got a trace on it? He's certainly not made contact to help us, for all he promised, has he?' He grabbed it up again and was about to dismantle it but Hebe took it from him.

'He had his reasons, so let's take it with us. I said in the wrong hands, I'm Death. I'm also a life-giver; and you've seen that.'

'So whose hands are the wrong ones?'

'3:16 for certain. My father's maybe…' She looked sad, mouth pulling down at the corners like a sad marionette. The pain lines were stronger than ever now. He should tell her, but he couldn't. Instead, he pulled her to him and held her tight. She laid her head on his chest and reciprocated, her small, bony elbows digging into him as she squeezed. 'I know you felt some desire for me the first day we were here, but you've never…' her voice was as small and bony as her elbows. Now it was his turn to say 'hush'.

'There will be a time and place,' he assured her, trying to convince himself too – except his strength was waning, and from the look of her, so was hers. How ironic to have found the love of his life and even have that love ask him to make love to her, but not actually have the capacity to do so. This new love was an old one – older than time, but without the luxury of having had time together. 'There will,' he insisted again, for both of them, as he held her even tighter. 'But for now, we need to get back on the run.'

Even as he said it, a noise made them jump and pull apart. Hebe went to the bedroom window and peered through the crack they'd created between the two halves of the curtain.

'A shadow,' she hissed. 'I saw it move across the yard.'

'Shit!' Luke muttered through gritted teeth. One of the vigilante teams probably. 'We need to get out of here and to the jeep.'

'How, if they're in the yard? They're already between us and the lock-up.'

Luke joined her at the window and she moved aside for him to peer though the chink. 'But so is the wheelbarrow,' he concluded as he stepped away from the window and felt in his pocket for the flip-lighter.

'You'll never be able to set it off and get past them,' Hebe shook her head. The chink of light allowed a tiny ray of sunlight to alight on her head and as her hair moved it caught several strands of silver amongst the gold that had appeared even since that morning. Luke's sharp intake of breath made her freeze and stare at him. 'What?' she whispered, ragged voiced.

He shook his own head, choking back the lump in his throat. The hollows in her cheeks had deepened too – no longer elegant fine-tuning derived from immaculate bone structure, but the hollows of decline and middle-age.

'Nothing,' he grimaced. 'Just thinking it through. We can do it. But you have to remember what I said, you make a run for it and don't look back. When you get to the jeep, you gun it – don't wait for me.'

'I won't go without you.' The set of her chin was mulish; a stubborn old-woman-child.

'We agreed.'

'No, you told me. I didn't agree. We both go together, or not at all.'

'You have a purpose. I don't.'

'We all have a purpose, Luke Maynard,' she smiled at him. 'Whether we know what it is or not. We go together or not at all.'

'In that case, I'll have to think of another way to set that wheelbarrow alight.'

'Why not let me?'

'How?'

'It's a fine evening, but there could be the chance of a thunderstorm shortly – maybe even a lightning strike…' she winked at him, and he had to physically stop himself from laughing out loud.

'Well, I suppose you might use those superpowers they're going on about,' he chuckled softly.

'OK,' she grinned. 'Five minutes…'

Five minutes later and the skies had clouded over. The azure blue of an almost summer evening had darkened to a moody purple, with black-rimmed clouds hovering in the distance. Even the air smelt moody and threatening. Moments later the first drops of rain began to fall, releasing the smell of musty wood loam into the awaiting turmoil, followed by the first crack of thunder. Several shadows flitted across the courtyard as the phone Luke had thrown unceremoniously into the rucksack, now slung over his shoulder as he waited by the back door, began to ring.

'Fuck!' he swore as he swung the bag from his shoulder and rummaged inside. Hebe remained unmoved, hands folded into each other, eyes closed as she connected the earth's biorhythm to her own. 'Sorry,' Luke added as an afterthought, suddenly mindful of how he foul-mouthed he must sound to Hebe, and that mattered now. He clicked to accept the call and Green's voice filtered through, tinny and distant.

'Get out of there, now!'

The call disconnected as the lightning strike hit the wheelbarrow and ignited the oil cans in a blaze of yellow flames. Luke grabbed Hebe and yanked her with him, out of the back door, shoving her ahead of him as the smoke mushroomed around the blaze and several running figures retreated to the edge of the courtyard.

'Run!' Luke yelled at Hebe, above the crackle of the flames. A plume of evil-smelling smoke rose high into the sky as renewed gluts of flame burst from the now incandescent wheelbarrow. They reached the door of the lock-up just as the wheelbarrow exploded, showering cinders and flaming ash high into the air and sending someone shrieking into the distance. The light from the fire illuminated the lock-up as Hebe reached the jeep. And then she froze.

'Come on!' Luke had already thrown the rucksack into the jeep and was struggling into the driver's seat. Hebe was staring at herself in the wing mirror – the one he'd so carefully steered her way from earlier.

'Oh my God, Luke! Why didn't you tell me? I'm old. I'm old and ugly.'

'Not you're not!' he paused too, the pain of her pain like a knife in his gut. 'You're beautiful. You'll always be beautiful.'

'But I'm not. What's happening to me?'

'Come on!' Another blast from outside and some shouts galvanised him into action. 'We have to go. We'll talk when we've found somewhere new to hide, I promise.'

She stared at him wide-eyed, then she gave herself a little shake and climbed into the passenger seat. 'Go on then, floor it!' she grinned weakly at him.

They drove for half an hour, eventually pulling into a derelict barn, full of rotting hay and abandoned farm machinery. The sky had darkened of its own accord by then, but the acrid smell of burning oil was still in their nostrils, mixed with the ripe aroma of decomposing hay and decaying animal feed. They dragged some of the sacks – the better ones that only had patches of green-grey mould adorning them – over to one of the drier mounds of hay and snuggled together under them.

'My joints ache and my hands are stiff,' she told him, as if it were a confessional and he the priest taking her confession. 'It's arthritis, isn't it?'

'Why do you say that?' he asked, trying to ignore his own joint aches and stiffness.

'Because I'm getting old, Luke. How old am I now?' She put her hands on either side of his face and forced him to look at her.

'Forty… fifty maybe,' he admitted eventually.

'I see. Why didn't you tell me?'

'I couldn't. And anyway. To me you will always look young.'

'Thank you, my love,' she kissed him gently on the lips and it took his breath away. 'Is that why we haven't made love yet? My ageing?'

'God, no. More like my inability,' he exclaimed. 'Whatever 3:16 gave me before I entered the facility, they also warned me would break down quickly if not topped up. I'm way past being topped up now. It's only a matter of time…'

'For both of us,' she concluded. 'In which case…' and she pushed the sack away from their entwined bodies and stripped off her top. 'Now is that time and place…'

Chapter 27

22:47, 31st May 2032: Hebe

I lay awake looking up at the stars through the gap in the barn roof long after Luke fell asleep, trying to rationalise my feelings. I couldn't. The only thing I could rationalise was the irrationality of how I felt – excited yet content when I should be feeling afraid and anxious. At least I had now grown up – really grown up – but ironically, now I needed to halt the process, regress even, if that were possible. The face that had looked back at me in the wing mirror had been middle-aged. How long had it taken to age from twenty to mid-forties? Seven days, more or less. That meant I'd aged at a rate of at least two years a day for the last week. If I kept it up, within another fortnight I'd be old, and another week could well see me dead – and that was if I didn't speed up even more. Three weeks, maximum, to do what I needed to do – what Luke called my purpose. But what was my purpose? I'd told him I was Death, destroyer of Life, but I am also Life, destroyer of Death. It all depends which way you looked at things.

I hadn't realised this until recently. Maybe I hadn't even known it until I actually said it to Luke. When Uncle Matthew found me and urged me to leave the complex, there was just a glimmer of something growing inside me – an idea, a kernel of truth. Since then, especially since I've been close to Luke, that seed has germinated and bloomed.

'Hey,' Luke stirred beside me, rolled into me and pulled me close. 'You should be sleeping,' he mumbled into my hair. The straw stubble scratched my cheek and lumpenly stuck into the hollow of my back, making it ache. I tried to unravel the knot it made by stiffening my limbs and arching my back. 'What's the matter?' He was more awake now, rolling away from me and scrutinising my face in the dim light the open roof allowed to trickle in. Starlight.

'Just thinking,' I replied, pulling him close again, but he resisted.

'Thinking about what?'

'How old am I now?'

'Oh Hebe,' his voice crumbled with his expression.

'I need to know.'

He sighed heavily, his breath ruffling my hair and warming my face. 'A little bit more than before – perhaps…'

'Well, at least I've stayed grown up,' I said, wishing now I hadn't asked. This wasn't a middle of the night conversation. It was plain daylight conversation when emotions were more under control and logic could prevail – even I with my limited knowledge of adulthood could see that. But a middle of the night conversation it was destined to be now I'd initiated it. Luke sat up, rubbing his forehead, and sighing again.

'I should have said something sooner. I get that now,' he said.

'I wasn't blaming you,' I began, but maybe I was – for trying to make it easier for me. This was never going to be easy. I could see that now.

'I know,' he replied, turning to me. His expression was pained, his skin grey in the half-light of the shadows. 'But you should. I was taking the coward's way out, not wanting to upset or scare you, but sometimes that is exactly what you have to do for the people you love, otherwise you're not helping them at all. I should have told you, not least because you're ageing far faster than you should and that needs a solution. The only solution I can see is to return to the lab and see what your father can suggest.'

'And you don't think that's the solution?'

'I don't know…' I tried not to show him how that made me feel, then he seemed to regain himself. 'No, I don't think that's the solution. I think he's part of the problem. And I don't understand why it even happened in the first place, do you?'

'No,' I admitted. 'One moment I was as I was, and now I am as I am.'

'Well, we have to stop the ageing process somehow,' he hugged his knees to him. They clicked in protest, reminding me that it wasn't only me suffering from the entropy I was causing.

'We can't.'

'You don't know that.' He let go of his knees and leaned back, lying full length alongside me again. He brushed the hair from my face and caressed my cheeks with his thumbs.

'I do. To everything its season.'

Chapter 28

23:20, 31st May 2032: Luke

Luke stared at her in despair, then jack-knifed suddenly in a spasm of coughing. He flopped back, exhausted. His limbs felt like rubber, floppy and useless, and his body weak and lacking control. He hadn't even got any meds left to help with it.

'You're much worse too, aren't you?' Hebe asked, her eyes gentle but probing. He tried to avoid their intensity, but even in the half-light, they reached into him and answered their unasked question for themselves. He nodded reluctantly.

'I should never have brought us both out of there. The only person who might be able to do something about this – and you – is my father. We have to go back.'

Luke shook his head. 'No, I'm not taking you back there for him – or anyone else – to virtually imprison you again. And in any case, he's not there. You didn't hear the earlier broadcasts, but he's moved out – left the lab – and gone to ground in a hotel called the Lombardy.'

'What?' Now it was Hebe's turn to sit bolt upright. She pitched forward onto her knees and turned back to face him just as the moon chose that moment to appear in the gap in the barn roof. It cast an unearthly white light on her face, turning her skin to alabaster and her body to marble. 'Do you know what that means?' she asked, her voice hushed and afraid.

'I… no…'

Both of them jumped as the phone in the backpack rang, cutting through the ominous silence that followed Hebe's question. Luke rummaged in the straw to uncover the backpack, now damp and stinking from the tender mercies of their hitherto bed. He pulled it out on the fourth ring, and held it up to his ear. Hebe leaned in so she could hear too.

'Luke?' It was Green's voice, harsh and strained. 'Are you alone?'

'What do you want, traitor?' Luke growled at him.

'I… I'm not what you think, really…' Green hissed back.

Luke held up a finger to his lips as Hebe motioned for him to hand her the phone. He shook his head at her, then put his hand over the phone and whispered, 'See what he has to say for himself first.' She hesitated, swaying on her knees like a supplicant in prayer. OK, she nodded at him. He released his hand from the phone and continued, 'And what is that?' as his knees sank into the rank bed of rotting straw, releasing a glut of putrid aroma, but neither of them flinched. The stench of betrayal was worse than any smell they might encounter in their make-shift hovel.

'Luke, I'm sorry. Jason's got a gun to my head – metaphorically. His security teams have squashed 3:16 – he only allowed me to enable their break-in as a means to destroying them. I should have known – it was all too easy, letting me disable the security systems, then letting you in…'

Hebe raised her eyebrows at Luke and mouthed, 'Yes, but by my mother…'

Luke frowned and shook his head but continued with his interrogation of Green. 'So it was all pre-planned?'

'Yes, I've been a nominal member of 3:16 ever since the start. It was Elise's idea originally – based on her belief that life is sacred – that's the true meaning of John 3:16 which was the basis of the group. She thought it could be used to exert pressure – gently – on Jason to stay within the boundaries of belief, but Jason's never accepted boundaries.' Luke looked across at Hebe. She was nodding. '…Only Christ can give eternal life and Jason Crane may have the same initials as Jesus Christ, but he's certainly no saviour. The man wasn't so bad – arrogant, pig-headed at times, and a bit of a control freak, with his own particular hang-ups around trust, but the Jason Crane we all know now isn't a man. He's AI with elements of a man's brain, which occasionally displace the purely rational of the AI master, but never to any overall benefit. Quite the reverse, usually they tend more towards the rigidly over-emotional – psychosis…'

'So you've been planning to betray him all this time?'

'No, not betray; save.'

Hebe frowned and her head tilted to one side. Luke tried to question her with his eyes alone, but couldn't. She was signalling something to him, but again he failed to decipher it. He babbled on, hoping to unravel what she was trying to tell him with more time.

'So was it you on the dark web chat, then, when I was asking about medication?'

'Yes, I had to know we wouldn't kill you before we even got you in here.'

'And the cure? Was it always going to be the ForEver Project?'

'God, no! The ReNewal unit. You would have been the first test subject. To be fair, I had no prior documentation to prove it would cure MND, but nor did I have any reason to believe it wouldn't either, given what I *had* seen it could do.'

'So who was my "proof" if there was no documentation?'

'My daughter, Katie.' Hebe clutched at Luke's arm then and they both lost their balance in the shifting mound of rotting hay. 'Who else is there? I thought you said you were alone?'

Luke held the phone out in front of him and Hebe and put it onto loudspeaker. 'You have a right to hear this,' he whispered to Hebe. 'I love you, but whatever we do has to be your decision too.' Her eyes were round and anxious, but she nodded and signalled for him to reply. 'Why do you need for me to be alone?' Luke continued.

'I haven't been entirely honest with you,' Green whispered, 'How is Hebe doing?'

'Hebe? Why?'

'If Hebe is now no longer regressing, it means her physiology could have changed to something more akin to progeria. That would mean Hebe is dying and so will Elise, but for different reasons. Elise's body is only propped up by the life support, but that's limited. While Hebe was around she seemed to be able to remain stable – some kind of balancing out between them, I don't fully understand how, but now Hebe's gone… I underestimated the extent of Hebe's moderation of Elise degeneration.'

'Oh no…' Hebe wailed but Luke plastered his hand across her mouth, stifling her.

'What was that?' Green demanded as Hebe sank back into the hay, her own fist stuffed into her mouth as she choked back her misery.

'So you've effectively put them both at mortal risk by sending Hebe out of the complex?' Luke asked loudly to cover Hebe's anguish, 'and made it my fault by getting me to take her.'

'Oh God, no!' Green's voice was shocked. 'No, I haven't. This isn't your fault, it's mine.'

'So why? What are you up to?'

'Nothing, nothing – only the right thing… And Jason could save both of them if we let him. We figured out what's wrong with Hebe's metabolism ages ago, but the progress she made was so intriguing...'

Green sighed.

'So, tell me,' Luke asked, his voice as cold and sharp as ice splinters. 'What is wrong with Hebe's metabolism?'

'She has a faulty overactive regenerative loop. It means she's been ageing at a ridiculously fast rate but then regenerating again physically, but in order to do so, of course she has to regress too. Over time her body became incredibly finely tuned as an organism, but it's not robust enough to do that indefinitely so now it's also rapidly burning out. That's why the regression stopped. She literally ran out of "juice". Or, I suppose, she reached the point where her body balanced, and then tipped over – like humans do at adolescence when the level of hormones are finally sufficient to force us into modification and maturity in order to be able to reproduce. Jason knew this would happen and that's why he wanted to get her into an AI body, but I was afraid of what would happen. We only had him as prototype and he's not been totally successful in so many ways – not least because I sabotaged some of the bio-engineering on him before the original transfer and I've never been able to fully rectify it. We needed another test subject first…'

'Fuck you!' Luke spat the curse in disgust. 'You lied to me about Hebe's condition and you decided I'd make a good test subject too – dying already and desperate for a cure, you already had me on the hook, didn't you? All that crap about dual functionality and then that the BioModule unit might not work. You already knew it wouldn't!'

'I'm sorry, I'm sorry. I didn't know you, but Hebe and Elise… they and Katie are my world…'

'But you said you and 3:16 and Elise are against the ForEver Project, so why would you want to use it on Elise and Hebe?'

'Elise was against it. I… I wasn't sure. I do believe in the sanctity of life, really, but I also believe in making science work and if it's the difference between someone you love living or dying, then… I wanted to make sure it was the only way. I mean, I've never been fully convinced it was just a biological aberration, and not some kind of fallout from Jason, but if she's still ageing then… Jason can still save them both but you'd have to bring Hebe back here. Maynard, please, you could do that. You could persuade her and then she and Elise could both survive, and so would Katie and me – although God knows I don't deserve to.'

'And Luke?' Hebe pushed Luke gently away and spoke aloud into the phone, her voice the coldest he'd ever heard it; smooth and treacherous as black ice.

There was shocked silence the other end, then Green replied weakly, his voice faint and shocked, 'Hebe, you heard all of that?'

'Yes,' she whispered, then, 'yes,' she repeated angrily. 'And what will happen to me without help?'

'Your body will… break down completely, age, die. Your brain… I don't know. That won't die but I don't know what will happen to it – what form … I'm so sorry, Hebe, I can't do anything… I should never have let the ForEver Project happen in the first place.'

They both listened with horror to the impassioned sobs coming from the other end of the phone until Hebe interrupted them. 'You haven't said yet what you can do for Luke?' she insisted.

'Luke?' The sobbing paused, became an awkward hiccup. 'Well, I suppose he could still have the procedure too.'

'So this is all ultimately about getting us all to agree to the ForEver Project. Let me go and suffer the effects of whatever this metabolic dysmorphia is so my only option if I want to live is to agree. Leave my mother in a state of such vulnerability that it is her only option too, and take advantage of someone who is already dying…' Hebe's eyes met mine and sent their loving apology to me, 'to test out the procedure on first because you anticipate they will readily agree to it for the same reasons?'

There was a moment of silence, then Green's voice slid down the phone. 'No, no – that's not it. I never wanted that. Look, Hebe, Jason will ForEver Project your mother whatever. And with two AI's, I'm sorry, but I can't stop him from doing anything then. We were barely holding back the floodgates with 3:16 because he was always wary of going too far in case they did exactly what they've done and stormed the lab, but now he's squashed them… well…it's only the possibility of you returning that's holding him back. If you don't - I can't be responsible… I'm sorry, but I had no choice. Katie, you see. He'd have turned off the unit in my Katie and then she'd die. Please, don't let Katie or your mother die, whatever you choose for yourself. I need your help…' His plea ended on a choked cry, and then the sound of despairing sobs. Even as I watched, Hebe's demeanour softened.

'Shhh,' she said. 'OK... I understand. It's hard denying someone you love a proper life. And how could you have stopped him anyway?' Luke thought for a moment she was talking to him, then he realised her words weren't directed at him but at Green.

'Hebe,' Luke tried to warn her, but she was already set on her course.

'Don't worry,' she continued softly. 'It's all right,' now her eyes were on Luke's and her words were meant for him. 'I'm precocious…' she smiled at Luke and his heart burst with pride and love at this strong woman who'd known little but childhood but was more of an adult than he'd ever be. Trust me, those eyes said. Just trust me.

'With all my heart,' he mouthed at her. Her smile acknowledged the understanding between them

'We'll come back, but secretly,' she continued into the phone. 'Then we'll see what can be done. Can you get us into the complex without my father knowing?'

'Yes, or at least I'll try,' Green's voice was suddenly strong and enthusiastic.

'OK,' she struggled to her knees and climbed down off the bank of rotting straw and away from Luke. 'This is what I want you do,' she said as she walked out of the barn and into the night. Luke watched her, struggling to hold back his grief and marvelling at her confidence and decisiveness – and how far from her being a forever child, Hebe had long ago grown into a woman right under everyone's nose.

Chapter 29

23:40, 31st May 2032: Hebe

'But I thought they were in a hotel – the Lombardy?' Luke looked confused as I returned to the barn. He was sitting on the edge of the rotting straw pile, chin on hands and elbow propped on his knees.

'That's the code name for my mother's suite. My father named it after the painting location of her favourite renaissance artists. Both Caravaggio and Leonardo did a lot of work there.'

'So the origin of that news report was…'

'My father,' I agreed. 'Or maybe Uncle Matthew, possibly.'

'Then…'

I knew what he was asking. Was this my father's doing? Or 3:16's?

'I don't know. I only know I need to get back into the complex and find out what is going on. My mother is completely vulnerable and my father completely uncontrollable…'

'I don't like this at all, Hebe. We went to great lengths to get out of there and now we're heading straight back in purely because Green tells you your father's going to do something dire to your mother. Is that really likely? I thought he was meant to dote on her – or can AIs dote?'

'AIs can dote,' I said firmly, remembering that look which always came over my father's face whenever he referred to my mother – whether he was being controlled by his AI or his human side. The look was always the same. 'But they can't always translate that into an appropriate emotional decision. It's easier to be rational than irrational for an AI.' I sat beside him on the straw and my weight made us sink together into it. For a while that was all I needed – him, me, and hope. But hope is a hard-won battle, and we hadn't even started our fight yet. 'How old am I now?' I asked as he brushed a stray strand of hair from my face. To me it had looked more silver than gold, but I doubted he would admit that to me.

'Older than you are and younger than you seem,' he replied, teasingly.

'And what's that in years?' I said, smiling.

'About…' he hesitated, 'about old enough for us to need to get a move on,' he replied eventually.

'That's what I thought,' I said, pushing him gently away from me and preparing to stand. That turned out to be not so easy with the shifting, sinking straw and newly arthritic knees. He pushed himself upright with more success than me and held out a hand to help me up. How the tables turn!

'So what's our plan?' he asked when I'd joined him and we were standing toe to toe on the muddy barn floor.

'My plan,' I began gently, 'is to sneak back in this evening.'

'And mine?'

'Is to get yourself to a hospital and find out what damage that drug you were given has done.'

'But I'll still only be thirty-six then, even with MND. You'll be late forties, heading for fifty, and by this time tomorrow you'll be older – and weaker – still. I don't know what the rest of the plan is, but it's not going to get you very far on your own if you're getting older and weaker by the minute. The damage the drug has done to me is irreversible, and like the man said, everyone is expendable. I am hereby exercising my choice to expend myself in your service, my lady, if you will accept me.' With that, he dropped down onto one knee in front of me. And what else can a damsel in distress do when faced with a knight offering her his services, but accept. Maybe he had come to save me after all, just as Uncle Matthew had told me.

'Someone is coming – someone who will help you, help all of us. Save us.'

'Who, Uncle Matthew?'

'A knight in shining armour – isn't that always who comes along and saves the princess?'

'That's only in fairy tales, Uncle Matthew.'

'Who says we aren't in a fairy tale right now? Your mother is the Sleeping Beauty, you are Rapunzel, trapped in the tower and your father is Rumpelstiltskin, forcing you to spin gold for him. Fairy tales are all allegory anyway.'

'And what are you, Uncle Matthew?'

'Tom, Tom, the piper's son, stole a pig and away did run – that's me.'

I murmured the line and Luke looked up at me questioningly. 'Just something Uncle Matthew said once – he likened himself to Tom the piper's son,' I explained, but I couldn't explain the strange mix of emotions in me as I said it; a mix of knowing and seeing and not wanting to see.

We didn't go back in the way we came out – much to Luke's relief. We went in the front door – literally. Uncle Matthew had opened up the main entrance door and we just walked straight in. The main reception area – new to me – but known to Luke as he'd originally entered this way too, was a mess. The main glass doors were intact and they opened with an expensive hiss to admit us. Uncle Matthew was standing just inside, piles of trash – old chip papers, discarded cans, puddles of split drink, congealing into a sugar-rimmed patina across the once highly-polished floor – surrounding him. He rose up out of the debris like a goblinesque hero, shirt rumpled and as stained as the floor, trousers creased and half-mast, face grizzled with the first showings of a beard and tired eyes, heavily under-bagged.

'Hebe!' he exclaimed as we entered and he waded towards me through the rubbish. I wasn't sure whether the smell of the place was from the rubbish or him. Either way, I tried not to recoil as he wrapped his arms around me and squeezed.

'Uncle Matthew,' I tolerated the hug but found I wanted none of the kiss on the cheek. Something was off, and it wasn't my imagination. 'Where's my father?'

'Ah,' a shadow darkened his face and he grimaced a pained smile. 'Ummm,' he sighed. 'Preparing.'

Luke joined us and stood protectively behind me, taking the weight of the rucksack off my shoulders, and swinging it onto his instead. I could feel the effort it took him, but he made not a sound. 'Preparing what?'

'The question should more realistically be preparing FOR what,' Uncle Matthew corrected him. He turned back to me. 'He's already moved her – into the ForEver lab. Ready.'

Chapter 30

23:50, 31st May 2032: Luke

'Ready?' Hebe grabbed Green's arm. 'For what?'

'Well, ForEver, of course,' said Uncle Matthew. 'But he's just taken a break – he's been getting very tired recently, ever since what happened in the lab… Anyway, if we hurry, we could get there before he comes back and maybe get her out.' He took Hebe's elbow and started to guide her towards the same inner door where Luke had bypassed the chip reader only a week ago.

'What's the sudden rush?' Luke interrupted, taking Hebe's other arm so she was pulled between them.

'What do you mean?' Green stopped short at the resistance now posed by both Hebe herself, objecting at being simultaneously pulled in two directions, and Luke's belligerence. 'The rush is to save Hebe's mother before Jason subjects her to the ForEver process.'

'And what's the sudden rush to do that?' Luke persisted.

'Why do you think, you fucking idiot?' Green exploded at him.

'Uncle Matthew!' Hebe exclaimed, pulling herself free of his grasp. 'There's no need…'

'There's every need,' Green hissed, icy cold. 'She's dying.'

'Dying? Oh!' Hebe's hands flew to her mouth as she choked back a cry of panic. It echoed oddly in the rubbish-strewn reception.

'But why? Why is she dying? Luke demanded. 'Surely on life support she could have lasted well into old age?'

'She could – if he'd let her. But she's regressing – I told you that on the phone. Without you to balance her out, as you age, she regresses. He set it up that way. I didn't believe it when he told me, but it's true. He's poisoning her through you.'

'Ahhhh.' Hebe let out a long low sigh. 'Now I understand,' she added. 'Not poisoning. Balancing,' she explained. 'That's where I get it from – the ability to feel others' pain. When my mother went into a coma, all that was left functioning was her most deep-seated brain function. Instinctive brain function – the crux of our humanity, if you like. She became an empath, absorbing everything there is in the atmosphere around us; the atoms and molecules. Everything is made up of atoms and molecules, you know,' Hebe turned to Luke, expression grim. 'Even emotions. So without me around to absorb my father's atomic discharges, she's absorbing them instead.' Hebe slipped from their grip of her and faced Green. 'Where is she? We need to get to her – now!'

'Well…'

'In the ForEver lab?' Hebe demanded. Green shrugged miserably as Hebe pushed past him so she could forge ahead through the inner door and into the first corridor. Luke rushed after her, with Green following, puffing and blowing behind him.

'Wait,' Green panted as he caught up. 'We need to be careful, there are booby traps.'

'Something stinks here, and it's not just the surroundings,' Luke commented, pausing for Green to catch up. 'What kind of booby traps?' he asked, drawing Hebe close to his side. This time she didn't resist, eyes wide with horror. Along the corridor walls, slogans and graffiti covered the walls – 'demons', 'kill the robot', 'AI means die' and similar inanities. To Luke it looked as if the defacement of the walls had been done using a mixture of faeces and blood, amongst other things. Certainly the smell would suggest so.

'One or two grenade bombs and maybe some tripwires and laser beams,' Green replied, chest heaving as he drew level and then ahead of them. The floor was less littered here as they neared the room Luke had been led to for the press conference, but the doors along the corridor had been beaten in, the jagged innards of the panelling on the doors standing out in bas relief against the smooth outer frames.

'Shit!' Luke put his hand over his mouth and nose to protect himself from the worst of the stench as they passed a room which had been particularly badly blasted. Lying on the floor in the middle of the room, a tangle of bloodied arms and legs described what remained of the occupants. 'And this was happening whilst we were playing cat and mouse downstairs?'

'So it seems,' Green replied heavily. 'If I'd known…'

'You wouldn't have let them in?' Luke demanded, barely able to speak for anger.

'Don't blame me, Mr Maynard. I wasn't the only one complicit with 3:16, was I?' Green rounded on him angrily, face flushed beetroot colour with rage and exertion. A bead of sweat rolled down his forehead from under his matted fringe and pooled on the inside of his glasses. No folding in on himself now, Luke noted. This man was totally at one with himself – if still socially inept and dangerously unattractive.

'But I didn't know what they or you had planned, did I? I was doing it solely for a cure. What were you doing it for?'

'Enough,' Hebe intervened. 'Arguing is going to get us nowhere.' She looked tired – far more tired than she had on entering the building. And older. Luke bit his lip. Older than she should look on the basis of the progression they'd calculated. This was Hebe on the verge of her golden years.

Green seemed to have noticed the change too. 'True,' he agreed, another bead of sweat following the trail the first had left. 'We need to hurry, come on.' He looked over his shoulder at Hebe and waved them on ahead of him. 'At the end of the corridor turn right and you'll come to the entrance to the courtyard. I've left it open ready.'

Luke took the lead, encouraging Hebe on. Her pace was less sure and slower with every step. Was it being back here that had accelerated things? She'd talked about her father giving off toxicity and as he now knew she absorbed her life force from her connection with everything around her; was she absorbing toxicity that was poisoning her too?

'Come on,' he gently urged her, trying to ignore the weakness in his own limbs and the dizziness that had started shortly after entering the complex, as if his brain was being interfered with. 'We're nearly there. Through the courtyard and off to the side to where your mother is.'

'No,' Green called ahead of them. 'Not off to the side. The ForEver lab. I told you, she's being prepared…'

Inside the inside sanctum, the walls were clean and the air filtered, yet still a sense of doom lurked in the air. In the courtyard, the grass seemed yellowed and rancid, the daisies shrivelled and the atmosphere odd. Even the air felt thick, heavy to breathe. Luke looked at Hebe as she stopped and held her arms out as if feeling the atoms around her.

'Hebe?' he prompted gently.

'It's all dying in here – everything is dying.' She turned to Luke and he could see there were tears in her eyes. 'We're too late.'

'This way,' Green pushed past them and beckoned them to follow him but Luke could have told him the way. The old familiar feeling of

Escher at play had already pervaded his body and his feet were itching to move. Hebe took one last sad look at the scorched grass and followed them, heavy-footed.

The ForEver lab door was standing ajar, and Green was already inside it when they arrived there. 'Hurry, hurry!' he urged them, slamming the door shut behind Luke, the last to enter. Luke's sharp intake of breath made his chest ache. It was all just the same – the scanner machine, the banks of computers and monitors, the racks of animal cages – but it was subtly different too. Luke scanned the room for the disparity. Then he got it. He'd always been in the machine, having it operate on him. This time he was standing outside it, looking at someone else's scan results plastered across every monitor in the room, but before he could get close enough to one of them to read the name of the subject, Green was hustling him towards the far end of the room and the small room with its viewing window and inner operating theatre. Green was holding out something green towards him, Clothes. Scrubs. Operating scrubs. They were going into the operating theatre itself.

'Come on,' Green was getting impatient with them, but time seemed to be slowing, taking longer and Green talking in slow motion. 'C-o-m-e-o-n…' Luke took the scrubs and watched in swimmy-headed bemusement as Hebe did the same, pausing to examine hers like they were intricately embroidered ceremonial garments. Luke slid one leg, then the other into the capacious green trousers, almost losing himself as he disappeared into them. Now he knew what this felt like. It felt like getting high – the only time he'd ever done it at university and long before Aaron had boasted to him about getting regularly wasted. He wafted into the inner room behind Hebe and hovered in front of the viewing window.

'That,' Green pointed to a flickering light on the computer monitor to one side of them, 'is Elise's brain signature being recorded ready for 3D printing.'

'So we haven't much time?' Hebe asked but her voice seemed to distort.

'No, he'll be here any moment,' Green agreed.

'Who will be here any moment?' Luke asked, marvelling at the stupidity of his question even as he asked it. Of course, he knew who Green meant.

Hebe stared at him, eyes dreamy and pupils wide and dark. She looked so old now – a beautiful old woman, silver-haired, paper-thincheeked, tiny lines networking the entirety of her face like a butterfly wing, her skin so pale it was almost translucent. Seventy? Seventy-five? Oh God, they hadn't had long enough, not by a million years… He tried to tell her how much he loved her – whatever age she was – but the words wouldn't come out. All he could hear was his repeated question.

'Who will be here any moment?' Oh, but it wasn't him speaking. It was the intercom, loud, vibrant, demanding, as the viewing window into the operating room transformed from opaque to clear.

'Oh shit!' Luke gasped – or so he thought. The face of Jason Crane was peering back at them, completely dumbfounded.

Chapter 31

00:10, 1st June 2032: Luke

'Matthew, what's going on?' Crane was staring at them through the viewing window as if they were strangers, then, 'Why are they in here? They can't be alone with the AI shells…'

'What?' Luke spun round but staggered off-balance as Green shoved him forward.

'Go on,' Green was trying to push Luke and Hebe towards the operating room entrance, but Luke resisted, staring at Crane.

Crane's expression changed from shock to dismay as Luke watched. 'Hebe? Oh, my poor child… look at you? What's happened?' His expression sharpened, and he frowned, then he beamed at them. 'But don't worry, we can fix you. We can fix all of you.' He laughed, surprised and disbelieving at first and then delightedly. 'Matthew figured it out. Is that why you've come back?'

Luke half-turned to question Green but Green's shove catapulted Luke into the back of Hebe and together they burst through the door from the viewing room and into the operating theatre.

'Ignore him. You need to go in, grab Elise, and get out of there!'

Green was hard on their heels, forcing them towards the surgical trolley that Elise Crane lay on, as icy as the room itself. Something was wrong – and not just with Green, with Crane too.

'Matthew?' Crane started towards them then froze.

'I don't understand,' Hebe steadied herself against Luke. 'Figured it out?' She too turned to face Green – and what he was pointing at them. The temperature of the room felt sub-zero to Luke. He shivered and then he saw the gun too. A cold sliver of real fear trickled down Luke's spine in response and he grabbed at Hebe, digging his fingers into her frail arms. 'What did you figure out, Uncle Matthew?' Hebe persisted but Luke could feel the tension in her body slacken. She knew already what

Green had figured out.

'Your cycle,' Green replied, waving Crane way from them with the barrel of the gun.'I figured out how your metabolic cycle works. You have two. Dual functionality: you and your twin – the twin you absorbed in the womb.'

'What?' Crane was stepping forward again. 'What twin?'

On the surgical trolley, the instruments gleamed like beacons. Luke wondered how quickly he could snatch up a scalpel and stick it into the heart of Green, or even Crane – he still wasn't sure who the villain was here, but the stink one or the other of them made had his stomach turning – had always had his stomach turning. The scalpel on the edge of the tray was closest, but maybe not big enough to sever arteries deep inside the chest cavity – and anyway, did Crane have a heart and arteries?

'The twin that was never born,' Green was explaining, a satisfied smile curling his upper lip. 'No, you didn't know about that, Jason, because I never told you. It was on the first ultrasound – the one they did before you dragged Elise out of the hospital and imprisoned her here. When we scanned again here, it had gone, so I guessed what had happened. The second foetus had died and been reabsorbed by the surviving twin.' He directed himself to Hebe and Luke. 'It happens in about twenty to thirty per cent of multiple gestation pregnancies. It's called vanishing twin syndrome. The survivor absorbs the cells of their twin in the womb, effectively becoming a blend, or chimera of themselves and their twin. Of course, that doesn't usually result in anything quite so extreme in results as Hebe, but then other instances don't have a parent who is a hybrid of AI and human tissue.'

'Why didn't you tell me?' Crane moved a step closer. He looked confused, contrasting emotions drifting across his face like the shadows cast by moonlight.

'Father,' Hebe looked concerned, stretching out a hand towards him.

'No!' Green responded, levelling the gun directly at him. 'You stay there, Jason. I've had enough fun and games with you.'

'Oh, and you think a bullet in me is going to stop me?' Crane laughed.

'Not just one, as many as it takes – and they'll stop you for long enough.' Green's smile extended, spread across his face and Luke was reminded uncomfortably of the Joker from the Batman movies he and Aaron had watched as kids. 'Especially if I don't put the bits close enough together to reattach.'

'Uncle Matthew, please,' Hebe was trembling now. 'Don't do this. Something's wrong…'

'Tell your father not to do this,' he countered. 'He's the monster here, the unnatural one.'

'No one's unnatural,' Hebe protested. 'We're all God's creatures, however we came to be made. He struggles – inside… That's what my mother would be telling you too.'

'But she's not. She's barely even alive, thanks to him,' Green spat venom at Crane. 'All these years, I've helped you, Jason. Helped you win over Elise, helped you set up this company, helped you become a billionaire whilst I wallowed in debt, helped you survive death, and then helped you with Hebe whilst I had to leave my own child to the tender mercies of her manipulative mother. I even killed for you…'

'They were your choices, Matthew,' Crane took another step towards him. 'I dragged you out of debt – and a criminal prosecution – not left you wallowing in it. I covered you for Kohn's death – not caused it, and I accepted your offer to help with Hebe, not coerced you into it. `Damn it, I even provided the BioModule units to cure Katie and Jane when you would have left them to struggle. You didn't have to be here. You chose to be here – and I've lived under the shadow of your control ever since I became what I am.' Crane abandoned Green and faced Hebe and Luke. 'Did he ever tell you he built a failsafe into the programming before it was used on me? Salt water in volume. That's what can kill me. One of the most common things of all in our world – sea water. Or chop me into bits and keep them all separated.'

'Don't listen to him,' Green spat at Hebe. 'Just unhook your mother and take her with you. You need to get her out of here. Then dual functionality will kick in.'

'But off life support she'll die and anyway, you said she'd been poisoned…' Luke objected, still holding Hebe tightly. He wondered if he let go whether she'd even be able to stand on her own now, anyway.

'She has, with his toxic possessiveness.' Green reached forward and pushed the trolley on which Elise Crane lay, serene and unmoving, towards them. 'She could have lived, but for his obsession with living forever himself.'

Hebe steadied the trolley as it bumped up against them, her hands the clawed hands of an old woman. Luke gasped in dismay as he gently turned her towards him and looked from her hands to her face. She had aged another ten years in as many minutes, whereas Elise Crane seemed younger than she had when they'd first entered the room. Her eyes read his.

'Yes,' Hebe said quietly to him, and the hubbub around them faded for a moment and it was only them, reaffirming their love in the face of death, then she dropped slowly and gracefully to the floor. 'But I'm absorbing the toxicity, so she doesn't have to now.'

'No! Hebe!' Luke struggled to catch her, his own body protesting too much to be effective. She slid the length of it, ending in a crumpled heap at his feet as he sunk to join her.

'You bastards, both of you!' Luke sobbed as he pulled Hebe's limp body into his arms and cradled her like a parent rocking their tiny child to sleep. 'You've sacrificed Hebe to the altar of your own ends, both of you – you,' he spat at Crane, 'to your damned scientific breakthroughs. And you,' he growled at Green, 'to revenge – because that's what this is all about for you, really, isn't it? You want revenge. He got the girl, the cash and the immortality. You got shit, so now you're going to turn everything he has to shit too.'

'No!' Green stumbled towards them, dropping the gun as he fell to his knees in front of Luke and stroked Hebe's silver-grey hair. 'No! That's not true. That's not what I intended. It's the biggest breakthrough since the ForEver Project itself. True symbiosis in order to completely heal. Hebe – it wasn't meant to go this far. If he'd only done what I'd told him to you could have just walked out of here with Elise but he always had to question, argue.' Green stared balefully up at Luke. 'You had the chance of immortality and you handed it back. You are a fool – even more than he is.' Green's eyes strayed momentarily to Crane, then flicked back to Hebe. 'I do have the cure. I do. He could have kept your father in check whilst I cured you, Hebe, and then you could have cured Elise. You could, you know. You have the power over life and death. You know that. Hebe…'

Hebe lifted her head the merest fraction. 'Not any more, Uncle Matthew. Not now my mother is dying. That's the thing about dual functionality. Now I am become Death, like her…'

'No! No! Do something!' Green tried to stand but his feet didn't seem to be able to find any purchase on the floor. Maybe it was the extreme cold? Luke's hands were already so numb he could no longer feel them, and Green's were also turning an unhealthy shade of blue. Only Crane seemed unaffected, but then he wouldn't be, would he? Luke reflected. He wasn't human. Except…

'I am sorry, Hebe,' Crane's voice was suddenly soft and sibilant as – briefly – his expression seemed to soften too, the harsh angles of his face transforming as if a mask had slipped away. 'I wish it could have been different to this...' his eyes seemed to be filled with tears, glistening in the harsh glare of the overhead arc lights.

Hebe lifted her head to look up at him. It hung from her tender neck like an over-heavy flower bloom, struggling to look up into the sunlight. Her expression was sad, sympathetic even.

'I know, Father,' she said gently, like she was comforting a distressed child. 'It's not your fault.'

'No…' Crane's expression crumpled to despair as he and Hebe stared at each other, then just as suddenly, both voice and features sharpened again, and his cool voice cut across Green's panic and Luke's misery. 'But there's no point in wishing when wishes don't come true. Fact and science are all I deal with now. That's all there is. And we have to say goodbye now, Hebe,' he said apologetically to Hebe as she slumped against Green. In Crane's right hand was the gun Green had dropped, but it was pointing straight down, at the floor, whilst his gaze was fixed on Hebe.

'I know,' Hebe whispered, raising her head the merest fraction to look up at Luke. 'Do it,' she said – barely more than a breath in sound. 'Tell him to do it,' she repeated.

'Do what? Luke asked, bewildered. His eyes met Green's and then Crane's.

'We've got the shells. It's only a matter of completing the process,' Crane explained to Luke's horrified expression.

'He's right,' Hebe's voice rasped. 'Neither of us will survive beyond the next hour as we are. There's only one way for both of us now. The ForEver Project.'

Chapter 32

00:25, 1st June 2032: Luke

'Are you assisting then?' Crane was coolly asking Green as if nothing had happened and they were merely back in the main lab, about to send Luke through the scanner again. Green looked as if he was about to object, then nodded miserably. 'Then we'd better put our young journalist friend here on monitoring.' Crane walked over to Luke and nudged at him with the barrel of the gun. 'You ever monitored brain function before?'

'Jesus Christ!' Luke exclaimed.

'No, Jason Crane,' Crane replied, smiling cruelly, 'but that's such an old joke, we don't use it anymore, do we Matthew? Here. You sit here.' Crane put the gun in his pocket and took Luke by the shoulders – an iron grip that bruised him through to the bone. Crane slapped Luke down into a chair in front of a monitor and spun the chair around so he was facing it, and away from the surgical trolley that held Elise Crane. 'You need to tell me if the red line goes below halfway, otherwise stay quiet and keep out of my way.' He pointed to a monitor with a blipping light similar to the one Green had shown them earlier, claiming it to be Elise's brainwaves. The monitor displayed two wavering lines, extending across the screen, two-thirds up. 'We'll do Elise first,' Crane was instructing Green.

'But...' Green objected, 'Hebe's...' Hebe was all but unconscious in the chair that had been placed alongside Elise's head, with Green supporting Hebe in it from behind.

'Hebe will have to be patient. I've waited three years to get my Elise back, and her AI shell is ready. Plus she's the original source. There's a few hours more left in Hebe,' Crane's lips were drawn into a thin line, and his eyes had narrowed to slits. 'And we can use your cure for Hebe, since you've now admitted to one.' Green's exhaled breath was loud and thready in response. 'Assuming that wasn't a lie?' Crane added.

'No, no...' Green's head bobbed backward and forwards and Luke had the distinct desire to go and beat it like he once would have beaten the speed bag in the gym when he'd tried to train as a boxer, before giving it up as barbaric and pointless. Beating Green's head wouldn't feel barbaric or pointless, but he doubted he would have had the ability to do so now. He only hoped he could hold it together long enough to see Elise Crane transferred and Hebe cured. After that, well, maybe now was the time to let go after all. There were many things he now understood, and he was grateful for that – but not so grateful that he wanted to perpetuate life inside an AI shell, if that was the only way left to survive.

Crane nodded at Green. 'Start connecting then,' he directed as he flipped switches on the machine in the corner of the room and a pump started up. Green stumbled across to the green-draped figure on the trolley, walking gingerly past the fire hose coiled next to it. For the first time, Elise Crane stirred – as if in protest – as Green angled the first tube attached to the machine and poked it into a tiny receptacle point Luke hadn't noticed before in her neck. He attached a second directly below it and the two tubes vibrated gently as fluid began to run through them – clear in one, deep, ruby red in other.

'Oh shit!' Luke couldn't help himself. 'Is that her blood?' he blurted out as the second tube filled with the red liquid and he realised the tube flowed into the machine and out the other side and across the room to the trolley. The surgical drape could have been covering either, but for Luke the shape under the green cover meant… 'Oh shit!' he said again as he remembered what he'd seen on the trolleys just before he and Hebe had escaped the lab complex – one draped in green and one in blue. 'But…' slowly it dawned on him. Hebe and Elise… He got up from his chair and hobbled across to the other trolley before Green or Crane realised what he was doing. His fingers fumbled with the drape, stiff and numb from the cold. It felt like cotton wool between his forefinger and thumb but somehow, he managed to peel it off the shape, like he was peeling a banana. What faced him as the drape fell away was the stuff of his worst nightmare. Not Elise Crane's AI shell, but Hebe's. 'You're putting Elise into Hebe?' he shrieked. 'Was that always the sick joke you had in mind?'

Green was with him in seconds, pulling him away. 'Shut up, shut up!' he hissed, trying to plaster his hand across Luke's mouth. Luke bit down hard on Green's fingers and Green howled and grabbed his hand away, cradling it in the other as he moaned and writhed. 'Damn you!' Green shouted. 'What the fuck do you think you're doing?'

'No, what the fuck do you think you're doing?' Luke demanded.

'Time to stop playing games now, Matthew,' Crane interrupted. 'He knows so let's get on with what we're meant to be doing,' he continued, voice like ice shards. 'If you can't assist properly, just keep him out of the way,' he instructed Green. 'I'll do the monitoring, you play the heavy.' Crane produced the gun from his pocket, dropped it on the floor and kicked it across to Green. In the middle of the room, Hebe stroked Elise's forehead and then raised Elise's hand to her lips and kissed it gently. Elise's eyes flickered briefly then settled as Crane attached the electrodes to her head.

'You're both in on this?' Luke gasped. 'You sick fucks!'

'Now, now, Mr Maynard,' Green was holding the gun to Luke's temple. 'You shut up, like the man said. We're doing what we always intended doing. That is Hebe's AI shell based on Hebe's genome. Everything Hebe can do, with the added bonus of being AI and having dual functionality. Like I said, the scientific breakthrough of the century after the ForEver Project itself. The perfect home for Elise and all her future progeny. Don't worry, there'll be so many Hebe's in the future, you'll be spoilt for choice…'

Chapter 33

00:46, 1st June 2032: Hebe

So here I am, back where I started. Not yet born and not yet dead. A child of the universe, part of its perfect formation and perfect failing. All beginnings have an end, even if they're forever. My father understands that too. It was in his eyes as he said goodbye. That, and relief.

I can feel her inside me now, struggling towards me, reaching out… Grasp my hand, I'm here. We can do this together… Oh, there you are... Now breathe and connect. I am Death, the destroyer of Life. I am also Life, destroyer of Death, and now we two are one…

Chapter 34

00:51, 1st June 2032: Luke

Luke grimaced at the pinch of the barrel as it pressed into his temple. He looked across at Hebe and desperately tried to catch her eye. She was still conscious, still upright, eyes open, but focused straight ahead of her, a half-smile playing across her lips. He tried to send her a thought, a plea. *Look at me, Hebe. Tell me what to do.* But his mind remained a blank. He sighed, a ragged exhalation of equal parts despair and surrender. In that moment, when his mind was blank and hopeless, Hebe's head turned, and she smiled at him. Briefly, her face was transformed – full of bright luminescence – and then all the life seemed to drain from it. Simultaneously Elise opened her eyes. Hebe turned away from him before Luke could say anything and instead, she and Elise locked gazes. The temperature dropped a notch lower and the air was filled with the condensation of his and Green's breath – great clouds of white steam. Not Hebe's though. Or Elise's. Hebe leaned forward and kissed her mother's hand again and then collapsed as Crane leapt into action, rushing back to the monitor showing the brain waves and frantically flicking buttons as the two wriggling lines glowed, then dimmed, then disappeared.

'Dammit!' Crane yelled, thumping at the monitor. 'Where've you gone?'

'No!' Luke wondered for a moment who was screaming above Crane's furious shouts and Green's whining, 'What's happened? What's gone wrong?' then he realised it was him. He knocked the gun away from his temples and elbowed Green out of the way. Green sprawled in front of him, but Luke leapt him, wondering how the hell his legs had the strength to even move, let alone hurdle a fallen body. He collided with Crane as he landed on the other side of Green's flailing arm and legs.

'Get out of my way,' Crane yelled, barging Luke and knocking him to the floor. 'Just do your job or they'll both die. Monitor that machine.

Look for a green wave form across it. Go!' he shoved Luke hard and Luke went flying towards the monitor Crane had just left.

'You bastard!' Luke screamed at him. 'Hebe IS dying.' Green tackled him from behind, sweating and stinking as he thrashed his arm about trying to evade him. A lucky hit winded Green and allowed Luke to practise a clumsy form of the rugby throw he'd mastered so well when he was young and athletic and not ill – one of the many attempts to prove himself better than Aaron in some way or another. But the throw backfired and Green grabbed him from behind, jamming his fist into Luke's mouth and squeezing at his throat. Luke gagged and then collapsed onto his knees, praying to the god of gods to give Crane and Green a horrific death as he watched Hebe's life slip away. Green held on tight as the final part of the process completed and Luke struggled to remain conscious as Green squeezed his throat. Through blurred vision, he saw the two wavering lines reappear on the monitor and under Crane's careful manipulation, merge and become one solid line careening across the screen. By the set of Crane's shoulders, Luke could tell he was pleased even before Crane stood aside from the monitor, grinning maniacally.

'You can let him go now. It's done,' Crane announced. He walked across to the central trolley and put his fore and second fingers to Elise's carotid artery, where the tube now hung as lank and lifeless as Elise herself. He nodded, apparently satisfied, then repeated the action with Hebe. Her hair hung in silver sheaves either side of her sunken face. He nodded again. Check her?' he instructed Green, and suddenly Luke was free and able to breathe again. He rubbed at his bruised throat and tried a couple of painful breaths. He wasn't sure whether it was the pain of grief or the pain of injury that made him wince in agony, but Crane was there, towering over him as he struggled to stand.

'You evil bastard! Don't you care about your daughter?'

'Daughter?' Crane laughed. 'You think I'm affected by histrionic emotional attachment just because she was genetically linked to me? She was a creation, and I can create many more now Elise will be functional again. But better – fully integrated, dually functioning for maximum achievement. No faulty overactive regenerative loops…'

Behind Luke, Green made a sound like he was gargling. 'Oh my God…'

Luke and Crane pushed past him simultaneous with the AI shell opening her eyes and saying in a surprised tone, 'Where am I?'

Crane barged Luke out of the way and flung himself to his knees by the side of the draped trolley. 'Elise,' he breathed.

All around Luke, the air seemed to catch fire – the fire of rage and frustration and revenge. His limbs raged too, with the last dregs of his strength. This was for Frieda and Hebe – and Aaron. All the times he'd failed, they'd failed, the world had failed them, now was the time to avenge them all – but mostly his Hebe. The scalpel was still lying, waiting, on the corner of the surgical trolley. Crane was kneeling in front of him, Green hovering in homage behind him.

'I'm sorry Hebe, I don't accept this is how it ends,' Luke hissed under his breath. Stepping lightly around Green, he almost skipped to the surgical trolley and had the scalpel in his hand before either Green or Crane had noticed him move – or so he thought. He might not be able to make an end of Crane, but he could of Green and then at least Frieda would be avenged. Crane, he could mangle pretty well and whilst he was reattaching the bits of himself Luke hacked off, Luke reasoned he would find a gallon of salty water for the bastard to swim in.

But Crane appeared to have a sixth sense and as Luke approached Green from behind, scalpel in hand, Crane sprang back onto his feet and knocked Luke to the floor. The scalpel flew across the room and clattered harmlessly against the wall as Crane landed square on Luke's chest and placed both hands around his throat.

'Enough, Mr Maynard,' Crane was saying as the blood pounded in Luke's head and his already bruised throat collapsed in on itself. 'This IS how it has to end…'

As Luke's vision faded and he struggled to take one last breath, the iconic moments of his life flickered in front of him. Aaron, grinning a gappy smile at him when they were about six and still best buddies, his first kiss – a sweet girl with blue eyes and flyaway red hair, the moment he collected his journalism degree, being diagnosed with MND, refusing to say goodbye to Aaron as his coffin was lowered into the ground, meeting Frieda and the challenging look she'd given him when he'd introduced himself, but most of all: Hebe. Hebe at four, staring up at him from the middle of the grass square in the courtyard and asking if he was there to save her. Hebe in her teens making inedible bacon and eggs. Hebe at twenty, making his heart race and his body throb with desire. Hebe in the rank smell of rotting straw that smelt sweeter than anything else on earth with her on it. Hebe, old and frail and still loving him. 'I'm sorry. I failed you after all. I wish I could have saved you…' he said to her – to all of them.

'Don't give up yet…' he opened his eyes, stinging salt tears streaming from the corners – but the hands around his throat had gone and Crane was lying next to him, eyes closed and apparently unconscious, surrounded by water streaming across the lab floor and Crane sinking, decomposing, fading away into it as the fire hose it was pumping from snaked around the room with a life of its own. Luke struggled to avoid the force of its jet but merely wallowed further into the sea of water it was creating, salty water... And standing astride him was the kind of vision the members of 3:16 would have wanted, but he'd never have expected to see. An angel, surely? An angel who looked so familiar – stately, Junoesque, glorious, glistening as her wet skin gleamed in the harsh light – completely naked.

'But…' he tried to sit up but this time his body completely refused to work and his throat closed over as he tried to speak. Slowly, slowly, he managed to turn his head just enough to see that, across the room, the AI shell was now lying on the floor next to Hebe's lifeless body. So who was this? Luke edged his head back so that he was looking straight up again. He stared in wonder at the angel, then recognition pinged through his body, through his head, through his soul. 'Hebe?' he asked tentatively, even though no words came out.

'Yes,' she smiled. 'Hello, Luke Maynard. I told you there was a special bond between us – me, my mother and you. Now my mother and I are one, as we once were. I forgot to tell you, didn't I? In the wrong hands I am death, the Destroyer of Life. But I was always intended to be Life, the Destroyer of Death. Now we are.'

He cried then, tears of joy and tears of regret, a baby's tears – helpless and hopeless, and as salty as the water he was bathing in. The words echoed through him, reverberating in his chest cavity even as he collapsed, body in complete spasm, breathing compromised and heart tachycardic.

'Oh God,' he managed. 'At least I got one thing right in my life. Makes it not so bad I messed the rest of it up.'

His eyes closed and darkness swamped over him. This was how it ended. He knew that. Frieda had explained it to him, all the doctors had explained it to him. ALS had finally kicked in and his heart muscle was failing. Amyotrophic lateral sclerosis: the end of days for an MND sufferer. But it was OK. He had helped Hebe be saved.

'Luke? Luke? He could hear Hebe's voice calling him again, but from a long way away.

'He needs the ReNewal module,' Green was shouting.

Luke opened his eyes for one last glimpse of Hebe. 'This is how it ends,' he whispered.

'No,' she said, smiling and shaking her head. 'No ReNewal unit, nor tech of any kind. This isn't how it ends,' and she pulled Luke towards her with what felt like superhuman strength. He dangled from her arms like a rag doll as he looked into her eyes. She kissed him, and his body tingled as the internal battle raged between MND and Hebe until he felt nothing: no pain, no fear, nothing. Hebe smiled down at him with all the light of wisdom fifty life transits of the biological process had built within her and as she stood, pulling him upright with her, he found himself steady too, healthy and glowing. Across the room he could see the pair of them reflected in the mirror on the wall and the calendar beside them: 1st June 2032. 'Now I have done what needs doing for you. And this is how it begins,' Hebe whispered.

Epilogue

12.01pm, 8th June 2032: Luke

'The disturbance we reported earlier at Crane Industries has finally been resolved with the relinquishing of the complex to the local police by the 3:16 Group. A number of arrests have been made, including Professor Matthew Green, who has been since charged with three counts of murder. The body of Dr Frieda Kohn, an employee of Crane Industries, was found in a cold storage area within the facility. Dr Kohn has been missing for over two years. In addition to this – and in a shock discovery – the lifeless body of his wife, Elise Crane, attached to disconnected life support, has also been found alongside the body of CEO, Jason Crane, who appears to have been killed in an acid attack. Enquiries are continuing, but one thing is certain, Crane Industries will not be developing any more of its ground-breaking medical products until a full ethics review has been conducted. A close relation of the tragic Crane couple, Hebe Crane, says that the complex will be shut down pending the outcome of the investigation – which may take many years to conclude, if ever, as most of the documentation supporting the company's products was destroyed in the 3:16 attack.

In other news, along with other instances around the world of unexplained recovery from chronic and terminal illnesses, the latest spontaneous recovery of a group of cancer sufferers in New Jersey has been hailed as a miracle...'

Luke turned the radio off, smiling as he watched Hebe wandering in and amongst the grasses on the meadow. Of course, it wasn't an acid attack. It was salt water that Hebe had caused to flow through the fire hose. And Green had surprised them both by willingly surrendering himself to the police with his own confession. There would be no more Revolutions for Hebe, but the revolution had already started through her as the atoms she exuded gradually filled and healed the world. Wherever she walked, it seemed to grow more lush, more green, more fruitful. An Angel. A Bringer of Life. A miracle of a sort. A ForEver Child.

Hebe must have sensed Luke watching her because she turned to face him, her wide, happy smile briefly eclipsing the sun before she once again became a silhouette against its brightness. The superb round of her pregnant belly proclaimed the indisputable truth that life remains the biggest ground-breaking scientific advance, and unconditional love what makes it possible without any intervention at all.

ABOUT D.B. MARTIN

D.B. Martin writes adult psychological thriller fiction and literary fiction as Debrah Martin, as well as YA fiction, featuring a teen detective series, under the pen name of Lily Stuart and children's books as Debbie Martin. She is also a painter and her book on writing and painting and the inspiration behind both, Savage Seas and Sfumato Skies, written under the penname of Debrah Martin contains many of her paintings.

You can find more about her work on www.debrahmartin.co.uk and sign up for news and updates on forthcoming publications here: http://eepurl.com/bkcUtH

And if you enjoyed this book – or any of her books, please do stop by and leave a review on Amazon.

BOOKS BY THIS AUTHOR:

Writing as D. B. Martin:

PATCHWORK MAN (Bk 1 in the PATCHWORK PEOPLE series) B.R.A.G. Medallion winner

Laurence Juste QC is the perfect barrister; respected, professional, always wins. But Lawrence Juste isn't who he says he is. He's a patchwork man, pieced together from half-truths and lies. Now his past is about to come back and haunt him as the patchwork man begins to unravel.

PATCHWORK PEOPLE ((Bk 2 in the PATCHWORK PEOPLE series)

No sooner does Lawrence Juste patch one hole in his fraying life than another appears. No-one is what they appear to be, and there's a certain irony in the fact that only someone even more deceptive than him can help – but they're already dead...

PATCHWORK PIECES (Bk 3 in the PATCHWORK PEOPLE series)

The wheel has turned full circle: the past is the present, the betrayed are the betrayers and the dead in Lawrence's world have resurrected. As his options diminish, the only way out is a lethal form of natural justice for the man for whom law and order were once king.

LADY LAZARUS

When Roseanne Grey jumps to her death on a cold December day, there's no apparent reason why – not even according to her psychiatrist. Detective Sergeant Darwin Grant is told to file the death as a simple suicide, but he's not so sure. There was a lot to know about Roseanne; none of it explicable ...

MEMENTO MORI (Bk 1 in the MIND GAMES series)

The enviable position of Deputy Director at the elite psychological treatment centre, ETHOS, comes with strings that Gaby McCray would prefer to ignore – until they threaten to compromise more than just her integrity. Can you be both good and evil, doctor and devil, simultaneously? Do you kill, or be killed to protect the answer?

THE BEHEMOTH (Bk 2 in the MIND GAMES series)

The truth behind the secret project psychologist Gaby McCray's eminent but mysterious father initiated lies deep within Gaby but as she comes to terms with who or what she might be as a result, the 'truth' changes once more. The deeper she digs, the more terrifying the prospect of what she has released as the Behemoth rises...

THE FOREVER PROJECT

His nickname of JC ("walks on water") becomes more than just a private joke when Jason Crane's ForEver Project – a means of combining robotics and biochemical engineering to extend life in the terminally ill - becomes more than just a project. He hadn't bargained on being the first test subject for it though – or what it might mean to him as a human, with or without a soul ...

THE FOREVER CHILD

If giving man immortality was incredible, then producing a hybrid child – part AI and part human is nothing short of a miracle. But the ForEver Project was never intended to produce a child, and miracles carry a price. For a Forever child the price is high indeed – for both them and the world they live in.

Writing as Debrah Martin:

FALLING AWAKE

The story of Mary, Joe and a world populated by love, betrayal and obsession – and what it does to those who live in it. Fantasy or madness? The impossible is only a breath away.

CHAINED MELODIES - B.R.A.G Medallion Winner

Courage isn't about facing death, it's about loving life – and life isn't always conventional. The unusual story of how two men find not just courage, but self-belief and the true nature of love as one transitions to female and the has to face their prejudices and fears. A different kind of love story. A different kind of life.

Non-fiction books:

WRITE, PUBLISH, PROMOTE

From first idea, through first draft and into print: Debrah teaches creative writing and publishing as well as practices it. Write, Publish, Promote is a distillation of ten years of teaching and writing – "Debrah is an excellent teacher. That first novel is nearer than ever..." say her students.

SAVAGE SEAS AND SFUMATO SKIES

Debrah is an artist as well as a writer. This book describes both oil painting techniques and combines some of her writing – short stories and poetry – with her paintings to demonstrate how to find inspiration through both to prompt creativity. And if you've never painted in oils and want to try – here's how...

Writing as Lily Stuart (YA fiction):

WEBS

Meet Lily: one smart cookie with a bitchy BFF, moody boys and crazy school friends. Life's a breeze by comparison to what happens when her mother starts internet dating with lethal results though. Step up Lily S: Teenage Detective.

MAGPIES

A boy with looks to die for – and Tourette's – tricky BFFs, and a gang of drug-dealers... THE teenage detective is back and looking for trouble – or trouble is looking for her. It finds her in the form of a childish rhyme, with a deadly hidden meaning.

www.ingramcontent.com/pod-product-compliance
Lightning Source LLC
LaVergne TN
LVHW091151150826
845672LV00005B/1109

* 9 7 8 1 9 1 5 1 2 0 1 6 8 *